The Millennium Journals:
Book 1–The Secret Library

Harold O. Hutchison

PublishAmerica
Baltimore

First printing

ISBN: 1-4241-4885-5
PUBLISHED BY PUBLISHAMERICA, LLLP
www.publishamerica.com
Baltimore

Printed in the United States of America

What has been will be again. What has been done will be done again; There is nothing new under the sun. Ecclesiastes 1:9

Job 41:12 –33

I will not fail to speak of his limbs, his strength, and his graceful form. Who can strip off his outer coat? Who would approach him with a bridle? Who dares open the doors of his mouth, ringed about with his fearsome teeth? His back has rows of shields tightly sealed together; each so close to the next that no air can pass between. They are joined fast to one another; they cling together and cannot be parted. His snorting sends out flashes of light; his eyes are like the rays of dawn. Firebrands stream from his mouth; sparks of fire shoot out. Smoke pours from his nostrils, as from a boiling pot over a fire of reeds. His breath sets coals ablaze, and flames dart from his mouth. Strength resides in his neck; dismay goes before him. The folds of his flesh are tightly joined; they are firm and immovable. His chest is hard as rock, hard as a lower millstone, when he rises up, the mighty are terrified; they retreat before his thrashing. The sword that reaches him has no effect, nor does the spear or the dart or the javelin. Iron he treats like straw, and bronze like rotten wood. Arrows do not make him flee; sling stones are like chaff to him. A club to him but a piece of straw; he laughs at the rattling of the lance. His undersides are jagged potshards, leaving a trail in the mud like a threshing sledge. Nothing on earth is his equal, a creature without fear.

Chapter 1

The battle raged on, sword clanging against sword, armor against armor, and everywhere there were the sounds of battle. I guess I had never realized quite how noisy war really is. And the smells of battle, the smell of smoke and singed flesh permeated the air. As a warrior, I love the sounds of battle, and I truly thought that I would never tire of those sounds and smells of battle, but today that would all change.

I listened to the sounds around me, somewhere off in the distance, a beast of some sort bellowed in pain and fear, and everywhere around me, men were yelling, screaming, some crying, yet, as consuming as those sounds were, one single sound somewhere close to me gave me the chills, chills that I had never experienced before on the battlefield, and that sound was the scream of a woman.

For one brief moment I wondered why on earth there was a woman was on the battlefield, and then it dawned on me, that scream had come from my beloved Mara, and chills ran all the way down my spine, causing my heart to sink within my chest. What was she doing down on the battlefield; she was supposed to be waiting on the hill with the others.

As I turned to run toward the scream there was a sudden, sharp stabbing pain high in my chest. I looked down incredulously at the dagger protruding from my chest, but somehow it didn't seem real. Dropping to my knees, I reached out to touch the hand of the woman who had fallen next to me, mortally wounded on this cursed battlefield.

As my breathing became labored, I coughed, a small splatter of blood stained the ground beneath me, and although I felt I could just lie down and sleep, I fought to stay conscious. Then, a sound, maybe a sixth sense, suddenly jarred me back to reality, and instinctively, I raised my sword to fend off one final blow from my unseen enemy, and when I did so I felt the resistance of my sword as it penetrated flesh and bone.

When my eyes lifted to face my enemy, to my horror, I recognized the face of that enemy, and as my enemy toppled over, there was a look of disbelief on the distorted face. He was so sure that he had destroyed us both. As I turned again to hold my lovers body, a blood-curdling screech diverted my attention, and through fading eyes I saw a horned apparition, clearly nine or ten feet tall, 30 feet long from nose to tail, regal, yet terrifying, lumbering toward me out of the wisps of smoke, eyes red like fire, spears and arrows protruded from its body like quills. Troops from each side were scattered in its wake as it ran over some, and knocked others into eternity with its mighty, spiked tail. As my eyes faded, I thought to myself, dragons sure do look clumsy when they're on the ground.

A constant, annoying screech jarred me out of my fog, beeping repetitively. My God, it's the alarm clock. I jolted upright up in bed, breathing heavily, and sweat was pouring from my brow. Instinctively, I felt my upper chest for the wound that I was sure would be there, but there was nothing. It was that dream again, the third time this month, and it was always the same, As I sat there breathing heavily, a soft hand reached up and touched my arm, further jarring me back to reality.

"Honey, are you okay?" a gentle, sleepy female voice asked. "Was it that dream again?"

"Yes dear, now go back to sleep. You don't have to be to work for a couple of hours yet"

"I would love to," she said, now slightly annoyed, "if you would shut off that blasted alarm clock."

I had not even noticed the alarm clock was still beeping incessantly.

"Sorry," I said, mashing down on the button to shut off the racket.

"You really need to see someone about this problem Henry. It's obviously starting to have an effect on your sleep patterns, and you've said yourself that you are becoming increasingly distracted at work lately."

"You're right dear," I said. "as soon as I can find some extra time on one of my days off, I'll go see my doctor, now go back to sleep."

I sat on the edge of the bed reflecting back on the dreams I'd been having. They seem so real; they feel so real, as though I had actually experienced the events of that battle, which of course is absolutely impossible, because this is

2005; I live in a small town in the Bitterroot Valley of Montana named Victor, and I'm just an average everyday paramedic working for the local hospital on their ambulance service.

I've never been a soldier; and I've never experienced a battle, yet for some reason I love everything to do with the military, and even as a child I played army incessantly. My dream as a child was to grow up to be an army man. It always seemed to be ingrained in me, although I don't know how that could be. As for swords, I've always had a love for swords, and have several in my collection, but in this day and age, I feel that I would be more likely to cut myself with one than I would an opponent.

All of a sudden, I realized that I was still sitting on the edge of the bed daydreaming again, and I thought to myself, enough of this already, I need to get ready for work, and so, on slightly unsteady legs, I made my way down the hallway to the bathroom. Man, I should not have had so many gin and tonics last night. It seems lately that I have been drinking way more than I should. I hope that doesn't mean that I'm becoming an alcoholic or something. It is just so relaxing to come home after a long stressful day at work, and relax on the deck with a nice cold drink.

Looking at myself in the mirror, I see a man whose life is at an impasse, Henry Olsen, a man bored with his life. I think it would be exciting to be in the midst of an epic battle, lives hanging in the balance, your heart pounding within your chest, adrenaline coursing through your veins, proud, fit, and strong. Ouch, damn it all, I just cut myself with the razor, that's going to leave a mark. This distraction is getting way out of hand lately. Wiping off my face, I climbed into the shower, turned on the water, and let the warm water cascade over my body, washing away not only the sweat, but hopefully, some of the thoughts that were going through my head.

A dragon, what in the hell was that all about? I've always had a thing for dragons, even to the point of having a dragon tattooed on my arm, and I collect dragon figures and pictures. Hell, every summer I even sell fireworks under the name of 'Red Dragon Fireworks'. Maybe that's all there is to this whole dream, fantasy thing. Maybe I need to just grow up and stop dwelling on dragons. And what about the woman in the dream, who is she, and who does she represent. It's all just a little bit disturbing. Good Lord, here I am daydreaming again, and now the shower is getting cold. I didn't realize I had been in here so long. I hope the water has time to warm up before Jane gets up or she'll need more than cold water to cool down, because she likes her showers hot.

Climbing out of the shower, I dried off slowly, letting the water evaporate to cool myself down. The day is already heating up. It is only June17 and it looks like it's going to be another hot summer. Hopefully we won't have another bad forest fire season this year. The past few years have been catastrophic, with fires destroying nearly 250,000 acres of pristine, nearby forest. It's nice and green in the mountains right now, and we have had some good rain recently, but that can change so fast. I just hope it doesn't dry out for a few more weeks until I can finish selling fireworks.

I take two weeks of my vacation every year to sell fireworks. It's a lot of work, but the money is good, and I get to see a lot of old friends that I only see once a year. In fact, it's as much a social event as anything, plus we get free fireworks, so how cool is that? After Christmas, the 4rth of July is my favorite time of year.

We hang around the booth visiting with customers, enjoying the look of wonder on the faces of both kids and adults alike. The days are long, with the booth opening each day at 8:00 am, and closing at around 11:00 pm, or whenever the customers stop showing up. Happy hour of course starts at around 7:00 pm when we start having a few beers, and although we don't flaunt it, I'm sure most people can tell we've had a few drinks. Maybe that's why the late night buyers always want to cut a deal on the price. But, it's good fun, and we take it all in stride.

The fireworks company called yesterday and said my shipment of fireworks would be arriving in a couple of days. We can start selling fireworks on June 24th, but until then I have a lot of work to do. Permits have to be secured, performance bonds posted, storage arranged, and the booth itself needs some serious attention, sweeping out all of the denizens that moved in over the winter, and a new coat of paint wouldn't hurt either. The fireworks come on a full size semi truck, so I'll have to make sure that I have a crew on hand to help unload, and that's where it pays to have good friends, or a loyal family.

My good friend Scott Mallory helps me out every year, and I don't know what I'd do without him. He has been with me forever, through thick and thin, good and bad, and even helped me through a nasty divorce, one in which I tried to commit suicide. Scott is a short, round, jovial fellow, always chuckling to himself, with a stocky build, a good-natured sort, and as true a friend as you could ever hope for. He is truly the one they must have spoken about in the Bible when they talk about a friend who sticks closer than a brother, and that would describe my friend Scott.

There is always so much to do, but that will all have to wait, because right now it's getting late, and I have to pull myself together and get ready to go to work. I can't believe that I've been so distracted lately. I really do have to do something about this before it gets out of hand. In my line of work, I can't afford to be distracted.

Quickly brushing my teeth, applying deodorant, and splashing my face with aftershave, I climbed into my ambulance uniform. By now, the wonderful smell of coffee brewing reaches out to me from the kitchen, and helps to bring me out of my daydream. Automatic coffee makers are such a blessing. I set the timer before I went to bed, and now the magic elixir awaits me. Coffee definitely makes life worth living doesn't it?

My workday starts at 6:00 am, and it is now 5:30 am. The morning is clear and cool right now, but, it is supposed to get hot today, around 90 degrees. These uniforms can get downright hot, so underneath our uniform tops, we have on tee shirts with our EMS logo, and we can wear these when we are not on a call. It makes life much more bearable during the heat of the day.

Filling my coffee cup, I headed for my old pickup truck, locking the house door behind me. Even in a small town like Victor, Montana, you can't be too careful. There's not normally much crime around here, but we do live less than an hour from a fairly large city, and there's no use in tempting fate. Besides, Jane feels safer with the doors locked.

The hospital I work for is in the town of Hamilton, Montana, and it was already breaking daylight as I drove the15 miles to the hospital. I love this time of day, when everything is coming alive, waking up, and starting to move. We only get so many sunrises in our lifetimes, and I plan to enjoy as many as possible.

I arrived at the hospital a few minutes early to find the night shift crew just finishing cleaning up and restocking the ambulance after a busy early morning, and they were looking a bit haggard. Apparently they had several emergency calls during the night and didn't get much sleep. The calls they rolled on were, an elderly female with a broken hip, a bar fight, which resulted in an unconscious patron, and then this early morning, rollover traffic crash. It seems that this guy swerved to miss a deer and rolled his new Jeep. It looks like he'll survive, but he did get banged up pretty bad. I hope this isn't an indication of how our' shift is going to be today, because after last night, I need to start out the workday with a nap in the crew quarters.

I jumped right in to help the crew get the ambulance ready to roll again, and we finished up just as my partner, Dan Erickson, arrived. The night crew filled us in on the night's activities, and then notified us that we'll probably be transporting this patient north to the regional trauma center in Missoula, Montana. That means we had better catch some quick breakfast out in the crew quarters before we get the page. It is now 6:05 am, and our day has already begun. I guess I'm not going to get my nap.

When you work in the emergency field, whether it be fire, police, or ambulance, you tend to eat your food fast, and today was no exception. We had no sooner sat down to eat, and our pagers went off requesting that we respond to the emergency room of the hospital to transport a serious patient to Missoula. Well, so much for breakfast. In the fifteen years that I have worked for the ambulance service, I can't begin to tell you how many meals I've had to cut short.

We picked up our patient at the emergency room, and got a briefing from the emergency room doctor on our patient. The patient is in stable condition, but he needs to go to Missoula for some reconstructive surgery and a long recovery, and that means traveling Code 1, no lights or sirens. Bummer man, we adrenalin junkies like to use the lights and sirens.

We loaded our patient into the waiting ambulance, and got started on the approximately one hour trip north to Missoula. The patient is sedated pretty well so it looks like he'll sleep most of the way. It's my turn to ride in the back of the ambulance with the patient, which is just as well given my recent lack of sleep, and concentration. It wouldn't be good to fall asleep driving an ambulance, and it's relatively foolproof riding in the back with the patient. The patient is hooked up to the most modern equipment money can buy, a heart monitor-defibrillator combination, pulse oximeter, I.V. pump, Dynamap blood pressure monitor, and all the bells and whistles, so if anything happens back here, some sort of alarm will alert you.

What would the ancients have thought of such gadgets? Soldiers and medics of old would have loved to have this stuff available, and as I think back to the battle I saw in my dreams, I think of the injuries that could have been repaired with modern day technology. Most people simply died of blood loss or infection. I also think about the woman who lay dying on the battlefield, who was she, and why was there a woman on the battlefield anyhow? I probably could have saved her life, knowing then what I know now.

A slow steady beeping jarred me back my senses once more. The heart monitor, good Lord I'm doing it again, off in a fantasy world. I have really got to get a grip here, because I'm starting to become a liability. I need to keep my mind on reality, on my job, and more importantly, on my patient, so I started to busy myself with checking the settings on the monitor, checking the flow rate on the I.V. drip, anything to keep my mind on the patient, and on the task at hand.

The rest of the trip was uneventful, taking vital signs every 15 minutes, running an occasional heart rhythm strip, double checking the I.V. drip, and everything is cool, only a few short episodes of daydreaming, not too bad. We delivered our patient to the regional trauma center, and gave our report to the receiving doctor. So far, it's hasn't been too hard a day. I can deal with this, and with any luck, I'll still be able to catch a nap on the trip back home.

As soon as we replace our supplies, put new linen on our gurney, and straighten up the ambulance, we'll be ready to head back south to Hamilton. My partner, Dan, suggested that we grab some breakfast when we get back to town, since we didn't have time to eat first thing this morning. That sounded great to me, because I was starving.

The trip back down the Bitterroot Valley is never boring or monotonous; in fact, the view is incredible, with the soaring Bitterroot Mountains close on each side of the highway, and the famed Bitterroot River running down the center of the valley. You'll see deer on nearly every trip, fisherman along the river, eagles, hawks, an occasional moose, and a myriad assortment of birds, rodents, and other wildlife. I don't think I'll ever get tired of this area.

My family has lived in the Bitterroot for 35 years, and although there have been a lot of changes, both socially, and economically, the splendor of the area never diminishes. The scenery is totally majestic, with mountains that seem to reach to the clouds, high plateaus, and vegetation so green and lush that it almost hurts your eyes.

With my partner driving the ambulance back down the Valley, I have time to admire the view around me, and I think back to the dreams that I've been having. The environment in which my dreams take place reminds me a lot of this area, with the high mountains, and the lush valley. This whole recurring dream thing has me so disturbed that I'm beginning to feel the need to talk to someone about this, and now seems as good a time as any.

"Hey Dan, can I talk to you about a something that has really been bothering me lately? There is this dream I keep having, and I really need your perspective on this."

Dan gave me an odd look and then said.

"You mean like going to high school in your underwear or something?"

Now it was my turn to look at him with a look of bewilderment, wanting to open my big mouth about the weird things he must dream about, but, I kept my cool, and said.

"No, nothing quite like that, I've been dreaming about fighting in an ancient battle, with swords, and spears, and things like that."

Dan started to get a slightly annoyed look on his face and then responded.

"So, what's so weird about that?"

Continuing, I explained.

"In this battle, there is a woman that gets killed, and I swear, it's someone I know, now, in this day and age. I haven't been able to figure out who she it is yet, but it's almost like she's been calling out to me lately, and it's really driving me crazy."

Dan still wasn't showing much of an interest, so I went on.

"During the battle, I get stabbed in the chest with a dagger, and I swear Dan, I can still feel the pain of it."

Now he was showing a little more interest, but continued to hold his tongue and listen.

"The wildest part of my dream is that just before I passed out, a dragon came crawling at me from out of the smoke."

Okay, that did it, Dan totally cracked up. He was laughing hysterically until he noticed I was serious, and that I was becoming a little annoyed myself, so he stopped laughing and said.

"You're not kidding, are you?"

"No," I said, "I think it's something that really happened, maybe in a past life."

Dan's face suddenly changed, and he got a more somber look, and said.

"Okay Henry, this is between you and I, and this conversation is not to leave the ambulance, do you understand?"

I nodded my head, and he continued.

"I used to have a recurring dream that also seemed totally real, and I didn't understand what was happening, so I mentioned it to a friend, and she told me about a hypnotherapist that might be able to help me come to terms with my dream. I've never talked to anyone about this because they would think I was crazy, but you brought it up, and it sounds similar to what I went through. The guys name is Doctor James Miller. He has a PHD in Psychology; he lives in Missoula, and does his practice out of his home. He's very good at what he does, he's personable, and you'll feel at ease just being around him, and best of all, his prices are good."

"I think I'll give him a call." I said as we were passing through my hometown of Victor, which lies about three fourths of the way between Missoula and Hamilton.

"Now, let's get something to eat, I'm hungry." Dan said as we pulled into the parking lot of Garfield's café, which is also in the town of Victor, and only about eight miles north of Hamilton, still well within our response time, and one of the best places to eat in the entire Bitterroot valley.

As we pulled up into the parking lot, and parked the ambulance, I felt renewed and refreshed somehow. I now had some direction, and maybe soon, some answers, and best of all, I no longer felt as if I was going crazy. It seems that I'm not the only one who has experienced dreams of past lives, in fact, there are others around just like me, and some, it would seem, closer than I expected.

This time breakfast went off without interruption, and while we ate, Dan wrote the phone number for Dr. Miller on a napkin, which I gladly put away in my pocket. After breakfast, it was back to work, driving the remaining eight miles to Hamilton. It was a little hard to concentrate the rest of the day, just thinking about hooking up with a hypnotherapist, but I wanted answers, and Dr. James Miller was the man I hoped could provide those answers.

Thursday the 19th was my next day off so I called the phone number that Dan had written down for me on the napkin a couple days before at the café. I had butterflies in my stomach as the phone rang on the other end. On the third ring, a male voice responded.

"Hello, this is Dr. James Miller, past lives counselor."

I was slightly taken aback, his voice was so mellow, so gentle, and so ethereal that I almost forgot to speak, but I managed to stutter and stammer enough to tell him my name, and explain the recurring dream that I've been having. He seemed genuinely interested, and excited to talk to me about it, so, I made the appointment for the next day at 1:00 pm. I was so nervous that I could hardly sit still the rest of the day.

That evening when Jane got home I held off on telling her about my appointment with the hypnotherapist until after supper. As usual, we sat out on the porch swing, drinking gin and tonics, enjoying the cool mountain air as it sinks into the valley floor just before dark, and then, with a little liquid courage under my belt I turned to Jane and said.

"Well, I did what you suggested about my dreams. I'm going to someone about it tomorrow. "

"That's good dear." she said, "What doctor are you going to see, because maybe he can also give you something to help you sleep at night."

"Well," I said, "he's actually more than just a doctor, he's a hypnotherapist."

Jane almost choked on her drink, and as soon as she was able to regain her composure; she turned to me and said.

"What on earth ever possessed you to seek out a hypnotherapist?"

I tried to explain to her what Dan had told me about his experience, and his beliefs about past lives. I could tell it wasn't going over so good, but she was a good sport about it, and finally agreed that anything was worth a try. She did strongly encourage me to seek legitimate' medical help if this didn't work out. The rest of the evening was spent quietly, avoiding any more unnecessary conversation. Inside though, I was excited about my appointment, and I was pretty sure I wouldn't get a lot of sleep tonight.

I woke up earlier than usual after a less than restful nights sleep. Episodes of sleep, mixed with dreams of work, dreams of dragons, and dreams of screaming women pretty much had me worn out by the time I got out of bed. After a shower and a shave, I grabbed a cup of coffee and sat on the deck reading the newspaper until Jane got up. She joined me a short time later on the deck with a cup of coffee, still wearing her bathrobe.

"Nice view." I told her.

"Yes, it is," she said, "I never get tired of looking at these mountains."

"I was talking about you." I said.

"Oh Henry, you are so sweet, I absolutely love you." she said, and with a quick kiss, off she went to get ready for work.

Whew, that should keep me in good graces for the rest of the day, I thought to myself, watching as she went into the house, strutting a little more than usual it seemed. I smiled to myself as I continued to read the newspaper and finished another cup of coffee.

After seeing her off to work, I kept myself busy with phone calls, making the last minute arrangements for the fireworks delivery. Then it was off to town for my meeting with the hypnotherapist. I was so nervous that I thought I was going to have a heart attack before I would get to Missoula, but I survived, and now I was here, parked outside of the doctor's house, even more nervous than I was on the trip down.

I arrived at the home of Dr. Miller nearly a half hour early, so I had some time to burn.

The house was a modest, split level home, nice, but nothing fancy. The yard was well kept, with large shade trees, and a covered deck on the back of the house. A white picket fence bordered the street, and a narrow sidewalk led the way to the front door. Venetian blinds covered the windows, apparently for the privacy of the Doctor's clients.

As I sat in the car waiting for my appointment time, I started to get a little nervous thinking about what would come out of this session and I began to think to myself, do I really want to know all of the dark secrets hidden away in the recesses of my soul? The things I had seen in my dreams were more than a little unnerving. Do I really want to live out those dreams in their entirety? Do I really want to experience the pain of the dagger in my chest, or the possibility of seeing one of my past deaths? Hell, do I really even believe in any of this? As I sat there pondering all the possibilities, I started to doubt the whole thing, and I thought that maybe I should just drive away right now and forget about all of this nonsense.

Just about the time I had myself convinced to leave, a man came out of the house. As he walked toward the street he had a distant, almost spooky look to his face. Another man stood at the door waving to him and said he would see him again next week. Obviously, the man leaving was a client like me, and the man at the door was Dr. James Miller. He was not what I expected at all.

I had envisioned a tall, dark, mysterious gentleman with a goatee and a mustache, maybe even horns, hell I don't know. This man was just a regular kind of guy, like anyone you would see sitting in a cubicle in an office building. He was dressed in tan slacks, with a brown sweater, brown loafers, a clean-shaven face, and close cropped hair. As a matter of fact, I was almost disappointed; at least he could have had a cape or something.

I must have been zoning out, because the next thing I knew, he was waving at me and he asked if my name was Henry. Damn, it was too late to run now, so I waved back, got out of my car, and strolled up the walkway to the man standing on the porch. He extended his hand to me and said.

"Hello, I'm James Miller, but please call me Jim."

Shaking his hand I introduced myself, and he showed me into his home. The inside of the home was designed specifically for comfort and mood. Hidden speakers playing soft music, mixed with the sound of a running stream, and the sound of birds chirping could be heard, quietly, as if off in the distance. An unseen fan somewhere simulated a light, refreshing breeze. The colors of the rooms were a neutral, pale green, and various plants and ferns adorned the room, adding to the ambiance of peace and tranquility.

Dr. Miller took a seat opposite to me. This was the first time I noticed his eyes, deep, iridescent blue, warm, understanding, and they seemed to be able to look right into your soul. As he started to speak, the tone of his voice immediately put you at ease.

"Henry, I would like you to tell me a little about yourself, and then tell me about the dreams you've been having." He reached over and turned on a small tape recorder.

"I'm going to record every session we do, so we will have an official archive of your events. Then, after we've talked awhile, I'm going to put you under hypnosis to see if we can get to the root of your dreams. So Henry, tell me about you."

I proceeded to tell him of my life, my job, my likes, my dislikes, and then to tell him everything I could remember about my dreams. When I had finished, Jim jotted down a few notes and told me to lean back in my chair, relax, and close my eyes.

"Now, clear your mind Henry, and forget about all of those things that are troubling to your soul. Feel your body relaxing as the cares of the world melt away. Listen to the water flowing, running over the rocks of a high mountain stream. Can you hear the birds chirping, telling the tales of the nature of the real world, wild and free, like your soul is right now? Do you feel the light breeze on your face, the same breeze that flows around the entire planet, giving life to every living thing? Now, imagine yourself lying beside that stream, lying in a beautiful mountain meadow, surrounded by towering peaks, green grass, blue sky, and soft, wispy clouds. Relax your entire body even more, becoming aware of every square inch of your skin, every cell. Relax, not a care in the world. I want you to feel yourself relaxing more and more, even getting sleepy. You are getting sleepy, relaxing deeper, deeper, deeper, and deeper."

Chapter 2

Screeching again, and yelling, what is all of that noise?

"Ethan, Ethan, wake up, wake up! Ethan please wake up, there's trouble down in the dragon pens. Ethan!"

I sat upright in my bed, my mind in a fog, trying to figure out where I was and what was going on, and as I looked around, I thought to myself, I have simply got to stop drinking so much wine.

'What is all that noise?' I asked myself again, looking about my bedchamber. The excited voice was coming from outside the door of my private chambers, and whoever it was, they were being very insistent.

The sun was just coming up between the twin mountain peaks outside of my castle window, and the purple velvet drapes were swaying in the breeze like dancing maidens. The woman lying next to me simply moaned, and rolled over, taking most of the bed coverings with her.

"Ethan, Ethan, did you hear what I said. There's trouble in the dragon pens."

It was Balon, my trusted friend and dragon tender. Balon is a short, stocky, good natured fellow, rather clumsy, prone to minor accidents of one type or another, always chuckling to himself, and although he was a man not normally given to excitability, he was now visibly shaken.

"Ethan, you must come with me, an intruder has gotten into the dragon pens and tried to poison the dragons. Captain Sardon has captured the intruder, but you must come quickly."

"Come in Balon, the door's unlocked." I said, running my fingers through my long unkempt hair.

Balon burst into the room, obviously out of breath, carrying on about spies, dragons, Sardon, and poison; at least until he saw that I was not alone. As soon as I could get him to calm down, he quickly repeated his version of what had happened down in the dragon pens, and it was then that the gravity of the situation finally sunk in. Then, I too got excited. As I jumped out of bed and headed for the doorway, until Balon excitedly blurted out,

"Ethan, stop, put on your robe." When I looked down it was obvious I wasn't quite awake yet.

"Oh my, this simply won't do." I said, and turning back, I grabbed my pants, shirt, cloak, sandals, and staff, and started dressing as we headed for the doorway. Turning once again to the woman lying in bed, who, now awake, was watching the proceedings with interest, I said.

"Marta, please let yourself out when you're ready, you know the way out, and I'll see you later at breakfast."

"As you wish, my Lord." she responded, now leaning on one elbow, taking in all of the excitement.

"Please forgive my intrusion Miss Marta." Balon said apologetically.

"It's okay Balon, duty calls." she responded, "I'll see you boys at breakfast."

As we headed down the hallway to the massive stone stairway that would lead us below the castle to the dragon pens, I couldn't help saying to Balon.

"My friend you would not believe the crazy dream I was having,"

Balon just looked at me with a puzzled look on his face, and kept walking. I hailed a trooper who was stationed in the hallway, and ordered him to come follow us into the caverns. He will provide an extra sense of security since I don't know what to expect once we get below. If there was one intruder, then there's usually more lurking somewhere nearby.

My castle is strategically located on top of a jagged mountain peak, overlooking a large plateau and a sweeping, luscious green valley nearly five miles below, and that valley holds the massive castle of King Malok. The mountain under my castle is honeycombed with caverns and caves, some of which have been utilized for the dragon pens. The caves we use for dragon pens open up to the cliff face, which provides perfect takeoff spots for the dragons, and the cliff itself is a vertical drop of nearly three thousand feet, which provides the ideal take off spot for my dragons.

Imagine if you will, a beast, 30 feet long from nose to tail, with a wingspan of nearly twice that long unfolded. They can't just lift off from the ground, because their wings are too long in comparison to their bodies. Dragons hunt on the fly, snatch their pray from the ground on a fly-by, and then land on a high peak or a rocky spire to eat their meal. When they're ready to take off again, they simply have to fall off of their perch, unfurl their wings and soar away. They are very ungainly on the ground, having to walk on their two legs and their folded wing tips, and once on the ground, they are vulnerable to attack. They would have to walk to a high point where they could get their wings unfurled enough to lift off of the ground. That is why my castle, with its unique caverns, and cave openings to the cliff face, are so important to my vocation. I am the Dragon Master. I raise dragons for service to the King's army. They are beasts of war, and they are an awesome force. My dragons are the reason why the King's army has never been defeated in battle.

My family didn't start out raising dragons for war; in fact, my grandfather first raised a single dragon as a hobby, a novelty if you will. My father was still a young man at the time, and was very impressionable. Aside from a few minor mishaps during the learning process, the experience was mostly positive. As dragon numbers worldwide continued to decline, my father became passionate about trying to save the dragons as a species, and started to raise a few of them to protect the blood line.

At that point in time, our castle was the only outpost in the entire region. We were isolated, self sufficient, impregnable, and certainly well protected by the dragons. The castle itself is only approachable from the main road coming up to the gate. A drawbridge protects the gate by spanning a seemingly bottomless crevasse, and sheer cliffs with drops of three thousand, to nearly ten thousand feet surround the rest of the castle, which means no one was coming into this castle uninvited.

Our peaceful way of life began to change when an envoy of King Malok arrived at the castle one day with a proposition, and as it turns out, it was a proposition that was not to be refused. It seems that the King was going to build his main castle in the valley below, and the envoy said it would be very profitable for my father, and his people. Now, my father, being a proud man, sent the envoy packing, stating that we had all we needed here without the King's generosity, which, as it turned out, was not the answer the King was looking for.

About a month later, while the peasants were working the fields on the plateau just above the valley, the King's army showed up, took all of the peasants as prisoners, and then laid siege to our castle. They could not take our castle by force, but they could starve us out in time. So, as a show of force on the part of my father, he turned loose the dragons, which of course, terrorized the King's soldiers. The dragons would not touch the peasants because they knew their scent, but the soldiers were fair game. The soldiers then threatened to kill all of the peasants, and thus, it didn't take long for our two sides to come to an understanding. We needed the produce from the fields below, we needed our peasants to work those fields, and the King needed the valley for his castle.

A deal was struck between my father, and the King. We would keep our autonomy, except for the fact that a garrison of the King's soldiers would be stationed in our castle to prevent any reoccurrence of hostility. In turn, we had to teach the dragons not to kill the King's soldiers. That was nearly seventy-five years ago, and now, the dragons themselves are in the King's service. Things certainly do change over time.

Raising a dragon is not a simple process. You don't really tame a dragon in the sense of the word. You have to gain their trust at a young age, provide their every need, treat them with respect, and never, ever, make them angry. After my father died, the job of raising and training the dragons fell upon me, as well as a couple of others, others such as my good friend and confidant, Balon.

It's really only by chance that you find out who is able to work with dragons. In fact, it's more of a case that the dragons pick you' to work with them, rather than you who pick to work with dragons. If they like you, you are accepted. If not, you'll die; it's as simple as that.

Basically, what we do here, is train the dragons who they should not' kill, which in this case, are the King's soldiers, myself, my staff, and of course, the local peasants, all of which are the clan of the Borg. Since the King and his soldiers were also of the clan of the Borg that was the only reason the dragons were willing to accept the King's soldiers as readily as they did all of those years ago.

We train the dragons to recognize the scent of a Borg, and this was done when the dragons were still quite young, unfortunately, with a few mishaps in the beginning. Any other scent, or tribe, is the enemy, that is, unless two things happen.

The first would be to parade members of any new clan past the dragons, and then hope for the best. The next step would be up to the dragons themselves. Dragons are very perceptive creatures, and may even be psychic. If they sense something good in you, if they sense that you are trustworthy, then they will accept you, and that is good enough for us. At that point, you will be accepted into our kingdom. If not, well, you know the rest of the story, meltdown, or the fiery furnace, so to speak.

Dragons have many ways to kill you, and all of them are quite nasty. The first of course, is that they just grab you up as they fly by with their eight-inch long talons, rip you to shreds, and eat you. That sounds gruesome enough, but, if you think that sounds bad, the next one is even nastier.

Dragons emit two different streams of venom from their back of their throat. Just the venom itself, when it comes in contact with the flesh, tends to melt the flesh from the bone, but more notably, when the two streams of venom mix with each other, and then mix with the oxygen in the air, it instantly ignites into an inferno, turning the hapless victim into charcoal. All of these are an unpleasant way to move on to the next sojourn, hence, we spend a lot of time with the dragons to gain their trust and respect.

Let's face reality, the dragons tolerate us only because they' want to, not because we want them to. There are not many dragons left in the world, they know it, and we know it. I believe that they know their continued survival, in this realm, depends on humans, and that is where I come in, I provide them with a protected place to live, at least until now it would seem. This castle, and these caverns, should have been the safest place on earth for a dragon to live.

Balon, the trooper, and myself hurried down the stone stairway, turn after turn, down three levels to a large, open chamber. The whole mountain is honeycombed with caverns of every shape and size. My ancestors carved stairways down through solid rock to tie each cavern into another. Some of the larger caverns were used as dragon lairs, especially the ones that are several layers down from the main castle, and away from its human inhabitants. This is the area where Captain Sardon had captured the intruder.

Captain Sardon, now there was a piece of work. Sardon is in charge of the Castle guard, appointed here by the King himself, sometimes, I feel, more to keep track of me, and my work with the dragons, than to actually protect us from anyone, because Lord knows we can protect ourselves without the help of the King's men.

The King has always felt a little threatened by me and my dragons. We live in a fortress on the mountain overlooking the King's castle. With our drawbridge up, we are for the most part impenetrable, and my dragons could raise havoc on the residents below. Unfortunately, we are all of the Borg clan, and my dragons are trained not to attack anyone with the scent of a Borg. So, I am at the mercy of the King, and his army. We now rely on the peddlers from the castle below for everything, and we would be totally isolated up here without food. Water is not a problem up here because the mountain, with all of the caverns, creates a lot of moisture from the circling air currents within.

There are natural springs all throughout the mountain.

We do have fairly substantial storage caverns full of grains and vegetables, which would sustain us for a few months, but a long siege, would still take a toll on us. The King also knows this, so, for the time being, we will be subjects of the King. My dragons will always protect me personally, but beyond that, I am still a subject of the King, even though I am master of my own castle. No wonder I drink too much wine.

Now, back to the subject of Captain Sardon, I suspect that the King didn't want Captain Sardon in his own palace, since that job only goes to the most elite, well trained, well mannered, and best groomed of all the king's troops, while the misfits, and miscreants are sent to my castle, and Captain Sardon definitely fits the profile. Maybe the King hopes the dragons will eat them all.

As for Sardon, he is not much to look at either, being kind of a frail individual, slightly taller than myself, skinny, with a scrawny little neck, a large pronounced Adams apple, and did I mention the fact that he has absolutely no personality. In fact, he seems a bit shady if you ask me, and I get the impression that he is hiding some kind of a dark secret deep inside.

As we approached the main chamber, the noise of the dragons' screeching was deafening. They were definitely upset, and I had never seen them act this way before. 'What was going on here?' I thought to myself.

As Balon and I turned the last corner, we could see Captain Sardon up ahead, about a hundred feet away, with a man on his knees in front of him, head bowed, with Sardon's sword pressed to the side of his throat. Although I could not say for certain, I thought I noticed Captain Sardon glance sideways in our direction ever so slightly, smiling imperceptibly. Just as I was about to hail the captain, we were horrified as Sardon thrust his sword through the throat of the captive in front of him. The helpless man fell sideways as Sardon pulled his bloody sword from his neck. Streams of blood spewed everywhere as the corpse toppled over, jerking in spasms on the cold stone floor.

"Captain Sardon!" I screamed at the top of my lungs, which caused the dragons to go into such frenzy, that it seemed at any moment, the dragons would break down the iron barriers from their caverns and charge into the hallways. I needed to get composure over myself, and gain control over the situation in a hurry.

Immediately, Captain Sardon fell to his knees before me, his face to the ground, saying,

"Forgive me my Lord; you know how bad I hate the Gogs. I've told you how they killed my parents and that was all I could think of, please forgive me."

Taken slightly aback, I said.

"This was a Gog clansman? How did he make it this far into the castle without being noticed by the castle guard? What was he doing here; you should not have killed him Captain, because we needed some answers. Has he told you anything? What did I hear about poison, tell me quick, I must know? Please Captain, rise, and talk to me."

It was Balon who spoke first, as he was standing right behind me.

"Ethan we must first calm down the dragons. You must let them see you, so they will know you are okay."

In my shock and dismay, I had nearly forgotten about the dragons, which were now in a volatile state of frenzy, volatile being the key word here.

"I will talk to you soon Captain. Meanwhile, gather some of your men and comb the castle for any more unwanted guests."

"Yes my Lord," Sardon said, bowing, and turning on his heels he headed upstairs toward the main castle, yelling for guards the whole way.

"Balon, let's go see the dragons."

As we headed down the hallway, I noticed a small vile, which had apparently fallen from the cloak pocket of the dead Gog clansman. I picked it up and placed it into my own pocket. The trooper who had followed us down into the caverns started to race after Captain Sardon, but I quickly stopped him,

"What is your name soldier?"

Bowing his head, he said, "My name is Valik, my Lord."

"Very well Valik, I want you to stay and guard this body. I do not want it moved until I return, do you understand?"

The guardsman bowed again, but with great concern in his eyes he said,

"Yes master, but my Captain has summoned us all, and I cannot disobey his order."

"I understand soldier, but I am in charge of this castle, and also of your Captain Sardon. I will speak to him on your behalf, now do as I have told you, it will be alright."

"Yes my Lord." he said, and assumed a defensive stance over the fallen clansman, his sword drawn, and his shield at the ready.

He was a formidable sight, standing slightly over six feet tall, long dark hair, closely trimmed beard and mustache, wearing the standard issue battle dress of a castle guard. These include a black leather vest, over a sleeveless, red silk undershirt, leather half helmet bearing the dragon circle insignia on the forehead, tight, black leather pants, and high top boots, very handsome, but very deadly, and as we walked away, I thought to myself, I think I need a private bodyguard, and I think Valik is due for a promotion. As if reading my mind, Balon spoke again, saying.

"Forgive my saying so Ethan, but I do not trust that Captain Sardon."

Still walking I replied, "Nor do I my friend, nor do I."

We approached the dragon pen gates cautiously, speaking reassuringly as we approached. It would not be good to suddenly appear in front of the iron gates only to be roasted, or at best, melted like a candle. I have seen both happen, and it was not a pretty sight. That is what dragons do, and these were raised to do just that, hopefully only to the enemy, but, when in a frenzy, as they were now, anything could happen.

As I approached the gate, I first had to clear my mind of all of the recent distractions. Dragons can sense danger, fear, love, trust, and especially deceit. Your feelings and emotions had better be true when you deal with dragons because I believe they can see into your very soul.

Dragon numbers are quickly vanishing. There are those in the world who want to eliminate all of the dragons that are left on Earth, including the Gog clansman who infiltrated the castle today. The Gog clan knows that we fight with the dragons, and to defeat King Malok, you must first eliminate my dragons. The Gog have killed most, if not all of the dragons in their own land, and now it would seem they want to kill my dragons as well, but why. There has to be something behind this brazen attack right into the heart of my castle. Not even the Gog could hate dragons so bad that they would risk their life to sneak into the dragon's lair itself. I don't like this at all, and I really wish I could have questioned the Gog clansman myself.

My seven dragons were raised from eggs that my father had gathered nearly 100 years ago from nests in the wild. Unfortunately, my father was captured, tortured, and killed a few years later as he tried to gather additional eggs in the land of Magog, which is where the Gog clansman live. But, before my father died, he had passed the legacy of dragon mastery down to me. I was raised with these dragons, we are the same age, they accept me, they love me, and they will protect me at all cost. I had hoped I could have done the same for them.

These dragons are still fairly young, as dragons go, with some dragons living to be 250 years old under good conditions. It is estimated that there are only a couple of dozen dragons, maybe less, left in the whole world, living totally wild and free. Occasionally a wild dragon pays us a visit, which really causes us some havoc, but even those times are becoming few and far between. I am afraid their years are numbered, and if the Gog clansmen have their way, the demise of the dragons could come even sooner.

As we drew near to the gates of the dragon pens, I called to each dragon by name.

"Feron, Thermon, Kracon, Ferose, Gahenna, Haden, Searon, everything is okay. I'm okay, be calm, I'm coming to the gate."

They were still pretty restless, but I could tell they were starting to settle down some, knowing that I was present, and that I was okay. I decided to add one more level of insurance before I stuck my head around the corner.

"Balon, would you speak to them also, they trust you?"

Balon has always had a way with beasts of every kind, be they wild or tame. I have never known any human who could walk up to a totally wild animal, reach down and pet it without losing an arm. They seem to have a natural trust in him, and that is why he has been so good with these dragons. From the beginning, they have accepted him without reservation.

It has been uncanny, there have been times when I lose my patience, and the dragons seem to be doing everything but what I need them to, and that's when I bring in Balon to restore order. And now was one of those times. Balon stepped ahead of me and also spoke to each dragon by name. There seemed to be an instant calming effect, and I felt that it was now safe to approach the dragons. Turning to look at Balon, I shook my head, and said.

"Sometimes I just hate you Balon. These are supposed to be my' dragons."

Tentatively we both peeked around the corner. Crowded near the gate was a sight that would have made a normal man's heart stop cold, dragons, terrifying, menacing, and yet regal all at the same time, but to Balon, and myself, the sight was beautiful.

Dragons, when on the ground, look very ungainly, seeming almost to be crawling at times to motivate. They can rise up and stand on their powerful hind legs, as they were now. Their front limbs have evolved into wings, and you can see the supporting arm bones within the leathery wings. To move on the ground, they have to walk with their wings, as well as their legs, which even though it's clumsy, it's quite functional.

The dragons still seemed to be visibly upset for some reason, and even with the both of us standing before them, something was still wrong, so I began to count heads. Feron, Theron, Kracon, Ferose, Haden, Searon, where is Gahenna?

"Gahenna," I called out. "Gahenna."

Balon also called out. No response. The dragons were now starting to mill about, so we decided it was safe to go inside.

"We need to go inside Balon, do you have the key?"

"Yes Master." Balon said as he pulled the key from his pocket, slid it into the hole and turned the key with a loud clank.

"Go easy and timidly Balon, I don't feel like being roasted today."

"Neither do I Ethan, not today, not any day," Balon said.

We stepped inside the cavern, trying not to show any fear or excess anxiety that might cause the same response from the dragons. As we moved farther into the cavern, we could see the large, motionless form of Gahenna lying near the back wall of the cavern. We approached cautiously so as not to upset the other dragons or suddenly arouse a possibly injured dragon. Both could be quite hazardous to our health.

Nearing closer, we saw no rising of her chest, no breathing, no signs of life. What had happened to her? There were no immediate, visible signs of injury. My heart sank in my chest; these dragons are a part of me, right down to my inner soul. It was truly as if I had just lost a part of my family, and the remorse I was feeling now was almost too much to bear.

Something is in the wind, I can feel it, and I believe this attack was personal. It was directed at my dragons, and at me, but to what end. For now, I will keep my suspicions to myself, but I think we are going to have to watch over the dragons a little closer in the future. I don't believe this was a random attack, and I don't think it will be the last. I think it is going to prove to be a wise decision to have a personal bodyguard.

I was suddenly aware of the quiet that surrounded us. As I looked around, all of the dragons were still, their eyes fixed upon us, and their lost sibling. They were grieving, and as I looked over to Balon, he had tears in his eyes. The Gog clansmen have done this, but how, how could they have gotten this far into the kingdom, not to mention this far into my castle? They have never seemed to be an overly intelligent lot in the past, and certainly never this bold, so something has changed, and I don't like it, I don't like it at all.

"Balon, you mentioned poison when you woke me up, how did you know of this?"

"Captain Sardon told me about it, just before he sent me to find you."

That's interesting, I said to myself, remembering the vial that had fallen on the floor after the clansman died, which means the vial would have still been hidden in his pocket after Sardon captured him, otherwise, why would he not have taken the vial away from the prisoner, since it was still a threat. And if the vial was still in the Gog clansman's pocket, how did Sardon know my dragon had been poisoned? I'm starting to smell a rat.

"Tonight, we must move the remaining dragons. Open the outer gates, and let them out to hunt. Then, close these gates, and open the level 2 gates for when the dragons return, because I want them a little closer to the castle where I can keep an eye on them."

"Yes master," Balon replied, and moved off to the iron chains and pulleys that would raise the massive outer gates.

My father, mostly to keep out roaming male dragons, had secured all of the cave openings to the outside with iron gates many eons ago. Since then though, they have served us well to keep out unwanted human guests also. How then, did the Gog clansman get in here? I suspect that we have a spy in our midst, and the very thought of it was unnerving. We must all be on our guard from here on out.

When Balon had finished raising the iron gates, I turned to the remaining dragons and spoke to them as one friend would speak to another.

"I am so sorry my friends, but we will get a chance to avenge the death of Gahenna, I promise you this."

At that, I walked to the gate leading to the hallway where Valik stood vigil over the slain Gogs clansman, and called out to him.

"Mr. Valik, please drag the body in here. Move very slowly, and show no fear or malice."

"Yes my Lord," Valik said, grabbing the dead clansman by his cloak, and then dragging him into the chamber of the dragons. Immediately, the dragons became tense and started milling about and growling. Valik dropped the body near my feet, bowed, and then started to back away toward the hallway.

"Mr. Valik," I said, "please stay close, I want the dragons to know you are my friend."

I reached down, grabbed the Gog clansman by his hair, and lifted him up so his face was exposed to the dragons, then, in a loud, stern voice I said.

"This, my friends, is the man who killed your sister, and he is our enemy. Take in his scent, and hunt down all who share that scent."

The dragons were starting to grow increasingly restless, and vocal, and I knew I wouldn't be able to control their anger much longer, so I spoke one last time.

"Come now my friends, fly, and hunt."

With that, I grabbed the dead clansman by the cloak, dragged the body to the open gate, and the cliffs beyond, and threw the lifeless body over the edge of the cliff into nearly five thousand feet of empty space.

"Now, fly away my friends!"

I stepped out of the way just in time as the frenzied dragons crawled past me and launched themselves over the edge of the cliff, soaring down the cliff face to intercept the falling corpse in their talons, then rising high into the air with the lifeless body, each dragon taking turns tearing the body to pieces, screeching incessantly. It was a sight that would turn a normal man white with fear. Balon, Valik, and I stood on the brink of the precipice, and marveled at the sight of the dragons circling and diving as they moved off into the distance.

Valik, I need you to handpick about a dozen men that you would trust with your life, and report back here to me. We need to take this dragon to a special place. Speak none of this to your Captain; I will take care of that. You are about to receive a promotion to my personal staff."

"Yes my Lord, and thank you, I won't let you down." At that, Valik bowed, turned sharply on his heel, and headed out the gate into the hallway.

As soon as he was gone, I turned to Balon, putting my arm around his large, bulky shoulders, and said.

"My true, dear, friend, thank you for always being by my side. I don't know what I would do without you. Right now, I have some chores for you."

"Yes my Lord," he responded, "what is it that you need me to do?"

"We must get the drawbridge down and the castle gate open for business. The peddlers will be waiting to set up their wares, and I want to convey the appearance that it's business as usual. If there are any more spies about, I don't want them to know that their plans have had any success. I hope the spectacle of the clansman being torn to bits was not too much for the peasants, because I certainly wouldn't want to start a panic."

"As soon as we get things cleaned up around here, I will need to go down into the valley to speak with the King about what has happened. When you're done Balon, meet me back here, there's something I want to show you, now go."

"Yes master," Balon said as he turned and followed out the same way Valik had left. Standing alone with the dead dragon, I touched the hard scaled hide of the magnificent beast, bowed my head, and said my goodbyes.

While I awaited the return of Balon, Valik, and the troops, I began to inspect the body of the slain dragon. Moving slowly around the body, I inspected every inch, starting at the head, with its short, slightly curved horns, then to the mouth, inspecting the rows of razor sharp teeth for any sign that she may have eaten something. Then I moved my way down the long neck, with its rows of raised scales that protect the back of its neck from attack, attacks mostly from other dragons. So far, there was nothing out of the ordinary.

Next, I worked my way down to the point where the wings attached to the shoulders. A dragon's wings fold in layers, with arm-like bones making up a sub substructure which supports a thick leathery hide. There is nothing vulnerable here. With much effort I stretched the first wing out as far as I could to view the chest area beneath. There was still nothing remarkable. Although I could use some help, dragons are fairly lightweight. Their bones are hollow to facilitate flight, otherwise, given their size, they would be far too heavy to fly, and even though help would be nice, I need to keep this as secret as possible, so I will forgo any help.

The dragon was lying mostly on the one side of her chest, and fortunately, when she died, her wing was partially outstretched. Getting down on my hands and knees, I crawled under the wing to inspect the chest. There was something, a small metal dart about six inches long, imbedded in the soft pit area just below the joining of the wing and the chest, the only possible vulnerable spot on a beast such as this. Our assassin knew what he was doing. But how did he deliver the poison dart? No one mentioned finding a blowgun, or a crossbow, especially not Captain Sardon.

Suddenly, I became aware of another presence in the chamber. Startled, I turned to see that Captain Sardon was standing at the gateway, and was staring at me with a look of disdain on his face. I realize now that I should have kept someone here with me. I am going to have to be a little more careful in the future.

"Finding anything interesting?" He asked.

"Nothing yet Captain, how about you, did you find any more uninvited guests in the castle?"

"We have found nothing sir, but since I have your ear, what is this nonsense about you taking charge over some of my men? You do not have the right, for they take their orders from me, not you."

"On the contrary Captain, I have every right to do as I please with you, and your men. You are on loan to me, by order of the King. You are here to protect, and assist me in any way I need. Or have you suddenly forgot your place and purpose"

I clutched my staff a bit tighter as I noticed Captain Sardon tense up.

Maybe I should learn to keep my big mouth shut. Sardon suddenly relaxed, bowed his head, and said.

"Please forgive me my Lord, I should not have spoken to you so irreverently, it was not my place. I am just upset about everything that has happened this morning, and of the foul presence of the Gog clansman. Myself, and my men, are at your disposal."

"Thank you Captain, but no one is as upset as I am right now, I have been with this dragon since it was first hatched, and I will miss her greatly. As for now, I will need about a dozen of your men to help me dispose of my dragon, and after that, I request that you assign Mr. Valik to serve me as my personal bodyguard. It would seem, lately, that I might need one."

"Yes, you are completely right Ethan. Again, please forgive my lack of protocol. Circumstances dictate a heightened state of security until this can be straightened out. I will make the proper arraignments to have Mr. Valik moved from the barracks to your villa. Would there be anything else?"

"No Captain, that is all, you may go, and thank you."

With that, Captain Sardon turned on his heel, and went out the way he had come. I paused for a few moments to listen as his footsteps cleared the hall and ascended the stone steps. Breathing a sigh of relief, I turned back to the chore at hand.

As I waited for Valik and the other soldiers to return, I went back to inspecting the body of the dragon. Returning to the wing pit area, I pulled the dart, wrapped it in my sweat cloth, being careful not to touch the shaft, or the tip, and placed it in my cloak pocket along with the vial that was dropped by the Gog clansman.

Continuing to work my way down the body of the dragon, I inspected the rest of the chest and abdomen, which are covered with tightly interconnecting scales. No way for a simple dart to penetrate this area. Even arrows don't stand much of a chance of penetrating the chest of a dragon. The softer underbelly has some vulnerability to a well-placed spear. The problem is, if you get close enough to put a spear into the abdomen of a standing dragon, you will probably be roasted soon after. I have seen lucky strikes on dragons flying close to the ground, with a spear penetrating the underbelly, but it is a rare occasion.

The tail of a dragon is a weapon unto itself. It can be fifteen feet long, with large spiny scales sticking up along its entire length, and three to five deadly spikes on the tip. When a dragon switches its tail, it is something you won't soon forget, if you live through it.

There are ways to kill dragons, but until now, those ways were usually a suicide mission. The most dangerous way to kill a dragon was for you to bury yourself under debris or in a hole in the ground, lure the dragon over the hole with a ram or sheep, and then stab the dragon up through the softer underbelly. Usually the mortally wounded dragon would tear the victim to shreds before it died, which was a nasty way for the victim to exit this life, and enter the next.

The next way to kill a dragon is to try to shoot them with large spring loaded spears, either on the ground, or with a lucky shot out of the air. These weapons look like giant crossbows, with bows carved from a single tree, requiring a dozen men to pull the bow back, and set the trigger. The arrows they shoot are ten feet long, and tipped with fire tempered iron broad heads, sharpened to a very long, narrow point, and razor sharp blades. Because of the difficulty in preparing the weapon to fire, you usually got one shot. After that, you were dragon fodder.

Now, it would seem, the Gogs have found an easier and more deadly method of dragon slaying. All they have to do is wait for a dragon to open his wings to stretch, take off, or fly overhead, deliver a poison dart, or a poison arrow, to the soft spot under their wing pit, and then hide. This poison is apparently very deadly, and very quick. This poison is a very real threat to my dragons, and to the King's army. I feel like I must notify King Malok immediately.

I had just finished with my inspection of the slain dragon when Balon returned, followed closely by Valik and his troops. Ropes were wrapped around the body of the dragon to secure the wings in close to its body. More ropes were secured to the head, neck, and body to facilitate dragging. Leading the way, we dragged the dragon out of the chamber and into the hallway, and then turning in the opposite way of the stairway, I led the procession to what seemed to be a dead end at a stone wall.

Turning to Balon, Valik, and the troops, I said.

"Men, you are about to see something that no other man alive today has ever seen, and I want you each to swear secrecy, and loyalty, first to me, and then to the dragons."

Each man knelt, and declared his loyalty.

"Rise now, and view the wonders of the earth, past, present, and future."

With that, I pulled a lone key, attached to a lanyard around my neck, felt along a crack in the face of the stone wall, paused, slid the key into the crevice, and turned the key. As if by magic, a large stone door slid sideways into the wall, revealing an opening into a long, sloping hallway, which disappeared down into the darkness. A stale, musky smell invaded our nostrils, as new air rushed past us into the passageway that had not been opened in many years.

"How did you do that," asked Balon, "are you also a magician?"

"No, my friend, it is all done with counterweights. It's science, not magic."

I stepped inside, feeling along the wall for one of the torches that had been placed there many years before. To one of the soldiers at the rear of the column, I said.

"Grab that torch off of the wall back in the main hall, and bring it up here."

When he had done so, Balon and I lit new torches, and instructed the men to pull the dragon inside the passage. When we were all inside, I took one last look into the main hallway to make sure we were not being followed, inserted my key into another lock on the opposite side of the doorway, turned it, and watched the secret doorway close behind us.

Moving back to the head of the column, I led the way down the gradually descending hallway, Balon behind me with his torch, then the troops dragging the dragon, and finally the last soldier with the other torch. The pathway went for a couple thousand feet or so before I spoke again.

"Please be sure to stay on the pathway gentleman, because you may not have noticed, but there is no longer a wall on your right side."

Lowering his torch slightly, Balon's light illuminated only the edge of an apparent precipice. You could hear a slight catch of breath from Balon, as well as a couple of the others. The pathway made a gradual turn to the right for another couple of hundred feet or so and then leveled out.

"Gentlemen, please stay in your places until I can get some light in here."

The troops watched as my torchlight moved off toward a wall that was about twenty feet away. I had to feel my way along the cold, dank stone wall for the chain placed there nearly fifty years before. There it is. I almost missed it with all the dust that had built up. The chain disappeared up into the dark void above, nearly two thousand feet in length, where it was attached to a small, well-camouflaged hatch, on an inaccessible southern facing slope of the mountain.

"Men," I called out, "prepare yourself for visions that no man has seen before you." Grasping the chains in my hand, I started pulling on one side, feeling resistance at first, as the chains strained against decades of dust, and then, as the chain began to move, rays of light started to penetrate the darkness, gradually increasing in intensity as rays of light ricocheted off mirrors and prisms, placed in unseen recesses along the walls, ceilings, and floor. Eyes were squinting as they adjusted to the near daylight brightness that filled the cavern. Everyone was so amazed at the miracle of the light, that they didn't notice the vision unfolding before them, until, with mouths agape, an audible gasp ran over the entire contingent of men as they became aware of the massive underground cathedral. Then, as the visions of the massive cavern began to unfold, Balon dropped his torch.

The first vision to befall the small group of men was enough to make the heart stand still, at least a dozen fully mummified dragons, standing side by side, wings unfurled, wingtip to wingtip, circling the walls of the massive cavern. It was a menacing sight to say the least.

I spoke as I walked back to the small group of men.

"These are the ancestors of the dragons we live with in the castle, placed here over time by my father, and his father before him. Some of these remains are five hundred years old. The natural dryness in this cavern preserves whatever, and whoever we put down here. The dragon we bring here today will take her place alongside these, and then there will be six more spaces left after today."

"Each dragon was meticulously mounted here to spend the rest of eternity. Maybe some future generation will find this place, when dragons no longer exist, and marvel at the beasts that once roamed the land. As soon as we put Gahenna in her place of honor, I will show you other wonders. From this point on, you are bound by your oath of honor, never to speak of this place, is that clear?"

Each and every man reaffirmed his oath.

Along one wall you could see the large pathway we had descended, disappearing back up into the darkness. It was probably good that the men had descended in darkness, because if anyone had been afraid of heights, he would not have made the trip.

We dragged the slain dragon to her place of rest at the end of the parade of dragons, then untied the ropes wrapped around her body. On the floor of the cavern was a pole structure in the shape of a stick man, fifteen feet tall, with a wye at the bottom. Ten feet up was a cross pole, about 40 feet long.

We laid the dragon out on the floor on her back, securing her to the pole with leather straps. The wings were unfurled, one at a time, each fold locked open with a smaller pole, and then the whole wing secured to the main cross beam. To attach the smaller poles, a small hole was cut through the leathery wing, just beneath the wing bone, so straps could be inserted to tie the wing to the poles. The neck was secured to the pole, with the head unsecured so it would droop forward slightly when the pole was raised, giving the illusion that the dragons were looking down on you.

Next, the legs were attached to the wye at the bottom to give the dragons a defiant stance. Ropes were inserted into iron rings at the top of the pole, and at the ends of the cross poles, with the other ends looped through iron rings placed into the stone walls of the cavern.

"Okay men, on the count of three, pull."

And as we did so, the dragon rose up before us, every bit as chilling in death, as it was in life. As soon as the ropes were attached to the wall, I said.

"I thank you gentleman for your help. Now, if you would be so kind as to join me in a moment of silence."

Although only Balon and I shared any real feelings for the dragons, the rest of the party showed their respect by bowing their heads.

As I stood there, I reflected back to the early years with the dragons, the good times, and bad. And I thought of my grandfather, who's dreams, and foresight, envisioned the cosmic connection between man and dragon, and to my own father who made working with dragons a reality. And now I could feel it all slipping away. My inner senses could feel a change coming soon, and with the events of today, combined with a nagging sense of impending conflict, I feel we are due to see some sweeping changes over the next few weeks, months at most. Something big is coming, and those changes have started right inside my own castle, and furthermore, I feel Captain Sardon is involved. From this point on, I must be very careful. I must pick whom I can trust, and I must watch over my dragons.

"Okay gentleman, please follow me, there is much more to see."

The cavern was huge, carved out over a millennium by volcanism, wind, and water. The inside of the main chamber was probably five hundred feet long, three hundred feet wide, and one hundred feet to the ceiling in the main part of the chamber. Nooks and crannies were etched into the walls, some as big as thirty feet wide. It was to one of these small nooks that we came to first.

The nook was recessed into the wall of the cavern about ten feet deep, fifteen feet wide, and facing the main hall of dragons. It was not readily visible until you approached it nearly head on. As we approached the small chamber, an audible gasp was emitted from the party of men, and some of the soldiers even reached for their swords. There before us were three grizzled old men, all three sitting on thrones, each one holding a tall sepulcher, with a crystal dragon head mounted on the top, just like the one I carry. An empty throne sat beside the others.

"Easy gentleman, they are no threat, this is my father, my grandfather, and the wizard who built this place and taught me the secrets of the universe."

Upon closer inspection, it was easy to tell that these three men were also perfectly mummified. The fourth throne is reserved for me when I die.

"I pray that one of you men here today will be around to place my remains here when my time comes. I picked Mr. Valik because I sensed his dedication and trustworthiness, and I trust that Mr. Valik picked you men for the same reason. The dragons accepted Valik, and that was all the proof I needed. Each of you will also face the dragons, and when that happens, be true, be trustworthy, be honest, and be sincere. If you are not, the dragons will see into your very soul, and you will not enjoy the results, do I make myself clear?"

"Yes my Lord," they all spoke in turn.

"Very well then, let's move on."

The next chamber we came to was slightly larger than the last. Inside the chamber was a large wooden table with an array of weapons displayed on it. Some were obviously very old, and most were objects never seen before in combat, while other objects were hard to determine what their use was for.

One object that was leaning against the wall drew the interest of the party of men. It looked like a large horn, fifty feet long, carved from the trunk of some sort of unknown, long extinct tree, wide at the top, fitted with a large drum head, covered with some sort of animal hide, then tapering down to the end, where it was fitted with an adjustable bellows.

"Why would a musical instrument be in an armory?" One of the soldiers asked.

"On the contrary," I said, "This is one of the most formidable weapons I have ever witnessed."

"How can that be," one asked, "It is nothing more than a drum?"

"Maybe it's a horn to call for help," another man joked.

"This is what is known as a harmonic weapon, young soldier. It is called the Horn of Gideon, and I have seen it defeat an entire army at one time, in fact, it can even render a whole city defenseless. Let me explain how it works."

"The bellows of this horn is pointed in the direction of the opposing army, while your own army remains behind it, or at least your troops must wear earplugs. Then, you simply start a drum roll on the head of the drum, with several musicians', so to speak, at the ready, so that the drum roll never ceases. The resonance emitted from this horn paralyzes the nervous system of anyone, or anything, in a cone shaped area directly in front of the horn, up to a half of a mile. Then, while your enemy is incapacitated, you simple stroll in, and have your way with them. Change the bellows to concentrate the harmony, and it can crumble castle walls, or bring down an unstable mountain. No one in the world knows this weapon exists, and I prefer it to stay that way."

"There are many more interesting objects here that I'll have to explain to you at a later time, but for now, we must move on, so if you'll follow me, I'll show you another cavern. We'll have to return to the surface before we're missed, but later, we will return here, and at that time I'll show you many more wonders. It's time to start training you in ways that have long since disappeared."

"In the days to come, I fear, we can not be too careful. I believe there are traitors in my castle, and if they are in my castle, you can bet they are in King Malok's castle also. I'm going to speak to the King about having you men assigned to be my personal guard.

Captain Sardon isn't going to like it, so until that time, you must all remain quiet. All you must tell your Captain is that the dragon was buried in one of the unused caverns.

Your silence in this matter is crucial, and you will be well rewarded for your loyalty."

We moved a short distance to another small cavern, which also contained a large wooden table. Upon this table were stacks of books, scrolls, manuscripts, and old parchments, some of which looked as old as the mountain itself.

"These, my friends, contain the knowledge of things past, present, and future. Some would consider these books magic; some would be considered heresy in a different time. All of the knowledge of the known, as well as the unknown world, is contained within these pages. These volumes can never be replaced, never duplicated, and there are many who would kill to possess these books. The clan that owns these books literally controls the world. That is how powerful this information is."

"In the days and weeks to come, you will learn many new things from these volumes. A new era is upon us, and we must be ready. Now, let's return to the surface, because we have many things to tend to."

"Balon, grab your torch on the way, and get it lit again. Soldier, grab yours also, and wait at the beginning of the pathway, it's time for darkness to return here."

As the men made their way back to the pathway, I took my own torch and went back to the chains that controlled the reflected lighting for the giant cavern. Pulling on the opposite chain as before, the cavern slowly slid into darkness. It was an eerie feeling to all of those present, knowing what secrets were hiding here in the darkness.

Returning to the others, we climbed the long pathway in silence, each man lost in his own thoughts, his whole world having been changed forever. Back at the secret doorway we paused, catching our breath.

"Let me make sure the coast is clear before I open the door. It would not look good to have a dozen men suddenly appear out of a solid stone wall. Remember, no one is to speak of this to anyone. Our enemies would love to know our secrets."

Moving to one side of the door, I blew dust away from a small crack in the rock. Leaning close, I pressed my face to the rock and peered through the crack to a small mirror placed on the opposite wall decades before, which gave an angled view to the main hallway. The hallway was clear, so, taking the key from around my neck, I slid it into the lock, turned the key, and the door slid open.

"Quickly now," I said, "everyone move out into the hallway."

As soon as we were out of the cavern, I quickly moved to the other side of the door, located the hidden lock, and turned the key. When the door was closed, I kicked some loose dust along the base of the door to disguise any possibility that anything was out of the ordinary.

After a short pause to make sure no one came suddenly into the hall, I bid each of the men a farewell, thanked them for their help, and handed each one a silver coin worth a weeks pay. As they moved off to return to duty, I called to Valik to hold back.

"Mr. Valik, I've spoken to Captain Sardon, and he's making arrangements to have your personal effects sent up to my Villa. When you arrive, ask for Marta, she is a very good friend of mine, and she will get you set up in your room. If there is anything else you need, just let her know, she will get it for you, and thank you."

With that, he bowed, turned on his heel, and headed off up the stairway.

As I turned to Balon, he gave me a look of disbelief, and said.

"What was all that about? You should not be so trustworthy Ethan, what are you thinking?"

"Just this, my one, true, trusted friend. I have foreseen ominous changes about to sweep over this land, and not everyone will survive it. What I am trying to do is gather a group around us that we can trust with our lives in the coming conflict. Today is the start of a testing process to find that group.

What I am going to tell you now is between you and me."

"I believe a time is coming very soon when this castle, my castle, is going to have to stand on its own. Events are unfolding just as I saw them in my dreams, and as you know, I have always had a gift of prophesy through dreams. I see a war coming, I see King Malok losing his kingdom, and I see a new kingdom arising, centered at this castle. There are many other things I have seen, some of which are very disturbing, and we will talk about those at a later time."

"As for Valik, and his men, I felt a trust for Valik from the first time I met him, and that trust was proven today by the dragons. Valik picked out the men that went with us to the caverns, so for now; I will trust those men too. Later, they too will be tested by the dragons, a test by fire if you will. There are those in this castle who want to see us dead, and I need to smoke out those enemies. The conflict has begun Balon, the death of Gahenna was the beginning of that conflict, and I fear we do not have much time to get ready to face that conflict."

Balon looked worried, so I put my arm around his bulky shoulders, and said.

"Let's go grab some food, I'm starving, and I need a nap."

With that, off we went up the stairs.

Emerging from the catacombs into the main villa was like a breath of fresh air. A lot had happened in the hours since we had gone below. Up here, life had gone on as though nothing had ever happened. The sun was shining bright, which was now hard on our eyes as we squinted to take it all in. My personal staff was busy with their daily chores, and outside in the main castle grounds, peasants and peddlers alike were going about the business of buying and selling. Up here, all was well, but behind the scene, evil was rearing its ugly head.

Balon and I headed for the kitchen to grab some food. Staff and housekeepers bowed to us as we passed, but none asked where we had been. It was not uncommon for their master to sleep in after a night of drinking or entertaining, and now that I think about it, that is really not such a good deal. We have all grown complacent, I could have been killed today, and no one would have known, or cared, for a couple of days. I'm betting that my enemies have already figured that out, so I'm going to have to radically change my lifestyle, and the sooner, the better. I guess it's time to become a little more responsible, and that thought was a little unnerving.

Arriving in the kitchen, my head housekeeper, Marta, was going over a few instructions with the kitchen staff. When she noticed us enter the room, she spoke a few last words to the staff and then walked over to Balon and me, greeting us first with a bow, and then to me she gave a big hug, saying.

"How are you today my Lord, can I get you some lunch?"

"Yes Marta, we're both starving, and it's been a long day already."

Marta has been with me for more years than I can remember. She has been my housekeeper, my friend and confidant, occasionally my lover, and I swear at times, my mother. In fact, she is considerably older than I am, but in this age, with a life expectancy of nearly three hundred years, she is still very young and attractive.

Three hundred years old seems so long now, but there was a time when nine hundred years was not out of reason. The sky is changing more and more all the time, and with that change, the result is a shorter life span.

Marta clapped her hands for the kitchen staff, and ordered them to bring fruit, bread, wine, and cheese. Sitting down with us at the massive wooden dining table she asked what was going on. As soon as the food was brought to us, we excused the servants so we could speak candidly, and as we ate, I explained some of day's happenings.

"Marta, some very disturbing things have happened today that have me very concerned. Gahenna was killed today by an intruder. I'm not sure how the intruder got into the caverns without being detected, but I think we have traitors in our midst."

Marta was visibly upset, for she too has been around the dragons for a very long time, and even though she did not share my sense of kinship with the dragons, nonetheless, she felt my feeling of loss, and with a hand on my shoulder, she offered her condolences.

After a short pause, I continued.

"Because of recent events, I'm taking on a personal bodyguard. His name is Valik, and he will be moving into the villa with us. I would like to have him put into one of the guest rooms within earshot of my room, and I would appreciate it if you would see to his immediate needs?"

"Yes my Lord," Marta said. "But, do you think you can trust this Valik?"

"I do trust him Marta, and so do the dragons, and that's good enough for me. And by the way, from now on, if you do not hear from me by breakfast each day, please send someone to check on me, for I fear my life is in danger."

Marta had a look of concern on her face, and she listened intensely.

I explained what had happened in the caverns, as well as my suspicions about Captain Sardon. I also told her about the dreams I have had, and what I feel those dreams meant.

Marta was becoming quite disturbed by the whole conversation so I decided we had talked enough about it for today.

When we had finished eating, I turned to Balon and said.

"I'm going to take a short nap in my chamber. Wake me up in a couple of hours, because I want to be down in the caverns when the dragons return. Tomorrow morning, we're going to take a trip down to the valley to speak to the King."

"Yes master," Balon replied, and then he turned and headed out of the villa to wander around the castle grounds. Balon is quite the socialite, and loves to wander around the castle grounds visiting with the venders from the town surrounding the King's castle. He picks up a lot of information from his visits, some useful, and some just gossip. I think some of that information will come in handy in the coming conflict. With Balon though, sometimes separating which information is fact, and which is fiction, can be the true test.

As I turned to leave, Marta rose and asked.

"Will I see you this evening my Lord?"

Turning back to her, I said.

"I'll have to let you know later Marta, I'm a little distracted right now about today's happenings, so for now, I have some very important things to attend to, and I do not wish to be disturbed. I'll call for you later if I change my mind."

"I understand, my Lord," Marta said, looking slightly dejected

Kissing Marta on the forehead, I headed down the hallway to my personal chambers. My chambers consist of several adjoining rooms, including a large comfort area furnished with overstuffed chairs and a huge stone fireplace. A bathing area, a sleeping room, and a study area with a large ornate wooden desk made up the rest of living areas. Once inside the privacy of my chamber, I went to my desk, pulled the vial from my cloak pocket, then the dart, and sat them both on the desk.

The Gog have gotten very bold it would seem. They must be feeling quite confident in their new strategy. I find it hard to believe that a barbaric race such as the Gog could come up with a strategy as complicated as this one on their own. Someone must be helping them out, but whom. My lack of responsibility over the years has led to this crisis, and now I am going to have to make up for it, if that is possible.

Before today, the Gog would only send out a few raiding parties into the outlying territories to steal food, livestock, and to take a few slaves. They were always too afraid of the dragons to venture very far into our lands.

Dragons seem to have a natural hatred for the Gog. I think that the dragons sense that the Gog would like to see all dragons perish from the earth, and indeed, the Gog have managed to kill most, if not all of the dragons in their own land.

A dragon can smell pray for several miles, and they have been trained to associate the Gog as pray. My dragons hunt our lands daily or at least during the daylight hours, and return to roost at night. Dragons used to hunt day and night, but unfortunately, my dragons have been domesticated far too long, and have lost their natural instincts. I believe that is how the Gog clansman managed to get this far into our land without being detected by hunting dragons. The Gog probably hold up in caves or holes during the day, and then travel at night.

I'm going to have to work with my dragons to restore some of their natural instincts. Otherwise, I fear they will not survive the good care they are getting. I wonder if my father or grandfather saw this coming.

Holding up the vial to the light from the window, it appears to be a simple, fired clay vial with a wooden stopper. Grabbing three more washcloths from the linen pile, I used one to cover my face, and then, using the other two to cover my hands, I twisted the stopper from the vial and peered inside. Even with the washcloth over my face, I could still smell the foul odor emitted from the black, tarry, liquid inside. I recognize the odor from a mixture the old wizard had once taught to me. He called the mixture 'Ravens Wart', made from a fluid secreted from a lizard found in the swamps of Magog. Very nasty stuff, and very deadly, killing its victim within seconds.

Since the Gog are kind of a barbaric bunch, without much education, I wonder where they learned this new trick. I sure wish Captain Sardon would not have killed the Gog clansman so soon. I would like to have questioned him first, but I have a nagging suspicion that Sardon did not want the Gog clansman questioned, and that scares me just a little.

The Gog are not a very talkative bunch, but there are herbs to loosen their tongue. I was an inquisitive lad, and the old wizard took me under his wing and taught me a lot of things before he moved on to the next sojourn. All of the old books and manuscripts in the secret caverns belonged to the wizard. He entrusted them to me when he died. The knowledge contained within the pages of those texts would forever change the path of humanity if it were to fall into the hands of someone who would abuse its power.

Power can corrupt even the most honorable of men, that is why even I have not been into the secret caverns of the wizard since he died nearly fifty years ago. With the events that I have foreseen coming, and the events that are already taken place, it would seem that I am soon going to have to use the knowledge that the old wizard trained and prepared me for so many years ago. He was a wise man, and he saw the changes coming a hundred years ago. I also should have seen this coming earlier than I did. but, I'm afraid too much wine over the decades has dulled my senses. It's obviously time for a change in lifestyle, so I can concentrate on the strategies I was trained for all those years ago. From now on, I need to be as sharp as I can be. It's time to go back to the ways of old, time to go back to the books.

Putting the stopper back on the vial, I removed the cloth from my face, walked over to my bedchamber, and moved my night table to one side. Beneath the table was a small rug, which, when pushed aside, revealed a small trap door. Lifting the heavy stone lid revealed a wealth of gold and silver coins, several rolled up parchments, a jeweled dagger, and an assortment of family mementos. It was here that I placed the vial of poison. It may just come in handy sometime, and I certainly wouldn't want it to fall into the wrong hands again.

Returning to the table I next inspected the dart, which I had pulled from the slain dragon. A simple, but effective weapon, a sliver of metal, very thin and lightweight, with feathers tied around the shaft so the fluff of the feather stuck out the back. When the dart is placed point first into a hollow reed, it doesn't take much breath to send the deadly dart flying to its target. It's amazing to think that a feather and a reed could bring down one of the mightiest creatures the Gods have ever created. Times certainly are changing, the era of man is arriving, and the era of dragons is disappearing. Sadly, I fear that things will never be the same again.

Wrapping the dart back into the cloth, I placed it also into the hidden space beneath the night table. Then, I replaced the stone trap door, then the rug, then the table, taking care that everything was placed exactly where it had been.

Moving out to the comfort area, I sat down on one of the soft, overstuffed chairs, and leaned my head back. As I closed my eyes, I thought about the events of the day, and the visions of the future. It has certainly been a long day already.

Chapter 3

Five, four, three, two, one, SNAP! I bolted upright out of my chair as if I had been shocked with electricity. My heart was pounding, my hands were sweating, and my eyes were as wide as saucers as I tried to focus on whom, and where, I was. Dr. Miller was sitting across from me on his chair with a look of total shock and disbelief. His face was ashen, and as he regained his composure, he managed to say.

"Everything is okay Henry, you can sit down. You are in my home office, you have been under hypnosis, but you are awake now."

It was all coming back to me in waves, threatening to overwhelm me. Now I really had to sit down, as I was getting weak in the knees. Burying my face in my hands until the visions in my head started to subside; I spoke as soon as I regained my composure.

"Doc, that was incredible."

"Yes it was," Dr. Miller replied, "I have never heard anything so graphic in detail in my life. This is something we are going to have to dig deeper into in the future. Most unfortunately though, we are out of time right now. Let's set up an appointment for the same time next week."

He then reached over and turned off the tape recorder, ejected the tape, and handed it to me, saying.

"This is yours; keep it in a safe place. You may want to refer back to it from time to time as a reference point. How are you feeling?"

"Other than a little shaky, I feel fine. So, I'll see you next week, same time?"

"Yes Henry, I'll mark you down in my appointment book. I'll be looking forward to seeing you and learning more about your past life." With that, we both stood, and after shaking hands, he saw me to the door.

"Thanks Jim, I can't wait to see you next week."

As I walked down the sidewalk to my car, I thought to myself, I bet I look just like the guy I saw coming out of the house when I was sitting in my car earlier, waiting for my appointment. I looked around, and sure enough, there was a fellow sitting in his car, looking very nervous, like he'd just like to call it quits and drive away. I'm sure I heard Dr. Millers' voice as I started to drive away.

"Hello, are you Mr. Johnson? Won't you please come on in?"

The hour drive back down the valley was spent in pensive, quiet reflection, replaying the events of the hypnosis session. Can this truly be real; could I have really lived that life in the distant past? Or was all of that just a product of a very active imagination? How can I know for sure? I suppose I never will, but it is exciting, and it does explain a lot of things in my life, my likes and dislikes, my fears, strengths, and weaknesses. If I couldn't concentrate at work before, how am I ever going to concentrate after this? It's a good thing I go on vacation next week, because this is going to be a very long week. I can't wait for my next hypnosis session.

I work three days on and four days off, twelve hours a day. Even though the days are long, it's sure worth it to get the four days off. You can get a lot done on your days off, which is what I have to do tomorrow. Fireworks sales are just a week away, and I have lots to do. One thing about being busy over the next few days, it will keep my mind off the recent, or should I say, past, events. What a crazy turn of events my life is taking.

I arrived home a couple hours before my girlfriend Jane was due. Instinctively I headed straight for the liquor cabinet to mix a drink. I stopped in mid mix, thought about my past life, and how drinking had dulled my senses then, and realized it was not doing me any good in this life either. Looking at the beverage in a new light, I walked over to the sink, and poured the liquid down the drain. That feels good; I wonder how long I can last. Opening the refrigerator, I grabbed a ginger ale, a glass of ice, and headed outside to sit on the deck, and I just sat there listening to the birds. As I leaned my head back, and closed my eyes to think about the things that have happened, I thought to myself, life feels really good right now.

I must have drifted off because the next thing I heard was Jane calling through the house.

"Honey, I'm home, where are you?"

As soon as I cleared the fog out of my head, and figured out where I was again, I called out.

"I'm out on the deck, come on out, it's too hot to be in the house."

Apparently I had slept about two hours, because Jane gets off work at five o'clock, and it was now 6:30. I guess I was must have been worn out from the ten thousand year journey I went on this afternoon.

Jane came out onto the deck looking tired, and then sat down beside me, saying.

"Would you be a doll and make me a drink too, it's so hot? I bought some steaks, but it's too hot to cook inside the house, so could you grill them on the barbecue?"

As I got up I thought to myself, I used to master of my own kingdom, but now I'm nothing more than a glorified waiter. It's interesting how things change over time. Kissing Jane as I stood, I said.

"What would you like to drink? I'm having ginger ale."

She gave me a puzzled look, and said, "A ginger ale, are you feeling okay?"

"I'm feeling wonderful, that's why I'm having ginger ale. Now, what will it be my dear?"

"I would like a gin and tonic of course, it's been a long day," she said with a slightly annoyed tone.

"It'll be coming right up," I said as I headed for the kitchen.

Now, don't get me wrong, I'm not giving up drinking, I still get a lot of stress relief from alcohol, but for now, I don't feel the need for a drink. I think when a person drinks just to drink, it's gone too far, and that's the point where we are in our life. It's time to make a change, and that change might as well start with me, one day at a time as they say, or in my case, one drink at a time.

Have you ever noticed how weak and run down you feel after you've had a lot to drink? It's the same principal behind our body going into shock from an injury. Injuries cause shock, most often from loss of blood volume. The result is that you don't have enough oxygen rich, nutrient rich blood reaching the muscles at the cellular level. Hence, your muscles, and your brain, no longer function efficiently. The same result happens with alcohol, but from a different process. Alcohol is a vasodilator, meaning it causes your blood vessels to expand, or open up. The result again is that there is not enough blood to fill the vessels, and not enough pressure to send that blood to all the cells. The result, is diminished strength, and diminished cognitive capacity. There are plenty of other deficits from alcohol consumption, but we won't go into those for now.

My point being to all this preaching is this; it's no wonder why we lose our psychic abilities, our motivation, and our direction from one life to the next. There are so many vices, so many distractions to steer us off course. We lose our strengths and abilities, mental, physical, as well as metaphysical. If I am to take any stock at all in past lives and the possibility that a dragons or a wizard could truly exist, then I need to somehow regain the powers that I have lost. I think the first step is to make the mind and body pure again. The rest will have to come from meditation, and hypnosis.

After having mixed a drink, I returned to the deck where Jane was now relaxing on the porch swing. I handed her the drink and sat down with her on the swing, and said.

"Let me finish my ginger ale, and I'll get the steaks started. Tell me about your day."

She began to give me a half hour dissertation on human interaction within the local government offices. By the time she was done, I was also worn out and needing a drink. It really is amazing how petty the human race is. Everyone is maneuvering for position, trying to climb the corporate ladder, stepping on anyone who might be in the way. Is this what man has ascended to, is this the lofty goal we all strive for, I think not. In fact, I think we are actually going backwards in our evolution.

Finishing my ginger ale, I stood up and said.

"I'll get the steaks going. Why don't you change into something cooler, and relax while I make supper."

"Oh, you are such a doll. But could you do me one more little thing, make me another drink."

"Okay dear," I said as I grabbed her glass and headed back to the kitchen. What I wanted to say was, "Yes your highness," but I kept my big mouth shut, made her a drink, and set myself to the task of making supper.

There is nothing comparable to a perfectly grilled steak right off the barbecue. There is something primordial about eating a chunk of meat cooked over an open flame. It is comforting to the soul, triggering emotions back to the very emergence of man upon the earth, when you had to stalk and kill your meal, and then cook it over an open fire. You can almost feel your forehead receding as you watch and smell the meat cooking. Okay, I think I just went a little too far back in history, and besides that, I think the steaks are done.

Dinner was pleasant, with the steaks being complimented by a potato, baked in the microwave, served with sour cream, and a cool garden salad. Conversation was sparse until she finally asked how my appointment went. Well, let's see how this goes.

"Jane, it was the most incredible thing I've ever experienced in my life. I was the master of my own castle, and I raised dragons to fight for the King. I was trained by a wizard, and had great powers. And, there is about to be a war that I may get killed in. Other than that, I have to wait for next week's session to learn more."

Jane now had a totally sour look on her face and said.

"You don't actually believe all that crap do you? And you can't be serious about going back to that quack, are you? I can't believe you paid good money for that. Maybe you should go see a psychiatrist, because I think you have some unresolved issues, maybe even some traumatic stress problems from your work. You know that you do deal with some pretty gruesome things. Hell, maybe you can even file a lawsuit, claiming a mental disability."

Now I was the one who had the sour look on his face.

"I knew you wouldn't understand. And thanks for the insight into my mental breakdown. Remind me never to bring the subject up to you again. Now, if you'll excuse me, I'll take my place as your personal valet, and do the dishes."

As I walked away, I thought to myself, I wonder where, in my past lives, her and I hooked up. It seems that we do tend to meet some of the same people over and over again in subsequent lifetimes, and next time around, I want to be sure to avoid her. Jane was still sitting there nursing her drink as I made my way to the kitchen.

I don't really mind doing dishes, especially when I'm stressed out. It's a good way to use up the excess endorphins that are released with increased emotional activity. And right now I've got a ton of endorphins coursing through my veins; in fact, I'm just about as stressed out as I can be. That seems to happen a lot between us lately, and to tell you the truth, we've talked many times about going our separate ways. It doesn't seem like we have a whole lot in common anymore, except drinking. We met at a party, and it would seem that the only time Jane is happy is if we're out partying or dancing. My interests in life go way beyond that, and with what I know now, drinking is hampering my development.

When I finished doing the dishes, I walked out to the deck to enjoy the cool air as night was beginning to fall. Jane was still there, working on another drink. She was starting to get a little tipsy now, and when Jane gets drunk, she gets on the fight, which makes her drink even more. It's like a light switch being tripped. One minute she's fine, the next, all hell breaks loose, and it looks like tonight is going to be one of those times.

Sure enough, as soon as I sat down, she started in on me about things that had no reference to anything we had discussed earlier in the evening. Of course, everything was my fault, from being insensitive to her feelings, to me wasting money, to her being overweight because we don't go out dancing anymore, and everything in between. After a proper yelling match, she stomped off to the bedroom, and I stayed on the porch swing to cool down.

What ever happened to me being the master of my domain? How can a person get that back? As I sat there fuming about the state of my world, I must have fallen asleep, because the next thing I remember, I was waking up on the porch swing to the birds chirping. The sun was already starting to come up, and my cloths were cold and wet with dew. When I looked over, I could see that one of the neighbor's cats was sleeping next to me on the other cushions. 'I am master of nothing', I mumbled to myself as I got up from the swing, which caused the cat to give me an indignant look for disturbing his sleep. In what life did things go so terribly astray?

I tried to sneak into the bedroom to grab a change of clothes, but Jane is a light sleeper, and of course she woke up. She can be like Jeckle and Hyde sometimes, and true to form, she said.

"Good morning dear, how did you sleep? I came down stairs during the night to apologize, but I saw you and the cat asleep on the porch swing, and decided to let you sleep. I'm sorry about last night, I was tired and upset."

"I'm sorry too," I said, but in my head I'm thinking that I don't want to keep living like this. It happens way too often lately, but staying composed, I continued.

"Come on downstairs, I'll put on a pot of coffee before I take a shower. I have to go into town today and pay the performance bond on the fireworks business. Then I need to submit the application for my fireworks license over at the City Hall. From there, I'll go find Scotty to help me clean out the storage unit. It sounds like the fireworks should be here this afternoon."

"Okay dear, I'll be right down. It sounds like we'll both be busy today. Thank God, it's Friday."

"Amen sister," I said as I headed down stairs with a fresh set of dry clothes.

Stopping by the kitchen on my way to the shower, I got the coffee pot ready to go, flipped the switch, and then hit the shower. Making the coffee before taking a shower has two benefits, the first being that Jane won't have to run the water while I'm in the shower. If you do, it turns the water in the shower cold, which is quite a shock to the system. The other benefit is a cup of hot coffee waiting for you when you get done.

By the time I was done showering and grooming, Jane was up, had a cup of coffee and was sitting on the deck reading the newspaper. I grabbed a cup and joined her, more to test the troubled waters than for the company. She started off by complaining about the latest news around the world, then about having to go to work, then about the coming hot day and the lack of air conditioning in our house. I let her ramble on, but all the while I thought to myself, 'Lord how I wish I could go back to my life in my castle.'

As soon as I finished with my coffee I stood, leaned over to kiss her on the forehead, and told her I was off to run my errands. It will be good to be out of the house while she gets ready for work. She is always running at least an hour late, which makes her totally stressed out and cranky every morning. Today would be no different for her, but for me, it's time to hit the road.

The first stop along the way was to pick up Scott at his trailer in a little town called Corvallis, about ten miles down the highway from my town of Victor, and about a mile off of the main highway to Hamilton. The day was heating up, so we needed to get things done early to beat the heat. Pulling into Scott's driveway, I honked the horn and as I waited for him to come out I looked at his home and yard. Scott lives in a small trailer in a large trailer court owned by his boss. He does all the yard work in the trailer court in trade for free rent, and then he works in his boss's wood shop to make money to pay the rest of his bills. It really is a pretty sweet deal for a single guy.

Scott has been single all his life. He had a girlfriend once about 25 years ago, but that didn't work out, and he hasn't had another one since. Not that he wouldn't like to have another one, it's just that now days, he has let himself go, but he still has high expectations in the quality of girl he wants to be with. Scott is a great guy, but he's probably going to die a bachelor, a fact that he seems to be quite comfortable with, and the sort of life that looks more and more appealing to me everyday.

As I was sitting there daydreaming, Scott came out of his trailer, and walked up to my truck. As he climbed into my truck, I must have really been daydreaming, because without thinking I said.

"Good morning Balon."

What a Freudian slip that was. Scott looked at me like I was retarded, and I of course felt retarded.

"Sorry Scott, my mind is on something else. Close the door and I'll tell you a story on the way to town." Now he did have a puzzled look on his face.

On the way into town I proceeded to tell him first about my dreams, which he had heard some of before, and then I told him about the hypnosis session.

The more I talked, the more interested Scott became, and he hung on every word, although sometimes he seemed to be daydreaming himself. When I told him that he was also with me in that past life, and that his name was Balon, you could see his jaw drop as if some great realization had just come to him. I told him I had another appointment with the hypnotist next week, at which time we would seek out more information on my, our, past life.

When I had finished talking, he said.

"That's the most incredible thing I've ever heard. I too have had some weird dreams over the years. I just thought maybe I ate something that didn't agree with me, but this explains a lot. I also have a thing for dragons, they fascinate me, and you know already how I have a way with animals. Just by you telling me about it, I can see, and feel, every move, every emotion, isn't that weird."

"Maybe it is Scott, I don't know anymore. I'm not sure anymore about what's weird, and what's not. I know what I've dreamed, but those are only dreams, and may not be real, although a lot of my dreams do come true. I know what I've felt inside, and that could be real, or it could just be wishful thinking. And then there's the world under hypnosis, I don't know what to think about that, because it feels very real. It explains a lot, and I want to believe it, but doesn't it seem too far-fetched, too incredible to be true. If it is real, then we are missing the most important truths this world has to offer. To be honest, I can't wait till next week's hypnosis session to learn more."

"After everything you've told me today, Henry, now I can't wait for you to find out more also, that way, I get to find out more about myself. And you can call me Balon anytime, Ethan."

As I pulled into the bank parking lot, Scott had a smile on his face and a far away, thoughtful look in his eye.

"Hang tight a few minutes Scott, while I run inside and get some cash to pay for the performance bond on the fireworks license. I'll be right back."

When I left, Scott was still lost in thought, undoubtedly thinking about dragons, castles, and deeds of daring. In this life, Scott has a very boring existence, but in that past life, it was anything but boring. Balon is basically Scott's alter ego, and I think knowing about his past life is definitely going to change his current life for the better, and mine too for that matter.

Having secured the five hundred dollars cash from my savings, we headed over to the Court House, and then to the city clerk's office. The city of Hamilton requires all fireworks booths to pay a five hundred dollar performance bond that guarantees that you'll remove your fireworks booth within seven days after the end of the selling season. Get your booth moved, and you get your five hundred dollars back. Take too long, and you lose your bond. This all came about because one year, someone left their booth on site for six months after the close of the selling season. Now, we all have to pay for their laziness. I make sure that my booth gets moved as soon as possible after I'm done for the year. I can't afford to lose the money.

Once inside the clerk's office, I requested a business license application, filled it out on the spot, and handed it back to the clerk, along with a site sheet, and of course, the five hundred dollars. She put my bond in an envelope with my name on it, put it in the safe, made out a business license, and I was on my way.

The next stop was about ten miles back down the highway toward home at my storage building. We had to move a few things around to make room for the shipment of fireworks to be spread out to inventory, and still have room to maneuver. With that done, we each grabbed a broom, and swept the place out good, along with a couple of spiders that were big enough to eat small rodents. God I hate spiders.

From here it was back to my house to wait for the truck to arrive with my fireworks. Back at the house we each grabbed a can of ginger ale and a glass of ice, and sat out on the deck. We continued to talk about the times of dragons and castles, and before long, it seemed like we were actually talking about something that had just happened in our not so distant past, rather than a fantasy dreamland that never existed, except in our heads. It all seems so far fetched, yet in the next breath, it seemed so real.

I was raised by Pentecostal, fire and brimstone, go to church three times a week parents. My feet are firmly planted in the ground, or so I would have thought. I would have a hard time accepting all of this if it wasn't for the fact that the bible talked about dragons in the book of Job, and talks about reincarnation in many passages throughout the bible. If not for that, I would have rejected the whole idea of a past life altogether. But now, how can a person deny the possibilities? Still, doubts will remain, for a while at least.

The sound of the phone ringing jarred us both out of our fantasy world and back into the real world again. I grabbed the phone, and the voice on the other end was that of the truck driver asking for final directions to my house. He was about twenty minutes away. After giving the driver specific directions, I hung up the phone, and told Scott the news. Then, I picked up the phone to call my mom to come over to be our scribe, and to count boxes as they come off the truck. My mom lives about ten minutes away, so she should be here in plenty of time. We talked again about the past while we waited in the driveway for the truck to arrive.

It was my mom who showed up first, parking her car around the corner on the side street to make room for the full size tractor-trailer rig to show up with the fireworks. I greeted her with a big hug, and asked her how she was, and then how dad was. Dad is nearly eighty years old now, and mom is seventy-five. Mom and dad own a ranch in the foothills of the Bitterroot Mountains, and have worked hard all of their life. Both are in great shape physically and mentally for their age, although dad is really starting to show his age now. It's been sad to watch the aging process on my dad, going from a strong, viable rancher, to a feeble old man who was fading away. It's too bad we don't live as long as we used to in the days of dragons, or in the days of the early bible characters.

The life expectancy during the age of dragons was easily two to three hundred years old, sometimes more. Biblical persons lived to be six to nine hundred years of age. At that rate, a man the age of my present day father would be of the stamina and vitality of a thirty or forty year old today. The differences in life expectancy from then till now had a lot to do with environmental factors, mainly in regards to ultraviolet rays, and ozone depletion in present day. Back then, a sort of greenhouse effect in the form of mist and fog covered the earth a lot of the time. That filtered out many of the suns harmful rays, and thus the human body didn't age as quickly as it does today.

An old prophet once spoke of the waters above being separated from the waters below. At one time, the earth was completely shrouded in mist and fog. This mist and fog watered the earth, simply by contact. The sun above the mist trapped in heat, and the flora and fauna of the earth grew to tremendous size. Over the countless eons that mist gradually gave up its tremendous load of water forming streams to flow from the mountains into the valleys, where they formed rivers, ponds, and lakes. The sunshine with its increasingly harmful rays was then able to shine directly on the inhabitants of the earth. Large trees gave way to smaller varieties more centrally located around areas that contained ample supplies of water, either on the surface, or now, underground. The life span of both man and beast gradually diminished over the eons. Add in the depletion of the ozone layer from pollution, and the result today is a mere seventy or eighty year sojourn on earth to try to attain the knowledge that was lost to mankind so long ago.

No sooner had my mom arrived and we exchanged our greetings, than the fireworks truck came around the corner off the main highway. I stepped out into the street and waved my arms so he would see us right away. A flash of his headlights acknowledged he had seen me, and now, the work was going to begin.

The big rig pulled up in front of the house, shut down the engine, and the driver climbed down from the cab, and greeted us.

"How is everybody doing today? Are you ready for your fireworks?"

As the driver opened the rear of the trailer, the sight was enough to make a pyromaniac break down and cry. The forty foot long trailer was filled with cases of fireworks front to back, side-to-side, and top to bottom.

"Those are not all mine, are they?" I said with my mouth agape.

"Oh no, yours are only about the first ten feet or so. There are about a half a dozen orders in there. You are just the first delivery on this truck. Then I'll try to get a couple more deliveries done today before I get a motel room."

"Thank God," I said with a sigh of relief, "I didn't know what I was going to do with that many fireworks; I only have a twenty foot storage unit. Well that's cool; I guess we better get at it."

The truck driver climbed in the back of the truck and started handing out cases of fireworks, calling out the corresponding number labeled on each case, which we would repeat as we grabbed the case, and my mom would check it off on the manifest. For now, we were simply stacking the cases on pallets in the driveway to be transported to the storage unit by pickup trucks. The big semi truck would never fit inside the gates at the storage area.

One hundred and forty three cases later, we were finished. As we took a breather, I signed for the delivery, and bid the driver farewell, and safe driving. We each sat back on a case of fireworks while we watched the big truck drive away. That was only part one of the job, now we have to load all the cases into pickup trucks, and haul them to my storage building. First though, it's time for another soda. The three of us went inside, grabbed a ginger ale and a glass of ice, and walked out on the deck to sit down, and chat.

We chatted with my mom for about twenty minutes or so while we drank our pop, and recuperated from the recent exertion. Then, we hugged, and said our goodbyes to her, and set ourselves to the task of packing the first load of fireworks into my pickup. My pickup is a club cab, so with the box loaded high, and the rear seat full, we could haul about forty-five cases at a time. Looks like it will take us about four trips. It's a good thing it's only about six miles to my storage unit.

By the time we had the third load hauled to the storage unit, we were pooped. We were taking a breather in the front yard when Jane pulled up into the driveway from work, and said.

"You boys look tired, but it looks like you almost have it whipped. How about I fix some hamburgers on the grill, a salad, and some fresh ice tea while you two finish with the last load. I'll get started now, and it should be done by the time you get back, and get cleaned up."

"That sounds wonderful dear. Let's get it done Scott, because I'm getting hungry."

With renewed energy we tackled the last remaining cases, and headed for the storage unit. En route I turned to Scott and said.

"Well she sure is in a good mood tonight, which is definitely a big difference from yesterday."

Scott just nodded his head and grunted his acknowledgement. Guys don't really have to verbally acknowledge each other; we have a psychic bond that goes without words. Besides, Scott has been around Jane long enough to know when to lay low, and when to keep his mouth shut. Yesterday would have been one of those days, but today seems to be safe to come back to the house without his cast iron pants on.

When we were finished putting the fireworks into the storage unit, we locked up and headed for home, weary, but happy to have this much done. The season was rapidly approaching, and I had such an odd feeling that this year was going to be something very special. I couldn't put a finger on it, but sometimes you can just sense things coming. I have always had that ability, my only problem is, I don't know what's coming until it shows itself. It seems that in my past life, I was keenly aware of exactly what was coming. This seems to be another example of how we tend to lose our metaphysical abilities from one sojourn to another.

There are just too many distractions in each modern life experience, too many new and wonderful things to distort the senses. I'm not saying that these new experiences are bad, it's just that you seem to have to give up one thing, or one gift, to gain another. Each one of us have to decide for themselves how much of that metaphysical spirituality they are willing to lose, or, how much modern day materialism you are willing to give up to get something back that is good for your soul.

The problem with most people these days is that they don't know, or maybe don't even care what sort of gifts they have already lost. They are too caught up in the earthly delights of today. In fact, most people would not be willing to give up any of their conveniences simply to have a mere spiritual gift. Now you know why the world is in the sad condition that it is in right now. They are all too caught up in actively trying to gain as many possessions as earthly possible, which, unfortunately, also means trying to take the other guys' possessions, no matter whether it's his shovel, his stereo, his wife, or his oil reserves. Where will it end you ask, well, I think we already know, the same place it has ended time and time again throughout eternity, war.

History constantly repeats itself, wars, and rumors of wars. After each war, there is an extended period of relative peace where the madness within us subsides, and the realization that wanting someone else's stuff was not all it was cracked up to be. We all find a small dose of spirituality for a short time, until we see something new that we just have to have, no matter what the cost. It will always be that way, it has always been that way, there is nothing new under the sun, what has been, will be again. Truer words were never spoken.

My, how my mind can wander sometimes, and before I knew it, we were pulling into my driveway, and I was hungry.

"Come on Scott, let's get something to eat, I'm starved," I said as I climbed wearily out of the truck, my back aching, and my body stiff from the exercise. I sure hope I was in better shape in my past life than I am in this one, because if I truly were in a war back then, I would have been toast with this current body. Man, am I hungry.

As soon as we got out of the truck, we could smell the hamburgers cooking on the barbecue grill. There is nothing more stimulating to the senses than the smell of a barbecue. I do believe its primordial, cooking a freshly killed animal over an open fire. Not only can you feel your forehead start to recede backward, but your nostrils flare out, hair starts growing all over your body, you start to walk hunched over, and speak in grunting sounds. Wait a minute here, that was a different movie, sorry about that, I do get carried away sometimes.

Jane yelled to us from the back yard.

"Come around back boys, and grab whatever you want to drink, because supper is ready."

Passing through the kitchen on the way to the back patio, Scott and I stopped at the refridgerator for a beverage.

"I'm having a beer Scott, how about you?"

"A beer sounds wonderful after that workout, thank you."

With beers in hand, we walked out on the back patio where Jane had a delicious meal set up for us on the bistro table. A stack of hamburgers, sliced onions, pickles, cheese, and fresh buns were placed in the middle of the table.

A large bowl of tossed garden salad and another bowl of sliced cantaloupe made my mouth start watering so bad I thought I was going to drown. This was going to be good.

"Not so fast boys, go wash up first, you two are acting like a couple of Neanderthals, now hurry up."

Jane stood there like a drill sergeant with her finger pointing the way to the sink. We both shuffled our way back in the direction we had come, grumbling like a couple of school kids, quickly washed our hands and faces, and then hurried back out to the table.

"That's better," Jane said, "now I can stand to be at the same table with the two of you, now dish up."

Jane was already finished with her salad, so we started digging in like we hadn't eaten in days. As we got our fill, I could feel my brow flatten out, the caveman hair retract back into the pores, and I thought I could feel myself sitting more upright in my chair. Well, not really, but it sounds good, right?

"Thank you for the great meal Jane," Scott said, "it was absolutely wonderful."

"Yes dear, it was incredible." I chimed in, so as not to be outdone.

Jane runs on praise, and she likes to be appreciated. That is how she has been all of her life. The best way to get her to respond is to praise her every move and she will open up to you like a new flower. So why do things go awry so often, you might ask. Because I am a male, and that makes me an idiot, just ask any female. Now as for us guys; just give us some peace and quiet for a couple of hours, and we'll be ready to do anything you want.

"Now Jane, you sit back, Scott and I will clear the table, and get stuff put away. Then we'll join you out on the big deck for drinks."

"Now that's an offer I can't refuse," Jane said as she picked up her drink, and headed for the cool shade on the big deck under the trees.

My house sits on a large corner lot, with a juniper hedge surrounding the perimeter of the property, which gives us a reasonable amount of privacy. There a half dozen huge cottonwood trees in the front and side yards that provide the most wonderful shade in town. I will never tire of sitting on that deck, under the shade of those trees. It is something that is comforting to my soul, and what more can you ask for.

Scott and I cleaned up the table, put the leftovers in the fridge, rinsed the dishes in the sink, and then put them in the dishwasher. We each grabbed another beer, and then joined Jane on the deck just as the sun was going down, and as the air was starting to cool down.

"What a nice evening," Jane said, "I could sit out here all night; don't you agree Henry?"

I agreed with her, but, remembering actually sleeping out here last night, I had a totally different thought altogether. Was that a dig, I wondered to myself, or maybe a hint? Maybe I was still in trouble. I guess only time would tell.

Finishing my beer, I spoke up.

"I need to give Scott a ride home; would you like to ride along Jane?" Although I knew the answer, I figured it was best to ask.

"No thanks dear, I'm going to watch a little television, and then get ready for bed. You go ahead, and please be careful driving, because you know how many deer there are out at this time of night."

"Okay, I'll be back in about a half an hour or so. Let's go Scott."

"Goodbye Jane, and thanks again for supper," Scott said as we were leaving.

"You're welcome Scott, and thanks for helping Henry with the fireworks, I hate helping with those things, and they scare me. We'll see you next week at the booth."

The ride to Scott's house was silent, each of us lost in our own thoughts, as well as watching for any deer that might try to cross the highway. Pulling into Scott's driveway I said.

"I'll see you next Wednesday morning about eight to start stocking the booth. Now, it's time to go back and face Jane. She's been really crabby lately. I think she's getting tired of me, and I feel as though the romance is gone from our relationship. She comes home late from work a lot, and seems to have to be out of town more than usual lately. I suspect she probably has another boyfriend, which I guess I can't blame her, since I'm not the kind of partying guy she would prefer. Jane's girlfriend is single and keeps telling her about all her fun nights out on the town, and about taking new guys home. I really feel Jane wants that kind of life again, like she used to have when she and I first met. I don't really like to party with her, because when she starts drinking, she can't quit, and then she gets on the fight. Oh man, I'm sorry to lay all of this on you Scott, I got a little carried away. I better get back home; I have to work early tomorrow. Good night Balon."

Scott smiled as he got out of the truck, and said.

"It's okay, I don't mind, good night Ethan."

Now that gave me the chills, hearing the name I was known by back in the days of the dragons. I smiled back, and told him goodnight, then headed back home to Victor.

The trip back home was again spent in quiet reflection. I very seldom listen to the radio, as it is way too invasive on my inner thoughts. I prefer the quiet and solitude to reflect on the day, and to solve any problems that may be troubling my soul, which right now seems to be a relationship problem. Neither of us is very happy in our relationship, our souls are becoming stagnant, and there's no excitement left in our lives. We seem to be bored with our lives, and bored with each other. We fight and bicker more often than not. We don't go out on the town anymore, because the closet town with any nightlife is fifty miles away, and we don't want to drink and drive, which puts lives other than just ours in danger. So, we come home at night, drink, stare at the television, which is also boring, and go to bed, where nothing happens either. Our life is cascading down into the gutter.

I don't blame Jane for looking elsewhere for excitement; I would do the same thing if I weren't so bored with my own life. I feel it all coming to a crescendo, and it doesn't feel good. The fights are getting more frequent and more severe every time. I don't think I can take much more of it, and it's like I don't even want to go home anymore. The closer I get to home, the higher my anxiety level climbs, and I'm sure my constant state of stress is at least partly to blame for my high blood pressure. As I drew closer to my house, and pulled into my driveway, I could feel my stress level beginning to rise. Our fight of last night has not been settled yet, and I suspect that the wounds are still raw. I guess I'm about to find out.

I parked the truck in the driveway and as I walked through the house, I grabbed a beer from the fridge, and then made my way out to the deck. Jane was still sitting on the porch swing drinking a beer. She looked visibly intoxicated, which usually means trouble. We will almost inevitably get into a major fight when she is drunk, and by the looks of her tonight, I would almost make bets on a major battle.

"That was a great meal dear," I said as I sat down, hoping to short-circuit any adverse thoughts she may have been harboring prior to my arrival. Unfortunately, it didn't work.

"I'm glad you liked it," She started out, "because I'm getting a little tired of being a maid around here. I don't appreciate having to cook and clean after you, and Scott. It seems that's all I'm good for these days. Lord knows we don't do anything together anymore. There is no more romance left in our life, no excitement. I want to go out dining, dancing, and partying like we did when we were first dating. Now we don't go anywhere unless Scott is with us. I don't know why you don't just marry him, instead of me, and don't give me that past lives crap, because the only past life you're about to know is the one you used to have with me."

Now, there is a scary thought, Scott and I getting married. I don't understand why that same conversation comes up in every relationship where one of the spouses has a close friend that hangs around too much. Of course now, I too have had enough to drink that I no longer have the good sense to keep my big mouth shut, so, here it goes.

"Do you know how ridiculous you sound? First off, Scott only comes around once a week, and sometimes not even that. Second, I cook around here once in awhile too, and I do the dishes more than you do, as well as vacuuming the floor. Three, Scott is not my type for marrying, or I would marry him because he, at least, doesn't give me any lip."

Okay, that last one might have been a little over the top, because Jane got up, stormed back into the house, headed upstairs to the bedroom, and slammed the bedroom door, screaming something about moving back to Missoula to live with her girlfriend. Looks like I'm sleeping with the cats again tonight. It's a good thing I don't have a doghouse, because I would be in it on a regular basis. It's amazing how a fight will sober you up in a hurry, and ruin a good drunk.

I sat there thinking about the last seven years of my life with Jane. It was not even as good as she thinks it was in the beginning, at least not for me. Jane is a very controlling type of person, which means we have always done only what she ever wanted to do. I pretty much put my life, my wants, and my personal desires on hold. She was happy, I was miserable, but yet I had to act happy, or she would be insulted. Looking back, I think it was wrong of me to allow that to happen, for me to be deceptive about my happiness, even more wrong than it was for her to be so demanding. She was being her true self, and I was not. I guess this has been a long time coming, and now it's time. A little time apart will probably be good for both of us. I only want to know one thing, why do these fights always happen on a night when I have to work the next day?

This time I spent a very sleepless night on the couch inside the house, instead of sitting on the porch swing under the stars. After checking my watch all night because I didn't have an alarm clock, I decided it was just as easy to go to the ambulance hall a couple hours early, where I could take a shower and shave. I have an extra set of uniforms there, which will save me the hassle of trying to sneak into the bedroom for a new set. By the time I get off work tonight, things will be settled one way or the other. I don't have the time, or the fortitude to carry the stress of this relationship any longer. Things will have to fall where they may this time.

I arrived at the ambulance crew quarters about 4:00 am to find the crew just getting back from a transfer to one of the nursing homes. They had picked up a resident of one of the nursing homes who had fallen during the night. After x-rays, and a thorough examination, she was released back to the nursing home. They looked at me like I was nuts, and asked me what I was doing there so early. I told them that things were a little tense at home, so I came in early to lay low. I told them that as soon as I showered and shaved, that one of them could go home early if they wanted, and it was up to them to decide who it would be. I left them to decide who it would be while I headed for the shower. My ulterior motive to sending one of them home was that it would open up one of the crew beds for me to catch a little sleep in until we got our first call. If I don't get some sleep, it's going to be a long, miserable day.

A half an hour later I emerged from the bathroom to find the coffee on, and one of the crew, Don, sitting at the table sipping on a cup of coffee.

"It looks like you're the one that gets to go home huh? Did Tom go back to bed?" I asked as I poured myself a cup of fresh coffee.

"Yeah, Tom went to bed for a couple hours before Dan gets here, and this will work out great for me. My wife and kids and I are going to the lake today when I get off. Now we can get up there before the crowds arrive. It's hard to get a good picnic spot if you get there too late. Thanks a bunch for taking over early, and I hope things work out with you and Jane. I'll see you next week Henry."

"Have fun at the lake Don, but you won't see me next week, I go on vacation to sell fireworks. But, if you get a chance, stop by the booth for a visit."

"Will do, see you then, and thanks again," he said as he headed out the door.

"You're welcome," I said, and as soon as he was gone, I set my coffee cup aside, left a note for Dan, who would be my partner for the day, and went into the sleeping quarters to catch some sleep. I no sooner laid my head on the pillow than I was sound asleep. It seems that when your normal sleep patterns are disturbed, your dream patterns also get messed up, and you tend to dream about weird things. Mine were definitely off the charts this time, with dreams about ancient pubs, shady characters, fights, and a beautiful peasant girl. Just when things started getting interesting, a voice jarred me out of my dream world.

"Henry, Henry, wake up, I'm hungry, let's go out for breakfast."

I sat up in bed and there was Dan, standing there with that annoyed look he sometimes gets. It was now about 9:00 am, so no wonder he was hungry. Dan gets a little cranky when he gets hungry.

"Hey, thanks for letting me sleep this long, I wouldn't have made it through the day without some sleep."

"No problem Henry, Tom told me you had a rough night. I'm sorry to hear about it. If there's anything I can do to help, just let me know, but do it while we're moving, because who knows when we'll get a page."

"Let's do it," I said as I jumped out of bed, slipping on my boots without bothering to tie the laces until I got into the ambulance.

"Wow, that sun is bright," I said as the garage doors opened up to face the world. All things considered, it was going to be a beautiful day.

"Where are we going to eat this morning?" I asked, even though it really didn't matter to me.

"I thought we would try the Coffee Cup Café today if you don't mind. There's a really cute waitress that works there," Dan said a little sheepishly.

I gave him one of those looks of understanding that only us guys know. There was no need to say anything more. Dan has been single for a couple of years now, having gotten out of a bad marriage himself, and it's nice to see him getting interested in another girl.

The Coffee Cup is a local, family owned restaurant that serves great home cooking with large portions. It's definitely nothing fancy, but the service is friendly, and fast. Like I said before, when you're in emergency services, fast service is what we need. Since we eat here on occasion, the waitresses know we could get a page anytime, so they bend over backwards to get us served quickly, and today was no exception. As we sat in one of the booths, Dan asked me how my session went with the hypnotherapist. As I related the story that unfolded during our first meeting, he was riveted on my every word, unlike the first time I had talked to him a week or so ago. In fact he had not even paid attention to the cute waitress as she walked by time after time, obviously trying to make her presence known.

When I had finished talking, he shook his head and said.

"That is one of the most incredible things I've ever heard, and the detail is extraordinary. Henry, the girl I told you about before, the one that told me to see the hypnotherapist; she related nearly the exact same story to me that you just did, from a slightly different perspective of course. She may be the girl in your dreams, you two really need to get together and talk, because this is crazy."

Our food had come almost without us noticing, and was starting to get cold, but like a moth to the flame, I found myself inexplicably compelled to ask the question.

"Dan, what is her name, if you don't mind me asking? I really need to know."

"I'm sure she won't mind me telling you, especially after what you just told me. Her name is Dee Ballinger, do you know her?"

My jaw dropped open, and the look on my face told him everything, even before I had spoken.

"I do know her Dan, very well in fact. She and I used to date each other for a short time about ten years ago, plus we had been good friends for many years before that. We both just kind of went our own ways, not breaking up, nor officially even going together. We had both recently became single after long term relationships, and our hooking up was more of a mutual support system for each other to make it through our grieving period. I've thought about her many times over the years, and I still have feelings for her. As a matter of fact, she comes and hangs out at my fireworks booth almost every day. I can't wait until she shows up again this year. You know I start selling in just a couple of days."

Dan was just finishing his breakfast, and I had not even started on mine. He was looking at me with a strange look, but all he could say was, "Incredible." With renewed vigor and a smile on my face, I ate my breakfast in record time. While I finished my breakfast, Dan was up at the counter talking with the waitress he was so fond of, which was nice to see.

Just as I was downing the last of my coffee, the pager sounded. That was great timing, it seems like all the stars are lining up in my favor, almost like divine intervention, or perhaps divine direction. Leaving cash on the table for our meals, we were out the door, and our day was off and running.

Between the ambulance calls, and the thoughts I was having about our conversation at breakfast, I had nearly forgotten about my woes at home. But as quitting time was nearing, the stress started to weigh heavily on my soul. Now, the problems at home were all I could think of, and I was dreading going home to face Jane. I was so preoccupied by the journey that faced me that I nearly forgot to join in on the briefing to the night crew when they came on duty.

"Don't worry about it Henry," Dan said, "You head home, and I'll brief the crew. Good luck at home and I'll see you in the morning."

"Thanks Dan, I'll see you guys in the morning." With that, I walked out to my truck, and headed for home. It would be the longest drive of my life.

It doesn't matter how beautiful the day is, or how wonderful your surroundings are, if you are depressed, stressed, angry, or just plain unhappy, the only thing you'll be able to dwell on, is the problem at hand, and that is what was going on with me right now. Here I am, driving down one of the most scenic highways in the country, 6:30 in the evening, 75 degrees, the setting sun starting to cast long shadows across the valley, and I'm too preoccupied with my own woes to enjoy it. This is not how I wanted to spend my life.

As I drove on, I thought to myself, it's as though something seems to be calling to me, I can't put a finger on it, but I can feel it, and I can sense it. I don't know if it's something spiritual, physical, or metaphysical, I just know it is getting stronger, and it's driving me crazy. Hell, maybe that's the whole problem, maybe I am crazy, or at least that's what Jane seems to think already. Oh yeah, I nearly forgot about Jane.

All of a sudden there was a knot in my stomach, I was just about home, and I don't know if I even have a girlfriend to come home to. As unhappy as we have both been over the last year or so, a time of separation would probably do us both a lot of good. The house we live together is too big, and too expensive to manage on my own, so if indeed we find ourselves going our separate ways, it might be a good idea to sell the house, or perhaps rent it out for awhile, at least until I can get my life settled. Wow, talk about stinking thinking, I'm not even to the house yet, and I've already got us broke up. I need to get a grip on myself before I get home.

As I drew near to the house, I noticed that the driveway was empty, so it's obvious that Jane isn't home yet. That means I can breathe a sigh of relief, at least for a moment or two. I need a little time to wind down, and gain my composure, because right now, I am way too stressed out to deal with her so soon. I parked my truck in the yard to leave her a parking spot when she does get home, and then I walked to the house. That's odd, there seems to be extra tire tracks in the dirt of the driveway, so tentatively, I unlocked the door, and went inside. It was immediately evident that something was not quite right. There seemed to be a few less pieces of furniture than there was when I left this morning.

Don't you just hate that sinking feeling you get in your stomach when things around you are falling apart? As I looked around, I saw a note on the counter. I felt sick to my stomach as I picked it up to read. The note was cordial enough, telling me that I have serious issues that I need to work on, that she is unhappy with her life, and how she needs to be on her own for awhile to work things out. She states that she will be back at a later date for a few more things. Meanwhile, she told me to take care of myself, and to have a good life. What a bunch of crap, right now I'm going to have a stiff drink, and then go find my buddy Scott. I am going to need his company once again to help me survive.

They say history repeats itself, but I didn't realize they meant every few years. It's like I never seem to learn whatever lesson it is that I'm supposed to learn. I do feel that if you're not following the path that is predetermined for you to follow, then you are doomed to keep repeating the same mistakes over and over again. Something, or someone, seems to be pushing themselves to the surface lately, and I seem to be the focus of that attention. Apparently, I have a date with destiny, and that destiny seems to be close at hand. I just hope I can survive that destiny. I wonder how many people get the chance to fulfill their destiny. This destiny appears to be very powerful, so things may get very exciting, very soon.

I drove back down the valley to Corvallis and to Scott's house. He was sitting on his porch drinking a soda when I pulled up. I got out of my pickup, went up on his deck and sat on his other patio chair. He could tell something was up, because as long as I have been with Jane, I have never come to his house during the week.

"Hey Henry, what's up, I never see you during the week."

"Jane left me Scott, and I'm feeling kind of rough. Would you be willing to stay at my place for a few nights so I have someone to talk to? I really don't feel like spending much time alone."

"You bet Henry, let me grab a few extra cloths and my shaving kit. I'll bring my own truck so I can get to work tomorrow, and I'll meet you at your house. Are you sure you're doing okay?"

"Yeah, I'm doing okay, it's weird Scott, it's like I know things are happening the way they are supposed to be, and I kind of feel at peace with it all. I've always had the belief that things happen for a reason, sometimes it just takes awhile to figure out what it is, and I'm guessing that this is going to be one of those times. Meanwhile, I'm going to have to endure a little pain and heartache for awhile, but, what the heck, I've been here a few times before, and lived through it?"

"We sure have my friend, and we will make it through this one too," Scott said as he put his hand on my shoulder. "I'll always stick by you, you can count on that. Now, let's head for your house, drink a few beers, and talk about dragons…Ethan" That brought a smile to my face.

"Thanks Scott, I mean Balon; you have always been my best friend, in this life, and the next."

With that, we both climbed into our respective vehicles, and headed for my house, where we sat on the deck, drank beer, and told stories of high adventure and daring, most of it fabricated and embellished, but exciting none the less. About midnight I told Scott that I needed to go to bed so I could make it to work tomorrow. Only two more days of work, and then I would be on vacation, and even though it was a working vacation, it was still a vacation.

"I need to get up at about five in the morning, what time do you need to get up Scott?"

"I'll just get up when you do Henry, that way I can go catch some breakfast before I need to be at work. I'll see you in the morning."

"Good night Scott, you know the way to the guest bedroom, and the bathroom, so I'll see you tomorrow."

We both headed our separate ways. The night would prove to be a restless one again. I guess I should be getting used to it by now, but mentally, I'm wearing out, so sleep would be a welcome distraction.

When you are breaking up with someone, the nights and weekends are always the hardest to make it through. That's the time when most suicides are likely to happen, and that's what happened to me when my first marriage ended.

My first marriage ended the day of New Years Eve. I used to be a very jealous man, and when she disappeared, I just knew she would be out partying with other men. That thought ate at me for two days before I decided to take an overdose of sleeping pills. It was the night of the second day, which in this case also happened to be Friday night, certainly another party night for my wayward wife. Scott was with me for the day as we searched all the local towns and motels for her. Just before evening, I ditched Scott at my home while I supposedly ran to the store for something. Unfortunately, what I went to the store for was two boxes of sleeping pills, and a bottle of whisky. From there, I drove up a mountain road to a place where my wife and I used to go and make love under the pine trees. The date was January 1, 1995; it was about ten degrees above zero, with over a foot of snow on the ground.

Out of the forty sleeping pills in the two boxes, I managed to wash down thirty-six, with about three quarters of the bottle of whisky. Now, in a drunken stupor, I decided to walk across the creek and out into the snow so hypothermia would make sure I would die. The only problem with my plan was that I had forgotten my bottle of whisky in the car, so I walked back through the partially frozen creek to the car to retrieve my bottle. Well, by now I was cold, so I got back into the car, and started the engine to warm up, and that's when I passed out.

Now here is where this whole saga gets weird. I should be dead now right, having bad dreams about snow, water, and whisky as Joe Blow in my next life cycle, but no, that's not what happened at all. By now, I had been passed out for several hours when something bumped my car, and woke me up out of my dead sleep, so to speak. I don't know exactly what it was, maybe an animal, maybe an angel, maybe a dragon, I don't know. What I do know is that now, after waking up in the dark mountains all by myself, is this, I no longer wanted to die. You might say I had a religious experience, or a revelation, I'm not sure even now, ten years later. Another thing I know, at this point, is that I have to try to get back to town, and to the hospital.

By now though, before I can head back to town, I have really got to go to the bathroom, so I open the car door, step out, and fall flat on my face. My legs are paralyzed, I can't walk, I can't even stand up, and now I'm scared. 'What have I done to myself this time,' I asked myself. I was able to prop myself against the car with my legs locked to urinate, and then managed to fall back into the car. Then, like an idiot, and by some miracle, I managed to drive back into town to my house, nearly wrecking several times along the way.

When I pulled into my driveway, my whole family was waiting there, including my son, and my mother, since I had left a suicide note. They managed to carry me to my mom's car, and took me to the hospital, which was a bit humiliating, given the fact that I worked for that same hospital. The hospital administration was very supportive, and paid for me to see a counselor for about eight months. I will always be grateful to that hospital, because I know in my heart, that if it was not for their understanding and support, that I would have found a way to later finish what I had started that night in the mountains.

The rest of that story is history. I thought many times during the next few months about killing myself, but I always thought back to the night in the woods, when something bumped my car and woke me up. I needed to stay alive for a reason, and I still believe that to this day.

I've had several bad relationships since my first marriage, which have probably helped prepare me for this setback. I believe very strongly that we are guided through each life by a preplanned destiny, and it is up to each person to choose whether or not to follow his or her destiny. I feel that when you stray from the plan, that you will have trouble in your life, and when you are on the right path, things will go well for you. The problem is, I have not yet figured out how to stay on the right path.

I know there are a lot of vices these days that lead you away from the path. I feel that most things, in moderation are okay, except for elicit drugs, and I feel there are some things that help you to find, and stay on the proper path, things like being kind, and helping the less fortunate. Beyond that, I'm just sort of blindly fumbling my way through life too.

I'm just now starting to realize that I am being led through each sojourn, and that if I would quit fighting against it, I would see opportunities opening up before me that would make me happy beyond my wildest dream. That is why I am looking at my current situation as a nudge by unseen powers, a nudge to go in a slightly different direction. I feel that something is leading me to the next steps in my journey, so I'm at peace with it.

I guess that I've always known something was not right with my current relationship, I was never at peace, never at ease, there was always something missing, and I think Jane felt it as well. That is why, this time around, I decided not to get married. Unfortunately, that lack of commitment probably contributed to the demise of our relationship. Right now though, I feel that since I am not in control of the situation, that there are powers greater than I am leading the show, and I'm okay with that.

I must have slept some during the night, because I don't remember much of it. I guess the alcohol must have helped a bit, because the next thing I knew, the alarm clock was screaming in my ear. Oh nuts, I forgot to get the coffee pot ready, now we're going to have to wait for it to brew. Life is just getting to be intolerable lately, isn't it?

As I walked past the door to the spare bedroom, I called to Scott that it was time to get up. A groan from the dark interior of the bedroom was all the response I needed. I knew Scott was easy to awaken, so I went on down the stairs to start the coffee. As I was adding the water to the coffee maker, Scott came down the stairway, wanting to know who put the cotton in his mouth during the night.

"Feeling a little rough this morning, are you?" I teased. "Go splash a little water on your face while the coffee brews, and I'll make us some toast."

Scott just mumbled as he went by. While he cleaned up, I made toast, set it out on the table, along with my mom's homemade raspberry jelly, and a steaming cup of hot coffee. When he came out of the bathroom and saw the food, he was a man reborn. We both ate greedily, sipping hot coffee, and listening as the birds were starting to chirp in earnest outside. Given all the problems and diversity surrounding my life right now, I was feeling quite wonderful and alive. The thought of feeling good was also making me feel a little guilty, and I thought to myself, 'Lord, I hope this guilt trip passes.'

Finishing our light breakfast, I turned to Scott, and said.

"I need to head for work, and I'll shower there, so, let yourself out when you're ready, and, can you come back over tonight?"

Scott stood up also, and said.

"I'm going to head out too Henry, and yes, I'd be glad to come back tonight. I'll catch you then."

Both of us filled a travel cup with coffee for the road, turned off the coffee pot, locked the house behind us, and headed our separate ways to work.

Today would prove to be one of the longest days of my life. It was one of those days where we had no calls, a day that just seemed to drag on forever. To keep from dwelling on my recent breakup with Jane, Dan and I talked about the visions of my past life. He wanted to know about the flora and fauna of the time, and about the dragons in particular. He stated that our mutual friend Dee talked about dragons all the time, and it seemed to Dan that it was more than coincidence that he now knew two people that so closely shared such common ground.

"Tell me what the dragons look like Henry," Dan asked with all sincerity.

"Well Dan, the best way I can describe them, is to say they are built much like a pterodactyl, with thick, light weight scales, and long wings that fold into their body. They don't have the long snout like the pterodactyl, but it's shorter, more like a dinosaur's head, with several spikes like horns on top of its head. No two dragons have the same horn structure, or number, some have four horns, and some can have six. The horns are about a foot or so long, with a slight curve to them. They have two rows of thick, hard, flat spines that stick up out of their back, kind of like the spines on some of the dinosaurs. Their abdomen looks like tires stacked on top of each other when they stand upright, and are nearly as tough as tires."

"The dragon's head is about two feet long from the back of their skull to the tip of their nose, and their neck is about five feet long to the shoulders of the wings. The torso is about eight to ten feet long, which then tapers another fifteen feet or so down to the tip of the tail. Each leathery wing is twenty to thirty feet long, with a sharp spike at the tip of each fold. Their legs are about eight feet long, so they have to walk on their legs and their folded wings; much like a bat does on the ground. They vary in color from a dusky brown or tan, to nearly black for the old males. They are very clumsy on the ground, but in the air, they are as agile as an eagle."

"Dragons have the sense of smell of a vulture, being able to pick out the scent of prey, or of an enemy, from several miles away. They have telescopic vision that can spot an object from the air, also many miles away. But, the most incredible thing about a dragon is that they are perceptive, nearly to the point of being psychic. When they look at you, you would swear they are looking directly into your soul. When you stand before a dragon, any emotion you try to hide will come right to the top to be exposed."

"It's weird Dan, but I feel that dragons have a soul, just like we do, and I think we are connected to them somehow on a spiritual plane. I know they are extinct as a species, but I can still feel their presence, like a spirit or something, I can't really explain it."

Dan now interrupted, saying.

"You don't have to explain Henry, because I've heard almost this same explanation before, from Dee. She believes the spirits of dragons roam the earth right now, and are available to her as guides, or mentors. To her, they are very real. She believes she can call one up anytime she wants. She says there are several dragons available to her, but there seems to be one dragon in particular that is her main spirit guide. You really need to talk to her Henry."

"Well Dan, I'm quite sure I'll be seeing her in a couple of days at the fireworks booth. Its beginning to feel like a date with destiny is arriving, and it's giving me the chills. Wait until I tell the hypnotherapist about this, because it will blow his mind."

"Amen brother," Dan said as he got up to leave the room, leaving me sitting at the dining table in the crew quarters of the ambulance hall, pondering my past, as well as my future, whatever that was going to be.

The rest of the day passed uneventfully, and when quitting time came around, I headed for home, a growing sense of excitement filling me as my vacation, and even more important, my next appointment with the hypnotherapist, was only one more day away. How was I ever going to make it through another day of work? My distraction level is at level that I have never experienced before. It's a good thing Scott was coming over tonight, or I would've gone stir crazy.

I have never been a person who could stand being alone for very long. I've always had to have someone in my life, even if it was the wrong person. I guess you would have to call me co-dependant. I wonder how this came about, if indeed I believe in my past life. I was the master of my own castle,

I was not married, although it seems Marta spent a lot of time with me, and I did have a house full of servants. Now that I think about it, I was never alone, even back then. Maybe that explains my need to have people around me all of the time. It's funny how you can answer your own questions if you just think about it for a while.

Wow, speaking about distractions, I'm already home, and I don't remember anything about the trip. I'll be glad when I get this all sorted out. Maybe it'll make it better, maybe it'll be worse, we'll soon find out. As I pulled up to the house I could see Scott's truck parked in front of the house. Scott has his own key, so he had let himself into the house. I sure do hope he left me a beer.

As soon as I got out of the truck, the smell of the barbecue reached out to me first. What is it about the smell of a barbecue that puts a person so much at ease? Maybe it is because a barbecue signifies leisure and enjoyment. As a matter of fact, I think the smell of a barbecue should be officially listed as a form of aromatherapy, because as soon as I stepped out of my truck, all my cares in the world lifted right off my shoulders. I was instantly at ease, happy, and most of all, hungry.

Walking around the back of the house, the sight that appeared before my eyes was enough to send me into the most wonderful state of uncontrollable laughter that I have had in many years. There was Scott, standing at the barbecue, wearing Bermuda shorts, a Hawaiian shirt, and an apron over the top of it all. He had a long neck bottle of beer in one hand, and barbecue tongs in the other, and he was grilling hot dogs. Now remember, Scott is not a small man, and the whole wardrobe probably would have worked if it had not been for the apron. Where is a camera when you need one? Somewhere in the middle of laughing hysterically I managed to say, "Honey, —-I'm home," and then I totally lost it again.

At first Scott looked a little hurt, but my laughter was contagious, and soon enough, a smile appeared on his face, and then he too started giggling. When he did the pirouette, that's when he lost it too. With tears of laughter in his eyes, he barely managed to say.

"I've been slaving over a hot stove all day, and this is how you treat me when you come home, I'm going home to mother."

That did it, we were both nearly doubled over with laughter, our stomachs hurt, and tears were rolling down our cheeks. Then I remembered the hot dogs were still cooking, or should I say burning.

"Scott, the hotdogs are burning!" I blurted out, and then started laughing again just as hard as before. Scott quit laughing, and looked upset, until my laughter got to him again. Putting my arm around his bulky shoulders, I said.

"Turn off the grill and I'll buy you dinner over at the Cantina. I appreciate the effort my friend, and next time, I won't interrupt you in the middle of cooking dinner. And Scott, get rid of the apron. I can dress you up, but I can't take you out."

As we walked out to the truck, we were still chucking like a couple of schoolboys. When we were both in the truck I turned to Scott once more and said to him, this time with all sincerity.

"Thanks for being such a good friend."

"You're welcome Henry," was all he said, but it was enough.

Dinner was as jovial as it could be, given the fact that my girlfriend of nearly ten years had recently left me. If it wasn't for the fact that it was a totally dominant relationship on her part, I probably would have been more upset, but as it is, I felt a sense of relief.

I was married to my first wife for twenty years, and when she left, I was completely devastated. Looking back, I can see that I was totally co-dependant upon her, and after she left me alone, that's when I tried to commit suicide. I remained single after that for three years before hooking up with Jane. In the meantime I dated several ladies, even going steady with a couple of them. Each time one of those relationships broke up, I was devastated again, but each time was a little less traumatic than the time before. That seems to be what has happened this time around, it doesn't hurt as bad as it used to, and since I never really got comfortable in this relationship, it was a lot easier to go my separate way. I'm not saying it is right, I'm just saying it gets easier.

After a good dinner and a few margaritas, we headed back to the house where we sat on the deck until around eleven, drinking beer, talking about fishing, fireworks, and women. In our slightly altered states of mind, we came to the brilliant conclusion that women were a lot of trouble, and that fishing for a living was a noble profession. Okay, none of this made any sense, but what does make sense these days. We were just two drunks, solving the world's problems, that is, just before we crawled to our respective bedrooms, and passed out.

It's a good thing my alarm clock is set to go off at the same time everyday, or this time I would have missed going to work altogether. When that alarm clock went off, it was such a shock, that I thought my heart would leap completely out of my chest. The alarm clock just kept buzzing as I lay there trying to figure out if I had died and went to hell, or if I was just having another bad dream. After about a minute of this, my brain finally got on track and figured out whom I was, then where I was, then, that I was indeed alive, and finally, that I had to go to work today. As soon as I made that last connection, I bolted upright in bed, and swung my feet over the side of the bed. Whoops, wrong thing to do, the whole world started spinning, and I swear a firecracker went off right between my eyes. I leaned over and put my face in my hands until the world quit spinning, and this time I only opened one eye at a time. It was much better this time.

Why do we do the things we do to ourselves? I know better, I even said so to Jane, not two days prior. I need to start practicing what I preach. I need to stop drinking, and get back in touch with my real self. And since I feel like crap, today is as good a day as any to stop drinking, or at least to slow down.

Standing on slightly unsteady legs, I realized I hadn't even gotten undressed last night. I guess that will save me a little time. Oh man, I didn't get the coffee ready last night again. I am really messing up lately. Maybe I'm more affected by Jane leaving than I'm letting myself believe, or maybe I'm just feeling sorry for myself. In fact, I'm quite sure that I look about as sorry as I feel right now. Oh, my head hurts, I have simply got to take better care of myself or I'm not going to be able to function, or get everything done that's coming up in the next few days.

As I strolled down the hallway I called out to Scott, partly to see if he was still alive, and also to see what time he wanted to get up. For the most part, all I heard was indiscernible grunting coming from the dark room, but I was able to make out that he was going to sleep awhile longer, and go into work late, which was probably a good idea. I wish that I could do that myself, but, when you are part of a two man team, if you don't show up, the ambulance is shut down until they can get the backup crew to cover while they call in someone else to work. Meanwhile, someone in medical need may be without care, so you go to work whether you're sick, tired, or just hung over. I've never missed a day in fifteen years, and I'm not going to miss this one either.

Making a beeline for the coffee pot, I noticed there was still a little bit of coffee left over from yesterday morning, so, being a true bachelor, I micro waved a cup of the cold coffee, poured it into my travel cup, and headed for work. With any luck, I'm going to go right back to bed in the crew quarters as soon as I get to the ambulance hall. Scott is just going to have to fend for himself when he gets up. He knows how to make coffee; at least I think he does.

Today is the last day of work before my vacation starts, so I just have to make it through today. Scott and I are supposed to start stocking the booth tonight so we can open early in the morning. Scott usually works mornings, but he can set his own hours. He manages a car wash, which needs to be cleaned and maintained several times a day, and he also mows all the lawns in a couple of trailer courts in the area. If we can get stocked up this evening, he can come to the booth just before noon to relieve me so I can get to my session with the hypntherapist. As excited as I am about fireworks, I have to say that I am even more excited to see Dr Miller tomorrow, and to learn more about my past life, and about the woman in those dreams.

When I arrived at the ambulance hall, the crew was just backing the ambulance into the bay. It looks like they were busy last night, so I hope today will be a quiet one. I joined them in the crew quarters to see how their night had went, and with an odd look from them, Jim asked me if I was okay, because I looked kind of rough. After admitting that I was just hung over, Jim suggested I go take a shower, and he would put a pot of coffee on before he left. My partner Dan had just shown up so we were set for the day. I thanked Jim and hit the shower.

When I came out of the shower to pour a cup of coffee, I felt like a new man. Dan was sitting at the table drinking a cup of coffee and reading the newspaper. When I came in, he put down his paper and asked me how I was doing, not so much physically, but emotionally. He was genuinely concerned that maybe I was going down the same path I did when my first wife left me.

"I appreciate your concern Dan, but actually, I'm doing very well with it this time. Right now, I'm way too busy to dwell on anything but getting my fireworks booth open, and of course, going to see Dr Miller tomorrow. I'm really excited about that."

"Oh that's right, I forgot you have another appointment tomorrow," Dan said, "I can't wait to hear about it. If it's okay, I'd like to stop by your fireworks booth tomorrow evening and find out how your session went. And Henry, you need to take care of yourself a little better."

"I'll be looking forward to seeing you tomorrow evening and telling you everything that happened with Dr miller. And I will take better care of myself Dan, which includes cutting back on the booze. Now, shall we get some breakfast, because I think I'm back in the land of the living?"

"You're on." Dan said as we grabbed our gear, and climbed into the ambulance. The sun was up, the mountains were looking particularly gorgeous today, and it was going to be a wonderful day.

It turned out to be a great day indeed, with three minor ambulance calls to keep us busy enough to make the day go by quickly, and before I knew it, it was time to go home, and to go on vacation. I bid the crew farewell, told Dan I would see him tomorrow evening, and jumped in my truck. I had a few errands to see to on the way home.

My first stop was to swing past the parking lot to make sure the fireworks company had delivered my booth, and sure enough, it was there. The fireworks booths are large, heavy wooden structures that are on skids. They are power winched up onto a flatbed truck, delivered to the site, and then unloaded by means of a tilt bed. There is no other way to move these booths around, so you're pretty much at the mercy of the movers. If something goes haywire, and your booth doesn't get delivered, you can lose a lot of money in sales. My plan is to eventually go into the fireworks business independently, with my own booth on wheels, but that is a ways down the road. At least for now, we're set up to stock the booth tonight. Now I have to track down Scott.

I wish I could have talked to Scott this morning before I left the house so we could have made a game plan. That's what happens when you let things get out of hand the night before. Oh well, I know most of the places he has to mow, so I'll swing by those first, and then I'll stop by the car wash. I wish that man would get a cell phone or something. What kind of guy goes his whole life without a telephone? Speaking of cell phones, I almost forgot about my own, I'll call the house and see if he is there.

Dialing my own home number felt really odd all of a sudden, because for the last ten years, whenever I called, Jane would be the one who would answer. Now I am starting to feel a little depressed. I guess I'd better try to talk to her when I get a chance, to see how she's doing. I thought I was doing really well until just now, but I can't let it get to me, I need to focus on the tasks at hand. I must have been zoning out because I finally became aware that someone had actually answered my phone, and was asking if anyone was there.

"Hey Scott, I'm sorry about that, I was off in the ozone for a second there. I'm glad I caught you, did you remember that we have to stock the booth tonight."

"I sure did remember Henry, is the booth on the parking lot?" Scott asked, sounding none the worse for wear.

"Yes it is, I just went by there, and everything is ready to go. I'll swing by the house and pick you up."

"Great," Scott said, "this time I've got supper ready for you when you get here."

"You're not wearing that apron again are you, because I couldn't take that vision two days in a row," I asked jokingly.

"Heavens no, I gave up trying to learn to cook, I just bought precooked chicken and potato salad," Scott said.

"Sounds wonderful Scott, I'm about five minutes away, I'll see you in a few."

Hanging up the phone I thought to myself, Scott is trying to take care of me like he did when my first wife left me all those years ago. I hope he's not as stressed out about this episode as he was the last time. I guess I need to talk to him, and reassure him that I'm not going to pull a bonehead stunt like that again. Scott is as good a friend as you could ever ask for, so I hope our friendship is not too hard on him. I'm more convinced than ever now that Scott truly was with me in my past life, because no casual acquaintance could ever be this loyal in one single lifetime.

As I pulled into the driveway, Scott was sitting on the bench on the front porch waiting for me.

"How's it going?" I asked as I got out of the truck.

"I think I'm going to live now, though I wouldn't have bet on it this morning. Remind me not to do that again, okay."

"Did you make it to work this morning?" I asked.

"Oh yeah," he replied, "but I didn't make it to the car wash until about ten, and then I only managed to do about four lawns before it got too hot. I swear I was sweating alcohol all afternoon, so I think I've got it all out of my system now. Come on in and eat, the chicken is on the table."

"Chicken sounds great; my mouth has been watering ever since you told me about it. Let's eat quickly, because we have a lot to do yet tonight."

As we walked into the dining room, Scott had the table set with paper plates, plastic cups, plastic eating utensils, and a large pitcher of ice tea.

"Wow Scott, that looks wonderful. And since you did all the food preparation, I'll do the dishes," I said as we sat down.

"Oh sure," Scott said, "now you volunteer to do the dishes, when we have throw away dishes, see how you are."

"My momma didn't raise no dummy," I said as we sat down to eat a quick dinner before we tackled our next big chore.

We had to eat fast because we have a lot to do yet tonight. We ate quickly and then started gathering the supplies we would need to get set up for the first day of sales tomorrow. We needed a stepladder, a hammer, extension cords, staple gun, assorted nails, screws, and other hardware.

Once we had our supplies, we drove both of our trucks to the storage unit to load fireworks, one full case of each type of firework, and then all of the cases of repacks, which are full of various mixed parcels of fireworks. From there we drove straight to the fireworks booth to start stocking shelves. The booth has lighting, and since it would be dark soon, the first chore was to run the extension cords to the power supply so we could work on into the night.

While I worked on stocking shelves, Scott worked on the outside of the booth, putting up the eight by ten foot vinyl wing signs, then a twenty four foot long top sign, and finally the posters all over the front of the booth. Each huge vinyl wing sign has the image of a huge dragon emblazoned upon it, as do most of the various posters. The booth really is quite impressive to see under normal circumstances, but after my journey back to the land of the dragons, the booth seems to hold a special significance that I really hadn't known about before.

We finished stocking the booth around midnight, and then we double locked the doors and the customer windows, and called it a night. We don't have to worry too much about burglars because we are in a major department store parking lot that is patrolled by the local police on a regular basis all night long. Plus, the locking systems on the doors and sale windows are pretty secure in their own right.

We were pretty exhausted by the time we got back home so we both headed straight to our respective bedrooms to get some much-needed sleep. Tomorrow was going to be a big day, and I was anxious to get started. Even though I was excited to be on vacation and selling fireworks again, I was even more excited about seeing Dr Miller tomorrow, and going back in time to my castle, my dragons, to the unknown woman, and the worrisome view of my own death. I just hope I'll be able to sleep tonight.

As it turned out, I guess I was more tired than I thought, because I slept soundly through the night, and even managed to sleep in until 8:00 a.m., which for me is late. It feels so peaceful and laid back to be on vacation, even if it is a working vacation like this one, and I think you actually sleep better. Strolling past the spare bedroom I called for Scott to get his lazy butt out of bed. The response I heard from the bedroom was one I'd heard a hundred times over the years from my own kids.

"No dad, I don't want to get up."

After doing a double take at the door, I told him he would be grounded if he didn't get out of bed, which didn't work on my own kids either, but by the grumbling I heard from the room, I knew he was stirring. What a wonderful day this was going to be, I could feel it in the air, and the excitement was building deep down in my soul.

"I'll get the coffee started Scott, so come downstairs when you're ready."

By the time the coffee was percolating, Scott was coming down the stairs, looking none the less for wear.

"Isn't it amazing how good you feel in the morning when you don't drink any alcohol the night before?" I said as Scott sat down at the table.

"It certainly is Henry, I feel great, and I'm ready to get started."

"I'll make us some toast, and as soon as we have our coffee, we'll get down to the fireworks booth, and get it open for business."

We ate our breakfast in record time, and loaded all of the supplies we would need to open up the booth, items such as the cash box, receipt book, tacks, staple gun, paper, pens, and calculators. Then it was off to the fireworks booth, with a quick stop at the bank for starting change and cash. Once we were at the booth, we unlocked the end doors, raised the sales windows, and another fireworks year was under way. It wasn't long before the kids started showing up to check out this year's firepower.

Kids are amazing shoppers. For the first several days they will price check every booth in town, only buying the best-priced fireworks. If they don't like the price, or if the product isn't good, they'll shop elsewhere. Even though kids can be a bit annoying those first few days, you still have to be nice to them, because they will tell their friends, and especially their parents, and those same parents come back during the last few days of the season to spend the big money on fireworks. So, we cater to the kids first, laugh and joke with them, make them good deals, and treat them like our best customers, so we can get their parents' business later on.

Now don't get me wrong, kids spend a lot of money. I don't know where they get so much money to spend, but they are a big part of our business. It's not like it was when I was a kid, where I had to mow lawns for a week to be able to afford a few packs of firecrackers. It's nothing nowadays for a ten-year-old kid to come in and spend forty dollars at a time, and a teenager may spend a hundred dollars just to impress his girlfriend. And the first booth open in the morning can make a couple hundred dollars before the other booths even open their doors. We got a late start today, but I will usually have the windows open by eight in the morning, and I will stay open at least an hour after the other booths close down for the evening. This tactic is what has kept me in the fireworks business for nearly twenty five years now.

The first few kids to stop by were just looking at prices, with some spending a couple dollars on firecrackers to get their neighbors excited. Occasionally, a tourist will stop and buy fireworks for the novelty of it, and then we get the big spenders who come up from the next state where fireworks are more regulated, and they'll spend hundreds of dollars for themselves, and their friends. Those are the sales that we wait for. The last four days of the selling season will be fully half of your total sales for the year. That's when it starts to get hectic, and you work your butt off. Other than those few days of chaos, it's fun to talk and joke with all of the customers that come in. Some of the people that come to the booth I only see during this time of year. I'm definitely a people person, and this is the highlight of my year.

My appointment with Dr Miller was at one o'clock, so at about eleven I told Scott to go on a break and get some lunch before I headed for Missoula. While he was gone, a couple of old friends stopped by to visit. These guys are rabid fireworks fans, literally spending in upwards of a thousand dollars a year. They'll go out and work different jobs during the day, then come back to the booth in the evening to buy fireworks. It's always good to see them every year. I have a lot of loyal customers like these two that won't buy fireworks anywhere else. That's what happens when you treat people right.

By the time Scott returned, it was almost past time for me to head for Missoula.

"Sorry," Scott said as he walked up, "the restaurant was busy, and I hurried as fast as I could."

"That's alright, I'll fire you as soon as I get back, just remind me in case I forget," I said as I headed out the back door to my truck. "Make lots of money, and I'll see you about four o'clock."

"I'll certainly try to Henry, and good luck. I can't wait to talk to you when you get back. Drive carefully," Scott waved as I pulled out onto the highway.

I'm going to have to call ahead if the traffic is slow today. Lord, I don't like to be late for an appointment, it stresses me out, and I'm already a little nervous about what I'll learn today. All the way to Missoula I replayed the events from the first session over and over in my head. Before I knew it, I was in Missoula, and pulling up to Dr Miller's house. He was sitting out on the front stoop enjoying the sunshine. He waved to me as I parked and got out of my truck.

"Hello Henry, I'm glad you could make it, I was beginning to worry that you were having second thoughts about all of this," Dr Miller said as he stood and shook my hand.

"There's no way I would have missed this session doc, in fact, all I could think about all week was getting back here for my next trip back in time. I've been excited and nervous about it all at the same time," I said as we walked into the doctor's house.

"To tell you the truth Henry, it's all I've been able to think about too," Jim said. "Our last session was so realistic, I've never had a client's past life experience come alive so vividly. I think there's something very special happening here, and I want to take this as far as it will go. In fact, most of my sessions last one hour, but what I would like to do with you is go at least two hours with each session, and longer if the flow is right. Otherwise, I'll bring you out of the hypnosis whenever there is a good stopping spot in the journey. I'll only charge you for one hour each time; because I believe we are going to learn some very exciting things in the next few weeks. So sit down, get comfortable, and we'll get started."

As I sat down in the recliner and leaned back, I again detected the sounds of birds, and the sound of a stream flowing lightly over rocks. The sound of soft music could be heard playing ever so quietly over the hidden speakers. A light breeze caressed my face as my head nestled back into the easy chair. Closing my eyes, I could feel my whole body beginning to relax, this time even quicker than the last time, and I felt an unexplained peace coming over me, like this was my destiny, here and now. After several minutes of relaxation, the doctor began to speak, ever so quietly, further putting me at peace.

"Now Henry, I want you to relax, feeling every inch of your body relax, every muscle, in fact, every cell in your body is at peace. I want you to concentrate on your breathing, feeling each breath flowing into your lungs, like the flow of the air around the earth, the same breeze that circled the earth so many years ago, when dragons roamed the earth, when you roamed the earth, Ethan!"

Chapter 4

"Ethan, where are you, Ethan!" I jolted upright from my soft cushion, eyes blinking, looking around the room to figure out where I was. I must have dozed off after analyzing the poison I had taken from the dead clansman. The light was already starting to fade, meaning I must have slept for hours.

"Ethan, where are you, you must come quickly, I'm afraid we might have trouble again."

It was Balon again, and he sounded as excited as he did when he woke me up the last time.

"I'm in here, what are you yelling about this time?" I said as I finally started to get my bearings. Balon rushed into the room, and he did indeed look shook up.

"Ethan, you wanted me to let you know when the dragons returned. They have, but one is missing, and the others look like they've been in a big battle."

Now Balon had my full attention.

"Which one is missing?" I asked as I jumped up and headed for the doorway, Balon trailing behind with his short legs.

"It's Thermon, she didn't return with the others, and I waited over an hour just to make sure," Balon said, slightly out of breath as he tried to keep up with me after already rushing up the two flights of stairs from the caverns.

"What did you mean when you said it looked like they had been in a battle?" I asked.

Balon worked to catch his breath as we rushed down the long corridor to the stairway down to the caverns.

"Several of the dragons have broken arrows and spear points stuck in their scales and all of them had blood on their talons. It must have been one heck of a battle."

"I'm only worried about whom they battled with, my friend, and by the way, why do you insist on waking me up with all this bad news today, it's really starting to get old, and besides that, you're ruining some really weird dreams."

Leading Balon down the hallway, we quickly descended the stone stairway to the second level where we had moved the dragons after the attack this morning.

"Has Captain Sardon been notified yet?" I asked.

"No my Lord," Balon said, "I haven't had time yet.

"Good," I said, "I don't want him to have any more information than is absolutely necessary. We're going to keep this quiet until we know exactly what we're dealing with."

We approached the dragon pens even more cautiously than before. These dragons have had a rough day, losing one of their numbers for sure, and possibly a second. It has been many years since my dragons have been in a battle, and anytime the dragons have been in a battle, they are very hyperactive for several hours after the fight, until the adrenaline wears off, and right now, we don't know for sure how long it's been since they battled.

Balon approached first, since he had been here already when the dragons returned. I called each one by name in a soothing voice, peaking tentatively around the corner as we had this morning. We were surprised at how calm they actually were compared to the earlier episode. It appeared that they were physically and emotional worn out, because they were all lying down, and barely paid us any attention as we opened the iron gates to the lair. Then, after walking inside, we quietly closed the gate behind us.

We approached each animal slowly, walking around each one, and examining them as best we could without disturbing them too much. It would not be good to disturb a sleeping, possibly injured dragon. I rubbed each dragon on the forehead and neck as I passed by them, a show of affection that I have observed them doing to each other many times in the past.

It was immediately evident that the dragons had indeed been in a battle with someone. Most all had tinges of blood on their talons, and some had blood around their mouths. Several of the dragons had arrow tips and broken shafts wedged in their scales, which I gingerly pulled a couple that looked loose, so I could examine them in more detail. As I examined each dragon in turn, I came upon a sight that was a little more disturbing, a spear point halfway imbedded in Searon's side, back slightly from the wing pit area. Someone either knew what they were doing, and missed, or just about got a lucky shot. I'm more inclined to believe the first idea, since the enemy seems to have found the dragon's vulnerable spot. There was no evidence of the poison darts in any of these animals, but we still don't know what happened to the other dragon, Thermon.

Now the most disturbing thing about the spear point imbedded in Searon is not that it is life threatening in itself, it is the fact that it will continue to irritate the dragon, in time turning her into an angry, unpredictable beast. Then the wound will probably get infected, and finally kill the dragon in a few weeks, after it gets sick and weak. This spear point is going to have to be removed and the sooner the better.

Waving Balon to the back of the pen, I said to him.

"We're going to have to remove that spear point before it causes us some serious trouble. I want you to stay here and console the dragons while I go back to my chambers for some medication and supplies. I'll be back in about fifteen minutes, so don't let anyone in here, do you understand."

"Yes, my Lord, I understand," Balon said as I headed back to my chambers.

As I hurried back to my chambers I examined the arrow tips I had removed from the dragon's scales, and looked at them closely as I walked. Weapons are very specific to the army that uses them, including arrows, and spears. Over the years I had the foresight to collect nearly every type of weapon known, and I did this for two reasons. The first is the fact that I love weaponry. The second is so that I will know my enemy when he appears, and know what he has to offer. It was obvious right away that these weapons belonged to the Gog army, and that made me nervous.

I guess I can blame myself partly for this latest confrontation between the dragons and the Gog clan. When I threw the body of the clansman over the cliff edge this morning, I told the dragons to hunt down and kill anyone that share the same scent, and that is exactly what happened. My mistake was to make a hasty decision without knowing what we were up against. It's my fault that Theron is missing. I sent the dragons to fight an enemy that seems to be prepared for the dragons. It would appear that I'm going to have to change my strategy from here on out.

After I had reached the top of the stairs and headed down the hallway to my chambers, I noticed Valik in the kitchen with Marta, getting something to eat. Calling to him from the doorway, I asked him.

"Mr. Valik, could I speak to you in the hallway please?"

"Yes my Lord," he said, immediately dropping his sandwich and following me out the door. Once we were in the hallway, I glanced around to make sure no one was within earshot, and turned to him and said.

"Mr. Valik, there has been another attack on the dragons while they were out in the field. It was the Gog clansman again, and this time there seemed to be a lot more of them, possible a large army detachment. Another of the dragons is missing, and another one is injured. We're going to treat the injured dragon before the wound worsens. What I need for you to do is to make sure the main gate is closed and the drawbridge is secured. Then gather a couple of your men to check out the castle grounds for anyone who doesn't belong here."

"Yes my Lord, it will be done," he said as he turned on his heel to leave.

"Oh, and Mr. Valik," I said as I stopped him in mid turn, "no one is to know about any of this, especially Captain Sardon, do you understand?"

"Yes my Lord, is there anything else?" He asked with all sincerity and concern.

"Yes there is one last thing," I said, "do not allow anyone down into the caverns until I return, and tomorrow I want you to accompany Balon and myself to town to see the King."

"Yes sir," Valik said with a hint of excitement in his voice. Then, he turned and disappeared out through the back of the kitchen. Marta had also disappeared from the kitchen, for she knew that the conversation between Valik and me was not for her to hear. Quickly I turned and continued down the hall to my own chambers.

Once in my chambers, I went to the door at the back of my bedroom. The door had a large padlock on it, which didn't appear to have been opened in a very long time, and indeed it had not opened in many years. A life filled with drinking and carousing had dulled my senses over the years and caused me to lose interest in all of the ancient arts which I had learned so long ago, the ancient arts of alchemy, and of sciences long forgotten, passed down to me by the old wizard. It would seem that recent events demand my renewed attention to those arts.

Opening an old trunk beside my bed, I moved clothing and personal items aside to reveal what appeared to be the bottom of the trunk. Pulling a small hidden pin from the outside of the trunk near the bottom, I reached back inside and lifted a board to reveal a hidden compartment. Grabbing a large key from the compartment, I unlocked the padlock, replaced the key, the board, the pin, the clothing, and closed the trunk. I guess it's time to assume the destiny that I had avoided for so long. Taking a deep breath, I removed the padlock from the hasp.

As the door swung open, I pulled a small chain, which opened a small hatch on the roof of the villa to let in enough ambient light, even though it was now dark outside, to find and light the old lantern in the middle of the large wooden table. As the light opened up the room to view, hundreds of bottles lined the shelves, each one containing different powders, herbs, dried plants, and dehydrated specimens of small animals, rodents, lizards, frogs, toads, and most of all, a baby dragon, having died shortly after hatching from its egg.

Grabbing a facecloth from a stack on the table, I put one over my face, and another one in my pocket. Then, I removed a small jar from one of the shelves, set it in the middle of the table, scooped out a small amount of a yellow powder, and poured it into a small vial, which I sealed with a cork. This vial I placed into my pocket with the other facecloth. Then, I removed my mask, and placed that also into my pocket. Replacing the stopper on the jar, I put it back onto the shelf, and grabbed a large set of iron clamps from the wall. Next, I grabbed another jar, scooped out a large dose of a brown sticky substance, and placed that also into a somewhat larger bowl, along with a small spatula. Looking around one more time, I extinguished the lantern, pulled the chain to close the hatch on the roof, then closed and locked the door to my workshop. On the way out of my chambers, I grabbed a vase, filled it with water, and put a stopper over the opening. Checking the hallway again, I headed down the hallway to the staircase, and made my way back down to the dragon pen.

Calling ahead so as not to disturb the dragons, or Balon, I entered the dragon pen to see Balon sitting on the floor, leaning back onto the injured dragon, which was sound asleep. I tiptoed over to Balon and motioned for him to stand, which he did ever so gently.

"You sure have a way with animals Balon, It's absolutely incredible. Put this mask on over your face, and make sure it's tight," I said as I handed him a face cloth from my pocket. Then, I removed the vial from my pocket. Balon looked at me with a look of concern in his eyes.

"It's okay my friend, I'm going to put the dragons to sleep for a short time while we pull that spear point. It won't harm them, and they'll wake up in an hour or so, none the worse for wear. We need to put them all to sleep so the others don't get the wrong idea that we're somehow hurting their sibling. They may want to protect her by injuring us, or worse. This is the safest way to do it. Now, secure your mask and we'll get started."

Ethan," Balon said as I started to prepare the powder, "it's good to see you back to your old self, and working with your potions."

"It's good to be back," I said, "It seems I no longer have a choice. Now, here we go." With that, I poured the yellow powder into the vase of water, and set it on the floor. Immediately, a yellow fog started pouring out of the vase, and began to fill the cavern. The dragons barely even stirred.

"Let's step out into the hall and let it work," I said, "this should only take about fifteen minutes."

Once out in the hall, we took off our masks where we were sure the fog could not reach us.

"Aren't you afraid someone might come down before we're finished here Ethan?" Balon asked as he was starting to pace nervously about.

"Relax my friend; Mr. Valik has orders not to let anyone down here until we return, so I don't think we have anything to worry about."

"You told Valik what we were doing down here, do you think that wise?" Balon asked with some concern.

"I trust Valik with our lives Balon, and it may well come down to that sooner than we think. You don't know all of the things that are in motion right now, so trust in me, and my judgment, if not in Valik."

"Yes my Lord, I just hope you know what you're doing," Balon said as he strolled over to the gate to look in on the dragons.

"Balon, wait, you don't have your mask on!"

It was too late, one good whiff of the fog and Balon collapsed like a rag doll, sound asleep on the floor of the hallway.

"I guess I won't need your help after all sleepyhead," I said, shaking my head.

Putting my mask back over my face, I dragged Balon back away from the gate, and laid him on his side with his head on his outstretched arm. By then, the fog had cleared enough for me to go back into the dragon pen.

The dragons looked very peaceful while they were asleep, but I'll need to work fast before the effects wear off. Grabbing the iron clamps and the gooey brown paste, I went up to where the spear point had penetrated the hide of Searon the dragon. Getting a firm grip on the spear point with the clamps, I rocked the tip back and forth, pulling with all my might to dislodge the metal shaft. Slowly, the spear point backed out of the hole between the dragon's scales. It looked like it was imbedded nearly five inches. I wondered how the spear had been delivered, but I figured it was probably by a giant crossbow. It would seem that the Gogs were prepared for possible trouble. This is very disturbing, it appears the Gog have come for the long haul. First thing in the morning, I must warn the King.

Once I had the spear point removed, I scooped up some of the brown paste with the spatula and spread it all around, as well as inside the wound. This is a special concoction that will not only kill germs, but will also seal the wound until it has a chance to heal. Quickly, I looked over the other dragons while they were still asleep, pulling at least a dozen more broken arrow points from scales and wings, applying the sticky paste any time I thought the wound might benefit from it.

Once I had finished, it was time to clean up the mess. Gathering up the vase that had produced the fog, as well as the bowl of paste, I simply walked to the opening of the cave to the cliff face, and tossed the whole works into the precipice. Better to be completely rid of any concoction that an enemy could use against us.

The dragons were starting to stir, so I thought this would be a good time to leave. I grabbed the iron clamp and went out into the hallway, locking the gate to the pen behind me. Balon too was just beginning to stir, so I sat down beside him until he woke up. He sat up and looked at me, still in a slight haze, and asked.

"What happened, how did I get on the floor? The last thing I remember was standing here talking to you, and oh, does my head ache."

"You walked over to the dragon pen without your mask on, and then you took a nap."

"Oh my, I'm so sorry master, what about the wounded dragon?" Balon asked in a worried tone.

"It's all taken care of," I said, "she'll be good as new in the morning. Now you lazy bum, if you can manage to stand up, we'll go upstairs so you can go to bed. In the morning, we go to town to see the King, and maybe check out some of the local establishments. It's been a long time since we've been to town. Now my son, rise up and walk."

Slowly Balon rose to his feet, a little shaky at first, and then more steadily. Once he had his bearings, we worked our way back up the stairway, with several pauses along the way for Balon to get his wind.

"What was that stuff?" Balon asked. "I feel like I have a hangover."

"Just a little trick an old man taught me one time. The powder is a mixture of several different plants, as well as a naturally occurring chemical. Mix those together, add water, and you saw the result. If you add one other compound that I won't mention at this time, you won't wake up at all. I would suspect that someday this type of knowledge will be used for evil purposes, so for now, that knowledge remains in my head, and in the books in the secret cavern. The knowledge in my head will go to the grave with me, and the knowledge hidden in the caverns will hopefully stay hidden for a long, long time."

As we reached the main floor, Valik greeted us, and he had his sword on his belt in case there was any trouble. You could see him visibly relax when he saw us, but there was a look of concern on his face when he saw Balon having trouble walking. His hand gripped his sword handle, and he asked.

"Is Balon okay my Lord, are there enemies down below, should I call out the guard?"

"Everything is quite well Mr. Valik; Balon just got his nose in the wrong place and took a little nap. He'll be fine as soon as the effects wear off. Could you please escort him to his chambers? In the morning I would like you all to meet me in the kitchen about an hour after sunrise. Then as soon as the main gate opens, and the vendors come in, we're sneaking out and going to town. I think it's best if we don't let anyone know who we are, so wear cloaks with hoods, and Mr. Valik, I trust you have concealable weapons you can bring."

"Indeed I do my Lord, and will you require any more troops to go along with us?" Valik asked.

"No, just the three of us will go," I said. "Any more than that would draw attention to us. There seems to be a lot of Gog clansman in the area, and I'm sure they would love to get their hands on me."

"Are you sure it is wise to go to town with so few of us?" Balon asked. "It might be safer to take a whole company of men with us for protection."

"As of right now my friend, we are the only ones who know that something is going on around here. If we start acting scared, then the whole population is going to be in a panic. I want to talk to the King first, since we are his subjects, and give him the opportunity to send out patrols to assess the danger. Meanwhile, we need to heighten the security within our own castle walls. The enemy has already penetrated our home once, and I feel there are still traitors in our midst, that is why I am taking the steps that I am. Everything must be done in secret for now, understand."

Both men nodded their understanding, so I continued.

"Mr. Valik, after you have escorted Balon to his room, go and find the troopers that you handpicked, and tell them to be on their guard for anyone coming into the castle that does not look like he belongs here. As this situation becomes worse, only registered vendors will be allowed inside this castle. Until I talk to the King though, we have to be discreet, so just have them observe who comes and goes for now, and then I want a report when we get back tomorrow. And again Mr. Valik, not a word to Captain Sardon, and I'll see you both in the morning."

"Yes my Lord," Valik said as he and Balon started down the hallway to the main villa, and to their respective rooms.

Since I had already had a good nap earlier, and wasn't tired, I decided to head for the kitchen to get something to eat. Their was still a light burning inside the kitchen as I approached, so I peeked inside, and there was Marta, sitting at the massive dining table, sipping on a cup of tea. Next to her was a place setting laid out with bread, cheese, and dried meat, as well as a steaming pot of tea.

"Expecting someone?" I asked as I walked into the dining hall and up to the table.

"Just you, my Lord, I figured you would be hungry when you finished down below. Is everything okay with the dragons, and what is going on around here? You now have a personal bodyguard, Balon looks totally stressed out, and you seem to have changed somehow. I'm starting to get a little bit scared by all of this."

Standing behind her, I massaged her neck, and said.

"Thank you for your concern Marta, there is a lot of things in the wind right now, but I think I have a handle on it. Thermon didn't come back tonight, and Searon came back injured. It looks as though the dragons had been in a major battle. I think there is a large contingent of Gogsmen in the area, and I don't think they are coming here for a visit. So I'm going to see the king in the morning to alert him. I would appreciate it if you would keep all this knowledge to yourself, and especially from Sardon. I believe there are spies in the castle, and I'm working on rooting them out. Everything is being done in secret, so promise me you will keep this to yourself, okay."

"Yes my Lord, but I'm afraid Captain Sardon was here earlier looking for you. I told him you were in the caverns. He asked if something was wrong, but I told him I didn't know. He said he would come back tomorrow to check on you. What will I say when he comes back, and you're not here?"

"Just tell him you don't know where I am. This is a big castle, and by the time he searches it high and low, we should be back from our visit to the King."

"He's going to throw a fit when he finds out," Marta said.

"That's alright," I said, "just leave Captain Sardon to me. This is my castle, and he seems to forget that fact on a regular basis here lately. I think that my being a drunk and a playboy all these years has given him the impression that I'm no longer a force to be reckoned with, or even respected any longer. Well, those days have changed, I've found myself again, and things are going to change dramatically around here in the near future. So, pour me a cup of that herbal tea instead of wine, and let me after that food."

Marta could only sit and stare at me while I ate the food set before me like I hadn't eaten in days. Even though evil plots were in the air, it gave me meaning and purpose in my life again. All those years of relative peace makes you listless, compliant, and soft. It's the intrigue, mystery, and danger that make a man feel alive. When I had finished eating, I turned once again to Marta and spoke.

"Thank you so much for having the food waiting for me, but, in the future, please remind me not to be so predictable."

Being predictable could prove to be the death of a person. The problem to date is that I have always been predictable, and now that is going to be to my advantage, except that I am going to do one more predictable thing right now, and here it is.

"Put away the leftovers my dear, and join me in my chambers," I said with a sheepish grin.

"I thought you weren't going to be so predictable Ethan," Marta said with a sultry look on her face.

I stepped up to her and took her in my arms, kissing her lightly on her lips, and said.

"Well, at least one more time, so I'll see you in a few minutes."

Then, I turned and walked back down the hall to my chambers. It would seem that all this intrigue is giving me renewed vitality, making me feel more alive. I like that feeling. It's time to be master of my own domain once again.

I was lying in my bed when Marta showed up about twenty minutes later. She had obviously gone to her own chambers first, because she came in wearing a lovely silk nightgown, which left little to the imagination. Holding out my arms to her, she slipped out of the robe and crawled under the covers with me. I blew out the candle and we made love with a renewed energy that we had not had in many years, and then slept soundly through the night.

It was Marta of course who woke up at the crack of dawn. She is used to getting up early to get the morning breakfast ready for all the servants and staff, and to get bread baking to serve with all the meals. I will never get tired of the smell of freshly baked bread. As she slid out of the covers, I suggested that she put on one of my heavier robes for the trip back through the villa to her own chambers.

"But everyone will know that we have spent the night together," she said as she donned one of my robes.

"Everyone already knows, my dear, we've been at this for ten years. Besides, you will cause a bigger stir if you wander the halls with only that silk nightgown on, now get out of here, and I'll see you in a little while."

"Yes my Lord," she said as leaned over and kissed me goodbye. Watching her walk away I thought to myself, she would have made someone a wonderful wife. Unfortunately, I'm not interested in taking a wife, which is not fair to her I suppose, but living in separate chambers does keep people from fighting with each other and getting disgusted with each others bad habits. Besides, I am still a playboy at heart, and to me, variety is the spice of life. Somewhere in the back of my mind, I feel like I am waiting for someone special to show up. I don't know who it is right now, but I think I'll recognize her when she comes around, and until that happens, I have no intention of giving up my wanton ways.

Taking my time, I got out of bed and cleaned up at the washbasin. The water was cold, but invigorating. After washing myself from head to toe, I trimmed my beard. put on a clean shirt and pants, and then gathered up my cloak, and staff. For safety and anonymity, a put a woolen sock over the crystal dragonhead on my staff. There's no use advertising who I am, especially when I'm wearing a cloak and hood for disguise. Looking at myself one more time in the mirror, I guess I'm ready to go to see the King.

As I left my chambers, I decided it was best this time to lock the door behind me. I would prefer from now on not to have anyone snooping around through my possessions, or finding a way into secret places that are not meant for eyes other than my own. Now to meet the others, have a bite to eat, and be on our way. This was going to be an exciting day, I could just feel it.

As I entered the kitchen, Balon and Mr. Valik were waiting for me, having a breakfast of bread, eggs, and freshly roasted meat, and as I entered the kitchen, the smell was wonderful.

"Did you guys save some for me?" I asked as I sat down.

"We wouldn't have if you'd have taken any longer," Balon said as he stuffed a large piece of bread with jam into his mouth.

"Sit down Ethan, and I'll bring you some food and tea," Marta called from the cooking area.

"Thank you my dear," I said as I sat down at the dining table. "At least someone around here loves me."

Marta put down a tray of wonderful food, and then poured me a large cup of sweetened tea. I ate greedily and then washed it down with the tea. When I had finished, Marta brought out a satchel of food to take with us on our trip.

"You can never be too careful, so take this food along in case you get delayed, or run into trouble. Now, you boys go, and be careful."

Balon grabbed the bundle of food, and we headed out of the villa, putting on our cloaks prior to leaving the building, and pulling our hoods over our heads. The castle grounds were busy with the activity of everyday life, buying and selling goods, people milling about and enjoying life. I turned to Balon as we walked and asked.

"Did you release the dragons this morning?"

"Yes my Lord," Balon said, "I opened the outer gates bright and early. They were not overly eager to leave this morning, so I just left them be. I figure they will go when they want to."

"Very good," I said, "I knew I could count on you. By the way, how are you feeling today?" Balon just looked at me and kept walking.

As we walked through the castle, we passed several guards and peasants, none of which paid us any attention. The early mornings this high on the mountain are fairly chilly, so having our cloaks and hoods on was not out the ordinary. We passed out through the main castle gate without incident, and headed down the long mountain path to the valley below, passing by several travelers in the first mile or so down the trail, and then only a very few for the next couple of miles. As soon as we felt it was safe to do so, we removed our hoods and cloaks until we would see someone coming, and then put them back on until they would pass.

The journey down to the valley takes about three hours by foot, but takes nearly twice that long to come back up, due to the dramatic climb in elevation. As we started to get within a mile or so from the King's castle, the amount of human activity increased with every step we took, so it was time to put the hoods back on until we got inside the King's castle.

When we emerged from the mountain and onto the plateau above the valley of the King, the sight of the massive castle of King Malok was overwhelming. The closer we got to the castle, the bigger the castle seemed to get. The castle itself was surrounded by a large metropolis, much like the ones that spread up around every castle, made up of shops and tent cities, shopkeepers, vendors, castle workers, peasants, beggars, soldiers, and their families. A ten-foot high wall surrounded the city itself with a large gate on each of the four sides. The large wooden gates would not be strong enough to withstand an onslaught by a determined enemy, but it did make the inhabitants of the city feel a little safer.

"I forgot exactly how big this place really is," I said, as we got closer. "Maybe the king has nothing to worry about. Maybe I'm just crying wolf, but I just can't deny the dreams I've had, and the feelings I've been getting. They've never been wrong before."

"I trust your insight Ethan," Balon said. "If you believe in what you're doing, then I believe it, and I'm behind you all the way."

"Thank you for the vote of confidence my friend, that's all I needed to hear. Let's go inside and see the King."

We entered the western gate to the city, passing first the beggars, then the prostitutes, and then into the area of the shops, vendors, and the pubs. One pub in particular caught my eye as we passed, I guess because it was called 'The Dragon Lair.'

"Remind me to stop in there for a drink on our way back through. Anyplace with a name like that has got to be good," I said as we passed by the seedy looking establishment.

It was easy to find your way through the city to the castle, as every roadway led directly to the castle in the center, so we just kept walking until we came up to the main gate. It was obvious as we approached the gate, that this was not your ordinary gate, it was huge.

Passing through the gate to the castle was enlightening. The gate itself was nearly sixty feet tall, which would have been a deterrent in itself, if it weren't for one thing; there were absolutely no guards at the gate. Anyone who wanted to enter the castle could just come and go as they pleased, including the enemy. This is a bad situation; the King has gotten far too complacent from the many years of peace. Maybe that's why the Gog have chosen now for their attack, they could be in the castle en masse before anyone even knew they were here. In fact, I fear that they are already here, just not in strength yet.

The King's villa was at the very center of the castle, with another wall surrounding the villa itself. Here at least there were guards at the gate. As we approached the gate, the guards stopped us with crossed spears, and asked what our business was. I stepped to the front, removed my hood, and said to them.

"I am here to speak to the King."

The guard rolled his eyes and retorted back.

"The King does not want any visitors, now be on your way before we throw all of you in the dungeon."

"The king will see me, or I'll see the two of you thrown in the dungeon.

I am Ethan, the Dragon Master. Now do as I ask and announce us to the King." Now I was starting to get a little annoyed at the lack of respect shown by the two guards.

One of the guards lowered his spear, and told us to wait there while he went to speak to the King. The other guard remained vigilant and held us at bay. About ten minutes later, the first guard returned and told us to follow him, and he would take us to the King.

As we entered the gate to the King's villa, it was obvious that the grounds were being well taken care of, compared to the rest of the city. It would seem that the King has lost contact with the rest of the populace, and was withdrawing into his own small enclave.

All this has the feel of self-destruction, and I'm even more convinced now that my prophetic vision about my own small castle becoming the center of power is not that far fetched.

The guard escorted us up to the villa, through the outer doors, down the long center hallway, and right out the back door to the courtyard. The King was seated on a large bamboo chair by a beautiful pool, in the shade of the large trees, with several lovely women fanning him. He was wearing a white robe that was not doing a very good job of hiding his large belly. It looks like the good life has been catching up to him, because he was getting very obese. In fact he was sitting there stuffing his fat face with spiced meats, cheese and wine, delectable pastries, and grunting like a swine. He looked drunk already, and it was not even noon yet, and the whole sight was beginning to nauseate me.

I told Balon and Valik to wait for me near the back door of the villa so I could talk to the King in private. As I walked up to the King, I bowed my head in reverence, only lifting my head when he bid me forward.

"Ethan, my good friend, to what do I owe the pleasure of a visit from the famous Dragon Master?" The King managed to say between mouthfuls.

With food spilling out around his lips, he truly did look like a pig. Gaining my composure, and trying not to look totally disgusted, I replied.

"Your Majesty, I'm afraid the news I bring to you is quite disturbing. May we talk in private?"

"Oh, very well," the King said in an annoying tone. "And it was such a beautiful day. Off with you girls now, but don't go far, the day is getting hot."

As soon as the ladies had left, the king motioned for me to have a seat.

"Now, Ethan, what is this all about?"

"My Lord, I believe we are about to be attacked by the Gog clan, in fact, they have already made an attack on my dragons, once for sure, and maybe twice," I stated in a serious, but subdued tone.

The King looked at me, at first serious, then with a smile, and then he started laughing.

"The Gog clan," he said between laughs, "they wouldn't dare come this far into our lands. For one thing, they don't have the intelligence to pull it off, and for another, your dragons are supposed to keep them out of my domain. That is what I pay you for, and that is why I allow you to continue to live on your mountain. I trust your dragons can do the job, or am I wrong Ethan?"

"Yes my Lord, they can do the job," I said, "but the Gog seem to have gotten smarter about things lately. They have found ways to kill the dragons more readily, and in fact, they have killed one of my dragons already, possibly killed another one, and wounded a third. And there is evidence that the dragons engaged a large number of Gog troops somewhere within our boundaries. I just think it would be prudent for you to increase your security here, and maybe send out some long range patrols."

The King listened intently while I spoke, and his face seemed to harden before he spoke.

"Listen to me Dragon Master, if you can't control your dragons, and keep them safe and fit enough to be of service to me, then maybe some changes will need to be made. I have tolerated your dragons only because they are of use to me, and you are only tolerated as long as your dragons are alive, understand. Furthermore, since when were you ever a military man to know what I should do with my army? I have neither seen, nor heard of any possibility of attack by the Gog clan, and if they did attack, they could never penetrate the defenses of this castle. What makes you think the Gog had anything to do with the death of your dragon?"

"Captain Sardon captured one of the Clansmen down in the caverns where the first dragon was killed," I said, feeling my own frustration starting to build.

"Captain Sardon, you say," the King mused, "now there's one to listen to. He's an odd one on a good day. He joined our army a few years ago, and specifically requested duty at your castle. That was fine with me, because I prefer a more refined soldier to be in my immediate service. Did you question the captive?"

"No my Lord, Captain Sardon killed him in cold blood before I got a chance to speak to him," I said in a submissive tone.

"So," the King said, "you really don't know for sure that the slain captive really was a Gog clansman or not. I think that from now on, you better have your facts together before you come to me with tales such as this, tales that would cause a panic amongst the populace. Until that time, I forbid you to speak of these things to anyone, and I will call for Captain Sardon to answer the question about killing the captive, and why he did not notify me about any such happenings at your castle. That will be all Ethan, I tire of this conversation, and I'm getting hot and hungry, now go away. Girls, where are you?" He bellowed as he leaned back in his chair.

I stood, gave a low bow, and backed away. The conversation was indeed over. He was not going to listen to another word, he was a fool. As I joined Balon, and Valik, the girls had returned with their fans, and the King was giggling away, gulping down wine, and taking a huge bite out of a block of cheese. He won't be quite so amused when the Gog army lays siege to his castle. The three of us turned to leave and as we walked, I spoke to my companions.

"We are on our own my friends; no one is going to look out for us. I'm afraid this castle will be lost out of complacency and indulgence. And speaking of indulgence, I think I need a drink. Let's go check out the 'Dragon Lair."

Pulling our hoods back over our heads, we continued back the way we had come. Out through the villa we strode, out past the two guards, who were now leaning against the wall in the shade, out through the villa gate, and down the dusty cobblestone streets of the bustling castle. We continued past ramshackle dirt brick homes, some with wooden roofs, some with sod roofs, past open sided tents used by vendors, out through the massive gate of the castle and into the increasing poverty of the city surrounding the castle, each layer of the city getting poorer as we moved farther away from the castle.

There, on the outskirts of town was the 'Dragons Lair', a seedy looking pub in a bad looking neighborhood, just my kind of place.

"Everyone be on their guard, one drink, and we'll be on our way. Mr. Valik, if you would come in about a minute after we do, you will be our element of surprise if no one thinks we're together. Balon, shall we proceed."

"Yes my Lord, but I have a bad feeling about this," Balon said as he fell in behind me.

"I'll see you in a minute my Lord," Valik said, "and I'll stand at the opposite end of the bar so as not to draw attention."

When we walked into the pub, it was like walking into a cave from hell, it was dark, smoky, and stunk of human flesh that hadn't seen bathwater in years. The bar was against the back wall, with tables and chairs spread about the whole area in no sense of arrangement. It was standing room only at the bar itself, and this was where we chose to do our drinking.

The bartender was a stocky man about six feet tall, overweight, with a full beard, unkempt hair, and missing half of his teeth. The other teeth were somewhere between a shade of brown, and black, and his breath smelled of garlic, or at least I hoped that's what the smell was. He came up to where we were standing and asked.

"What'll it be lads, beer or wine?"

"Is the beer cold?" I asked.

"Of course not, do you think you are in the King's villa or something," He laughed in a thunderous roar, obviously more amused with his own humor than anyone else was.

"I'll just have a mug of wine then," I said as I turned my back to him to look at the crowd.

"Same for me," Balon chimed in.

The bartender just grunted as he reached under the bar, and brought out a bottle of wine and two metal cups.

"Pay for what you drink, leave the rest, and if you need anything else, just let me know."

About that time, Valik walked in and stood at the far end of the bar, so the bartender went down to take his order. All of a sudden, the bartender bellowed out.

"Now here's a man who drinks a real man's drink, beer, and warm beer at that."

He turned and poured a huge mug of beer from a large wooden barrel on the back bar, slamming it down on the bar, causing foam to splash all over the bar top. Valik threw him a coin, leaned back against the wall, and drank deeply from his mug.

Mr. Valik is a smart soldier, I thought to myself. His back is to the bar and he's close to the door, so he can see everything that goes on in the whole place. He only has to defend what is directly in front of him, and he is close to an escape route. He is going to work out quite nicely.

As I stood there sipping at my wine, I noticed that a commotion had started in one corner between several rough looking men and a demure, very attractive young woman, one who obviously didn't belong in a place like this. One of the men was grabbing at her dress and trying to pull her onto his lap, and she was obviously trying to push him away. I started to tense up when Balon whispered to me.

"Let it be Ethan, this is not your concern."

He was right, so I went back to sipping my cup of wine. About that time things started to heat up in the corner, and now it got our full attention when we heard the woman say to the men.

"I just came in here to ask if anyone knew how I could find the Dragon Master, not to be groped and fondled by the likes of pigs like you."

And to put a little emphasis on her point, she kicked the man trying to grab her right in the groin, doubling him over in pain. That's when the man standing next to her punched her in the face and knocked her to the ground, kicking her in the ribs while she lay helpless on the floor. Then a couple of the grimy slobs picked her up from the floor, throwing her across the table, and started to undress her to have their way with her, and that was it, I'd had enough.

I dropped my cup of wine on the dirt floor, clutching my staff, and strode across the floor in what seemed like the blink of an eye. Balon was in a panic, and shouted.

"Ethan, No!"

But it was too late, I was on them, and I was at full swing when I hit the one attempting to straddle the young woman. Just about the time the crystal dragon headpiece struck the man on the back of the head, the sock fell off, revealing the crystal image of the dragon to the whole place. The first man fell into a heap on the floor, and while the man standing next to him stood staring at the crystal dragon, I swung and hit him right between the eyes, knocking him senseless, and leaving a lasting imprint of the dragons face in his forehead.

As I turned to take on the next challenger, I was startled by the booming voice of Mr. Valik yelling for me to duck, and out of some ingrained survival instinct I ducked, which was a good thing, because a small dagger whizzed past my head and stuck in the wall behind me. A split second later, Valik's own dagger found its way into the chest of the man who had thrown the dagger. Another man tried to make it out the opposite door, but Balon tripped him as he went by with his own staff, and then put him to sleep with a blow to the back of his skull.

The three of us then moved to the center of the room, back to back, staffs at the ready, pulled back our hoods, and waiting for any more challengers, but there were none. Everyone in the room sat or stood, mouths agape, staring at us, at me in particular, and an audible murmur spread around the room, saying.

"It's the Dragon Master, it's really him."

"I thought he died long ago," another man said.

We started to relax our defensive stance, and while Balon and Valik kept watch, I leaned over the injured girl, and asked if she was badly injured, helping her to sit upright. Other than a little blood around her mouth, and some bruising, she was a very beautiful lady.

"Are you really the Dragon Master?" she asked.

"I am, but who might you be my dear?" I asked, wondering with suspicion why she would be seeking me out.

"My name is Mara, and I come from a land far away from here. I have sought you out over a lifetime and more. I have called to you from many lifetimes gone by, and now I have found you, and I have much to tell you.

"Dragon Master!"

It was the bartender this time, causing us to tense up again.

"The King's soldiers will hear of this soon and come looking for you. A man slipped out the back during the fight, so you must leave quickly. We will get rid of these bums but you must go." He had a sense of mounting concern in his voice.

"You are right," I said, "thank you my friend; I will not forget your kindness."

With that I threw him three gold coins, worth a month's wages to a normal man. As patrons started dragging bodies out the back door, I offered my hand to the girl and asked.

"Can you walk?"

She took my hand and stood, a little wobbly at first, and then bending over in obvious pain, with a look of nausea washing over her face, and then when it had subsided, she said.

"I will force myself to make it; there is no turning back now."

She looked me in the eyes, and it was as though she could see into my soul. Her eyes were beautiful, and there was a look of adoration on her face like none I had ever seen on anyone before in my life and for some reason, it seemed vaguely familiar. It was as though I knew this girl, but that couldn't be, for we had just met.

The girl grabbed up her rather large travel pack, groaned in pain, and dropped it again.

"Let me get that for you," I said as I shouldered the heavy pack. "Now, we must get out of here quickly."

As we started out the door, Valik reached down, pulled his own dagger from the mans chest as he was being dragged out the door, wiping the man's blood on the man's own cloak, and then kicked him once for good measure.

"Nice touch," I added as the last of the bodies disappeared out the door.

Once more the bartender interrupted and said.

"Dragon Master, you have always been my hero, and that is why I named this pub after your dragons, thank you for coming in, it has been a dream come true."

Grabbing the man's wrist in a warrior's handshake, I said to him.

"Come see me at my castle anytime, and thank you for your help in cleaning up this mess. Did you know these men?"

"No my Lord, they just started hanging around here within the last few days. In fact, there seems to be a lot of strangers in town lately, and quite an unsavory lot of characters too I might add."

It was just as I had suspected, the Gog will take this city and its castle before the defenders even know they are here, and I felt I needed to warn someone, so I turned back to the bartender, leaning close so that no one else could hear, and said.

"Listen my friend, I believe a battle is coming, and I think these strangers are the first of that army. I think they are going to slip in a few at a time until the main army approaches, at which time they will raise havoc throughout the city, as well as the castle itself. You would do well to let a few close friends and family know to seek higher ground before that happens. There may even be a place for your pub at my castle, so come and see me real soon."

"Thank you my Lord, I will heed your advice," he said as he shook my hand, and quickly went about pouring water on the blood and sweeping it in among the copious dirt already on the floor.

As we slipped out the west gate of the city, it was about mid afternoon, and it would be a long walk back to my castle with the injured girl in tow. We would not make it back to the castle before dark, and there were many ideal ambush places along the path back up the mountain. A new plan was in order, so I guess it was time to reveal another of the Dragon Master's secrets. I do hope our newfound friend is not a spy, because my dragons will not treat her as well as the thugs in the pub. It's time for another trial by fire.

We made a slower than anticipated climb from the valley floor to the plateau above, and we had to make many stops along the way because Mara couldn't breathe very well. I would say she must have some broken ribs.

At the point where the plateau meets the base of the mountain, we stopped for a break in a thick grove of trees by a creek, and all of us sat down, except for Valik, who insisted on keeping his guard up at all times. I could not have made a better pick when I chose him to be my bodyguard.

"Mr. Valik,' I said, breaking the silence, "I forgot to thank you for saving my life back in the pub, I am forever in your debt."

"You are most welcome my Lord, but you owe me nothing, you would have done the same for me with no thought of reward. Besides, I did it as a soldier would protect his commander, his King," Valik said, puffing up his chest.

"Mr. Valik, you already have a King, King Malok," I said, testing the waters.

"Not after what I saw today, my Lord. In fact, I venture to say that within a week's time, maybe two, King Malok will no longer be in power, and I believe you know it as well. That's why you are building a group of loyal followers around yourself right now, am I right?"

"You read the battlefield quite well Mr. Valik, I do indeed expect King Malok to fall from power. He is weak and stupid. As for myself, I have no desire to be a supreme ruler, or King, or anything like that. My dream is of a self sufficient community dedicated to making each other happy, like it was in the days of my great grandfather, before King Malok moved in and changed the flow of Earth's harmony. He is as bad as the Gog in his own way."

"How do you plan to do this great thing," Mr. Valik asked, "since you have no army?"

"Do you remember the trip into the secret caverns with the slain dragon?" I replied.

"Yes my Lord," He also replied.

"The things you saw there are only a small part of what is hidden and waiting to be revealed. Not only are there weapons both ominous and threatening, there is other technology hidden there that will sustain our realm forever, as long as it doesn't fall into the wrong hands. You have seen today that the King is weak, and will probably be defeated, and that is going to leave a vast hoard of the enemy on our doorstep. My weapons are more than a match for the Gog army; I just need a few good, handpicked men to teach how to use them. There is no way to stop the coming conflict, but there is a way to decide the ultimate outcome, and to decide how the future is to be shaped afterward. I must admit though that there are things in the chamber that even I do not know what they do, and I hope that together we will solve the puzzle."

"I think that is where I come in." It was the girl who spoken, as though she knew all along what we were talking about.

"What did you say?" I asked, as if I really hadn't heard what I thought I did.

"You heard me correctly," Mara said, sitting on the edge of a fallen log. "The weapons you speak of came from my home realm, a realm long ago sunk beneath the waves of the ocean. Those weapons, as well as all of the other wonderful things in your possession were brought here by a great man by the name of Zander, who saw the end of our civilization coming, and took it upon himself to whisk away some of that technology for safe keeping in a foreign land, this land. He is the wizard you speak of, and he was also my great, great grandfather. He sought out another great man, the man who wanted to save the mystical dragons, and that man was your great, grandfather Ethan, a man who had left our land a thousand years before the wizard."

"Are you telling me that I am not a Borg?" I asked. "Then who, or what am I, and who are you?"

Now I was really getting mixed up, and I didn't like the feeling.

"You and I are Atlanteans," Mara stated, "or at least we are decedents of the Atlanteans, since our lands have been gone for thousands of years. What is left of our culture is spread out all over the earth now, but a small group of us have managed to track down some of the remnants of our people. We maintain a library of all our past history, our achievements, our failures, our technology, our art, and most importantly, our genealogy."

"You mean a library such as the one in the caverns?" I asked.

"Not quite," said Mara. "The library I speak of is as big as a small city, and contains at least one of every item ever conceived of by all of the known peoples on earth at that time, plus a few items from beings not of this earth. It also contains a copy of every book, every poem, and every song ever written."

"Why is genealogy so important to you?" I asked.

"We know that our souls never die, that they drop back to the earthly plane whenever conditions are right for them to do so, or if there is a pressing need for them to return. We try to keep track of where and when some of those souls drop back to the earthly plane again. We have been trying to pre dictate before our death, exactly when we wish to return to the earthly plane following our death. It's not an exact science anymore, like it was in the days when Atlantis was flourishing. We used to be able to predict, and even influence when we would return to the earth, down to within weeks, maybe months, but now after so many decades, we have lost so much of our heritage that we are now only accurate to within a few decades. Take you and me for instance, I willed myself to drop back to earth with you, but you dropped about fifty years before I did, so we still have some work to do."

"Wait a minute," I said, "you willed yourself to drop with me and that means we knew each other before this lifetime. That explains a lot about the feelings I've had about someone calling to me. How well did we know each other in our past life, if I could be so bold to ask?"

"We were lovers then, we were lovers before that, and I predict we will be lovers again in this life, if fate doesn't step in again," She said as she suddenly turned her eyes away, a hint of a tear in her eye.

"What do you mean, if fate doesn't step in again, what happened to us in the past?" I pleaded.

"Let's please talk about it later Ethan, I have found you again after a thousand years, let me enjoy it while I can, because I know that there is again turmoil in the wind, and that turmoil may well separate us again, and right now my heart is soaring, and breaking at the same time."

Now she did start crying, so I went over to her, lifted her chin with my fingers and looked into her beautiful, tear-filled eyes. It was then that I knew everything she had said was true, our souls knew each other, and then we kissed, a kiss so deep, so meaningful, so powerful, a kiss that spanned a thousand years or more, and then she fainted. I caught her in mid fall, and lowering her to the ground, I called out.

"Balon, bring me a wet cloth from the creek, and make it quick."

Balon nearly tripped over his own feet trying to get to the creek. He was back in a flash, and handed me the wet cloth. Mara was starting to come around but I still wiped her brow with the damp cloth, and as she came around, I smiled at her and said.

"Welcome back, I missed you." With that she sat up, threw her arms around me, and held on tight.

"You sure have a way with the girls," Balon said as he took back his face cloth and wrapped it around his own neck, allowing the cool damp cloth to revive his own spirit.

It was Valik who spoke up next.

"Forgive me for saying so my Lord, but we need to get moving. I've seen dust on the trail ahead of us, and also behind. You would be a great prize to catch in the open. How are we going to get back to the castle unseen?"

"Just follow me my friends," I said, "because we're not going back the way we came."

Helping Mara to her feet I led the procession across the creek and away from the main trail. The path we were following was not much a trail at all;

in fact, it was actually more of a game trail, overgrown by the thicket. Once we were clear of the thicket, we were working our way up a steep ravine, paralleling the creek, staying high along the boulder strewn hillside. Going was tough, even if you weren't injured, but Mara was holding her own, although she needed to stop frequently to catch her breath.

"Are you sure you know where you're going?" Balon asked, also getting short of breath.

"Trust me my friend," I said, "it's been a great many years, and the trail is almost gone, but I will know the place when I see it. We just need to make it to the place I'm trying to reach before dark, so we need to keep moving."

As we climbed out of the steep ravine, the ground leveled out into a beautiful valley, about three hundred yards wide, and a half a mile long, while the sides of the valley were walled in by nearly vertical cliff faces. The small creek we had followed earlier now opened up into a wide, meandering deep blue stream, teeming with fish. Lush green grass grew throughout the valley, and tall groves of trees provided cover and shade. The look on each persons face told the story, they were in awe.

As we followed the stream to the back of the valley, Balon again spoke up.

"Ethan, how is this going to get us back to the castle, we're headed for a dead end? We have no way to climb these cliffs, and even if we did, how would we know where the castle is?"

"Balon, why do you always have such doubts, have I ever let you down before? Let me tell you first where we are. Do you see the cliff wall at the back of this valley?" I asked.

"Yes," Balon replied.

"At the top of that cliff is another valley, many times the size of this one, with walls three thousand feet high, the valley floor strewn with boulders, debris, and bones. It's not a place for humans; it's a place only the dragons know."

"It's the valley below the dragon pens," Balon blurted out, quite excited with himself. But then his face went blank again and he said.

"But how does that help us out, you said it is not a place where humans go. I don't understand any of this Ethan."

"My friend all will be revealed in just a few moments," I said as we came to what seemed to be the end of the trail.

The trail ended at the back of the small valley, where a cliff rose straight into the sky, with a massive waterfall, cascading over a thousand feet down the cliff face above, creating shimmering rainbows in the now setting sun. If it hadn't been for the fact that our enemies were probably hunting us, and we really needed to get back to the safety of the castle, this would have been a great place for a picnic. I let everyone marvel at the beauty of the scene before it was time to show them the way home.

"Follow me fellow adventurers," I said as I started to walk into the waterfall. Everyone just stood there.

"Follow you where?" Balon asked.

It was Mara who took the initiative, and taking my hand, she followed me beneath, and behind the waterfall. Reluctantly, the others followed along. Behind the waterfall was a small cave, which had been totally hidden from view by the falling water and mist.

Removing the key from around my neck, I felt along the wall for the opening that had been grown over by moss so long ago. A slight indentation gave me an idea where to dig away the moss. There it was the keyhole. Inserting the key, it took two hands to turn the key, but sure enough, a huge stone door nearly fifteen feet wide, and ten feet high opened up with a hiss, sealed from decades of closure to the outside world.

"I knew that was going to happen," Balon said as he stepped through to find a torch he now knew would be stashed on the wall inside. We all just looked at him as he went by, and shook our heads. Lighting three torches, I turned to find the keyhole on the opposite wall, inserted the key, turned it, and watched as the massive stone door closed behind us.

"Now we're safe, my friends. It is still a long, hard walk, but we can now take our time. I will lead the way, Mara behind me, then Balon, and Mr. Valik bringing up the rear."

"I'm getting hungry Ethan," Balon said, "how about we stop and eat first. Marta packed us a great lunch."

"We need to get some distance behind us first, so let's walk for an hour, and then we'll take a break and eat. Do you think you can last that long, I mean, I wouldn't want you to waste away to skin and bones," I said jokingly.

"I'll force myself along," Balon said, "but if I pass out from exertion, you'll have to carry me home.

"Or I could leave you down here for the bugs, really big bugs," I teased. Balon's pace quickened noticeably.

"That's not funny Ethan; you know I hate bugs, let's go, what are we waiting for?" Balon said. He was not amused. We all laughed, and then trudged onward, and upward.

After about a half hour, Valik spoke up.

"Why is this pathway so wide my Lord?"

"It was made for another marvel which you haven't seen yet, a chariot that does not require live beasts to pull it. In fact, it flies like a bird, sort of," I said sheepishly, since I myself was not sure how to run the machine.

Valik chuckled, "Flies like a bird," he mocked, "not likely." Then he suddenly remembered whom he had spoken to, and suddenly apologized.

"Forgive me master, I meant no disrespect."

"None taken Mr. Valik, it would seem hard to believe, but you will see many more wonders before long."

It was Mara who spoke this time. "Ethan speaks the truth, and these chariots do indeed fly. My people used them for hundreds of years to get from one place to another in a short time. Technically they do fly, but they will only climb to about treetop height at best. They are a very simple machine, relying on large magnets, which repel the earth's natural magnetism. Small magnets when placed against each other will repel each other, if only a small distance. The huge magnets underneath these chariots repel the earth's own magnetism, up to a distance of about fifty feet. There were even larger ships in my world that could raise heavy loads to a distance of several hundred feet. It was an amazing period of history."

"What happened to it all?" Balon asked.

"Several factors caused the demise of our culture," Mara began, "Internal conflict began between different key individuals. Then, people of each frame of mind started to gather around the man they thought shared their point of view, and soon the country was divided. The conflict grew until violence threatened to destroy everything. Each side developed amazing weapons until our whole civilization seemed doomed. Then, nature herself said 'Enough', and ended the conflict for us with earthquakes, volcanoes, and tidal waves, and then the entire continent slipped into the ocean. Those who could escape did so, some by leaving earlier, like the wizard you speak of, others escaping only with their lives to be scattered and devoured by the world."

"Are there other stashes of technology like the one I have Mara?" I asked.

"Only a couple that we know of, besides the ones in the library under the lions paws." Mara said, but then she added, "It is best for all mankind that our technology did not survive. There are those in the know who are actively seeking to find those stashes to use for their own gain, evil gain, and that includes your stash. I believe the coming conflict to this area is a result of those seeking to find your weapons. You must be on your guard at all times from now on Ethan; those weapons must not fall into the wrong hands, even if that means that they have to be destroyed."

"You said that someone is actively trying to find and take my stash also?" I asked.

"Yes there is Ethan, why, have you suspected someone?" Mara replied.

"Yes, there is a Captain in charge of the castle guard at my castle. His name is Sardon," I said as we decided to take a break. Mara stopped in her tracks, as if someone had put a hand on her chest.

"Did you say Sardon?" Mara asked, looking shocked. "Sardon is in your castle?" she asked. "You are in grave danger Ethan, how much does he know of the weapons, does he know where they are?"

"He doesn't know anything about them," I said, "nor does he know of the secret cavern. But tell me, what do you know about Sardon, and how might he be responsible for what has been going on around here?"

"I knew I didn't trust that guy," Balon said as he pulled a loaf of bread from the satchel, tore off a chunk, and then passed the loaf around, followed quickly by a block of cheese.

"What sort of things have been happening Ethan?" Mara asked.

Over the next half hour I explained to Mara all that had happened with the death of the first dragon, to the possible death of a second, and the buildup of Gog troops in the area, and finally about Captain Sardon, and his unmerciful behavior with the captive. Everyone ate and rested while I talked.

Then Mara began again. "Sardon, as he is known now, is a covetous sort. He wants what he can not have. He seeks power, riches, and he especially wants to possess me. And he will not rest until he gets what he wants. He is a patient man up to a point, but, if it looks like he 's not going to get what he wants through deceit, he'll resort to violence. He has placed himself in your castle years ago to try to learn your secrets. That hasn't worked, and time is getting short, so he'll start getting bolder. He needs to get his hands on the secrets of the cavern before the battle starts."

"That's why Sardon was down in the caves the day the dragon was poisoned, he was looking for the secret caverns. And he's the one that let the Gog clansman into the dragon pens. They want to eliminate the threat from the dragons so they can carry out their attacks on both castles. We need to step up our agenda to learn how to use the weapons, all the while keeping our work secret. Tomorrow, we'll use the chariot to secretly go out through the bottom entrance, and then we'll practice using the weapons in the Valley of the Dragons below the castle. Right now though, we need to get going, otherwise people are going to be getting worried, and restless. And by the way Mara, what did you mean by Sardon wanting to possess you, are you two lovers?"

I asked this last question because I was feeling kind of injured, since she seemed to allude to the fact that she was my long lost lover, and all of a sudden I was feeling pangs of jealousy building up inside of me, although I had no right to do so.

"The feelings are only one sided my love. He has been in love with me in every one of my lifetimes so far. He pursues me through the ages in the same way that I pursue you. Sardon knew I was coming here to find you, but he managed to find you quicker than I could. He may become more unpredictable once he discovers I'm here, so we must all be on our guard. And don't worry Ethan, I always have, and always will, be totally in love with you."

Mara's eyes met mine once more, and when I looked into her eyes, there was no more doubt in my mind. I knew she had spoken the truth, and I could feel my love for her taking over my very essence like it was something that had always been there, which of course, it had.

We made good time walking until we seemed to come to another solid wall, a dead end. Balon started grumbling something about all this work for nothing when he suddenly stopped as I reached down inside of my shirt for the magic key around my neck.

"Oh you of little faith, Balon," I said as I found the keyhole, turned the key, and the wall opened with a rumble.

"Would I lead you astray my friend?" I asked. Balon didn't answer but instead he just rolled his eyes.

"Do you know where we are right now my male companions?" It appeared we were inside a massive cathedral, since the lights were not reflecting any light back to us.

"I do believe we are in the wizard's cavern," Mr. Valik said.

"Very good my friend, you're right, and that means we're almost home. Unfortunately, since it is dark outside, the mirror lighting will not work in here right now, so we won't be able to show the treasures here to Mara. Tomorrow we'll come back here with some of your handpicked troops Mr. Valik. Training day is upon us, but for now, let's go home."

I led the way up the long pathway to the lower caverns of the castle, and to the dragon pens. The rest of the walk was made in silence, each person lost in his or her own thoughts, thoughts of the conflict in town, of the nemesis that was Sardon, of the coming conflict with the Gog army, and of all the wondrous information Mara had enlightened us with. When we are in private, I must ask Mara more about our past lives together. I hope we will be able to talk about it for many happy years to come. How wrong I would be.

We reached the top of the pathway, and to the secret wall leading into the lower levels of the castle. Moving once again to the far wall, I pressed my face to the wall, looking through the hidden view port to look for anyone in the hallway.

"Captain Sardon," I whispered, "he's in the hallway with a couple of troopers. They're examining the walls, looking for cracks. Mr. Valik, take a look, and tell me if you recognize those troopers."

Valik pressed his face to the wall, adjusting slightly until he could get a clear view from the hidden reflecting mirror, and still get a good view of the men in the hallway.

"Yes my Lord, I do recognize the swine, they transferred here with Captain Sardon when he came up from King Malok's court. Trust me to say that I will pass the word about the two of them. Don't be surprised if they meet with an unfortunate accident. It looks like they have given up, and are going back down the hallway to the stairs." Valik stepped back to let me resume the watch.

I stepped up to the wall, and looked through the view port; it looked to be all clear.

"Let's give it ten minutes or so, and then we'll go," I said, leaning back against the cool stone wall next to Mara. Grabbing her by the hand, I rejoiced when she squeezed back. It felt so natural, so right, that I really felt like I'd known this girl forever.

After about ten minutes, I moved to the peephole, and looked again, confirming that the hallway was still clear. Removing my key, I inserted it into the hole and turned it. The heavy stone door slid away, opening up into the castle caverns and cool, sweet, fresh air.

"Okay everyone; let's move out into the hallway while we have a chance," I said, almost pushing everyone out into the hallway, then extinguishing the torches in a barrel of sand just inside the secret passage. Moving quickly into the hallway, I inserted my key, turned it, and watched as the door closed tight. Now, I too could breathe a sigh of relief. Life used to be so simple when there weren't any troops here to guard our every move. We used to be able to come and go throughout these passages without all the secrecy, leaving the door wide open if we so desired. My goal is to regain that independence, and I hope that goal will soon be realized.

We started down the hallway to the stairway that would take us up to the villa. The dragons were roosting on the next level up, and now would be as good a time as any to let the dragons meet Mara.

"We need to check on the dragons, would you like to join us Mara?" I asked.

"I certainly would Ethan, I haven't traveled over half of the earth surface to miss this chance, let's go see them."

"Prepare yourself before you go inside. Show no fear or loathing, no malice, for the dragons are somewhat mystical, and they will see you for who or what you are." I said as we topped the steps to the next level.

"I'm not scared Ethan, I sense the dragons spirit also, maybe from lives gone by, I'm not sure. They call to me in dreams and visions, and I understand them." Mara said, and it appears that she truly believes it. I hope she's right, for her sake.

As we approached the dragon pens, we started to talk to them as we usually do so we wouldn't spook them, but stopped in mid sentence when up ahead we could see five dragon noses pressed up to the iron gate, watching us approach.

"They act like they knew we were coming," I said as we approached.

"They did know we were coming," Mara said. "I sensed them as we entered the lower hallway. They've been waiting for us." With that, Mara walked ahead of us directly to the gate.

"Mara, wait, it's not safe!" I said as I rushed ahead, afraid for her life.

"Don't worry Ethan, we're old friends," She said as she reached through the bars and rubbed each dragon on the nose and chin.

What happened next was something that I never would have thought possible from a beast that was known to the most fearsome force on earth. It sounded as though they were cooing at her, as each dragon tried to get in a better spot to be touched. They were acting like puppies.

"I've never seen anything like it Balon, and I thought you had a way with the dragons. Balon. If you would open the gate my friend, we'll get acquainted."

"I will if you say so my Lord," Balon said as he unlocked the iron gate, and let it swing open. The dragons backed up, giving way as Mara walked in amongst the supposed terrifying beasts. She hugged each one in turn, talking to them as if they were long lost friends, telling them everything was going to be okay now, and they were listening. I knew they had an understanding, but this was more than that, this was a bond. I knew in my heart that my soul mate was here, the thing that had been missing in my life, it was here, she, was here, and I was happier than I had ever been in my life, in this life anyhow.

The dragons moaned and cooed as if they were talking to her, which maybe they were. Balon, Valik, and I just stood there staring in awe at the spectacle before us. Soon she turned and spoke to us.

"I know where their sister is, she was badly injured out on the plain of Sarin, beyond the Talon pass. There was a massive army encamped there, all sharing the scent of the man who killed Gahenna in the pen below. The dragons attacked at random before the Gog knew they were there. Apparently they assumed their spy would have killed most of the dragons, and probably would have if Balon had not discovered Sardon and the spy outside of the dragon pen when he was making his morning rounds." Continuing, she said.

"The dragons attacked relentlessly, ripping through the panicked troops like cultivating the crops. Attack after attack decimated them until they were able to rally and coordinate a defense against the dragons with the giant crossbows. It wasn't until their sister was struck down that the dragons broke off their attack. They circled above their fallen sister to keep away the human scavengers until darkness forced them to return here. I am so sorry Ethan, and to you too Balon."

"The dragons told you this?" I asked in utter amazement.

"Not so much in words," Mara said, "but in images, from their brains to mine. I sense things in pictures, which to me become words. The same works for them in reverse, they understand me in the same way. I told them to avoid the battle now at all cost until the time is right. We can't afford to lose any more of them. We have the weaponry to deal with the Gog army without them. They will find the opportunity for their revenge. They now know Sardon is the enemy they seek, and they will not be at peace until he is dead. And by the way Ethan, they said they are glad to see you standing in your fathers footsteps once again. They said you have been gone from yourself for a long time."

"You are amazing Mara, it's no wonder we're together lifetime after lifetime," I said.

All of a sudden, a look of sadness came across her face, and I asked.

"What is it Mara, what's wrong?"

"Nothing my love, I will tell you about it later, right now I'm just happy to be with you. I'm tired; I think I need some rest Ethan."

"You're right my darling, let's close up here and get back upstairs, people will be worried about us. We'll have a lot of explaining to do, but no word about how we got back into the castle. In fact, Mr. Valik, go to the front gate, and bribe the guards to say that we came back in through the main gate. Here is a couple silver coins for the guards, and a gold coin for you for all your help today, including saving my life."

I handed the coins to Valik, and even though he gestured that it was not necessary, I insisted until he took them.

"Thank you my Lord, but you do not have to pay me for everything I do. I pledged my loyalty fully to you without reservation or reward," Valik said.

"Thank you Valik, but take it anyhow, you might want to buy something good one day, now go my friend." With that, he turned and headed up the stairs to the main castle.

"Balon, close the gate, it's time to go," I said.

Mara said goodbye to the dragons, then Balon locked the gate. The dragons were still looking at us through the bars as we climbed the stairs.

"Is anyone hungry," I asked, "we could stop by the kitchen and have Marta make us some dinner?"

"No," said Mara.

"No," said Balon.

"Okay, I'll show you to my chambers Mara, then I'll go tell Marta we're home," I said as we reached the main floor.

"We'll see you tomorrow Balon," I said as Balon turned to go to his own chambers. Then Mara and I headed down the hallway to my chambers. Reaching the chambers, I unlocked the door, and the two of us went inside.

"Make yourself at home Mara, you can have the bed, and I'll sleep in the lounging area." I said, trying to act proper, but hoping for something totally different.

"Ethan, I've waited for this moment all of my life and you will not sleep in the lounge area. Hurry back my love."

Mara went off to the bedroom, and I headed back down to the kitchen area, my heart racing like a schoolboy going on his first date. I swear I was breaking out in a cold sweat as I walked down the hallway, and I nearly forgot what I was doing by the time I reached the kitchen.

Entering the kitchen area, there was no one to be seen, so I continued through the kitchen and dining room area to Marta's chambers, and tapped lightly on the door. After a minute or so Marta opened the door a crack, and when she saw that it was me, she threw the door open and hugged me, starting to cry.

"We heard there was a fight in a pub in town, and that someone may have been killed. There was a rumor that it was you, and I was so upset. I thought I would never see you again, don't you ever scare me like that again." She said still holding me tight.

"How did you hear about the fight?" I asked, holding Marta out to arms length.

"Captain Sardon told me, he said some of the peasants brought the news when they returned from town," Marta said, still with concern in her voice.

"What really happened Ethan?" She asked.

"I'll tell you about it tomorrow Marta, but right now I have to get back to my own chambers," I said impatiently.

"I thought you could stay here with me tonight Ethan, I'm so upset, and I need the company," Marta said in an almost pleading voice.

"I'm sorry Marta," I said, "but I have a guest tonight, so please set an extra place for breakfast in the morning."

Marta looked hurt. "A guest Ethan, who is she, someone local peasant girl, or some little whore you picked up in town?"

"You seem to be forgetting your place Marta, you work for me, and we are not husband and wife. I trust you will remember that in the future," I stated.

Marta was visibly upset, visibly injured. "I will not make that mistake again, my Lord, now if you'll excuse me," She said as she stepped back and slammed the door in my face.

Wow, that didn't go quite according to plan, I thought as I turned to go back to my own chambers, feeling sad and guilty at the same time. I hate feeling guilty. This is supposed to be the happiest day of my life, a dream come true, so why do I have to feel sad. Marta and I have only been occasional lovers, nothing serious, or at least that's what I thought. She must have thought there was something more to our relationship, and that is probably my fault. This is going to make things a little awkward around here for a while. Little did I know how awkward it truly would become?

By the time I got back to my chambers, the sudden remembrance of the beautiful woman waiting for me inside caused me to totally forget Marta for the time at hand. My heart was again pounding from excitement as I entered my chambers. I felt like a kid again, and it was an incredible feeling. I closed and locked the door behind me.

Entering the bedchamber, the female form of Mara could be seen beneath the covers, illuminated only by the dim candlelight from a lone candle on the nightstand.

"Come to bed my love," Mara said in a sweet, sultry voice.

My heart nearly leapt from my chest, and I was shaking as I removed my cloths and boots. Blowing out the candle I slid beneath the covers, feeling the warm silkiness of the woman beside me. I don't know what time it was when we finally went to sleep, but it sure didn't seem long until there was a heavy pounding on my chamber door that caused me to bolt upright in bed. I'm sure getting jumpy lately; it seems the only way I get woken up lately is to some sort of crisis. 'What now,' I thought to myself.

"I'll be there in just a moment," I yelled to whoever was so insistent outside of the door.

The pounding continued as I slipped my pants on, and pulled the covers over the beautiful woman still lying in bed. 'This had better be good.' I thought to myself as I headed for the door. Reaching the door, I asked.

"Who is it?"

"It's Captain Sardon, and I must ask that you open this door immediately. I must speak with you," He sounded rather agitated today.

Opening the door with my guard up, Sardon stood there looking very stern.

"What can I do for you today Captain?" I asked, although I knew why he was here.

"What is the meaning of you leaving the castle without checking with me first? You know the danger that you have been in lately, what were you thinking, how can I protect you if I don't even know where you are?"

He was really wound up today, his face was red, his neck veins were bulging, and his oversized Adams apple was bouncing up and down like a bouncing ball. Trying to hide the fact that he looked even more ridiculous when he was excited, I calmly responded to him, saying.

"I appreciate your concern Captain, but for the exact reason that you mentioned is why I left this castle under a disguise. I do not trust anyone within this castle, for the enemy has already penetrated my castle once, even into my private villa and to the dragon pens below, which as you well know, are only accessible from within my villa. Besides, I had my own personal guards with me, and we were fine." I was trying to make light of the whole situation before Sardon blew his top.

"Well, by the sounds of things in town, it doesn't sound to me like things were fine," Sardon said, like he was trying to gloat on some bit of information.

"In fact, we heard there was a fight in a local pub, and there may have been some foul play where someone might have been killed. We thought it was you, since someone mentioned that the Dragon Master had been there."

"I assure you that I am none the worse for wear, especially for someone who had supposedly been in a fight in a pub. As you can see, there is not a scratch on my body anywhere. You know how rumors are Captain, where exactly did this fight take place, and who supposedly died, did they find a body?" I asked; now being slightly belligerent myself, while still trying not to goad Sardon into an argument that would be premature at this point in the game.

"Interestingly enough, the fight was at a pub called the Dragons Lair, surely a place that would lure you in, and it was three unknown travelers who died, or supposedly died, and no, fortunately for whoever was involved, there were no bodies found, according to the report I got from the dispatch messenger this morning. But I assure you that I will continue to look into this myself. And by the way, why did you go to town yesterday, and how did you get back into the castle last night?" Sardon asked, fishing for information.

"You sure do ask a lot of questions Captain. First off, what I do is none of your concern, but since I have nothing to hide, I will tell you." Of course I was going to embellish the story just a little.

"The fact of the matter is I went to see the King to voice my concerns about the presence of the Gog in the area, and to tell him of the loss of my dragon. And as for returning to the castle, we came in through the main gate. You can ask the guards who were on duty."

"I already have asked the guards," Captain Sardon replied, looking even more annoyed. "And how was your reception with King Malok?" He also asked in a defiant tone.

"Let's just say it was not what I had hoped for," I said, not wanting to let too much out of the bag. "Now if you will excuse me Captain, I have a guest that I must get back to."

That peaked Sardon's interest, especially if he had heard the rumor about the fight being over a girl. He tried peeking past me, hoping for a glimpse of who this girl might be, but the rooms were separated, thank goodness. It was not time yet for the two of them to see each other. I wasn't sure if the meeting between the two would force Sardon's hand, but at some point soon, I am going to force Sardon's hand, and Mara might just turn out to be that catalyst.

"Forgive my intrusion my Lord, I will let you get back to your guest, but please, for your own sake, notify me when you decide to leave the castle. It really is for your own good. And by the way, two of my men were missing at roll call this morning, you wouldn't happen to know where they may have gone do you?" He asked.

"I'm afraid not Captain, I went straight to bed when we got back to the castle. Besides, I have a hard enough time trying to keep track of my own affairs, let alone helping you keep track of your troops. I trust you will find your men Captain, now, if you'll excuse me."

I stood there as Captain Sardon turned and headed back out the door, watching as he disappeared down the hallway. Closing the door, I locked the door once again until we were ready to go to breakfast. Today was going to be a busy day, but first, one more rendezvous with Mara to get the day started on a better note.

Returning to the bed, Mara was lying in bed leaning on her hand. "I take it that was Sardon; I recognized his voice, even after all of these years. I'm not sure I'm ready to see him face to face again."

"We'll postpone it for as long as possible Mara," I said as I lay down on the bed facing her. "Besides, we have the advantage with him not knowing you're here. He thinks I'm still the lazy drunk he's been manipulating all these years, and as long as I keep letting him think that, we can continue to prepare our defenses and plans for the future. For now, all I want is you, my love."

"Five, four, three, two, one," Snap!

Chapter 5

"Oh bummer Doc, it was just starting to get interesting. Couldn't you have waited just a few more minutes?" I said as my consciousness clawed its way out of one world and into another.

I really didn't want to come back, I enjoy my previous life much more than I do this one. In that life I was master of my own domain, life was intriguing, dangerous, exciting, but here, it's the same crap, just a different day.

"I'm sorry Henry, but we've run out of time. Do you think Mara is the girl from your dreams?"

"It would certainly seem so," I said, "but it's too bad, she seems quite incredible, and I hate the thought of her getting killed. Do you think there is a way to prevent it, or is my dream a record of history?"

"That's what we're here to find out Henry, so, same time next week?" Dr Miller asked.

"Yes Doctor, I'll be here, and I can't wait, I'll see you then," I said, and as I stood, I handed Dr miller a check for the cost of my appointment, and shook his hand.

Dr. Miller escorted me to the door and we said our goodbyes. As I walked down the sidewalk, I noticed the next customer was waiting for his appointment. I wondered to myself what sort of epic journey he was soon to embark on.

I climbed into my car and opened the windows. It was really getting hot out during the afternoons now. Thank God for air conditioning. As I drove back down the valley, all I could think of was Mara. I felt like I was in love with her all over again, even though this was a totally different lifetime. Life just isn't fair, how can I stand to be in love with someone who's been dead for thousands of years? If she sought me out back in those days, maybe she will seek me out in this life also, and who knows, maybe she already has. If Mara does seek me out again, will I recognize her, have I seen her already? These are questions only time will tell.

By the time I got back to the fireworks booth, I had relived over and over again the experiences I had learned in this week's hypnosis session. I now know who the girl was that was in my dreams, but I still only have a vague guess about how she died. I'm sure it had something to do with the upcoming battle with the Gogs, but how could we have been so careless as to let it come to that? Only further hypnosis will be able to bring out the truth. Lord, I can hardly wait till next week, but as for now though, I need to sell some fireworks.

As I pulled into the parking lot, I could see that Scott had a few customers, mostly kids on bicycles. Kids cruise through checking all the prices, and to see what new kind of stuff each booth has gotten in this year. Its great fun talking to the kids about fireworks, because they get so excited. Now that I think about it, I still get excited about fireworks too. I remember doing the same thing when I was a kid, checking all the fireworks booths to marvel at the wonderful things they had. Only problem was, back in those days, we didn't have much money, so all I really got to do was look. It was still enough to get me excited about fireworks.

I originally got into selling fireworks through the local Jaycee chapter when I became a member of that organization. One of their yearly fundraisers was to sell regular fireworks to make enough money to buy the really big fireworks that they shot off for the public over at the fairgrounds. As a Jaycee member, you also got to go light off those big boys, the ones with the big booms, and the huge airbursts. From that point on, I was hooked, and that was twenty years ago now.

I sold fireworks for the Jaycees for about four years until I got out of the organization. At the time, I was working at a job that didn't pay very well. I became a little disgruntled at work one day, and had a disagreement with the boss, who exercised his rights as a boss, and fired me. So, then I was out of work, summer was coming on, and I needed to make some money. I contacted the company that provided the fireworks for the Jaycees, and asked if I could sell fireworks for them as a privateer. They said yes, so I built myself a tiny little booth that I had to empty out each night for security. In fact it was so small that one afternoon a windstorm came up and I had to pull my truck up to the back of the booth and tie it down to my bumper to keep it from blowing over. I made just enough money that season to squeak by until I landed a real job.

The next spring, the fireworks company approached me to sell for them under their national title of Red Dragon Fireworks. They would provide a huge booth for me, deliver it to the site each year, and pick it up, provide the fireworks, which I could return what I didn't sell, and provide half of my lot rent and advertising. I jumped right onto that with both feet, and I've been doing it for that company ever since. In fact, my whole family ended up in the business. My little sister ended up with a chain of four booths, my brother started one in his hometown. My mom and all of our kids take turns working in each of the booths. What do you think drew us to the business, money, firepower, or maybe the dragon logo, we may never know? I just know that we have a fascination with dragons, and now I know why.

I pulled up to the back of the booth, locked my truck, and entered the booth through the side door. Scott was looking a little tired.

"How's business been?" I asked.

"It's been steady, how was your session?" Scott asked.

"It was incredible Scott, I'll tell you about it between customers. If you need a break for a while to get some dinner, now would be a good time to do it, because we'll get a rush after suppertime. That's when people will want to get a few of the pretty fireworks for the evening. So go ahead, it's my turn to watch the store." I sat down as the kids on the bicycles took off to check on the other booths.

Scott got out of his chair and said. "I think I'll take you up on that offer. I'll go get a bite to eat, and then I'll go get a couple of lawns mowed when it cools down a bit. I'll be back in time for the evening rush."

"Sounds good Scott, I'll see you in a few hours," I said.

It was about 4:30 pm now, so he should be back about 7:30. That should be absolutely perfect. I watched as he drove away. At least Scott could do his other work as he sees fit, mow a few lawns, hose down the car wash bays, nothing that requires a time clock. That's not something that would work in Scott's life; it's not in his lifestyle. That's also why he likes to work at the fireworks booth with me, the hours aren't regulated, he can come and go as he needs, and he makes a little money doing something he loves.

It is amazing to me that Scott still likes fireworks at all, because about twelve years ago an errant firework took out one of his eyes. He gets along very well with one eye, and still loves to play with fireworks, but not many people would have the fortitude to keep at something they love after a devastating accident such as his. Scott is an amazingly resilient individual, both in this life, and in the life in which I knew him as Balon. I believe he will always be dependable, trustworthy, and as loyal as any friend could ever be, in this life, that life, and the next life to come.

The next hour was pretty quiet, people were getting off work and heading home for supper, so now would have been a good time for a nap. In fact, I was just starting to nod off when a car pulled up in front of the booth and parked. The driver looked familiar, which proved true when the girl Dan and I spoke about stepped out of the car and started walking to the booth. She still looks as good as she ever did, it's like she never ages, and she has always looked the same. She was smiling as she approached the booth.

"Dee, you look as gorgeous as ever, how have you been," I asked, "I've missed you since last year, and I was hoping you would stop by to see me."

She was blushing now and replied. "You really missed me, thank you, and I missed you too. I was hoping you would be doing this again. I only get to see you once a year, and that's not enough."

Seizing the opportunity I added. "I think about you all the time, but you know how life is, too busy to keep up with old friends."

Dee and I have known each other for over twenty years, and were even lovers for a short time about ten years ago. We were both fresh out of bad relationships, and fell right into each other's arms. Unfortunately, neither of us was ready to commit to another relationship, so we soon went our separate ways, not breaking up or anything, just going different directions and not coming back to that intimate point. We remained close friends all those years even when we were with other lovers. As for myself, I never forgot about her, and would often think about her and wonder what it would have been like if we had stayed together.

Dee responded by saying. "Henry, that's so weird, because I've thought about you often over the years too, and I've sensed someone calling to me over those years, but I didn't know who it was. I've told you in the past that I can sense things; I am what they call an Empath. My God, it was you, all this time, it had to be you."

She looked as though she was about to faint, lowering her head into hands, and leaning her elbows on the counter. I quickly jumped over the counter to support her so she wouldn't fall.

"Are you okay Dee?" I asked, though the déjà vu I myself was feeling was almost to overwhelm me also.

"Let me help you around the side of the booth and you can come inside and have a sit. Besides, I have some things to talk to you about that you might find interesting."

As I helped her around the end of the booth and helped get her into a chair, I thought to myself, 'could this be her, could this be Mara from the past?' My God, I was being flooded by thoughts and emotions that were threatening to make me crazy. I have to think this through logically, because there has to be another explanation.

Dee sat in the chair and I pulled up another chair and sat down in front of her. She lifted her eyes and looked into mine, and in a shaky voice she started to talk.

"Henry, I have been in love with you ever since we met twenty years ago, I've never known why, and I've always been able to hide it from myself. Then, when we became intimate ten or so years ago, my love for you grew by ten fold, but still I denied it. I wasn't in a position to face that sort of commitment at the time. I've had nothing but one bad relationship after another ever since, and during every bad relationship, I dreamed that you would come and knock on my door, sweep me up in your arms, and rescue me like a prince would rescue a princess, but you never came, and I just survived one bad experience after another. Now, you tell me you've thought about me all these years, and all I want to do is cry. I've wasted so much of my life chasing down something that was nearer to me than I ever could have imagined. Henry, where have you been all my life?" She asked as she started crying.

I leaned forward and hugged her, letting her cry, then, lifting her chin with my finger to look in her eyes, we leaned into each other for a long, deep, passionate kiss, mixed with salty tears, and pent up emotions. As I broke off the kiss, her eyes rolled back, and then closed almost dreamily, and, she fainted. 'Not again' I thought to myself, that's exactly what happened to Mara when we first kissed. I held her for a moment until she regained her senses, and as she shook her head slowly, all she could say was,

"Whew, what happened?" But then as she looked up, she knew, and she threw her arms around me once more and hugged me even tighter than before, saying again.

"Henry, I missed you so much. We do need to talk more, but right now, I have to pull myself together, and go home to feed my kids. We'll be back later tonight to talk."

A quick kiss on my cheek, and she was off to her car, turning completely around to look back at me, smiling, and then almost as suddenly, a look of despair crossed over her face. It suddenly struck me that it was nearly the same look of sadness that I saw on Mara's face in my past life. Dee turned quickly, got into her vehicle, and drove away, leaving me standing there wondering what else life had to reveal to me.

The next couple of hours saw business pickup markedly, slowly at first, and then building to a steady flow of customers looking for entertainment. Thank goodness Scott finally showed up about eight pm, because I was starting to get frazzled.

"Looks like I got here just in time," he said as he entered the booth and immediately started helping customers.

Scott looked tired and hot, but he's always willing to jump right in and lend a hand. As soon as we had a break in the action Scott went back out to his truck and brought in a large cooler. Subsequent trips brought in bags of ice, six packs of pop, and finally a case of beer.

"Now you're talking," I said, "I was beginning to think we were living in a desert, I was so thirsty. How'd the lawn mowing go?"

"It went as good as lawn mowing can go I guess," Scott said, "but I built up one heck of a thirst, so I picked up a few supplies to last for the next day or so. All we'll have to do is refresh the ice each day, and we'll be set. For now though, I'll stick with pop until business slows down a little, how about you, care for a pop?"

"You bet, pass one on over here," I said, licking my parched lips.

Taking a soda, I popped the top and drank deeply, feeling the cool liquid flowing all the way down my throat until it hit the bottom of my stomach.

"Oh, that's good, I didn't realize how thirsty I was getting until you showed up with the refreshments. By the way, guess who showed up?"

"Let me guess," Scott said, "Dee?"

"No fair, you know she always shows up, but wait until you hear the rest of the story. Let me start with my session with Dr Miller."

I proceeded to tell him about the events of the past life experience, including the fight in the pub where we met Mara, who was apparently the girl from the dreams on the battlefield. Then I told him about the visit from Dee earlier, and my suspicions that she is Mara reincarnated. Scott listened intently, nodding his head, and then he responded.

"It all makes perfect sense you know. If indeed there is something to this past lives theory, and if friends and loved ones tend to follow each other through the ages, then Mara would definitely seek you out in this lifetime also. Even though you two are a few years different in age, it would appear that you two are narrowing the gap in how many years apart you drop back into the earthly realm. At this rate, your next life together will only be a year or so apart. It's rather exciting I think."

"Wow Scott, you're really getting a grip on this past lives thing. And you're almost correct about narrowing the time period when we drop back to earth. I believe that it also depends on whether or not your partners die at the same time. If you set your return sojourn too soon after you die, you will run the risk that your soul mate will live beyond the date set for your return, especially if one of you dies early, before your time so to speak. Then you spend eternity trying to catch up to each other again. I wonder if that is what Mara had meant when she spoke about fate messing things up. She was pretty vague about it then, so next time I go under hypnosis, and back to my past life, I'll have to try to remember to ask her more about it."

Continuing, I said. "You and I seem to have gotten it down pretty well over the centuries it would seem. We both must have died at roughly the same time. I'm not sure I want to know how, but I guess it would be interesting to find out. It will also be interesting to learn who the other players from our past will turn out to be."

I had no sooner finished my sentence than Dee and her kids showed up. It was like looking at an old friend that you hadn't seen in years, and in this case, it could have been a few thousand years.

"Hey guys," I said as the small group walked up to the booth. I've known Dee's kids since they were babies, and have treated them to fireworks all the time they were growing up. They are really starting to grow up fast, with her son Chad now being about fourteen, and her daughter Chelsie being about ten. Dee smiled as she walked up, which was almost as quickly replaced by a frown. There was something definitely bothering her. It was almost the same frown that I had seen on Mara's face during the hypnosis session. I will make it a point to find out what is bothering her, and Mara, because it is something very deeply seeded, and probably related.

"Hello Scott," Dee said as she walked up to the booth.

She and Scott have known each other even longer than her and I have known each other. As a matter of fact, Scott is the one who introduced the two of us nearly twenty years ago. The first ten years of our friendship was just an occasional meeting at a party, or out at a bar, and then about ten years ago, we both became single after long-term relationships. Then one night after partying together at a bar, we went home together, and the chemistry was ignited. Unfortunately, that intimate relationship only lasted a month or so, and we both went on with our lives. But, I now believe that our lives were forever sealed together from that time forward. The problem was, we weren't together long enough to learn anything about each other, so, we never realized the cosmic connection we shared yet at that point of our lives. It would take another ten years of yearning for each other from a distance to finally come back to this point in time.

Dee walked up to the booth and leaned on the counter in front of me while the kids worked along the counter staring at all the fiery delights on the shelves. She had a slightly serious look on her face, and leaning forward so no one could hear, she said to me,

"Henry, we need to talk about a few things, and please don't say anything until I've finished. First off, I have a boyfriend right now, he's not much to look at, but he's nice to me. His name is Mike, and he works with me once in awhile at the shop. It's nothing serious at this point, but I don't want to break off another relationship, especially if you and I aren't compatible."

Continuing she said. "I know it sounds crazy, but I believe that you and I have been together in a past life, in fact, I believe we've been together in several past lives, and each one of our lives together ended with an early death for one or the other of us. Because of that, I'm afraid to let my guard down again for another relationship with you in this life. I'm scared about what will happen this time, because I remember one of my deaths as being very tragic, and I can't face that again. I know you think I'm crazy, but I know these things are real, at least they're real to me."

I couldn't wait any longer, and I had to interrupt.

"Dee, my love, you don't know how right you are, in fact, I don't think you're crazy at all. Now, let me tell you a story."

I proceeded to tell her about the recurring dreams I've been having, about how I've been seeing Dr. Miller and how I'd been undergoing hypnosis to get to the roots of the problem. As I continued to tell her about my castle, and the dragons, her mouth was agape, her eyes wide, and her hands were trembling. I told her about our past life meeting at the pub, and I thought she was again going to faint. I told her the story right up to the end of the last session with Dr. Miller, and then I asked her what she thought.

Her voice was shaky as she started to talk.

"Henry, what I'm going to tell you is going to blow you away. I too, have a thing for dragons, I collect dragon figures, and as you remember, I told you that I could sense things. Well, one of the things I can do is sense dragons all around me, and like spirit guides, I can talk to them, and they help me to get through life. I too believe strongly in past lives, and I've told you that I believe you and I have been together many times over the eons. When you mentioned the part about you and I meeting in the pub, I know that scene, it is one of my recurring nightmares. I remember getting assaulted in that pub, and I remember you rescuing me. But, I also remember that I died a tragic and violent death, and that scares me still. These memories are still a dominant part of my life, and it affects my every waking moment. I've shut them out as much as possible, but now I feel them all flooding back in, and I'm having a hard time coping with them. I hope you are up to helping me get through these memories as you have in lives past, otherwise, leave me alone, so I can continue to shut those memories out of my head."

Looking her in those beautiful eyes, I said to her with all the sincerity I could muster,

"Dee, I believe I was in love with you in the lifetime I mentioned before, I believe that I am in love with you in this lifetime, and whether or not we end up together in this life, I will always be there for you to share your troubles with. I'm fresh out of a bad relationship again myself, so it's a little early to know my true feelings, but knowing what I do now, I'm sure that at some point, we'll be together again. I don't think we can deny it. That's probably why neither of us can manage to stay in a relationship for very long, our fates are predetermined."

I was just starting to get dreamy eyed enough to kiss her again when Dee suddenly went cold, leaning back away from me. As I stood there wondering what had happened, a tall geeky looking guy rode up on a bicycle, pulling up next to Dee, and saying.

"Hello dear, how are you doing? I got here as soon as I could. Are we ready to buy some fireworks?"

Then Dee turned to me and said.

"Henry, I'd like you to meet my boyfriend Mike, and Mike, this is one of my oldest friends, Henry."

"How do you do, Henry, it's nice to meet you," he said as he extended a half limp hand to shake.

Shaking his hand, I responded.

"Nice to meet you too, Mike, I've heard so much about you."

Mike was definitely a dorky looking fellow, tall, skinny, with a long scrawny neck, and a very pronounced Adams apple. In fact, as I stood there looking at him, a dreadful realization swept over me, this was Captain

Sardon, from the past life. He was here again too, but why, are we all so interconnected cosmically that we are all spending eternity chasing each other around.

I must have been staring because Dee broke the silence by asking.

"Henry, are you okay?"

"Oh yeah, I'm sorry, Mike just reminded me of someone I used to know, and I totally spaced out there. I guess that's what happens when you get old. But, I'm back now, so, what can I get for you guys?"

The next half hour was spent making small talk about fireworks, and picking out things the kids wanted, and then the items the adults wanted. Every few minutes, Dee and I would catch each other staring at each other, then looking away quickly so as not to be obvious. This was going to be difficult on both of us. I believe in fate, so whatever is supposed to happen, will indeed happen.

When they had finished picking out the fireworks they wanted, Mike said it was time for them to go, so once again we said it was nice to have met each other, and they loaded Mike's bicycle into Dee's car. She waved goodbye to both of us, and then as they were getting into the car, Dee hesitated before she got in, and, looking back at me she silently whispered the words to me, "I love you." Then she too climbed into her car, and they drove away.

After they had gone, I turned to Scott and said.

"Can you believe the dork she's with? But, do you want to know what is really scary, all I could think of while he was standing here, was that this was Sardon, in the flesh, back to be my nemesis. And if it is indeed Sardon reincarnated, what is he doing here, is he here for me, or for Dee? I feel like I need to warn her, but will she just think I'm being jealous and critical?"

"I felt something wasn't quite right about that guy too," Scott said, "but by the way Dee looked at you, I don't think you're going to have to worry about competing with Mike for Dee's affections for very long. It looked quite obvious to me that she is totally in love with you, again. Give it a little time, I think you'll see her come around, and as for Mike, or Sardon, or whoever he is, we'll just watch him close, just like we had to all those lifetimes ago."

"You know Scott, if I didn't know better; I would say that in one of your lifetimes, you were some sort of sage, because sometimes you have a wisdom and insight that is remarkable. Thank you for your input, I will take your advice, and wait for things to shake out"

About that time, two more cars pulled in to buy fireworks, so it looks like it's time to get back to work. Sometimes it's good to be busy, if for no other reason than to keep your mind off of the things that stress you out, which in this case was Sardon, I mean Mike, weaseling in on my girl. I wonder if he knows who he is, and if he does, what is he looking for in this life?

The evening kept us busy until about 10:30pm, and then fizzled out so to speak. So, we decided it was a good time to close up shop and drink a couple of beers while we counted up the day's earnings and restocked the shelves. After closing the counter windows and securing them, we locked ourselves into the booth while we counted the money. We had just finished counting when there was a knock on the door, immediately putting us in defense mode. I always have a club handy in the booth in case of problems, because even in a small town, you never know when someone might want your money more than you do. Scott tiptoed to the back door in case he had to sneak around the back of the booth to pounce on a robber. As soon as he was ready I said.

"Yes, who is it?"

"It's Dee; can I come in and talk to you Henry?" The sweet female voice responded from outside.

"You most certainly can Doll," I responded, trying hard to contain my excitement. I opened the door and there she stood, looking a little distressed but still very beautiful.

"Come on in, would you like a beer?" I asked, offering her a chair.

"I would love one," she said as she took a seat.

"Scott, bring Dee a beer please," I said as I pulled another chair up close to Dee, and sat down facing her. Scott had a nice cold beer ready in a flash.

"I'm going to head for the house, and let you two have a talk," Scott said as he turned to leave. "It looks like you two have some private issues to talk about, so I'll see you when you get home Henry."

"Take the cash home with you Scott," I said as he started to leave. "that way I won't forget it."

"Okay," he said, "I'll see you in awhile."

As soon as he left, I closed and locked the door again, as much for privacy as it was for security. Then I went back and sat down next to Dee, who was staring at the floor.

"How are you doing, is everything okay?" I asked, even though I knew it wasn't. As a tear rolled down her face, she sat her beer down, leaned forward and put her arms around me, holding me tight, and then started to cry softly.

"It's not fair Henry, I've wanted you for so long and you weren't available, and now that you're available, I'm seeing someone else. I'm sorry I had to ignore you when Mike showed up earlier, but he's a very jealous guy.

I don't know what to do with myself, and my feelings for you. Oh God, I do love you Henry"

She lifted her head to face me, and our eyes met, searching each other's soul down to the very depths. And once again our lips met, this time a long, drawn out kiss that seemed to go on forever, until once again I felt her start to go limp, and I broke off the kiss. Her head hung as though she was a rag doll, so I continued to hold her as she moaned a little, then shook her head and said."

"I don't know what you do to me, but every time we kiss, my head swirls with visions and emotions that seem to come at me from every direction, and every place in history. It is the most incredible sensation I've ever felt, and I've never felt this from anyone else in my life. I absolutely love you," she said again as she rested her head on my shoulder.

"Just hold me for awhile, and then I better go."

We continued our embrace for several minutes, each of us lost in our own thoughts, myself, remembering the scenes played out during the recent hypnosis session which were still fresh in my mind, and her thoughts, one could only guess at this point. How much does she actually remember of our past life together? When we finally broke off our embrace, we looked each other in the eyes, and almost simultaneously said, 'I love you.' Then just as quickly, she said she had to go, and turned to leave. But before she left I said to her.

"Please come and see me again tomorrow, maybe during your lunch hour. I can't bear the thought of not seeing you again, and if Mike gets too much for you to handle, let me know, and I'll take care of him. I dealt with him in my past life, and it looks as though I'm doomed to deal with him again in this life, but if you'll just trust in me, and follow your heart, I'll take care of the rest."

Stopping in her tracks, she turned to face me, and there was a look of dismay on her face, and then she asked.

"What do you mean you've dealt with Mike before in a past life?"

"This is going to sound weird," I said, "but both Scott and I recognize Mike as a fellow we knew as Captain Sardon from the lifetime with the dragons. He was the Captain of the guard in my castle, a traitor to the king, and someone who was trying to steal secrets from the hidden caverns. I believe that you knew him prior to that from the land you lived in, and furthermore, I believe he was the man responsible for something terrible that happened to us in that life. I don't know what exactly happened yet, but we're getting closer to it in the hypnosis sessions. I know you're probably thinking

I'm just saying bad stuff about Mike so I'll have a better chance with you, but this is very real to me right now, so be careful. History tends to repeat itself, but I also feel that knowledge is the best deterrent."

Dee had a look of shock on her face but she gathered her composure and said.

"I do believe you Henry, I've sensed something about Mike for a long time, but I couldn't put my finger on it. If what you say is true, both of us could be in danger again in this life. I've never completely trusted Mike, but I didn't know why. I've talked to him at length about past lives, and he too believes in it, but I don't know how much he can put it all together without help. I'll take your advice and be careful around him, but I'm especially worried about his reaction if I break up with him, because that could be the trigger for our trouble in this life. He has a very quick temper, and I'm afraid of how he might react. I'm just so confused anymore, my emotions are a mess, and I really need to get home to the kids, especially before Mike tries to call or stop by the house."

As she turned again to leave I asked.

"Will I see you tomorrow?"

"I'll be back to see you Henry, because a team of horses could not keep me away from you now, and you know already that I love you with all of my heart." With that, she turned quickly, let herself out the door, and was gone.

I sat there for several minutes as I listened to her car drive away, and pondered on the happenings of the day, from the session with Dr. Miller, to the emotions I was feeling now about Dee, and whom I felt she represented in the past. It was a lot to take in all in one day, and I was worn out. It's time to call it a day and go home.

I turned off the overhead lights, double locked the doors, and made one more check around the entire booth to make sure everything was secure. Then I jumped into my truck and drove the fifteen minutes home, replaying the day's events over and over again in my head until I thought I would go crazy. I hope I will be able to sleep tonight, because my mind is racing, and I'm quite sure Dee is feeling the same way right now.

Before I knew it, I was pulling up into my driveway. Scott had the porch light on for me. As I went inside, there was a short note from Scott, saying he was tired and had gone to bed. I was still a little wound up so I grabbed a glass, filled it with ice, and mixed a gin and tonic. Then, I headed out to the deck to unwind, and to enjoy the cool night air.

Just as I was walking out to the deck, I noticed the light on the answering machine was blinking, indicating that there was a message. Pushing the play button, I was shocked to hear Jane's voice on the tape, saying she would like to stop by and talk to me tomorrow. She said she would stop by the booth tomorrow evening to chat about our future. Great, one more thing I have to worry about. Little does she know, I don't think there is a future for her and I written in the cards, at least not one that I'm aware of, from a past life perspective, or a present one either for that matter. Time will tell what the future will bring, but I've come to the conclusion that your destiny is written in the stars, and you only have so much control over them. So, I'll deal with Jane as fate plays it out and there's no use getting too excited about it. You really are just along for the ride in the merry go round called life.

Taking my drink out onto the deck, I sat down on the porch swing and took a deep pull from my glass. The night was still warm and humid, and the gin and tonic was so quenching. I just sat there in the dark, enjoying the stars, and thinking about how much my life had changed in just one day. I was also thinking about the girl who was such a hidden part of my life up until today, Dee, AKA, Mara. Were we meant to be together in this life like we were in the past, how would I know? Why couldn't I just go back in time to my castle, to my dragons, to Mara? I'm beginning to wonder if I ever should have gone to see Dr. Miller in the first place. Maybe ignorance would have been bliss, or at least it would've been a lot simpler. I could have just left my life to chance, no divine destiny, no tragedy, no deception or intrigue, just the here and now, just a miserable, meaningless existence. Man, am I ever starting to get melancholy. It must be time to go to bed.

Finishing up my drink, I checked my watch; it was nearly 1:00 am. I had better get some sleep so I can stay awake at the booth tomorrow. Scott will go to work for a while at his regular job so I'll have to open the booth and hang out there for most of the day by myself. Early in the season like this isn't so bad, and since it doesn't get real busy until the last five days, I'll be able to handle it by myself without any problem. I'll take my laptop computer with me, and a couple of movies to watch if it gets boring. But for now, it's time for bed.

I went back into the house, closing the sliding glass doors and locking them, put my drink glass in the dishwasher, and shut off all the lights. As I went upstairs, I passed by Scott's room and all I could hear was snoring. I guess the day must have pooped him out as well. It's nice to have someone else in this big old house, because it would get awfully lonesome if you were here by yourself. I crawled into bed, thinking once again about all the things that have happened today, until sleep crept up on me without me knowing about it.

Dragons, Sardon, fighting, a huge battle, and then a woman's scream. MARA!!! I bolted upright in my bed, and I was sweating profusely. It was just starting to break daylight. Looking around the room, I realized it was that dream again. It had been almost two weeks since I've had that dream. I guess with all the recent revelations, the dream is starting to come to life again, calling to me like I siren. I have got to find out what happened in that long ago life. I've got to know what happened to Mara. How am I ever going to last a full week until my next appointment with Dr. Miller? I guess I really do need to keep going to him for awhile, at least until I find out what has happened to me, and to Mara, in that long ago time.

All of a sudden, Scott rushed in through the door, with a worried look on his face.

"What's the matter Henry, I heard you yell out, and it scared me to death. I thought maybe a burglar had jumped you or something. Are you okay?" he asked with genuine concern.

"I'm sorry Scott," I said, "I didn't realize I had yelled out. I just had that bad dream again, the one I've told you about before, about the woman screaming. I believe it's Mara, whom I also believe is Dee."

"I thought those dreams were going to go away with these hypnosis sessions," Scott said, "so why are you still having them?"

"Because I still haven't found out what happened to us in that past life," I stated, "and until I do, I guess I'll keep on having the dream until I do find out. I can't wait until next week's session, because I'm going to be worn out by then if this keeps happening. I guess since I'm already awake, I might as well fix a pot of coffee and take a shower. I'm sorry I woke you up. If you want to go back to bed, I'll wake you up when I finish with my shower." I got up out of bed, and started past Scott to go make the coffee.

"I'm awake now too, Henry," Scott said, "so, I think I'll get started early on the lawns today to beat the heat. Then I can hang out with you in the shade of the fireworks booth when it gets hot outside. By the way, what happened with Dee last night, she looked a little upset?"

As we walked downstairs, and while I made a pot of coffee, I explained the emotional conversation between Dee and me, leaving out the part about the kissing. I also explained how she was afraid of Mike, as well as afraid of a commitment with me, and finally about her deep seeded fear of tragedy that she believes has happened repeatedly between her and me throughout history. Then I dropped the bombshell on him about Jane coming to the booth tonight to talk.

"Well," Scott said, "you'll just have to take things easy for now. You know as well as I do that if you and Dee are meant to be together, then nothing can stop it, not Jane, not Mike, not you, or myself. And as for Jane, who knows what will happen there, you two were together for a long time. It might be a little soon to hook up with Dee until things are settled with Jane. All I'm saying is be careful, because this could get complicated and messy."

"Thanks Scott," I said, "I know you're right, I'll take it slow and see how it goes. I don't want Dee to have an emotional crisis either. I do love her, so I'll give her some space. I'm going to hit the shower, so I'll see you later at the booth."

As I headed into the bathroom, Scott was pouring a cup of coffee. I thought about what he said, and I knew he was right when he said to take it slow. Scott has been a good friend, in this life, and beyond.

After a nice long shower and a shave, I put on a new set of cloths, and grabbed a pair of shorts and a tank top to change into this afternoon when it gets hot. While I sipped at my cup of coffee I gathered up the cashbox, my laptop computer, and a couple of movies to watch during the day when the booth isn't as busy. Then, pouring the rest of the coffee from the pot into a briefcase thermos, and a travel mug, it was time to head for the booth. I need to make a stop along the way at the grocery store for some more ice for the cooler, some lunch makings for later, and something for breakfast now.

After the brief stop at the store I pulled up behind the booth, and then did a quick walk around the booth to make sure everything was secure. Then, I unloaded everything into the booth before opening the windows for business. Now it was time to sit back, drink my thermos of coffee, and eat my breakfast while I waited for the first customers to show.

It didn't take long for the first vehicle to pull up, some tourists from out of state traveling through. Fireworks are not allowed in most states, so for many tourists it is a treat to stop by a real fireworks booth. Tourists like to start traveling early in the day to beat the traffic and the heat, so I always like to be the first booth to be open in the morning, and it has proved to be to my advantage on more than just a few occasions over the years.

It stayed fairly busy until about noon when the heat and the need for food slowed things down for awhile. At about 12:30pm a car pulled up, which I didn't pay much attention to until I noticed Dee get out of the car and start walking toward the booth. Just seeing her made my heart soar with excitement, I couldn't help myself, and I hope she feels the same way when she sees me.

"Hey gorgeous," I said as she waked up, making her blush, "I'm so happy you came to visit me. Can I get you a pop, or make you a sandwich or anything?"

"A pop would be perfect Henry," she said as she leaned on the counter, "but I'll pass on the lunch for now. I've found that my appetite is gone lately, because I can't think about anything but you, and the messy situation I feel I'm in right now."

"I'm sorry Dee; I didn't mean to put you in an uncomfortable situation. What would you like me to do about it, because I can't help how I feel about you? I will give you all the space you need, and if you need to stay away from me, I'll understand. Besides, Jane said she was going to stop by the booth tonight to talk, so I don't know what will come of that either, especially since you're not available right now. I hope you'll keep coming to see me, but I'll understand if you don't."

Dee looked a little dejected but recovered quickly and said.

"Don't write me off too quickly here Henry, because life has not been all that good with Mike, and I don't want to be with him on a permanent basis. I'm totally in love with you, I always have been, and always will be. And I too believe in our past lives together, so the chances are going to be real good that we'll end up together in this life too, I don't think we can deny that. For now, my love, I like the feeling of being in love with you, I feel like a kid again, so, let's keep seeing each other, even if it's in secret, until we know what this life has to offer us, okay."

"Come around the end of the booth so I can give you a hug you beautiful hunk of woman," I said as I waved for her to come around to the door.

As she made her way around the booth, I met her outside the door, taking her in my arms, holding each other tight, as though we would never see each other again if we let go of each other. At that point, Dee raised her eyes to meet mine, and the kiss that followed made us both weak in the knees.

"Come inside; because we better sit down before we fall down," I said as I held her around the waist and escorted her into the booth and offered her a chair. Just about the time we sat down, Scott showed up, and he too came inside and sat down.

"You two look happy," Scott said, obviously noticing something between us.

"We've come to an understanding." And that was all I had to say.

Dee smiled, and blushed, and Scott smiled as well. We all sat around and made small talk while Dee was there for the duration of her lunch break. Then when it was time for her to go, I walked her out to her car, kneeling down beside her door after she got into her car.

"Will I see you tonight my love?" I asked.

"You know you will, I can't stay away, but if Mike shows up, please be cool, and don't stare at me with those lovesick puppy dog eyes, it would be a little obvious. I'm not quite ready to deal with Mike on that level yet, okay?'

"Okay," I said, then leaned forward and gave her a quick kiss on the cheek, and then I told her I loved her, closed her car door, and watched her drive away. When I walked back to the booth, Scott looked at me and said.

"I thought you two were going to take it slow? It looks to me like you guys are falling head over heals for each other."

"In a way we are going slow Scott. We're going to see each other in secret until we see if things are going to work out between us, and to see what shakes out with the partners we are currently with. Neither of us is happy in our present situations, and we both believe in our destiny, past and present, so we also believe it is inevitable that we will be together, it's just a matter of time. Until then, we are just going to enjoy each others company, out of sight of Mike, and Jane of course."

"Just be careful Henry," Scott said, "I don't trust that Mike character, and I don't know why yet, but the feeling is very strong."

"I will do so my friend, and thank you for watching out for me," I said with all sincerity. "Now, fix yourself a sandwich, I bought a bunch of lunch making materials this morning before I opened up, they're in the cooler."

We both made ourselves a sandwich and sat there and ate them while we waited for the next customer. Business was slow that afternoon, with only a few kids showing up to buy fireworks. It will get busy again after the adults get off work, have supper, and their kids bug them to go shopping. Until then, we'll relax and enjoy the views of the Bitterroot Mountains barely a half mile to the west. We even dozed off in turns a time or two as we sat there. About 6:00pm a horn sounded on the highway in front of the booth. Looking up, we noticed Dee driving by on her way home from work. I can't wait to see her this evening. I hope Mike doesn't show up with her, because that would bum me out.

It didn't take long for the customers to start showing up for evening entertainment. We were staying fairly busy when Dee's car pulled up in front of the booth, which made my heart leap, until I noticed Mike was with her, as well as her kids. I was feeling a few pangs of jealousy at that moment, but I knew I had no right to feel that at this point in time, but I couldn't deny it was there. I am going to have to be careful not to let that jealousy show.

"Hey guys," I said as they approached the booth. Dee tried to keep her cool, but kept stealing glances in my direction, as I did in her direction. This is not good, I thought to myself, but we kept up with the ruse, hoping no one would notice. Scott helped them to pick out some fireworks while I helped a couple of other customers. When I was done I walked over and struck up a conversation with Mike while Dee and the children finished their transaction.

"It looks like you guys are going to have a little fun tonight," I said to make small talk.

"Yeah," Mike said, "these guys are nuts when it comes to fireworks. As for myself, I could take them or leave them. I don't know what they see in them, it seems like such a waste of money if you ask me."

"There are a lot of people who feel the same way you do," I said, "and if they had their way, there would be no more fireworks, and we would lose another of our freedoms. Then where does it stop Mike? As long as fireworks are available, people will keep buying them, and I'll keep selling them."

My last words held just a slight hint of defiance, which I think Dee picked up on, because before Mike could open his mouth in reply, she said she was finished and it was time to go. Lucky thing for the little pencil neck *#@!*/ /. Maybe there's a little jealousy behind my attitude, I don't know. I have a feeling our time will come, just like it must have in the past.

When they had driven away, Scott handed me a folded sheet of paper, saying.

"Dee handed this to me with her money while you had Mike occupied, and told me to give it to you after they left. By the way, what was that little spat between you and Mike, I thought you two were going to get into it for a minute?"

"In another minute, we were going to get into it," I said. "Deep inside me, I don't like that guy, maybe it's just a jealousy thing, but it feels a lot deeper than that. I can't quite explain it Scott, but there is something there, maybe something from a long time ago. I think that we'll find out soon enough, but for now, let me sit down and read this note."

Taking a chair, I sat down and unfolded the note and started reading.

'My dearest Henry,' the note started.

Well, that sounded like it could go either way, a dear John letter, or a love note. Only one way to find out is to read on.

'It has been the joy of my life to be near you the past couple of days, to hold you, to kiss you, to feel your broad shoulders once again. I believe we have been lovers many times over the eons of time, and it feels so natural to be in love with you once again. Please forgive my hesitations at jumping straight back into your arms, for there seems to be something fearful deep down inside of me that I can't explain, about having an unbridled relationship with you. I feel something dreadful has happened to us in the past and it scares me to go through it again. I love you with all my heart and soul, but give me a little time, and I'll come around as I start to feel more comfortable and safe. Until then, just continue to love me, and I will come to see you every chance I get, which includes this evening after Mike leaves, and after the kids go to bed. I can't wait to see you and feel you in my arms once again. I'll be down about eleven, all my love, Dee.'

"What did she have to say?" Scott asked as I lowered the letter and stared off into space with a dreamy look on my face. I just started to tell him when I noticed a familiar car pull up in front of the booth, Jane's car. My heart sank to my knees, and without thinking I said to Scott.

"Oh Oh, here comes trouble."

As soon as Scott became aware of who was coming you could see his face go pale, as if he too was going to catch heck right along with me. He started to fidget in his chair as Jane, and her girlfriend from Missoula got out of the car and walked toward the booth, strutting along as if they were God's gift to men.

"Well hello Henry," Jane said as she walked up to the booth, as though I was supposed to be happy to see her.

"Jane," I responded, "what can I do for you?"

"Aren't you glad to see me?" she asked, feigning like she was hurt.

"Not exactly," I said as a matter of fact. Now she did indeed look hurt. Jane does not respond well to anyone who does not love her every move. She is quite narcistic, and wants everyone to love her.

"Don't you even miss me a little bit Henry?" she whined. "I've missed you. I wanted to talk to you about maybe getting back together again, what do you think?"

'I think I need to think about that one for a while Jane. To tell you the truth, you hurt me when you left, and now, I'm kind of enjoying the freedom myself. I'm not in a position emotionally to deal with anything but the fireworks booth for now, so let's talk more after the season is finished. That will give us both some time to think about things before we make another rash decision."

"You want to wait to make a decision about whether you want me back or not?" she asked incredulously.

"Obviously you didn't love me that much to start out then did you?" Now she was starting to get angry.

"Well, I wouldn't take too long to make a decision if I were you, because I just might find someone new while you're 'thinking about it.' Have fun selling fireworks, because I'll be partying hard, my dear." With that, she and her girlfriend strutted back to the car and drove away.

Scott walked up next to me as we watched them drive away, and I said to him in a seriously non-serious tone of voice.

"That went well don't you think."

Scott just looked at me with a look of disbelief, turned around, went to the cooler for another beer, then went back to his chair and sat down shaking his head, mumbling to himself all of the way. Following his lead, I too went to the cooler, grabbed a beer, went back to my chair, and sat down. Neither of us said another word for nearly a half an hour, both lost in our own thoughts.

Business pretty much died out early that evening, so I told Scott he could go home early. He said that would be great because he wanted to swing by his house to pick up a fresh set of cloths. I told him I was waiting for Dee to come back so I would be home late again.

I was just closing the windows when Dee showed up, so she helped me to finish securing the booth. We had no sooner got inside the booth and closed the door when this time Dee threw her arms around my neck and kissed me with an urgency that could only come from two lovers being apart for a long time. When we finally broke off the kiss we were both weak in the knees. She raised her eyes to meet mine and the words she spoke nearly made my heart stop in my chest.

"Henry, I want you to make love to me, right now, right here."

I wanted to shout for joy at the top of my lungs, do a wolf howl, and dance a jig, but, I kept my composure, and in a shaky voice, all I managed to say was,"

"Okay."

How's that for keeping your cool, and except for the fact that I nearly passed out, I did manage to tell her I would go get a blanket from my pickup to put on the floor. I won't go into all the details, but suffice it to say, we made love with the urgency and clumsiness of two teenagers after prom night, first quick and needy, then settling down to pure passion and pleasure. I certainly hope no one walked by the booth during that time because they would have gotten an ear full.

It was after midnight as we lay in each other's arms, rejoicing in the love we had for each other when Dee finally broke the silence and said she needed to get back home and check on her kids.

"By the way," she asked as she stood up and started to gather her cloths, "did Jane show up for your talk tonight?"

"Yes she did," I replied, also standing up to face her. "She wanted to get back together and work things out. Her girlfriend is probably getting tired of living with her too."

"What was your reply to her?" Dee asked with just a hint of concern in her voice.

"I turned her down, and said I needed to think about it for a while, and that until fireworks season was done, I couldn't possible deal with anything more."

"What was her response to that?" Dee asked.

"She got mad," I said, "and then she told me if I took too long, she would find someone else, and then her and her girlfriend left without saying goodbye."

"What do you think you're going to do about it when fireworks is done Henry?" Dee asked with a definite air of concern.

"That is going to depend on you my love." I stated. "It will also depend on what happens between you and Mike. I love you Dee, and I will wait for you as long as I need to, as long as we can get together once in a while to hold each other in our arms. I know it is difficult on us both, but now we have each other again, and I'm never going to let you go as long as we both shall live."

"That's the part that bothers me," she said. "because we never seem to live long enough to enjoy a long life with each other."

"Then we will enjoy each other while we are alive," I said. "We will make as much out of every day that we are together, and celebrate every moment we get to spend with each other. Let's not waste any of the time we get to be together on worrying about what happened before. Our fates are sealed ahead of time, and we can't change that. All we can do is to make the most out of the time we have together. So, will I get to see you again tomorrow?"

"That's a silly question." she said as she took me in her arms, our still naked bodies pressed together, feeling so delightful in the cool night air. "You won't be able to keep me away anymore my darling." she said as our lips met once more in a long kiss.

When we finally broke off our embrace I asked. "Would you like to go for one more round before you leave?" This time there was no shakiness in my voice, just love and passion.

"Save it for tomorrow big guy," she responded, "I have to work tomorrow, and I need to get home to the kids."

With that she gave me one more quick kiss on the lips, and put on her cloths. I did the same as I took in the beauty of her body while she dressed. She looked up once while I stared at her and she just smiled, and I swear my heart skipped a beat. I followed her out to her car, and gave her a hug.

"I'll see you tomorrow night Henry, and I love you," she said as she drove away into the night. I floated back to the booth with a heart so light that I think I probably could have flown like a bird if I had wings. This feeling of love is incredible, and I hope it never goes away.

I grabbed the cash box, turned off the lights, and double locked the door. As I pulled away from the parking lot I noticed a lone figure at the far back corner of the parking lot, peddling away on a bicycle. Even though it would seem odd for someone to be riding a bike this time of night, the town of Hamilton never seems to sleep. There are cars and people running around all hours of the night, as well as a couple of weirdoes and homeless folks who wander the streets and alleys at night picking up anything with a little value. So at this point, I didn't pay much attention to the solitary figure riding away into the night on a bicycle. I was tired and just wanted to get home to bed, and the thoughts of tonight's events clouded my mind from anything except Dee.

When I got home, I was so tired, all I could manage to do was bring in the cashbox, lock the doors to the house and go straight to bed. I will have to wait until morning to take a shower, for tonight, all I want to do is sleep, and dream about Dee, and that is what I did, because the next thing I knew, Scott was knocking on the bedroom door and saying it was time to get up. It was getting late, and he was off to do lawns. He said he would see me later at the booth.

This would prove to be the routine for the next five days, work the booth during the day, Scott would show up about mid afternoon, Dee would come over at lunchtime, and again with the kids and Mike about 7:30pm, leave, and then return to make love about 10:30pm. Mike seemed to be becoming increasingly confrontational on his visits to the booth, which I tolerated only because of Dee, but it was obvious that he was starting to suspect something. Maybe I was starting to feel guilty or something, but I knew one thing, I was not going to be able to curb my tongue forever.

The night before my next meeting with Dr. Miller, Dee and Mike were there picking up a few fireworks for the kids, and the conversation somehow got around to cars. Since I have never seen Mike in anything but the passenger seat of Dee's car, I asked him what kind of car he drove. The response he gave me would make my heart sink right down to my shoes, and cause my face to turn white.

"I don't own a car," he replied, "I only ride my bicycle."

He had a smirk on his face, and if it wasn't for the shock I was going through at that moment, I'm sure I would have wiped that smirk clean off of his face.

"Are you alright Henry," Scott asked as he watched my face go pale. "You look ill."

"I'm fine," I responded, "I just think I need to get something to eat. It's been such a busy day that I haven't had time to eat yet, but I'll get something pretty quick." That was my cue to walk away from Mike before I gave anything more away.

When they had left, Scott walked over to me and asked. "What was that all about Henry, I've never seen a look like that on your face as long as I've known you?"

I related the story of the first night that Dee came back to the booth after leaving the note, avoiding all the juicy details of course. But then I told him about the bicycle that I saw ride away, and then I told him that I've seen that same bicyclist twice more since then, always at the back of the parking lot between the businesses.

"I think that bicyclist is Mike, spying on Dee and me every night. I think he's on to us, and that's why he is getting so confrontational when he comes here with Dee. I'm going to have to warn her tonight when she comes over, because if everything we suspect about Mike, aka Sardon is true, then Dee, or myself, could be in grave danger from this screwball."

Now Scott's face was kind of ashen too, and he said, "You be careful Henry, you could be playing with fire. This could come to a head soon, for better or worse, and you need to be ready for anything. Maybe tonight, instead of going home, I'll park way at the back of the parking lot and watch for him with the binoculars."

"Sounds great Scott," I said, "and you should leave right at dark, drive around a few blocks so he thinks you've left for the night, then swing back around and park over there with the night employee cars."

"Sounds like a plan," Scott said.

The rest of the evening stayed fairly busy, and then when darkness started to fall, we set our plan into motion. Scott left the booth, got into his truck, and drove away. A little while later, I noticed a vehicle back into the employee parking area, and turn off its lights. So far, everything is working according to plan. At 10:30, I closed the booth just as I have every night so far, and a short time later, Dee arrived just like clockwork. Entering the booth, she threw her arms around me and kissed me hard, expecting another session like before, only this time I broke it off early and held her at arms length.

"What's the matter Henry?" She asked with a look of concern on her face. As I related the story of the bicyclist in the dark, and our suspicions about who it might be, her face also went ashen, and she started pacing the floor and moaning, saying.

"What am I going to do now Henry, I'm scared, he's been acting really strange, and kind of mean lately, and now I know why. How am I ever going to face him again, he's probably out there right now, watching and waiting, what am I going to do?"

"Well, do you love me Dee?" I asked.

"Yes," she replied, "why do you ask?"

"Maybe it's time for you to make a decision," I said, "and make a commitment to be with me on a permanent basis. Let him go, he's a bum with no job, no car, and lives with his mother. I have a good job, a nice home, and I've loved you for ten thousand years. What more is there to think about?"

"You know that I want you Henry, but you also know our suspicions about Mike being Sardon, and that someone has always come between us in the past. It's not that death itself scares me, because I know I will be back in another lifetime, but what bothers me is the mode that brings about my death. My death has always been violent, and I can't bear the thought of it coming. I know I'm being silly, and weak, but I just can't shake it."

"I understand Dee," I said, "but if you stick with me, I may or may not be able to prevent it, but whatever happens, we'll face it together. Think about it tonight my love, then we'll face him together, and send him packing." I pulled her to me and held her in an embrace of security, while she rested her head on my chest, and cried softly.

"How can I be so happy, and yet so sad at the same time?" she asked.

"Changes and hard decisions will always cause anxiety," I replied. "but good things can come with change.

"What about you Henry?" Dee asked, "what are you going to do about Jane?"

"If you are willing to be with me for the rest of our life, then I will stand by my decision to not let her come back, and you know as well as I do that it won't be fun dealing with Jane either." Lifting her chin with my finger to look into her eyes, I continued.

"Think about it tonight, and let me know tomorrow evening. I won't be here at lunch tomorrow because of my appointment with the hypnotherapist, so I'll see you tomorrow evening, okay."

"Thank you Henry, you know I'll choose to be with you," she said, "but you know I'll need a lot of support emotionally for a while, so I'm going to trust you with my heart, and possibly with my life, are you up to it."

"I'm up to it Dee, I promise," I assured her. Then we kissed each other deeply, and held each other tightly for several more minutes. Then she said she needed to go home, so I walked her out to her car.

"I'll see you tomorrow night," I said, "and I love you with all of my heart."

"I love you too," she said, and as she pulled away I could see her straining to look around the dark parking lot trying to spot the hidden spy whom we knew would be lurking back in the shadows.

I walked back to the booth, grabbed the cash box, and locked the doors. I climbed into my truck and started the engine, but instead of driving away immediately, I hesitated for a few minutes until I saw Scott's lights come on in his truck, and waited for him to drive over to where I was parked. When he pulled up we both opened our windows to talk.

"You were right Henry," Scott started, "it was Mike, hiding right over by the corner of the building. He showed up within minutes of Dee's arrival. He definitely has your routine down pat, but he had no idea I was there watching him. I think next time we should pull a switch on him and catch him at his own game. We should be waiting for him in his little hiding spot."

"Sounds like fun Scott," I said with a hint of sadistic excitement, "but then what do we do with him?"

"That depends on him Henry," Scott said, also showing a sadistic side.

"Let's make plans tomorrow afternoon when I get back from Missoula," I said.

"That's right, I forgot you had your next appointment tomorrow," Scott said. "I can't wait to hear about the next installment on our life with the dragons. I'll make sure I'm here by 11:00am so you can get an early start. For now, I'll meet you at the house."

"See you there," I said, and we both drove off and I followed Scott home. What an interesting day this has turned out to be. Wait until I tell Dr. Miller about everything that's happened since I saw him last, especially about Dee, and my belief that she is Mara reincarnated. There are so many questions yet to learn the answers to; questions that may also help Dee understand some of her fears too.

When we arrived at the house, we were too hyped up and hungry to go to bed right away, so we decided to cook some T.V. dinners in the microwave and drink a beer out on the deck. The night was warm and the stars were shining with an intensity I haven't seen before. Maybe it's just because I'm feeling so alive lately. There is nothing like a new relationship and a little intrigue or danger to bring out all of your higher senses, and make you appreciate everything around you.

After we finished our beers and ate our dinners we had finally unwound enough to go to bed. Tomorrow was going to be an exciting day and I wasn't sure if I would get any sleep or not, there was so many things going on in my head. I could feel a deep anxiety that I'm sure must be Dee going through a hard time at home worrying about Mike's behavior and his reaction to her wanting to dump him. Then the excitement about tomorrows' session with Dr. Miller was enough to keep me awake all by itself. Well, I still need to try to get some sleep or I'll regret it tomorrow.

"Good night Scott, I'll see you in the morning," I said as I turned off the lights and headed upstairs to bed.

"Good night Henry," Scott replied as he also shuffled off to bed.

The birds woke me up the next morning before the alarm clock ever went off. I have several huge trees in my yard, which are a haven for nesting birds. Sometimes the mixed chorus that starts up at 5:30 in the morning is almost too much to handle. Now don't get me wrong, I love birds, but someone should have programmed the little goobers to start singing at a more reasonable hour of the day. And so, after listening to the mismatched symphony for about twenty minutes, I decided since I'm not sleeping anyhow, I might as well get out of bed, make a pot of coffee, and go out on the deck to enjoy the sounds of nature. If you can't beat them, join them, as they say.

I was sitting on the deck drinking my coffee when Scott came outside carrying his cup of coffee, still looking like he was half asleep.

"Can you believe how noisy those birds were this morning?" he asked as he sat down on one of the deck chairs. "I ignored them for as long as I could, but they finally won out."

"That's why I got up so early." I replied. "They seem to be particularly noisy today, but that's okay, we have a busy day today so we might as well get started early. You can fix yourself some toast if you want before you go, but I'm going to hit a fast food joint on the way to the booth."

"That actually sounds like a good idea Henry; I think I'll do the same thing. One thing good about getting an early start like this is that I can get a lot done before it gets too hot. Besides, I need to get to the booth early so you can get to your appointment in Missoula, you don't want to be late for that."

"Lock up when you head out Scott; I'm going to get going so I can make a deposit at the bank after I eat, and before I get to the booth," I said as I got up from my chair and started for the kitchen.

"I'll just head out with you right now," Scott said as he too got up to leave. "I'll see you about eleven." He went out the door with me and headed for his truck.

I grabbed the cash box and the bank deposit, locked up the house, and got into my pickup. Once I got to town, I grabbed some fast food breakfast, coffee, and a cinnamon roll, then stopped at the bank to make my deposit, and headed for the booth. As soon as I got to the booth, I did a quick security check, opened the windows for business, and sat down inside the booth to finish my breakfast.

By this time of the selling season, business starts to pick up dramatically, so I called my mom on my cell phone to see if she would come and help Scott while I supposedly ran some errands in Missoula. I can't tell her I'm seeing a hypnotist about past lives experiences because she is a very religious lady who doesn't believe in such nonsense. She only believes that God made the earth in five days, made us humans on the sixth day, had a picnic on the seventh day, end of story, we don't need to know any more. So, I will keep this a secret for now, there's no use giving the poor woman ulcers thinking her son is possessed by Satan.

It wasn't long before the first customers started showing up. The early morning hours are usually busier than the afternoon when it's so hot, so I stayed pretty busy until my mom showed up about 10:30, and then Scott about 11:15. I quickly ushered Scott aside and told him not to mention to my mom that I was seeing a hypnotist or anything like that, but to just play dumb and say he didn't know what all I had to do in Missoula, just that he was watching the booth while I was gone.

I hung around till about 11:45 and then headed for Missoula. I was definitely excited to get started on today's journey back to the days of dragons, but at the same time, I was distracted by the fact that Mike knew about Dee and I seeing each other. If indeed he was Sardon reincarnated, we could both be in danger. Mike and Sardon both share the same personality traits and demeanors, and both seem to be a brick or two short of a full load, which makes them unpredictable. I must be on my guard at all times from now on.

I arrived at Dr. Miller's house about fifteen minutes early, so I sat on the tailgate of my pickup and listened to the sounds of the city, thinking how noisy our world was in comparison to the days of old. It's really no wonder that people have lost their psychic abilities over time; there are way too many distractions. You can't think, you can't meditate, and you can't hear your inner spirit talking to you, giving you guidance.

I must have been daydreaming pretty well because the next thing I knew, Dr. Miller was calling to me from his front stoop. I snapped out of my fog and hailed him back as I closed the tailgate and walked up to the house.

"I'm sorry Jim; I was daydreaming and enjoying the shade under the trees."

"That's quite alright Henry," said Dr. Miller. "It's a little early but my last appointment cancelled so I thought I would check and see if you were out here. This way we can start a few minutes early and talk about your week, so come on in and we'll get started."

I followed the doctor inside and took up my usual position on the easy chair with Jim taking the chair across from me. Picking up his clipboard he asked me.

"How has everything been going since I saw you last week?" I thought he was never going to ask.

"Well doc, you simply aren't going to believe all that has happened," I started.

Then I proceeded to tell him about Dee and her beliefs in dragons, as well as her belief that she has spent several past lives with me. Then I told him about her boyfriend Mike, and our belief that he is Sardon reincarnated, and what a jerk he is turning out to be. I also told him about the affection that Dee and I are developing for each other, and all the while he was feverishly writing notes on his tablet. When I had finished with my story, he lowered his notepad, and then looking over his glasses he responded.

"You sure have had a full week it would seem. Be careful not to rush into anything too hastily until we can get all of this sorted out in our hypnosis sessions. Promise me that you won't make any hasty decisions until that time, okay Henry."

"I promise Doctor, but it's going to be hard you know," I resigned.

"I know it will be hard, but patience has its own rewards," he replied. "Now, are we ready to get started on today's journey?"

"Doc, I've been ready since I left here last week," I stated.

"Then let's get started," he said. "Now lean back in your chair and get comfortable, take a deep breath, let it out slowly, close your eyes and relax. Feel yourself sinking down into your chair, soft, comfortable, relaxing, so relaxing. Now feel every part of your body relaxing, every cell is at peace. Go to your peaceful place along that stream in the mountains, the sun is shining, a slight breeze on your face, the birds are chirping, you can hear the stream flowing among the rocks of the stream. You are feeling very relaxed now, very sleepy, sinking deeper, deeper, deeper.

Chapter 6

"Ethan, Ethan, wake up my love."

Now that was a whole lot better way to wake someone up. I opened my eyes to see the heavenly face of Mara leaning over me, smiling, her hair cascading down to tickle my face. I must have fallen back asleep after Sardon left. I remember coming back to bed, and, oh yeah, now I remember. I reached up and pulled Mara to me for a deep passionate kiss.

"Hold on there big guy," Mara said as she teasingly pulled away, "you're wearing me out. Besides, one of your servants was here to announce that breakfast was ready, and I don't know about you, but I'm starving."

"Oh girl, you're torturing me, but, you're right, I am a little hungry, and we do have a lot planned for today. I'll get cleaned up, change cloths, and we'll be ready to go."

I got out of bed and washed up, and then put on some cloths that would be rugged enough for the trip I had planned for us today, along with some sturdy boots. The sun was shining in through the window; the towering mountain peaks in the background looked even more majestic today than I had ever noticed before. I imagine it's because Mara is here with me today, but nonetheless, the view was stunning. And speaking of views, the view as I watched Mara moving about the villa getting ready, and it was enough to keep my attention fixed upon her like I was under a spell.

I must have been in a trance because the next thing I knew, Mara asked me why I was staring at her like that. I simply responded that her beauty was mesmerizing me, at which point she smiled, smacked me on the chest, kissed me on the cheek, and said.

"I love you Ethan, now let's go before the breakfast gets cold."

Teasingly, she turned, flipped her hair over her shoulders, and headed for the door, me trailing along behind like a love sick puppy, Enough of that, I'm Lord of my domain, I thought to myself, so I ran up to her before she could get to the door, stepped ahead of her to slow her down, and said.

"Not so fast there my love, remember, I'm Lord of this here castle, I can't have you leading me around like the love sick puppy I am. What would my servants think, or my subjects, or the troops, and not to mention the peasants? So please, walk beside me as an equal, and at least give everyone the illusion that I'm still in charge of my senses."

Showing the intelligence, maturity, and cultural understanding that I knew she possessed, she smiled, took my arm proudly, and said.

"Yes my Lord, forgive my forwardness, I will be a proper lady, but just you wait till I get you alone again, then I'll make it up to you." She had a sultry grin on her face as we walked down the hall.

My heart just skipped a beat, and I broke out into an instant sweat. I must maintain my senses here, there is so much danger brewing that I can not let myself get too distracted by this incredible lady. I believe she is here for a reason, but if I'm not careful, one or both of us could lose their life, and in the worst case, a lot of other people could lose their lives too.

As one of the servants passed by I stopped her and said.

"Please send someone out to find Mr. Valik and Balon and have them join us in the kitchen for breakfast."

"Yes Master," she said, bowing, and then hurried off to do my bidding.

As she left, Mara said. "I hope you don't expect me to be that submissive do you?"

"No my love, I only ask that you be respectful of my position, especially in public, and I will never ask you to be submissive. You are my equal in status, and my superior in the ways of the mind. Each of us have talents and gifts that compliment the others talents and gifts. I think with all of the various people that are being drawn to us lately, I believe they are being drawn to us for a reason, and that we will have a team that will prevail in this coming conflict. We must all do our part as a member of the team to survive what is coming. We are equals in this team, and no one person is better than the other, including me, fair enough."

She looked me in the eyes, and spoke. "Now I know why you are to be King one day Ethan. You have a foresight and a perception of people and things around you that will make you triumph over every obstacle. I knew I was right about you, and forgive me for saying so, but you are wrong in one aspect, you are more than an equal to all of us, you are Lord of your realm. You may have lost track of your importance over these many years, but I feel you have it back now in a big way. You are going to be a powerful force in the world soon, and I am proud to call you my Lord."

She had a dreamy look in her eyes that made my heart soar just to look at them. I took her in my arms, kissed her, held her tightly for a few moments, and said.

"God how I love you Mara," I said, and started to kiss her again. This time she put a finger between our lips, and said.

"Can we eat now my Lord, I'm hungry?"

I laughed, grabbed her around the waist, and led her through the door into the private dining area of the kitchen set aside for myself, and my guests. Several servants were waiting, and so was Marta, arms crossed, with a look of disgust on her face.

"It's about time Ethan," Marta said defiantly, "or do expect me to stand around and wait for you all day long. I do have other chores to do around this castle you know."

She clapped her hands and the servants jumped like they had been slapped, and then hurried about bringing food, hot tea, and dishes. Marta had a definite look of hatred on her face.

"Good morning Marta," I said, trying to break the ice, "please set a couple more places, I'm expecting two more guests for breakfast."

"Yes, I heard," she stated, "I have already made plans for them. Now, if you don't mind, I have other things to attend to. The servants can get you what you need, now, may I go?" She started to turn to leave but I stopped her in mid step.

"No, you may not go Marta; I'm not through with you yet. This meeting is going to involve your participation as well, now, please sit down."

Marta had a shocked look on her face, but, knowing her place, she sat down opposite from Mara and myself, a look of fire in her eyes.

The problem with Marta is that she's pretty much had the run of the castle for many years, and that claim was unfortunately reinforced during all the years that I was lost in the debauchery of drinking and carousing with the local women. I was partying so much that I didn't have the time or the inclination to run my own castle, I just didn't care at that point, and so, Marta just sort of took over those duties. I fear now that it has gone to her head and she is not willing to relinquish that role back to me. It's my own fault, but I am going to have to reestablish my authority over this castle, and Marta is not going to like it.

Balon and Valik were just walking in which helped to ease the tension in the room. After greeting them, I invited them to sit down, and as soon as the servants had brought out the food and tea, I asked them to please leave the room and close the door, so that we could talk in private. As soon as they had gone, I started to speak.

"I will start with you first Marta, so that you can attend to the chores you are so anxious to get to, as well as the new chores that I'm going to assign to you today."

She started to complain, but I silenced her immediately by holding up my hand. She sank back into her chair, resigning herself to the self-imposed humiliation of having to actually submit to me.

Continuing I said. "First of all, I want you to meet Mara; she is my guest in this castle and will be treated with the respect of visiting royalty."

Marta interrupted, and with a smug look on her face, she said.

"I've never seen visiting royalty carry on the way you two were in the hallway before you came into the kitchen."

Now I was getting angry, so I stood up and banged my fist on the table, causing everyone to jump, especially Marta, who acted as though she had been slapped, and then I addressed Marta directly.

"I will not tolerate this continued insubordination from you Marta. This is my castle, not yours, and I am its Lord. Furthermore, I am master over all who wish to dwell here, including you. I thank you for watching over me all these years while I was acting so stupidly, but those days are over, and I'm back to face some grave responsibilities that are challenging our very survival. From this moment on, this castle is going to be run like it is under siege from an enemy force, which I believe that it is."

"I believe the enemy is approaching these lands with the intent of destroying everyone and everything within these lands. Furthermore, I believe there are enemies within this castle as we speak. We have identified a few of them already, but I'm sure there a lot more and we will find them also. I have a plan for that which we will discuss later. What I do not want is domestic enemies also within these walls, and that means you Marta. I need to know that I can rely on you to do your part here, and not try to be subversive behind my back. Can I rely on you Marta?" I demanded, still standing, and looking directly at her.

Her glare had now subsided and she was now looking more injured than defiant. She responded by saying.

"Yes my Lord, you can rely on me, and forgive me for being so bold." Her head was bowed a little, like a school kid having been chastised in front of their classmates.

I sat down in my chair to relieve the tension, and then continued.

"As I started to say before, this is Mara, she has traveled many thousands of miles over many years to find me, and is now going to be a big asset in helping us overcome the threat confronting us. She has some amazing psychic abilities with the dragons that are going to prove priceless, as well as some other talents that are going to help us to destroy the invaders."

"Furthermore," I continued, "Mara and I have a connection that goes back several lifetimes that only the wizards could explain fully, but suffice it to say, Mara is my friend, my partner, and my lover, and I will not tolerate anyone trying to stand in the way of that, nor will I tolerate anyone being disrespectful to her in any way, do I make myself clear."

Balon and Valik spoke their approval right away, while Marta just sort of mumbled her acknowledgement. You could tell her emotions were based on jealousy, and jealousy is a dangerous beast all on its own. I felt sorry for her, but this is how things are going to be from now on. I'll just have to watch her closely to make sure she doesn't try to do something deceitful that would jeopardize this castle, or anyone in it, such as me, Mara, Balon, or Valik.

"Okay, now down to business, Marta, this is for you, and then you may leave. I want you to start ordering in extra amounts of nonperishable foods, especially grain, flour, dried fruits, vegetables, dried meats, salt, and so on. If anyone starts to ask questions, tell them we are going to host some major celebrations, in honor of the moon, or whatever else you can think of. I'm sure they will believe it, given my past lifestyle of partying for reasons of even less importance."

"If this castle comes under siege, we want to be able to hold out for as long as possible. Fill the storage caverns below as quickly as possible, because I have no idea yet how soon this conflict will take place. Buy everything you think we'll need to hold out for an extended period of time. Send some of your most trusted servants to buy whatever we need from the vendors so it doesn't look like it's just the castle itself that is stocking up. We want to keep it low key for as long as possible. I think we probably have a week at the most to get ready. Do I make myself clear Marta?"

"Yes my Lord," she responded, but added, "what did the King have to say about this?"

"He did not believe me, in fact, he told me to remember my place as a subject to him, and then nearly threw me out of his villa. I think we are all on our own here Marta, I'm sorry to say, so please, get us ready for a siege. You were here for the last one, so use that knowledge to make amends for any mistakes that may have made the last time, okay."

"Yes my Lord," she said as she got up, bowed, and left the room.

"Mr. Valik," I said, now turning to address him, "I now need you to handpick two of the men you would trust with your life, and meet us in the hallway close to the secret doorway, because we're going to do some training today."

"Yes my Lord," he said as he rose to leave.

But as he started to leave, I stopped him, and said.

"By the way, Captain Sardon stopped by my chambers this morning, and he said a couple of his men didn't show up for roll call this morning. He asked me to ask around to see if anyone had seen them."

Valik just sort of smiled at me, and said. "Imagine that, they didn't show up for roll call. If I see them, I'll tell them to report to Captain Sardon immediately." With that, he turned crisply on his heel, and headed out the door.

"Balon, my friend, as for you," I said, putting my arm around his bulky shoulders, "have the kitchen servants make a lunch big enough for six people, for the whole day, and then meet us at the dragon pens. We have an exciting day ahead of us, now go."

"Yes my Lord," he said, and was off to the kitchen.

"Well, my love," I said as I turned to look into the beautiful eyes of my beloved Mara, "I need you to speak to the dragons before we release them for the day. I'll let you know what to tell them when we get there, are you ready for a journey?"

"I'm ready Ethan, this is what I was born to do, and you my love, are who I was born to do it with. We can't put this off any longer, our destiny waits, so we might as well meet it head on."

We both rose, and then arm in arm we went down the hall, descending the stone stairway to the dragon pens below. The journey had begun, destiny was being played out, and our predetermined fates awaited our arrival. It was scary, yet exciting all at the same time.

Before we even got close to the dragon pens, the dragons were waiting at the iron gate, trying to peek down the hallway to see us coming, or should I say, to see Mara coming. It was uncanny how they responded to her presence.

"It looks like your fan club is waiting," I said to Mara as we drew closer to the gate.

"I know," she said, "I could sense them waiting for me, they knew I was coming before I got here, isn't it sweet."

She stopped in front of the gate and reached inside to pat each dragon on the nose while I unlocked the gate, then they all moved back so we could enter, just like they had real manners and personalities.

"It's amazing," I said, "absolutely amazing. I thought Balon had a way with the dragons, but you my dear, are on a whole different level."

"So are you, my Love," she said, "you just didn't realize it, but the dragons did, they understood you all these years, and they tried to talk to you, but you couldn't hear them. Come up close to me, close your eyes, and clear your mind of everything going on around us right now, including any worries or fears you might be having right now. Now, point your mind like a finger toward the dragons, and listen with your mind, not your ears. You will see' what they are saying, you'll see it in pictures. Can you see them?"

All of a sudden my mind was nearly overwhelmed by the visions I was seeing, the dragons, the Gog army, the killing of the dragon in the valley of Migido, the killing of the dragon by the poison dart, Sardon standing with the Gog clansman, S A R D O N!!!

My eyes popped open like I was about to be attacked, and I instinctively spun around to the iron gate as though I expected the assassin to be standing there with the dart gun, my eyes were wide, my heart pounding in my chest, and as my hand went for my short sword, sweat broke out upon my brow. I quickly became aware of my surroundings, and as I regained my composure, I looked into the faces of five dragons that looked back at me as if to say, 'What took you so long.'

"I saw," I managed to stammer out, "I saw the whole thing, from the battle in the Valley of Migido, to the assassination of the dragon here in the pen by the Gog clansman, and by Sardon, the rat, he was here when it happened, he was helping the intruder. I'll kill him myself the next time I see him."

Now I was angry, I was angry with Sardon for being so treacherous, and angry with myself for not knowing about him ahead of time. I was also angry with myself for my years of inattentiveness to the dragons. They have had to suffer for my transgressions, and now it is up to me to try to make up for it.

"We don't have time to deal with Sardon right now Ethan," Mara said, her hand resting gently on my arm. "Right now we have some work to do to protect ourselves from any further treachery. You started your plans into action this morning, and we need to buy some time. Killing Sardon now would upset the whole plan, and probably bring the King's troops down on us before we have all of our resources in place. You must have patience my love."

"You're right Mara," I said, "forgive me."

Then turning once again to the dragons I said.

"Forgive me my friends, my lack of integrity over the last few years has led to this tragedy, and now we must all pay for my short comings. I am indeed sorry, and I beg for your forgiveness."

With that, all five dragons lowered their heads close to my own, as if showing equality, and submission. I was forgiven.

Balon was the first to arrive, carrying two large satchels of food, and a large bladder of water. He was clearly winded from the heavy burden. Dropping the load on the ground, he let out a big sigh, and said.

"I hope someone is going to help me carry this stuff from here on, or I'm not going."

As if on cue, both Mara and I said in unison.

"The dragons said they would gladly take care of the food for you."

We all looked at each other, and then Mara and I broke out in laughter, while Balon just stared at us like we were crazy. I decided to break the tension and said.

"Balon, please open the outer gates to release the dragons." While he was doing the chore I had asked him, I turned to the dragons, and spoke to them.

"We are going to be traveling through the Valley of the Dragons below the castle, and going all the way to the Talon pass to try to get a view of the Valley of Migido, and a possible look at the Gog army. We're going to be flying in a strange craft, and trying out some dangerous new weapons. Please stay high in the air so you don't get injured, and do not come down to help us unless we call for you. Watch over us for any unseen danger, and let us know what you see. Now go, hunt, be careful, and we'll see you in a few hours."

The dragons turned, crawled to the open gate, and then launched themselves over the edge of the precipice, diving straight down until the air got under their wings, at which time they soared high up into the air, circling higher and higher, until finally moving off into the distance until they disappeared from view.

"I told you that you were awesome when it comes to talking to the dragons," Mara said, putting her arms around me. "All you needed was the right frame of mind."

"And the right teacher," I added. "Now, we better get down below to meet up with Valik and his troops."

We all grabbed part of the provisions that Balon had brought with him, and went down the hallway to descend another flight of stone stairs to the next level of caverns. As we reached the bottom of the stairs, we could see Valik and his two handpicked troopers waiting for us partway down the hall. Mr. Valik was showing his intelligence and good judgment by not waiting all the way down the hallway in front of the secret doorway. The troopers were dressed in light battle gear, with short swords and leather helmets. Battle ready troopers are an awesome sight, and these guys were no exception. I'm glad they were on our side.

As we approached, the troopers with Valik bowed their heads slightly, and then stood at attention.

"Good morning men and thank you for joining us today. We're going to show you some exciting new things, as well as some very deadly ones, plus we're going to take a little journey to the valley of Migido to get a look first hand at what we're facing."

"My Lord," One of the men interrupted, "the valley of Migido is over a hundred miles by road and trail, and we're not equipped for an extended journey."

"Son," I started, "the way we're going is only about thirty miles as the dragon flies, and we won't be walking, we'll be flying." When I said that, jaws dropped on everyone except Mara and me.

The troopers started mumbling to themselves when the man who spoke up before spoke again.

"Forgive me Lord, but how can that be, are we going to ride upon the dragons' backs?" He looked a little concerned, as did the others.

"Not hardly," I began, "even I wouldn't trust that kind of a flight. You are going to see some very interesting things today, including a chariot that flies through the air like magic, and some weapons that will make the hearts of the enemy stop from fear, so, the sooner we get started, the sooner you'll see these things, so, let's start our journey."

I started down the hallway, followed by Mara, Balon, Valik, and the two troopers. Reaching the secret door, I quickly looked around to see if anyone was watching, and then inserted my key into the lock, and with a turn, the heavy stone door slid out of the way. We grabbed several torches, lit them, and then, inserting the key into the opposite lock, watched as the door slid closed.

The walk down the pathway to the wizard's cavern was done in complete silence, except for the sounds of our footsteps on the stone path. No one spoke a word, with each person lost in his or her own thoughts about what they were going to see today. Reaching the bottom of the pathway, I told everyone to stay where they were while I got some light into the cavern. Finding the heavy chains, I pulled on the one that would open the trapdoor high on the mountaintop, allowing light to bounce off mirrors and prisms until the whole cavern was awash in light. Again, there was an audible gasp from each person, even though they had seen the cavern before, all except Mara, who could only stand and stare in awe at the sight before her, mummified dragons, wings spread wide, menacing, awesome, and regal.

"Incredible!" Was all she could manage to say for the first several moments, and then, as I walked back to the small group, she asked.

"Are these the ancestors of the dragons you now care for?"

"They are," I replied, "and if you'll follow me, I'll show you a few more ancestors. Balon, please keep your torch lit and hang it on the wall behind you, and the rest of you can douse your torches."

I led the way through the cavern to the first room, the room that held the bodies of my Grandfather, my father, and the wizard. Mara drew close to the mummified figures with the interest of a scientist.

"This is so incredible," she said. "The natural dryness and the air currents mummify everything down here, right?"

"That's correct," I replied. "The wizard pointed it out to us while he was down here. He found out quite by accident; by leaving fruit sit here while he was gone to the surface. He would be gone for extended periods, and when he returned, the fruit was perfectly preserved, it never rotted. So, he experimented first with the dragons that died over the years, getting good results, and then when my grandfather died, he became the next experiment. You can see the results to this day, perfect preservation. When I die, I have left instructions with these men to place me on the empty throne next to my father, and if the gods are willing, and I have a son, he will continue the legacy."

"A son?" Mara said, looking me in the eyes. "Do you entertain the thoughts of one day ending your wanton ways and raising a family?"

"I do since I met you Mara," I said, returning her gaze, and then I continued, "When this conflict is all done, I want you to be my Queen."

"I would love to be your Queen," Mara replied, throwing her arms around me, giving me a quick kiss on the lips, and then just holding me in her arms.

"Here, here, hail to the King and Queen!" Valik shouted out, raising his fist in the air in a salute, followed in unison by the other troopers with him, and then Balon took up the chant.

"Hail to the King and Queen." It was enough to give us goose flesh all over.

"Thank you gentlemen," I said, "I will try to live up to your expectations."

"We have no doubt that you will be the greatest King that ever lived," Mr. Valik said as he patted me on the back. "You have already proved your worthiness to us in every move you make, my Lord."

"We might be getting a little ahead of ourselves here," I started, "but we must first survive the coming conflict, which means we need to get on with our training, and then a little reconnaissance of the enemy, so, let's keep moving."

We moved on to the next cavern, the cavern containing the armory.

"Gentlemen, please grab the horn of Gideon, and set all of the parts out in the main cathedral to be picked up on our return."

Next, I grabbed an object in a large cloth bag that was leaning against the wall, laid it on the table, removed the bag to reveal another object, approximately four feet long, that looked like a telescope with a large bowl shaped structure on the top, back portion of the tube. The bowl itself was about a foot in diameter, and the inside of the bowl was very shiny, highly polished to a mirror finish, with a prism and a powerful lens at the bottom of the bowl where it connected to the main tube. The bowl had a protective cover over the top, and another cover over the front lens. I handed the object to one of the soldiers and said.

"Whatever you do, do not uncover both of the protective shrouds of this weapon at the same time; unless of course you are ready to kill anything in front of the weapon, do I make myself clear?" I was totally serious when I spoke to the soldier.

"Yes my Lord," he said, standing nearly at attention when I addressed him," your orders are completely clear."

"Very good," I responded, "now set this out with the other weapon. Balon, please stay with the weapons while the rest of us go and get the chariot."

"Yes my Lord," Balon responded, assuming a stance that a soldier would assume on guard duty. It looked a little ridiculous, given his physique and stature, but it made him feel important, and that's what counted.

I led the way farther into the cathedral until we came to another cavern, this one much larger than the last, and there before us was a vehicle like none the world had ever seen.

The vehicle before us was round, nearly fifteen feet in diameter, with a hand rail about four feet high surrounding the craft so you wouldn't fall out, and a center console with its own support railing, which contained the control levers. The craft stood about three feet off the ground on six, thick metal legs, with eighteen inch, flat metal pads on the bottom of each leg to keep the craft from sinking into the dirt. The whole craft was made of the same shiny metal that the telescope type weapon was made of, with an opaque floor covering thousands of octagon shaped crystals. The craft now sat on sets of rollers so it could be rolled in and out of the cavern. Turning to the men with me, I said.

"Help me move the craft out into the light of the main cathedral so it can charge up a little."

With a bit of effort, we managed to get the craft rolling out of the cavern and into the main cathedral. The rollers had flattened out over time which made them difficult to start rolling, but, as soon as the craft started to get into the light of the cathedral, it started to vibrate on its own with a barely audible hum, which of course spooked the soldiers helping to push the craft, and caused them to jump back away from the craft.

"It's okay," I reassured them, "it's just the craft gaining power from the sunlight, charging up the crystals in the floor. It won't take long to charge the craft enough to power it out of the mountain and outside into the open sunshine. Once outside, it will fully charge up, giving it even more power, and give it enough of a reserve charge to get us back home even if it gets dark.

"Where did all of these crystals come from my Lord?" Valik asked. "I have never in all of my travels seen such perfectly uniform crystals, not to mention the sheer numbers of them."

"I can answer that question," Mara said. "they came from a supposedly extinct volcanic mountaintop on Atlantis. The whole mountain seemed to be made of crystals, and once we discovered the power of the crystals, that was when our culture started to advance so rapidly. Unfortunately, we advanced technologically faster than we advanced mentally and spiritually. That was when the subversive countercultures started to flourish, with men like Sardon."

"Tell us more about this crystal mountain," said one of the troopers as we finished moving the craft out into the main cathedral.

"Okay," Mara continued, "the ancient Atlanteans used to think the mountain was haunted, and wouldn't go anywhere near it."

"Why did they think such a thing?" asked the trooper.

"Because the mountain would make strange noises all of the time. My people used to say it was singing to them, trying to lure them to their death, like the old tales of the Sirens calling sailors to their deaths in the ocean."

"What sort of strange noises?" asked the other trooper.

Mara continued, "It was hard to explain until later on when we finally learned what it was, but at first it just sounded like noises, or as we called it, singing. What it turned out to be was voices, voices from around the world, and around the universe. That was why we couldn't understand what it was, because it was languages we had never heard before. Later, we would learn how to use the mountain to communicate with peoples from around the world, as well as creatures from other worlds."

"What do you mean when you say, creatures from other worlds?" Valik asked.

"That was how we learned how to use the crystals from the mountain," Mara started. "One day a strange craft landed at the base of the mountain, occupied by odd little creatures. To make a long story short, signals from the mountain itself had drawn the other worldly visitors to our planet to check out the source of the signals, and after a lot of initial barriers and fears, our people became friends with the visitors, and they are the ones who taught us how to build all of these wondrous things."

"What happened to the visitors since then?" Valik asked.

"They visited us often for several decades, and then they would come only occasionally, and then hardly at all. After the cataclysm, we never saw them again, except for the occasional report of lights in the sky, which may or may not be them."

"And what of the mountain, and all of the crystals?" asked one of the troopers.

"We mined the mountain of its crystals for hundreds of years, using them ourselves, and stockpiling them around the world, until finally the mountain itself rebelled against us, and the supposedly extinct volcanic mountain came back to life, starting at first with major earthquakes, as though it was trying to shake us off of the earth like a dog does fleas. The earthquakes then opened up fissures into the molten center of the earth itself, and soon our continent was torn apart and sinking."

"It took some time for the end to come, so many of the more affluent people were able to barter escape to places around the world. The rest of our people perished when the remainder of our continent sank beneath the waves. Everything else is history, our people, and our descendants are scattered around the world, not even realizing their heritage any longer, save for the few of us who continue to study our ancestry, and seek out our past, like Ethan and myself."

As we stood there listening to Mara, and looking at the craft, it slowly became evident that the craft was starting to lift slightly off of its rollers, no longer even touching the ground.

"How can this be?" asked one of the soldiers, bending down on one knee to look underneath the craft.

"Is this some sort of magic?" asked the other trooper.

"No, my friend, its science, not magic," I said as I grabbed one of the handles along the bottom edge of the craft, and as I did so, I started to pull the now weightless craft along with me, all by myself, and back to where Balon waited for us with the weapons. The rest of the soldiers followed along, mouths agape, completely mesmerized by all of what was happening around them. Only Mara was showing no sign of anything being out of the ordinary.

As we approached Balon, he showed no concern until we got closer and he too noticed that the craft was floating about a foot off of the floor. He kneeled down to look underneath the craft and he too had that same mesmerized look on his face, his mouth also agape. Just as Balon was about to speak, Valik interrupted and said.

"Science, not magic."

Balon just looked at him, mouth still agape, and shook his head.

"Let's get going," I said as I reached along the bottom of the craft and pulled out one of the sets of steps that were recessed along the underside of the craft.

Helping Mara to climb the steps while I steadied the craft, I instructed one of the soldiers to climb up next, which he reluctantly did. Then I instructed the others to hand the weapons up to the first soldier and had him secure the six pieces of the Horn of Gideon with lashes attached along the floor, and then finally the telescope looking weapon.

"Please hold onto that last weapon until I get aboard," I said to the soldier who was handed the weapon.

Then after the other soldier, Valik, and Balon climbed aboard the craft, I pushed the step back under the craft, and then I sort of jumped, and crawled up onto the craft myself. Taking the weapon from the soldier, I removed the cloth bag it was in, and then, moving to the railing on one side and slightly forward of the center console, I slipped the small post on the bottom of the weapon into a hole in the railing. The weapon could now be rotated nearly 360 degrees, with a stop on both sides so it could not be pointed at the driver standing at the console, nor too far to the rear where other passengers may be standing. There was a similar mount on the opposite side of the craft, as well as one on the rear.

"Mara," I said, "if you would be so kind as to control the craft until we get outside, I'm a little rusty at this, and men, space yourself evenly around the railing, and hold on until you get your legs used to the movement. Let's move ahead to the back wall and the next door."

Mara grabbed the lever at the console, and ever so slightly pushed it forward. With a slight lurch, the craft tipped nose down and moved forward, floating about a foot off of the ground. Once we reached the back wall of the cathedral, I jumped down from the side, inserted my key into the key hole, turned it, and the heavy stone door slid open to reveal the wide pathway leading down into the darkness. Mara maneuvered the craft through the doorway and stopped while I grabbed the torch that Balon had left for us, and then I closed the secret door, and climbed back aboard the craft.

"Please turn on the lights Mara," I said as I felt my way along the rail. Finding the small lever, Mara flipped it forward, and the area ahead of the craft was bathed in soft light, showing the pathway clearly.

"Once the craft is fully charged," Mara stated, "the light will be brighter, but for now, this will have to do until we can get outside. The light from this torch will keep the crystals charged until then. Now everyone hold on, because here we go." With that, Mara tipped the main lever forward, and we started moving down the pathway.

"Okay gentlemen," I started to explain, "I'm going to explain the workings of this craft so that any one of you will be able to take over the craft if someone else is killed or injured. Each person will get their turn operating the craft for the same reasons. First of all, this craft works with very powerful magnets, all placed under the craft in such a way that they repel the earth's natural gravity. The lever that Mara is using to control the craft simply tilts the magnets one direction or another to push the craft in the direction you wish it to go. Normally, the craft will only go the speed of a fast runner, but with the assistance of the crystals in the floor, and a light source to charge those crystals, there is nothing on earth that can keep up with us, except perhaps the dragons."

Continuing, I explained." Sunlight is the best source of light to charge the crystals, but in this case we can get enough light from the torch to gain minimum speed and lift. The other benefit from a good light source is that we will also gain a significant amount of height from the ground, which is good when someone is shooting arrows at you. Here in the tunnels of course, we don't need a lot of height, but once in the open, we will have to be on our toes for any sign of danger, and we will want to be able to climb to our maximum height at the first sign of danger. There shouldn't be anyone in the Valley of the Dragons, but beyond that, everyone we see is to be considered a threat, and should be killed immediately, I don't want any word of secret weapons to get back to the enemy, as we want this to be a complete surprise, do I make myself clear on this issue? Everyone we see has to die."

Looking around, all the men in unison nodded their approval to the plan. Getting my first looks into the faces of the men with us, all showed few signs of the anxiety they had first displayed when they climbed aboard the craft. In fact, it appeared that some of the men were even starting to enjoy the ride, and I'm sure I could detect their chests swelling from the pride of being involved with such equipment and intrigue. All was coming together nicely.

We were just coming onto a large flat area that I knew was the exit point to the Valley of the Dragons, so I turned to Mara and said.

"Turn to the left and stop just short of the wall."

"Another secret door?" she asked as she performed the maneuver perfectly and stopped just short of the wall.

"Yes my love," I said, "this is the doorway to the Valley of the Dragons, which is three thousand feet below the castle above. Once we are outside, we need to stay close to the cliff edge to remain out of view of the castle above. We don't want anyone to see us before we can get out of sight farther along in the canyon. And if you don't mind, I'll have you keep operating until we get out of sight, then we'll all take turns practicing before moving on to spy on the enemy."

I jumped down from the craft, and then moved to the wall to find the key slot. Since it had been a great many years since I had came this way, it took me a few moments to find the keyhole under all the ages of dust. Once located, and with a little effort to push the key into the slot, and actually turn the heavy key, the door swished open to the outside, bathing us in bright sunlight, causing all of us to squint hard against the light. As soon as our eyes had readjusted, I motioned for Mara to move the craft out of the tunnel, and as soon as she did so, the crystals in the floor started glowing brightly, and what was before a barely perceptible hum, now increased to a much more audible tone, not uncomfortable, but definitely more perceptible.

Once the craft was outside, I closed the heavy stone door, and climbed back aboard, taking my position at what was to be known as the 'Dragon's Breath' weapon. We had exited the mountain just above the waterfall where we had entered the mountain the day before. Here the stream resumed its slow, meandering course from the valley ahead. The valley here was about a half a mile wide, with nearly vertical cliff walls to the west side, and walls that rose up to my castle above that actually leaned back over our heads, making them impossible to ascend. It was close to this overhang that we would travel for the first several miles to keep out of sight of the castle.

The craft was nearly at full power now and moving quite fast as we worked our way deeper into the Valley of the Dragons. Everyone seemed to be enjoying the sensation of flight, and they were even getting comfortable enough to move about without losing their balance. There were lashes attached to the railing so you could secure yourself to the craft for fast moving or evasive maneuvering if the need arose.

We were just passing the base of the castle when I spotted something unusual all over the rocks ahead. Drawing closer it was evident that there was blood, flesh, and bones splattered all over, but what caught my attention was the clothing that remained partially intact, it was the uniform worn by the castle guard above. As we passed by I looked at Valik and the troopers, who were looking everywhere else but at the two bodies and me, so I said.

"I guess we know what happened to the two troopers that Sardon was looking for this morning."

Valik opened his mouth to say something but before he could speak I said.

"It looks like they must have had a guilty conscience for spying on me, and jumped to their deaths, isn't that the way you men see it?" I asked, looking back to the gruesome scene now fading away behind us, and then back to them.

"Um, yes, I'm quite sure that must have been what happened, my Lord," Valik said, and then he started whistling some incoherent tune, looking around to avoid direct eye contact.

I just smiled, and turned my face into the breeze, and was enjoying the ride when I noticed something else lying amongst the rocks. I asked Mara to slow down a bit so I could get a closer look at the object. My heart sank when I realized what it was; it was the dart gun that the Gog clansman had used to deliver the poison dart to the first dragon. No wonder I couldn't find it that morning. Apparently Sardon disposed of it over the cliff before Balon and I arrived in the cavern. That traitor will pay dearly if it's the last thing I do.

Continuing on into the valley, we were cruising five to ten feet off the ground, and at a fairly brisk rate. Mara grew up using one of these craft, and she was definitely good at it.

We went about five miles farther into the canyon until we came into a fairly open meadow, at which time I instructed Mara to stop. It was time for all of us to practice handling the craft. Mara reached down to another lever, pulled the handle back, and a set of shutters closed between the crystals, and the now noticeably clear floor under our feet. The craft slowly lowered to hover about a foot above the ground. Mara now began the training session.

"The shutters block the sunlight from reaching the crystals, thereby reducing the power to the craft. We are still able to maneuver with the magnets, which is what we are going to do until you get used to controlling the craft at reduced power. The third lever here on the console flips the magnets over so they no longer provide lift for the craft at all; otherwise it could wander off by itself if no one kept a hold of it. So, Mr. Valik, you're first," Mara said, motioning for him to come over to the console.

Valik looked a little pale, but he was also an obedient soldier.

"Take the control lever in one hand only," Mara began, "using a touch as light as a feather. If you move the lever too hard or aggressive, you won't be able to control it and we'll crash and die. Do you understand?"

"Yes my Lady," Valik stated, taking the control, and looking very nervous.

"Now, we are not at full power," Mara continued, "so you won't be able to lose control even if you wanted to, so, using the lever, simply tilt it the way you want the craft to go, and have fun. Take it away Captain Valik." With that word 'Captain', Valik's face beamed, and his troopers cheered him on.

Valik did a marvelous job controlling the craft, as did one of the other troopers, even to the point that Mara opened the shutters and guided them through some faster maneuvers. Now Balon and the other trooper were a different story, having a hard time using finesse to control the craft. Both men were burly types who normally use their brawn to make things happen, not finesse.

"Okay you two," Mara said, "we'll keep working with you guys later, and remember, if either of you have to fly this craft, do it only with the shutters closed for better control." Both men nodded their approval, and relief.

"Your turn now Ethan, my love, show us what you've got."

I moved to the console, leaned back against the support railing, and took a hold of the control lever. With my other hand, I opened the shutters, feeling the craft rise, and come alive beneath my feet.

"Hold on tight," I said, and when everyone had a hold of the railing, I pushed the lever forward to an exaggerated position and the craft tilted forward and took off at a pace faster than anything Mara had tried thus far, causing her to let out a squeal. The other men's eyes were as big as saucers.

As soon as Mara realized that I knew what I was doing, and was in complete control, she let out a raucous yell, and with a laugh, she shook her hair in the wind and held one hand high in the air. It was not long before the rest of the party joined in and they too were yelling and enjoying themselves, at least until one of the dragons did a close up fly by, nearly scaring us out of our senses. As we realized what was happening, we again took up our gleeful yelling as one by one, the dragons swooped over our heads to rise high above, doing rolls and somersaults, showing off too, and proving to us that they still held mastery over the skies.

The Valley of the Dragons is a long, crescent shaped valley, about thirty miles long, narrowing as it reaches higher into the peaks, where it rises above the Valley of Migido, and the Talon Pass. The unique shape of the valley itself shows the dragons their way back to the castle and to the caves high on the cliff face. From their vantage point high in the sky, the dragons need only to recognize the crescent shaped valley, and follow it home to their roosts in the caves beneath the castle.

The Talon Pass is at the far end of the Valley of the Dragons, and will be a thousand feet below us when we emerge from the backside of this valley. We will have a perfect vantage point to look down on any unsuspecting enemy troops who might be below us.

The Valley of Migido is a huge valley nearly a hundred mils long, and will be another three miles by winding trail below the Talon Pass, and we hope to be able to see as far out onto the plains as possible for any signs of enemy troops.

The valley of Migido is a mostly barren landscape that separates the Land of Magog, where the Gog call home and the lands which my people call home. I'm surprised the Gog army was brave enough to attempt a crossing of that valley because of the danger from the dragons. Only a large army with the confidence to take on the dragons would dare enter those lands, and from all indications so far, the Gog army has figured out a way to kill the dragons. They must figure the ratio of lost troops to lost dragons is worth the price.

The trail from the Valley of Migido, up through the Talon Pass is a trail just wide enough for wagons, and for troops riding three or four abreast. Even at that rate, it would still take considerable time for a large army to wind its way through the Pass, and I want to be there when they try to march through, because after they clear the Pass, there is nothing between them and the valley holding the King's castle, 'My' valley.

Once the Gog army has entered the Pass, I think the sonic weapon can slow them down, and we will be unapproachable from our vantage point above them because of the sheer rock walls on both sides of the Pass. That is the beauty of this place, it is only accessible from the Valley of the Dragons, and the Valley of the Dragons is only accessible from inside my mountain castle, and the Pass below us is how the Gog army must come to lay siege to King Malok, and here is where I can ambush them.

Geologically recent earthquake fault lines and upheavals created these impenetrable canyons, valleys, and peaks. Time has yet to erode the edges of this land to make nice smoothly rounded mountains like other places on earth. The sheer ruggedness of this place is the reason my father and grandfather chose this land to settle in, and all was well until the arrival of King Malok. Now that I know that he and I are not of the same bloodline, his fate is his own to bear. The battle I plan to wage is for my own protection, not King Malok's. As a matter of fact, I'm counting on the King falling from power.

We had traveled about twenty miles into the valley when I slowed the craft down and then stopped, saying, "This is what I'm looking for, gentlemen, it's now time to learn how to use the weapons."

Pulling the lever to close the shutters, the craft settled down to hover just above the ground, and then I pulled the lever to flip the giant magnets so the craft would set down fully on the ground. I wanted a stable platform from which to work.

Laying my hand on the Dragon's Breath weapon, I said.

"This weapon my friends, is the equivalent of the sun on earth. I want you to watch that group of dead trees at the base of the cliffs over there, and whatever you do, do not get in front of the weapon."

The group of trees I spoke of was about three hundred yards away, maybe a dozen trees in all, positioned at the bottom of the cliff, amongst a large rockslide. I had chosen these particular trees because the rockslide above the trees would limit any danger of fire from the intense heat that this weapon would produce.

Reaching around to the front of the weapon, I removed the protective cover, revealing a thick, powerful lens. There was a small lever on the underside of the weapon, which could be pulled with your fingers. Pointing the weapon in the direction of the trees, I looked through a smaller tube on top of the weapon to get the general sight of the target, and pulled back on the lever. As soon as I pulled the lever, the cover of the bowl shaped unit on top flipped open, gathering and concentrating the sunlight which bounced the light through a prism at the bottom of the bowl, which then bent and concentrated the beam of light even further into the tube through a series of perfectly shaped crystals, nestled one against the other inside of the tube, and the result was a two inch thick beam of hot, white light that streamed out of the front of tube, across the three hundred yards of space to the trees, shearing them off and engulfing them in flames. All of this happened in less than the blink of an eye. Releasing the lever closed the lid of the bowl, and the beam stopped.

Looking around, everyone except Mara had a look on their face like they had just seen a ghost. Soon, mumbling turned to words of wonder, and Valik was the first to speak.

"That was incredible my Lord, how long has this technology been around, and what happened to the army that developed it, because they must be the most powerful army on earth."

It was Mara who answered the question for me, since I really did not know all the answers.

"These weapons were developed by my ancestors, and Ethan's, and they have been around for a couple of thousand years. We did not have an army; the weapons were designed to kill the large beasts that roamed the world at that time. Then, when the earthquakes came and our lands started to sink beneath the waves, a very few of these weapons were whisked away to be hidden throughout the world, such as this one, and one other, that came here with the wizard, and Ethan's grandfather. There are only a few of them known to exist, and Sardon wants control of them, and you can see why. Whoever controls these weapons will become a very powerful man."

"Now gentlemen," I interrupted, "it's time for each of you to learn to fire the weapon. Mr. Valik, you are to go first."

Each man took his turn at the weapon, and each time the weapon was fired, the men gained a bigger fondness for its power. I showed them how to sweep the weapon across a broad area to incinerate large groups of men, horses, houses, or whatever multiple targets might be presented. The weapon has an effective range of over a mile, depending on how tightly the tubing, and thus the crystals, are compressed. Beyond that range, the target would get severe burns, but death could not be guaranteed. This weapon was definitely a crowd pleaser, and everyone was impressed.

"Next," I started, "we need to try out the sonic weapon, which is officially known as the Horn of Gideon, so lets get it unloaded and put it together."

I showed the men how to lay out each section of the horn', with the first section raised up on it's stand with the drum head attached, and the last section with the bellows, also on a smaller stand that could be moved and pointed in the general direction of the enemy. This weapon does not have to be accurately pointed to any one place as it will broadcast its devastation over a wide area in front of the bellows. Since we would not be able to demonstrate it's power on living beings, I planned to show them what could happen to an unstable mountainside like the rock slide area before us, which was still smoldering from the recent testing of the Dragon's Breath weapon.

As soon as the weapon was put together, I asked everyone to stand behind the drum, and then, taking the drumsticks in hand, I began a slow, steady drum roll. Almost immediately we could all feel a slight pressure on our eardrums, as well as a pressure on our chests. I stopped for a moment to speak.

"You can feel the pressure on your eardrums already and we are not even in front of the horn, but, if you were in front of this weapon, you would soon lose control of your bowels, and with continued exposure to the sonic vibrations, loss of muscle control would be next. If exposure continued, damage to the internal organs would lead to death. Now, let's adjust the bellows, close them down slightly to concentrate the sonic vibrations."

This time as I started the drum roll you could almost see the vibrations rippling through the air, and the mountainside ahead started to crumble, only slightly at first with a rock here and there rolling down the hill, and then more and more until a whole section of the mountain gave loose and came down as though an earthquake had just taken place. In fact, I stopped the drum roll when it looked as though the landslide was going to overtake our position and cause us to leave in haste.

"Well," I started to say in a slightly nervous voice, "you can see what this weapon is capable of. Now, let's secure this equipment on the craft and go pay the Gog army a visit. If we can catch them in the pass, we'll see if we can slow them down a little with a small man made earthquake, and hopefully kill a few in the process. If they're not there yet, we'll still create an earthquake to block the pass to slow them down so we can finish gathering enough supplies to weather a siege of our castle, and perhaps save a few lives in the valley of King Malok"

As soon as we had everything reloaded, I instructed Mr. Valik to take over the controls and take us on up to the Pass. Tentatively, he took his place at the control console, still a little unsure of himself, but willing to take the challenge. He moved the lever to flip the magnets back to the lift position, and then without yet opening the shutters, he moved the craft forward on magnet power only to get a feel for the controls until his confidence level rose. Then he opened the shutters to the crystals, causing the craft to rise to its limit of fifty feet above the ground, steadily increasing the speed to match his comfort level and we were off and running once more to meet the enemy.

It was mid afternoon when we reached the top of the Valley, and the place where we could get a good view down into the Talon Pass area. Shutting down the craft, we packed the Horn of Gideon to the edge of the rock face overlooking the Pass. After confirming there was not a major army within the Pass as yet, we went about finding a good place to put the Horn of Gideon, which took a little more time than we had planned, but once we found a good vantage point, the weapon was set up much more quickly than before.

The weapon was aimed at the opposite rock wall on the far side of the pass, an area that looked a bit more unstable than the rest. Now it was time to bring down the house, so to speak. Just as we were making the final adjustments to the bellows, Balon spoke up.

"My Lord, there is a large cloud of dust rising from the far end of the pass, and what looks like fog, or smoke out on the plains of the Valley of Migido, what do you suppose it is?" I knew right away what it was, and it made my heart skip a beat.

"That my friend," I began, "is the dust and smoke from the Gog army, and it must be huge to put up a cloud such as that. I'm afraid we don't have much time."

Looking around, I could see the concern on the faces all of the people there with me. But continuing, I added.

"I know it looks hopeless and scary my friends, but I have confidence in the weapons we possess, for there is nothing on earth to compare with them. I don't hold out much hope for King Malok's castle to withstand an attack by that army, but once the Gog are in a position where we can use our weapons on them, they will not stand a chance."

"The positions we want them in is in the King's valley below the plateau, or on the narrow road leading up to my castle, or even outside my castle walls where they will die by the thousands. What we have to make sure of is that these weapons do not fall into the hands of Captain Sardon or the Gog clan. As soon as we have enough food and supplies stored in the castle caverns, we are going to kick Sardon and his allies out of my castle for good. Now, let's get to work."

Just about the time I was going to start the drum roll, one of the troopers blurted out. "Look, down below, a large scouting party coming up through the pass."

Ducking down, we watched as nearly fifty Gog soldiers on horseback worked their way up the pass, scouting out the trail, and no doubt looking for dangerous ambush spots. Boy, are they about to get a surprise.

"Wait until they are farther up the pass so none of them can escape," I said as we watched the slow stealthy progress of the troops below. As soon as the scouting party below had reached the point of no return, I turned to one of the troopers Valik had picked out, and said.

"Mr. Damon, if you would do us the honor of being the first to dispatch a group of enemy soldiers," I said as I handed him the drum batons. He just smiled as he took the batons, and then started a slow, steady drum roll.

The first to notice something wrong were the horses. The horses started to fidget, and then to buck wildly, throwing some of the soldiers from their backs. Next you could see some of the soldiers grabbing at their ears and trying to tear off their helmets, and all the while you could see rocks starting to roll off the mountainside above them. Some of the soldiers tried to gain control of their horses and turn to flee, but the pressure building inside their heads made them lose their balance, and while still trying to cover their ears, they were bucked off of their panic stricken horses. Soon, an entire slab of the cliff face above the dying soldiers sheared of, crashing down into the pass, burying horses and soldiers alike.

Mr. Damon had already stopped the drum roll when the mountain came crashing down, which was okay, since the deed had already been accomplished. We all stood in awe as two lone horses scampered back down the pass. We watched them go until all of a sudden, Mara spoke up.

"Look, down below, more soldiers."

Apparently another, larger contingent of soldiers were coming up to secure the pass until they heard the landslide above, and possibly some of the odd sonic vibrations emitted by the Horn of Gideon. No matter, they were in full retreat back down the slope to the valley below. It would take a few days for them to get enough courage to come back up the pass, and even longer to clear enough debris to bring their army through. That will be enough to buy us the time we need to prepare for war. We had drawn first blood, and now it was time to get back to the castle.

"That should slow them down a bit, but I wish we could have gotten a crack at those other troops," I said as I broke the trance.

"Let's get this stuff loaded up and get back to the castle. Besides, I'm starving. Is anyone else hungry?"

Everyone agreed they were starving, since in all the excitement of the day, no one had eaten since this morning. As soon as we were done securing the

Horn of Gideon back on the craft, we brought out the bags of food and water that Balon had prepared for us and we sat down and ate greedily. When we were done, I turned this time to Mr. Damon, and said.

"Mr. Damon, It's your turn to control the craft for the trip back to the mountain entrance. I want everyone to learn how to fly this craft like they were born to it, which you never know, because you may very well have been."

Climbing aboard, Mr. Damon took the controls, and as though he had done this all his life, he worked the levers like a pro, flipping the magnets into place, opening the shutters, and gliding the craft back down the steep slope from the peak and back down through the Valley of the Dragons, past the area where we tested the Dragon's Fire weapon, then hugging the overhang cliff face past the castle, past the suicide' troopers who were with Captain Sardon, and then right up to the secret doorway to the mountain, all the while with my dragons circling high overhead, nearly out of our sight, but with us well within their sight, watching over our well being like guardian angels.

As we approached the wall of the cliff, Mr. Damon slowed the craft to a halt, and then closed the shutters. We all looked at each other in amazement, and nodded to each other.

"Excellent job, Mr. Damon," I said, "I think we've found our pilot. Are you sure you've never been on one of these crafts before, because you sure took naturally to this one."

"Thank you my Lord," he responded, "but I've never even seen one before today. It just felt so natural to me, like I knew exactly what I was doing, I can't explain it."

I think I can," Mara spoke up, "I think we've found another long lost Atlantean, so welcome back Mr. Damon." Mr. Damon was grinning from ear to ear.

"Balon, my friend," I said, nearly startling the poor man, who looked at me like he had done something wrong.

"It's your turn to drive, take us inside, and back to the cathedral."

"Are you sure about this Ethan?" He stammered. "You could really let someone else do it you know, I won't mind." He was really acting nervous about this, but I needed him to learn.

"Balon, my friend," I explained, "you and I spend a lot of time together, and if I get hurt in battle, I may need you to get me back to the safety of my castle if no one else is around, or in case they have all fallen in battle, so, I need you to do this for me. We are only going to be moving on the magnets alone, so there's no way you can get into trouble. Now, take the controls while I open the doors."

Reluctantly, Balon did as he was instructed, with more than just himself looking a bit nervous, but, with the shutters closed over the crystals, we would only be able to crawl along at a walking pace. He would do fine.

I jumped down from the craft, and opened the heavy stone door, waving for Balon to move on through, while Mara stood by his side to coach him through. Balon tilted the lever forward, and, after nearly running me over, and bouncing off the doorway, he was safely inside. Closing the door, I climbed back on the craft, and we resumed our lurching, sometimes bouncing off the wall ascent back to the main cathedral, that is, as soon as Balon remembered to turn on the lights to see where we were going.

Once we were safely back inside the cathedral, Valik and his troopers jumped off the craft, and kneeling down, they kissed the ground, saying they didn't think they were going to survive.

"Very funny," Balon said as he pulled the lever to flip the magnets, allowing the craft to settle down on its legs.

"Not bad, my friend," I said, "we'll keep working on it. Let's just leave the craft parked right here, since we'll be using it again soon to check on the Gog army. Now, light a couple of torches while I turn off the lights, it's time to get back to the surface."

The long walk back up the pathway to the castle was again spent in silence, each person pondering on the things they had seen and done this day. Mara and I held hands as we walked; enjoying the companionship and love we shared for each other. As soon as we reached the top, I checked the peephole to make sure there was no one in the hallway before I opened the doorway. Seeing that the hallway was clear, I opened the door, while the torches were stuck into the sand to extinguish them, and as soon as everyone was through, I closed the heavy stone door.

Moving several yards away from the door, I stopped everyone to make plans for tomorrow, telling each one to meet again in the morning for a briefing on the plans for the day. Speaking to Mr. Valik, I said.

"Mr. Valik, please survey the troops stationed here in the castle, I want to know who we can trust, and who we can't, who will stand with us, and who might be against us. Then, I want you and your handpicked men to keep a close eye on Captain Sardon. I don't want any more surprises from that one, understand."

"Yes, my Lord," He replied, "it shall be done." All three troopers bowed, turned sharply, and headed up the stairway to the castle above.

Turning to Mara and Balon, I said. "Let's stop to speak to the dragons before we go up, I want to know what they thought about the events of the day, if that is okay. Both nodded their approval.

We climbed the stairs to the next level and then started down the hall towards the dragon pens. It was obvious that they knew we were coming, because they had their noses pressed up against the metal gate to the hallway. They must have flew directly back to their roosts when they knew we were back inside of the mountain. It would seem that since Mara arrived, their psychic senses have turned on to a degree I had never seen before, and it was almost eerie.

Drawing up to the gate, Mara reached in to pat the dragons on their noses while Balon opened the gate. The dragons immediately backed up to let us in like they had developed real manners. In reality, they had a respect for Mara that was uncanny. They accepted her as an equal.

It seemed almost immediately that the telepathic images from the dragons started filling our minds, coming so fast it was nearly overwhelming. There were mixed emotions coming from the dragons, they were amazed at our flying machine, thrilled about the ambush of the dreaded Gog troopers in the Talon Pass, but quite disturbed about the new weaponry they had seen displayed today. I got the inner feeling that the dragons were starting to realize their own mortality.

For as long as anyone could remember, dragons were the Lords of the earth, unstoppable, and undefeatable. Occasionally, one by one, man has found a way to kill them, if only by pure luck. Now, within just days, two more of their kind have been killed, and now it would seem, weapons existed that could literally make them extinct in a matter of days. It was all very disturbing to them.

Now it was my turn to communicate back to them, most of the time with my voice, but filling in with thoughts that I hope conveyed my true being. I started out by telling them how much I have cherished their friendship and loyalty all these years, and how ashamed I was for neglecting them during my recent years of self-indulgence. Then I told them how much I was going to need them in the coming days to defeat the Gog army, but, when the battle was done, that they were free to go wherever they desired, hopefully to find mates so their species could continue to propagate

I explained to them that I didn't plan on there being many of the Gog culture left alive after the battle to threaten the dragon species any longer, and furthermore, I didn't plan on King Malok being in power when this was through either. The King was a worthless, lazy, fat slob who was going to let his own people perish out of arrogance, and stupidity. He would never again be in control of my people, or the dragons, or myself. We would all be free, free to live our lives how we saw fit.

The dragons stood before me, stoic, regal, and sad. They didn't know what to make of the concept of freedom; they hadn't realized that they were not free until now, for they had never known life any other way but the one they were living now. It would get some getting used to, but they had never before ventured beyond their territorial boundaries. I sense they have always desired to see what was beyond, but they also knew that danger, and death awaited them beyond our borders. But soon that would change, soon the blight upon the earth that is the Gog will cease to exist, and once their vast army is defeated, the rest of the peoples of the earth will swallow the remnants of them up. The Gog will never again be strong enough to wage war upon the inhabitants of the earth, be it human, or dragon.

Now, I bid the dragons good night, giving each one a hug around their strong necks, telling them to rest, because the battle draws close. The next few days are going to be busy with preparation. Mara and Balon both gave the dragons a hug, and then we locked the gate, and went up the remaining stairs to the villa. At the top of the stairs, I asked.

"Shall we get something to eat, because I'm starving?"

Mara and Balon both agreed that they were hungry too, so off we went to the kitchen. Entering the kitchen, two of the kitchen helpers were sitting down, apparently waiting for us. Both rose, and bowed as we entered, saying that Marta had instructed them to tend to our needs upon our return, and that they had prepared food and drink for us. When I asked where Marta was, they said she was tired, and had retired to her chambers for the evening and did not wish to be disturbed, but that she would see us in the morning. I think I understand what the problem is, and I will honor her request not to be bothered tonight.

The food was brought to us along with herbal tea, and we devoured the food as though we hadn't eaten in days. Balon finished his food quickly, and then asked to take his leave, that he too was very tired from the excitement of the day. We both bid him good night, and he went on his way. Finishing our meal, I said to Mara.

"Let's go to our chambers, I have something else to show you."

It was weird saying our' chambers, because I had never shared my chambers with anyone for more than a night or two, and now I was entertaining the notion of sharing the rest of my life with this woman. It all felt so natural, like it was preordained, which I'm sure that it was.

Taking Mara by the hand, I led her back to our chambers, and once inside, I locked the door behind us so as not to be disturbed. Leading her to the bedroom, I moved the nightstand to reveal the secret compartment hidden underneath, took out the old key, and unlocked the two large padlocks that secured the door to my secret room. Grabbing a lit candle, I went inside to light the oil lamp on the heavy wooden table, and as the light engulfed the room, the sight to behold was jar upon jar of herbs, plants, and colored powders, along with preserved specimens of small creatures, some of which have never been seen before, or since.

Mara's eyes lit up like a child with a new toy when she saw the pharmacy before her. She entered the room slowly, looking around to take it all in, picking up a dusty jar here and there to examine its contents, commenting more to herself than to me, but in general, she was amazed and delighted with the abundance and variety. Finally, she spoke to me.

"This is the best and most complete collection of old world cures and remedies I've ever seen, or even heard of, at least outside of Atlantis. Where did they all come from?" she asked. "You know that a lot of these compounds have disappeared from the earth, and that some of these specimens are also extinct. This is absolutely incredible."

As she continued to look around, I explained what I knew about how I came into possession of these marvels.

"Some of these herbs of course are still around if you know where and when to look for them, while others were gathered by my father before he died. Some of these were gathered locally, while still others were gathered by my father in the land of the Gog, when he was searching for dragon eggs. Then there were some of these herbs, potions, and specimens that were gathered by my grandfather, and some that I heard were brought here by the old wizard, which I now know was your great grandfather, making them a product that would only have been found on the island of Atlantis, which is now long gone."

"Do you know what all of them are for?" asked Mara.

"Most of them," I replied, "but not all of them, how about you, do you have knowledge of herbs and potions?"

"But of course," she replied, "I studied them exclusively at the Library of Knowledge and Enlightenment; it is one of my favorite subjects. There will come a time when the world will hunger for the study of cures, potions, and herbs. Right now, it's still feared by a lot of people, uneducated people who are afraid of what they don't understand, but that won't always be the case. There will be some dark times between now and then, when this knowledge will actually carry a death sentence, so it's important that our knowledge is passed down from generation to generation, and pharmacies such as this are preserved, hidden away from the ignorant and the non caring."

"Do you think these things should be moved down into the secret caverns?" I asked.

"Yes I do," Mara replied, "there are only a few collections this complete left in the world, and it would be a tragedy to lose even one of them."

"So there are other collections?" I asked.

"Yes," Mara said, "the biggest one of course is in the Library of Knowledge and Enlightenment, along with copies of the books you have stored in the cavern below, and many more. In fact, all knowledge, from throughout the world, up to the present time, is documented, catalogued, and stored within the walls of the library."

"Where is this library?" I asked.

"It is in the land of the great river," she began, "and hidden beneath the paws of the great beast."

"Why are you speaking in riddles?" I asked, "for I have held nothing back from you."

"I'm sorry Ethan," she replied, "I'm only speaking the way I was taught to respond when asked about the Library. The land where the Library resides as yet has no name. It is in the land first visited by the beings from another world, the land by the great river."

"And what about the great beast you spoke of?" I asked.

"The great beast," she began, "is a great stone beast, carved in honor of the visitors who gave us so much of the knowledge we possess today. Beneath its paws is a secret, underground library containing all the books, manuscripts, potions, powders, and knowledge of all mankind, as well as some knowledge passed down to us from the beings who live beyond the stars."

"When you speak about beings from beyond the stars, do you mean the same ones you mentioned who were from another world?" I asked.

"Yes I do," she responded. "It is rumored that beings from beyond the stars came to our land of Atlantis when we were still nothing more than animals ourselves. Over the eons, they nurtured our species, caring for us, teaching us, and visiting our land, often at first, then only occasionally, and then not at all. We never knew what became of them, but every once in awhile you hear of someone who thought they had seen strange lights in the sky, perhaps it was the beings checking up on us. Maybe one day they will come back to visit us, when we need them again."

"I would like to one day visit this land you speak of." I said, looking around at the small collection that I had so cherished all of these years. The Library Mara speaks of must be enormous, and quite wonderful.

"Once this conflict here is resolved," Mara said as she walked up to me, wrapping her arms around me, then, looking me in the eyes, she continued, "I will take you to see this marvelous place, and together, we will learn all the secrets of the universe."

"I would like that," I said, as I kissed her.

"Let's go to bed," she said, "it's been a long day, and I'm getting tired."

"Sounds good," I replied. "Now let me turn off the lantern, and then tomorrow we'll gather all of these things into baskets and have the men return them back to the caverns where they will be safe. You go ahead to bed. I'll finish here, lock up, and meet you there."

Looking around one last time, I felt a renewed appreciation for the items within this room, and for the knowledge that they represented. I blew out the lantern, closed the door behind me and locked up, replacing the key in the compartment under the nightstand, then replacing the nightstand.

Mara was already in bed, so I blew out the candles and slipped under the covers, feeling her warm, silky nakedness beside me. Life was good right now, even with the dangers that loomed ahead. I felt more alive now than I have all my life. Wrapping my arms around Mara, I pulled her over on top of me and kissed her longingly.

"Five, four, three, two, one," SNAP.

Chapter 7

"Oh man, doc, you sure know how to mess up a good dream," I said as I looked around the home of Dr. Miller. "Things were just about to get interesting."

"Now Henry, there's always next week," he said, furiously jotting things down on his notepad. "There was some very interesting information in this week's session, don't you think? These weapons you described like that sonic weapon, and the Dragons Breath, now that one is probably a precursor to the laser of today, and the sonic weapon, the Horn of Gideon, that sounds remarkably similar to the technique the Israelites used to bring down the walls of Jericho. Their technique was a little simpler, and took days instead of seconds, but the idea was the same, and after thousands of years, I'm surprised the technique could be revived at all. I would have to say that someone was reincarnated from a time that had witnessed just such a weapon. It is just so interesting, I can't wait to hear more next week, but for now, our time is up, so I'll see you at the same time next week."

"Sounds good doctor," I said as I stood to leave, shaking his hand as I left. He followed me to the door, so he could invite his next client in, who was waiting outside by the front gate. The client looked as anxious to get started as I had been. I nodded to the fellow as I walked past to my car, and said.

"Happy journey," at which the man responded.

"Thank you, I certainly will," and inside he went with Dr. Miller.

As I walked to my car, it seemed like it was a more beautiful day than I had remembered before I entered Dr. Miller's house. It was definitely hot out, but everything just seemed more pleasant. It's hard to explain, but I think knowing your own past, knowing your strengths and weaknesses, and knowing what mistakes you've made, gives you a sense of peace and empowerment in the present.

I drove back down the valley, reliving once again the things I had experienced in the hypnotic state, applying what I had learned while I was asleep, and trying to compare those visions with what drives my personality in the present, and it all makes sense, my likes and dislikes, my fears and strengths. What amazes me the most is the fact that so many people who are close to you, seem to follow you through each sojourn. We really are tied together on the metaphysical level.

As I approached the fireworks booth, it was obvious that it was very busy, with customers lined up across the entire front of the booth. It looks like I got here none too soon, as my mom and Scott looked frazzled. I quickly parked my truck and hurried into the booth, waiting on the first customer I came up to. Mom and Scott looked relieved to see me. We waded through the customers fairly quickly, and at the first lull, I told my mom she could go home, and thanked her for the help. I felt sorry for her as she hobbled back to her car to drive the fifteen miles home, because she looked exhausted.

One thing about working in a fireworks booth is that it is really hard on the feet and legs. You are on your feet for twelve to fourteen hours at a time when it gets busy, and you are standing on a wooden floor. If you don't have good shoes on, you can literally be limping by the end of a busy day.

As soon as my mom had left, and we had an extended break, I told Scott about my session with Dr Miller and the events I had experienced while under hypnosis, including the exotic weapons, and what those weapons might represent today. It was amazing that a culture so many thousands of years ago could have a technology as advanced as it seemed to have been. It would seem that cultures come and go, along with their knowledge and technology, only to be rediscovered, or reinvented thousands of years later. I suppose the same will be said about our culture in a few thousand years when someone finds some of our devices, only to wonder what they could have been used for. I'm sure some of the things we have nowadays will totally baffle our distant offspring of the future. Maybe it will take a hypnotherapist in the future to decipher early versions of what they are using in their time, even if they think the people of old were too dumb to know of such things. The Bible tells us that there is nothing new under the sun, and what has been, will be again. That verse can have a lot of applications.

Scott listened to me with great interest, though he did seem a little too tired to get a good grasp on everything I told him. The rest of the evening was a steady flow of customers, trying to get their fireworks before the mad rush that was going to come in the next couple of days. There were only three more days until the fourth of July, and the selection gets pretty scarce as it draws closer to the fourth. There are always a huge percentage of fireworks buyers who wait until the living end to buy their fireworks, and then they complain when we don't have a decent selection left. Nearly seventy percent of our total business is done in the last three days of the fireworks season, as compared to the first seven days, so it can get pretty intense those last few days.

When Dee didn't show up at her regular time, I started to get a little concerned, and if it hadn't been for the fact that we were quite busy, I would have been totally stressed out. As it got closer to quitting time, I mentioned to Scott that I might have to drive out to Dee's house after we closed to make sure she was okay. Then, just as we were locking up for the night, Dee's car pulled up out front, and my heart began to race with excitement, but she did not immediately get out of her car. When she didn't get out of the car, I turned to Scott and said.

"Lock up for me Scott. I'm going out to see what's up with Dee."

"You got it," he said, and began to secure the booth.

Walking up to the car, I could see Dee inside, head lowered, with tears falling down her face. I tapped on the window, and she opened her door, quickly trying to wipe her face, but not having much luck. She stepped out of her car and grabbed a hold of me, burying her face in my chest.

"What's wrong?" I asked, wondering what could have happened.

Between sobs, she managed to say, "Mike came by the house today and was acting crazy, screaming at me, calling me a cheat, and threatening me."

"What do you mean when you say that he threatened you?" I asked, ready to go out and find the S.O.B. right now.

"He's crazy Henry, he said if he couldn't have me, no one would, and then he said he would deal with you too. I'm scared of what he might do, and I'm afraid for my kids, what am I going to do?"

Stroking her hair, I lifted her chin to look into her eyes, and said.

"Let me worry about Mike, I'll take care of him quite soon my love, and I know just where to find him. I won't deal with him tonight, but tomorrow he's due for a big surprise. As for tonight, how about I come to your house for the night, just in case he tries to pay you another visit. We could even leave my truck here tonight, and you can drop me off back here on your way to work in the morning."

"That would be wonderful Henry," she said, looking up at me with those beautiful eyes, "I would definitely feel safer with you there tonight."

"Just let me finish up here Doll, and then I'll let Scott know what's going on."

I turned and walked back to the booth, glancing over toward the store to see if I could see Mike hiding in the shadows. I could not see him, but I could see what looked like a bicycle tire visible. I continued on into the booth as though nothing was out of the ordinary. Once inside the booth, I spoke to Scott.

"Scott," I said, "I'm going to spend the night at Dee's house. It seems Mike is threatening her, and me, so I'm going to hang out there in case he shows up. Won't that be a surprise? Meanwhile, I want you to take the cash box home, and then meet me here in the morning before you go to work."

"Okay," Scott said, a little apathetic at first.

"One more thing," I said to Scott, "I'm going to leave my truck here, so that it's not parked outside of her house in case he does show up. But, I don't want him to see me get into Dee's car, so, as soon as you leave, drive straight toward the corner of the store so he has to take off and escape. Then, I'll jump into Dee's car, and we'll be gone."

"How will you make it back here in the morning?" Scott asked.

"Dee will drop me off here on her way to work in the morning."

"Sounds like a good plan, so, I'll see you in the morning," he said as we locked the doors and windows.

I walked out to Dee's car and stood by her door until Scott got into his truck and started driving toward the dark corner where Mike likes to hide. The results were immediate, first the bicycle tire disappeared, and the headlights from Scott's truck as he drove by the corner revealed the lot was empty. It was now time for us to make our escape too.

Dee scooted over to the passenger seat and asked. "Would you drive please Henry, I don't feel up to it?"

"You bet," I said, sliding into the drivers' seat, with Dee snuggling up close to me as I drove, holding my arm tight. Dee lives about three miles south of town, so if Mike did wish to show up at Dee's house, he would have to ride his bike a long ways in the dark, making him tired and vulnerable if he wanted to cause any trouble.

We arrived at Dee's house, and went inside. Dee fixed us each a drink, and we sat on the couch together, listening to soft music, and holding each other close while we sipped our drinks. After a short time, Dee stood, took me by the hand, and led me to the bedroom, where we made love until the wee hours of the morning, sharing a sense of need, mixed with a sense of danger, making the sexual experience even more intense. We were so exhausted that if Mike had showed up, I don't think we would have heard him even if he had beat on the side of the house. In fact, the next thing we knew, Dee's son knocked on the bedroom door, telling Dee it was time to get up for work. From then on, it was a mad house of frenzied activity, with Dee getting ready for work, her kids wondering how I had gotten there, and I wondering what had happened to my life in the last few weeks.

Dee got ready quickly, and we were off to town, dropping her daughter off at her ex's house, and then dropping me off at the fireworks booth, where Scott already had the sales windows open for business. Kissing Dee goodbye, I asked her if I would see her again tonight, at which she replied.

"Of course, you can't keep me away now Henry. Besides that, you know that I'm totally in love with you."

Before she left, I said to her. "Could you make arrangements for the kids to spend the night without you, so you could come and spend the night at my house?"

"I think I can arrange that," she said, saying her daughter could stay at her dad's house, and her son would probably love to spend the night with a friend. She said she would call and make the arrangements from work today, and then see me at lunch. A quick kiss and she was off to work.

Joining Scott in the fireworks booth, I apologized for being late, and thanked him for having the booth open for business. He said he got bored while he was waiting so he decided to open up, which was a good idea since he'd already had a couple of customers. It was going to be a very busy day, but he said he would have to go mow a few lawns before it got hot. I told him to go ahead, but to come back as soon as possible. He assured me that he would, and off he went.

As I sat waiting between customers I thought about the days of dragons, about Mara, about Dee, and about the recent problem with Mike. He seems just unstable enough to be dangerous, and that made me nervous. I definitely didn't trust him, and I'm afraid a confrontation is in our future, so I must always be on guard.

Time went by pretty fast waiting on customers and the next thing I knew, it was nearly 1:00 pm, and Scott was just pulling into the parking lot. He looked hot and tired, so I handed him a soda as soon as he walked in. About fifteen minutes later, Dee pulled in for her lunch break, and I offered her a soda also, which she gladly accepted. It stayed pretty busy so I wasn't able to visit with her as much as I wanted, but enough to know that she was feeling a little better about this thing with Mike.

Under normal circumstances, you wouldn't dwell on a past relationship for too long, but these are not normal circumstances. If Mike really is Sardon from the past, he tried to murder one or both of us then, and has probably tried many times throughout history. Given a history like that, there would be a good chance that he would try to do it again. Even though Dee is feeling better about it, I don't share her sense of security. Something in the back of my mind is nagging at me, causing my personal danger alarm to sound, and only time itself will tell the tale, only time.

Dee's lunch break was over way too fast, so I walked her out to her car, but before she headed out, I said to her.

"I can't wait to take you home with me tonight, I feel just like I was back in high school again. The house is a little empty of furnishings right now, but I still have the essentials, like the hot tub, and the bed of course."

Dee gave me a lustful look, and said. "Henry, you're incorrigible, you have a one track mind."

"Yeah, so what if I do?" I said as I gave her a kiss to go. "I'll see you tonight.

"Okay," she said, "but, I need to run home first and get a few cloths for tomorrow, and some sexy lingerie for tonight, then I'll be down to help you out."

"Yeehaw," I said with a holler, "I won't be able to think about anything else all day now, so thanks a bunch." With that, she threw me that sexy look one more time, and drove away. As I turned around to walk back to the booth, Scott just looked at me like I had lost my marbles.

"What?" I asked, lifting my hands in fake bewilderment. Scott just shook his head and went back to stocking shelves before the next rush.

The rest of the afternoon was busy, with a steady stream of customers coming up to buy the myriad assortment of colorful fountains, mortars, and firecrackers. When I did have some down time, all I could think about was Dee in her lingerie; it was very distracting. At one point as I was zoning out, Scott told me to snap out of it and get back to work. All I could do was smile back at him.

"I'll spend the night at my own house tonight," Scott began, "that way the two of you can have a romantic evening alone, and then I'll meet you back here in the morning. Since the last two days are going to be crazy, I'm going to skip lawn mowing. Otherwise there would be no way for you to keep up with sales while I was gone. Also, maybe Dee could help out on the fourth, since she should have the day off."

"That sounds like a great idea Scott," I stated, "I'll ask her tonight."

The rest of the afternoon was busy and before I knew it, Dee had arrived to help out, and since it was busy, she jumped right in to help. Of course, having her there in the booth, and thinking about her coming to my house for the night, had me totally distracted. I really had to concentrate on what I was doing so I wouldn't give someone the wrong change. Dee just made things worse by teasing me all evening, brushing up against me, winking at me, and giving me quick, sultry smiles when I would look her way. It was driving me crazy, and by the time it was time to close down for the night I was a basket case.

After bidding Scott good night, this time, to give Mike a good show, which we knew was hiding in the shadows of the store, we left Dee's car at the booth. She grabbed her overnight bag from her car, got into my vehicle, and then the two of us drove off together. Meanwhile, Scott did the drive by past the store to run him off. Who knows, maybe it's foolhardy to mess with the guy like this, but again, only time will tell.

The drive to my home in Victor was playful, almost causing us to go off the road, so by the time we got there; we were ready to jump each other's bones. But, we forced ourselves to go slow to prolong the pleasure of each other's company. First, we soaked in the hot tub for a half an hour or so, sipping on wine, and looking at the stars between kisses and groping. Then, after a shower, I was sitting on the couch with a glass of wine when Dee came back down the stairs wearing some very sexy lingerie, doing a pirouette before me to show off. My mouth was hanging open like an idiot and all I could say was.

"Oh my God Dee, you are so beautiful."

She held her hand out to me, which I took into my own, stood up, and she led me upstairs to the bedroom, and what a glorious night it was.

A woman's scream jolted me out of a sound sleep, and I bolted upright in bed, sweat pouring down my brow. Looking around the room, the sun was shining, the birds were chirping loudly, and Dee was sleeping quietly beside me. That dream, the woman screaming, I'd had that dream again. It had been quite awhile since I had that dream, and I was hoping that I wouldn't have it again, now that I was going to the hypnotherapist. I guess that was wishful thinking since we really haven't reached the point in my sessions to find out definitively who the girl was, and exactly what had happened to her. So, I guess until I deal with it in one of my hypnosis sessions, I'll continue to have the dreams. Well, it was time to get up anyhow, and I still need to get Dee back to town in time for work.

Leaning over, I kissed Dee on the cheek, which caused her to smile, and open her eyes ever so slightly. She put her arms around my neck and kissed me deeply, saying.

"It is so wonderful to wake up to you like this Henry, I could really get used to this."

As she tried to pull me down on top of her I had to resist, and say.

"Hold on my love, we don't have time for that. We need to get you back to town in time for work, no matter how much I want to take you up on the offer, so get up, and I'll make coffee."

Dee had a pouty look on her face, and then she smiled with a totally lustful look and said.

"I have an idea, let's take a shower together, and then we can make love, and shower at the same time."

"Why that's a marvelous idea," I said, and that's exactly what we did, awkward, slippery, and absolutely wonderful, not to mention time energy saving.

I made a pot of coffee while Dee got ready for work, then we grabbed a couple of travel mugs of coffee for the road, and headed for town. Pulling into the Parking lot, Scott was already there, and had the booth open for business.

"It's about time you two showed up," Scott said, "I was beginning to think I was going to have to do this job all by myself today. And by the way, you two are glowing like the sun; you must have had a good night."

"Yeah," I replied, "and an equally great morning." Dee shot me a lustful glance, and said.

"I need to get to work boys. I'll see you at lunch time." And with that she got into her car and drove away, throwing me a kiss as she went. All I could do was smile as she drove away. I just stood there staring until Scott broke the spell.

"Hello, earth to Henry, it's time to go to work here, we need restock from the storage unit. If you think you can concentrate on your business long enough, I'll run to the storage unit for more fireworks, and by the way, we left all the cash here last night, what would have happened if someone had broken in?"

Now the spell was definitely broken. I need to get a grip here, how could

I have been so stupid. Thinking with the wrong head, that's how I can be so stupid.

"You're right Scott," I said sheepishly, "I need to concentrate on my business, there's only two days left, so thank you. I'll watch the booth while you get some supplies, and Scott, help keep me in line from here on out, especially with the cash box at the end of the day, I can't be losing my head now."

"You got it," Scott said as he headed to his truck, "And I'll hurry back, anything else you need while I'm out?"

"Yeah," I replied, "how about picking me up a breakfast sandwich, I'm starving."

"Will do," he said, "I could use one myself. I'll see you in about forty five minutes."

He drove away in his truck, and I sat down to wait for the first customer, and I didn't have long to wait. In fact, I stayed quite busy, enough so that I didn't realize the time had went by so fast, and before I knew it Scott was back with supplies, and none too soon, because we were running out of things quickly.

Between rushes of customers, we hurriedly ate our breakfast, restocked the shelves, and had sat down for only a few moments, when Dee pulled up. The morning had zipped by so fast. I sent Scott to a local fast food joint to pick us up burgers and fries, and while he was gone, Dee helped me with customers. When Scott returned, we let Dee eat while we worked so she could get back to work on time. Scott and I could eat anytime between rushes. I hadn't really even gotten to talk to Dee before she had to leave, except for a few stolen pets when I could sneak one in. Sometimes the teasing makes it more fun later. As Dee was ready to leave, she gave me a quick kiss, and said.

"Thanks for the lunch Henry, it was interesting."

"I'm sorry it wasn't a little more romantic," I replied as I walked her to her car, "but I need to make money now so we can play later."

It's okay, I understand," she said, "I actually enjoyed myself, plus it's just nice to be near you, even if it is in a work setting."

"Thanks, I feel the same way," I said. "Are you going to stop by tonight?"

"Of course," she responded, "as soon as I pick up the kids, and get them some dinner, then we'll be down. I'll see you this evening."

"See you then," I said, "and thank you for the incredible night last night."

I leaned through the window and kissed her goodbye, and watched as she drove away. By then, a couple more cars had pulled in and it was time to go back to work. The afternoon was steady, and as evening approached, it continued to get busier and busier. Dee showed up about eight with the kids, and it was so busy that I had her help us out. I gave her kids some fireworks to light off in the parking lot to keep them busy while Dee helped out.

It stayed busy until about ten, at which time Dee said she really had to get the kids home, so I gave her a quick hug, and a short kiss goodbye. She doesn't have to work tomorrow, so she said she would be down to help. Besides, I always buy pizza and beer on the night of the fourth as we finish up sales, then we watch the big night display put on at the fairgrounds, which is only a few hundred yards from our booth. Besides the display going on at the fairgrounds, the whole parking lot around my fireworks booth will be ablaze with private fireworks shows, and it is truly an amazing sight. It is by far the most exciting night of my year, every year.

We closed the booth about eleven, more out of exhaustion than lack of customers. Tomorrow will be the biggest sale day of the season, and it will be busy, so we need to get home, get some rest, and be back here bright and early in the morning. I have a feeling deep inside that tomorrow will be an exciting day. I had no idea how right I would be.

Closing up the booth and securing it, we left Scott's truck at the booth, and took mine home. Glancing in the direction of the shadow area of the store, there was no sign of Mike, or his bike, so maybe he finally got the hint and gave up. I'm too tired to worry about him right now anyhow, and by the time we got home, all we could manage to do was go straight to our rooms and go to bed. Tomorrow would come way too soon, and, sure enough, morning came way too soon.

After a pot of coffee, we headed for town, stopping at the storage unit and picking up as much of the remaining fireworks as we could load on the truck. Today will be too busy to make a run back here for restock, so we took as much as we could haul. A quick stop at the fast food place for breakfast sandwiches, and we were off to the booth.

As soon as we opened for business, the customers started to arrive, since it was a day off for most everyone. Dee showed up about noon, and her kids occupied themselves with fireworks, and then went off to browse in the department store. Business stayed brisk, and about 6pm I ordered pizzas to be delivered, and sent Scott to get plenty of beer. The big party was about to begin, and the excitement was building in the air. You could start to hear a rising crescendo of fireworks going off all over the city, as the evening progressed. Now is the time when my heart starts to race, and my pulse quickens. I dearly love fireworks, and my time has arrived.

As evening approaches, I take a few packs of firecrackers out on the parking lot and light them off, a whole pack at a time. The effect is contagious, and everyone within earshot starts to do the same thing, which of course is good for business. As night falls, the explosions increase in frequency and intensity, with rockets and mortars bursting in the air. You can smell the burnt gunpowder, and you can feel the electricity in the air. Soon, a huge cannon shot at the fairgrounds signaled the beginning of the show and we all migrated out of the booth to get a clear view of the night sky over the fairgrounds. The night display was just starting to reach its apex.

Dee and I were outside of the booth, standing side by side, holding hands, and enjoying the show. It was kind of chilly tonight, so we both had our coats on. Sometime during the noise and chaos of the show, I felt a tug against the side of my jacket, and a red-hot burn along my side by my armpit. At first I thought perhaps a stray firework had hit my coat, which has happened more than once over the years in this parking lot. Fireworks are notoriously infamous for going astray on occasion, so I really wasn't too concerned until I checked my coat to see if it had gotten burned, and that's when I saw it, a neat little round hole through the side of my jacket, 'a bullet hole.'

Immediately, I turned to look back toward the shadows of the store where Mike is usually lurking, and as I turned, I pulled Dee with me, almost knocking her to the ground in my haste. She gave me a look of anger for a second until she noticed the deep concern on my face.

"Get into the booth!" I yelled over the noise and confusion. "I think I've just been shot, hurry, and get into the safety of the booth."

We both ducked our heads and raced to the safety of the fireworks booth where Scott was still inside waiting on customers. As soon as he seen our faces, he knew something was wrong. Dee's kids were sitting on the counter watching the show, and she immediately called them off the counter to hide behind the wall.

"What's wrong?" he asked, "you look like you've seen a ghost."

"I nearly did see a ghost," I said, "I almost saw my own ghost. I think I've been shot."

"You mean by a stray firework?" Scott asked.

"No," I replied, panic still in my voice, "I mean by a real bullet, from a real gun. I think it came from Mike's favorite hiding spot. I need to call 911."

I quickly pulled off my jacket, and held it up to the light to view the perfect little bullet hole through my nice leather jacket. Now I was pissed off, I paid a lot of money for that jacket.

"My god Henry, you're bleeding," Dee shouted, panic in her voice.

I looked down at my tee shirt, and sure enough, a large bloodstain was evident on the side of my shirt. I felt my face go pale, thinking maybe I was bleeding more inside than out, but when I raised my shirt, it was evident that the bullet had only left a short, three inch furrow along my side below the armpit, an almost clean miss, almost that is.

"That was too close for comfort," I said, trying to be lighthearted about it, but inside I was feeling a little ill.

The customer Scott had been waiting on was white as a ghost also, and then a look of dread came over his face as he realized his family was in the parking lot watching the display, and the realization that there was a mad man was loose with a gun. He immediately dropped his fireworks and ran off; grabbing his kids, and hustling his wife into their car, tires screeching as he drove out of the parking lot.

Meanwhile, I got on the phone to 911, and told them I had been shot, where I was, and who might have done it. Well, that started a panic within the town, as six police cars came screaming into the parking lot from every direction. Dee pointed to the dark corner Mike had been hiding in by the store, and several of the cops drew their weapons and raced off to secure the area. Other police and sheriff vehicles were arriving now, and sealed off the entire parking lot, with all of the fourth of July revelers still inside, which pretty much put an end to the party.

Once the area was secured, and there was no sign of the gunman, the ambulance was allowed in to check on me. I told the police I was okay, but they wanted official documentation of my injury pending prosecution of the offender. Of course my partner Dan was on duty, and when he showed up, he just had to give me a hard time.

"I can't leave you on your own at all without you getting yourself in trouble," Dan said as he put a dressing over the wound. "So what sort of trouble are you into now?"

"Just an ex boyfriend kind of problem," I said, knowing well enough not to bring up any past life information, which would land me in the funny farm if the police officers heard about it.

One of the officers came up and said he needed me to be evaluated at the emergency room for official documentation, and then he needed to ask me a few questions. He was going to have to take my coat as evidence, but would return it in a few days after it was photographed, and tested for residue and such things. It's still summertime, and I shouldn't need it for a while, so I agreed.

I instructed Scott to close down the booth, secure the cash box, and meet me at the emergency room. Dee asked if she could ride with me in the ambulance, and since Dan was a mutual friend, he readily agreed. The officer in charge said he would make sure Scott was cleared from the scene as soon as he closed up and they interviewed him. Dee's children would ride down to the hospital with Scott.

The ride to the hospital was uneventful. It was odd to be on this side of the ambulance for a change, instead of being the caregiver. Dan asked how Dee had been, and asked how the hypnosis sessions had been going, so in the short trip to the hospital, I gave him as much information as I could remember, and he was totally amazed by what he heard, hanging on every word. Since we were already at the hospital, I told him I would fill him in more when I returned to work in a couple of days.

Inside the emergency room, I was an instant celebrity since I knew all of the doctors and nurses. Mostly I got more teasing than sympathy for having to come to the E.R. for such a minor scratch, and because the cause of my injury was from a jealous boyfriend. It wasn't long before the detective showed up to take mine, and Dee's statements. He told us they still hadn't found Mike, but that the shot had definitely came from the shadows of the store. They had found the empty shell casing right where Mike would have been. The detective said there would be an all points bulletin put out for Mike's arrest. By the time the detective was done with us, so was the doctor, who released me to go home. Scott and the kids were in the waiting room when Dee and I came out of the Emergency room.

"I think you guys all better spend the night at my house tonight just to be safe," I said, "at least until they find Mike. I have plenty of room, and besides, you don't have to work tomorrow. As soon as we get up in the morning and have a nice breakfast, I can bring you back home, and then Scott and I will get the booth cleaned out and tore down. What do you say?"

"Yes mom, please," Dee's daughter was the first to speak out.

"Yeah mom," replied her son.

Then it was Dee's turn to speak. "What can I say, of course we'll stay. but I don't have anything to wear; do you think it would be safe to stop by my house before we go to your house?"

"No," I replied, "I don't think it would be safe, at least not until the police find Mike." Then I whispered into her ear, so no one else could hear me. "Besides, my love, you won't be needing any cloths tonight." That's when she smacked me with the back of her hand, right on my wound, causing me to wince in pain.

"Oh my God," she said, "I'm sorry, I didn't mean to do that."

I grabbed her into my arms, pulled her close, and said. "Oh now that's going to cost you my love, just wait till I get you home."

Her daughter just giggled, and everyone else was smiling as we headed out to my truck for the ride home. It's a good thing I have an extended cab truck, because it looks like I'm going to need it, which suits me just fine. All of a sudden I have a ready-made family all over again, and it feels good.

By the time we got home, it was nearly 2am, and the kids were asleep in the back seat. Scott was awake in the passenger seat, but was being very quiet, deep in thought I'm sure, and Dee had her head leaning on my shoulder, with her eyes closed. I wasn't sure if she was asleep or not. When I pulled into the driveway, I announced our arrival to everyone, and even though it was dark, you could see enough of the house to tell it was a very nice house. Neither of Dee's kids had ever seen the place before, and Dee herself had only just seen the house the night before.

"Wow, cool house Henry," exclaimed Dee's daughter, as she jumped from the truck and ran to the door.

"Yeah, cool," responded her son, admiring the high peaks of the Victorian style roof as he walked up to the house.

"Your house is very beautiful," Dee said, still holding my arm as we walked up to the door. "You are very lucky to have such a nice place."

"Thank you," I said as I fumbled for my house key, placing it in the lock, turning the key, and letting the door swing open. Switching on the lights, there was an immediate gasp from the kids.

"Wow, look at this place, it's wonderful," her daughter again exclaimed.

"Take a look around," I said, placing my key on the counter. "Scott, show the kids to their rooms upstairs, and would you mind taking the new bedroom downstairs tonight."

"I don't mind at all," Scott replied, as he led the kids up the stairs.

"Would you like a drink before we go to bed?" I asked.

"After tonight," she responded, "I would love one."

"Would you like beer, wine, or a mixed drink?" I asked.

"I would like a mixed drink," she said without hesitation, "and the stronger, the better."

"You got it," I said. "Meet me out on the deck, and I'll bring one out for all of us."

While Dee went out to sit on the deck, I mixed drinks for Dee, Scott, and myself. By then, Scott and the kids had come back down stairs. It would seem that the kids were totally rejuvenated, so I told them to pick out a soda from the fridge, and meet us out back on the deck. I handed Scott his drink and took one out to Dee, and then I sat down beside her in the dark under the stars. Scott and the kids followed close behind.

"This is absolutely wonderful, Henry," Dee said, "except for the part about you getting shot I mean. It's wonderful and scary all at the same time. I could have lost you tonight, right when it seems that I had found you again after all these years. It seems that something bad always happens to us when we're together to split us up and keep us from being happy. I hope this was the end of that cycle, because I can't bear to lose you again, either by your death, or mine."

Dee held my arm tightly, and leaned her face onto my shoulder. The cool, wet moisture of a tear found its way to my skin, and I put my arm around her to comfort her. It would seem the events of the night, along with the total exhaustion of being up so late was starting to take its toll.

"Everything is okay right now, Dee," I said, "you have to live for the moment, and tomorrow will take care of itself, but for now, let's go to bed, I'm beat."

"Okay," she said, "kids, head for bed."

"And you too, Scott," I added, "since you're the biggest kid of all."

"You don't have to tell me twice," Scott said.

Everyone shuffled their way off to their respective rooms. As soon as Dee and I hit the bed it was obvious we were way too tired to make love, so we just held each other tight, and it wasn't long until we were both sound asleep.

The sounds of birds chirping woke me up as usual. The huge trees in my yard harbor a host of birds all summer long, and it would seem they do indeed get up early, whether it's to catch worms or not, I couldn't tell you. Usually I just get up when they do, but sometimes I shut the window so I don't have to listen to them. As for today, I let them sing, and I just lay there and listened to them. It's funny how a near death experience can change your outlook on things that you normally took for granted.

I was also aware of the wonderfully silky nakedness of the woman lying bedside me in bed right now, and it was more than I could stand, so I rolled over and started to caress the beautiful woman lying next to me.

"Oh, not now Henry, I'm tired," she said, in a less than convincing voice. But, with a little more caressing, she responded with earnest, and after a wildly passionate lovemaking session, Dee went back to sleep while I got up to take a shower.

After an exhilarating shower, I made a pot of coffee, poured myself a cup, poured the rest into a carafe, and started another pot. I took my cup of coffee and went out to the deck to enjoy the cool morning air, listen to the birds, and ponder the events of my life, past, present, and future. It wasn't too long before Scott joined me on the deck with his cup of coffee, since he is also an early bird. We both just sat there, listening, thinking, and not speaking. Guys can do that, we have an unspoken language, a language of peace and quiet.

Dee's son, Chad, was the next to wander out to the deck, still looking tired. He too sat down, not saying a word for the longest time, but soon, as kids do, he had to say something.

"When's breakfast, Henry?" Well, did you expect him to say anything else?

"I'll get started on it right away," I responded, "I'm starting to get hungry myself. We'll let the girls sleep until breakfast is ready. Scott, do you want to help me out?"

"You bet," he said, and we both got up and headed for the kitchen.

"Can I get in the hot tub Henry?" Chad asked as we were walking away.

"Sure you can," I said. "Do it while we fix breakfast."

Scott and I set about the task of making a great breakfast, cooking up mounds of bacon, poached eggs, toast, and home fried potatoes. Sometime during the process, Dee's daughter made a pass through the kitchen, and before she could even ask, I told her Chad was already in the hot tub, so she could jump in with him while breakfast was cooking, and with a small squeal, she was off to the hot tub. Both kids were already wearing shorts, so they could drip dry while we ate breakfast out on the smaller deck off of the kitchen where the table and barbecue is set up.

Soon, the smell of breakfast brought Dee downstairs, wearing only one of my long tee shirts, and what a sight it was.

"Wow girl," I exclaimed, "you look gorgeous in the morning, I think we might have to skip breakfast."

"Well you'll have to skip it by yourself," she replied," because I'm starving." She came into the kitchen, gave me a big hug and a kiss, poured herself a cup of coffee, and walked past me to go out to the deck, my eyes fixed on her the whole way, with my mouth hanging open like a retard.

"You're killing me girl, absolutely killing me," I said as I reluctantly went back to finishing the breakfast.

"Scott," I said, causing him to jump, because apparently he too was a bit mesmerized by the view.

"Scott, would you please set the table outside. Then put out the carafe of coffee. And would you bring out the jug of orange juice in the fridge?"

"You got it," Scott replied, jumping on the chance to change the awkward scene we were having at that moment, and he set about the task with fervor.

It wasn't long before the breakfast was ready, so I called everyone to breakfast. The kids had already gotten out of the hot tub, and were sitting in the sun. The mention of breakfast brought them running to the back deck, and to the wonderful breakfast set before them. I waited for Dee and walked to breakfast with her, putting my arm around her waist, and of course, trying to cop a feel as we walked.

"Now stop that Henry," she said, "the kids might see you, you bad boy. I'll deal with you later."

"Promise?" I said as I patted her on the bottom, and then hurried past her to the table, bringing about a very short chase scene that caused the kids to giggle when we got to the table.

Breakfast turned out to be a very pleasant time of food, jokes, and laughter, and when it was over, Scott and I cleared the table and put the dishes in the dishwasher. Meanwhile, Dee and the kids got showered and dressed, and then it was time to go to town. It was agreed that we would all meet back here this evening for a steak dinner in celebration of the end of fireworks season.

Once we got to the fireworks booth, I walked Dee and the kids to her car while Scott opened the booth, all the while looking over my shoulder toward the corner of the store where Mike was hiding. I don't like that feeling of always having to watch over my shoulder for danger. That sort of thing can make you paranoid, and I don't like being paranoid. I like to be in control of my surroundings at all times. There is no use worrying about Mike right now, because we have work to do, and that means repacking boxes.

We will use several of the old empty boxes to pack fireworks in after we count the returns. As long as the displays aren't open, we can send them back for full credit. The open displays usually get sold for a discount to the steady flow of customers who show up after the fourth looking for deals while you're packing up. We will sell full displays also if they want them, but with the reduced price, it's hardly worth wasting our time trying to pimp the stuff off when you can just send it back as soon as you get it all packed up. It's worth selling the open packages because otherwise you have to keep everything that's open, and unless you have a cool, dry place to store them, they aren't much good the next year.

As soon as the fireworks were packed up and inventoried, we took down all the signs, and swept out the booth. Then we loaded all the fireworks in the truck to take to storage until the fireworks company sent its big truck around to pick up the returns from all the booths. After we took the fireworks to storage, we made a trip to the bank to make a deposit, and then to the post office to send a final check to the fireworks company. After a trip to the market for steaks, pop, beer, corn on the cob, and potatoes for baking, we headed back to the house to relax.

After all the late nights getting home during the selling season, it felt weird to be home in the daylight. I came to the conclusion that the lawn was in serious need of water, and mowing, so, I will water tonight, and mow tomorrow. As for right now, it's time for a beer.

After putting away the groceries, Scott and I grabbed a cold beer, and went out to the deck to relax. It wasn't long before Dee and the kids showed up, and after a short gab session and refreshments, Scott, Dee and I got dinner started. The potatoes were rubbed with olive oil and put into the oven to bake, the corn on the cob was wrapped in aluminum foil with butter, and the steaks, which had been seasoned as soon as we got home, were ready to put on the grill. Meanwhile, the kids were back in the hot tub, and this time they came prepared with bathing suits.

The dinner was fantastic, the perfect culmination of two weeks of very hard work, not to mention the drama of last night's gunshot. It had truly been an interesting vacation. I had called the detective earlier in the day to see if they had found Mike yet, but so far, he had eluded capture. It was only a matter of time until they would catch him since he really had nowhere to go. Meanwhile, law enforcement would make regular trips past both of our homes to watch for him.

The detective didn't think we would have any more trouble from Mike because they felt he would be on the run, thinking he had mortally wounded me, especially since the ambulance had showed up for me. For now, we had the advantage, but, that could change later when he learned I wasn't seriously harmed, and if he wasn't caught soon, he could come back to finish the job. We will have to keep our guard up for awhile longer until Mike was behind bars.

The rest of the night was spent with the adults sitting on the deck, and the kids watching television or playing video games. Tomorrow, it was back to work so we all went to bed at a reasonable hour. I would be up first to be to work at 6am, then Scott would wake up Dee at 7am on his way to work, and

Dee would have to get the kids up and be gone by 8am. If everything went according to plan, it would work out just fine.

Since Dee and I would not see each other for a few days, we made the most of our last night together, enjoying each others body until the wee hours of the morning, which made it a little difficult to get out of bed at 5am, but well worth it.

The alarm went off bright and early at five, well, at least early, and, after resetting the alarm for 7am, I kissed Dee goodbye, and told her I would call her this evening, and see her in a few days. I started the coffee pot before I got into the shower so it would be done by the time I was finished getting g ready for work.

It was not until I got out of the shower that I got a good look at the bullet wound on my side. It was an angry looking furrow etched into my upper side, about three inches long. It didn't really look infected, but I would have the emergency room nurse check it out for me since I would be there anyhow.

I finished putting on my uniform, grabbed a cup of coffee for the road, and headed for work. It felt odd going back to work after being off for two weeks, and I wasn't looking forward to getting back into the routine of patient care, no matter how rewarding it was. I think I'm starting to get burned out. It happens to every health care worker, because working with sick or injured people is demanding, both physically, and emotionally. It's not a job for everyone, some people last a month or so, some not even that long, so it's rare that a person actually reaches retirement age if they work directly with patient care.

And so it was, I was reevaluating my life on my way to work this day, and I'm beginning to think it's time for a change. Maybe the shooting has caused me to think about my future, I don't know, but something has changed in me. I'll have to ask Dr. Miller about my feelings when I see him in a few days.

The workweek went smoother than I thought, thanks to good training. It seems that when called to action, your training and instincts take over and you get the job done. I was a bit of a celebrity for the first day or so, but even that wore off quickly. My wound was healing nicely, Mike had seemingly disappeared from the face of the earth, work was busy enough to keep my mind occupied, and before I knew it, my three-day week was over. Tomorrow was Thursday, and I would go to see Dr Miller again. Boy was he going to be surprised by the things that had happened since I had seen him last.

Scott was still coming over in the evenings to keep me company, and I would talk to Dee for an hour or so each evening. Both of them were excited to hear about my next meeting with Dr Miller, as was I, so it was not surprising that I didn't get much sleep that night. Scott and I sat out on the deck until nearly midnight before going to bed, and after much tossing and turning, a managed to get a few hours of sleep.

The next morning I was up bright and early, coffee in hand, when Scott finally crawled out of bed. Obviously he wasn't nearly as excited about things as I was. It's amazing to me how some of us know deep down inside that we have been around before, and that someone close to us in our present life was probably close to us in a prior life also. But a guy like Scott doesn't seem to be aware of his past, or is too caught up in the present to even care about the past. Then again, guys like me could just be nuttier than a fruitcake, and everyone else could be normal. Nah!!!

After a pot of coffee, and some toast, Scott hit the road for his workday, and I worked on getting a few bills paid before heading off to town for my appointment with Dr. Miller. It was proving to be a nice leisurely day that is until the phone rang. The voice on the other end was not what I wanted to hear this early in the day, it was Jane, and she wanted to talk.

"What can I do for you Jane?" I asked impatiently.

"It doesn't sound like you're too happy to hear from me," Jane started, "I thought by now you would be missing me, after all, we were together for a lot of years."

"Yeah," I said, "and they were some of the most stressful years of my life, and that I do not miss."

"From what I've been hearing on the news," she replied, "things aren't much better for you right now either. How's your wound doing?" There was a hint of venom in her voice, and all of a sudden, any trace of missing her vanished into thin air.

"The wound is healing just fine," I said, "thanks for asking. Is there something you want to talk to me about Jane, because I need to get to town for my appointment with Dr. Miller?"

"Are you still seeing that quack?" she asked with a nasty tone of voice.

"Yes I am," I replied, "if it was any of your business."

"You know," she started in again, "all of our troubles began when you started going to see that freak. I have a good mind to turn him in to the state as a fraud, what do you think of that?"

"I think you can do whatever you want to do," I replied with a little venom of my own, "But I doubt it will do you any good. And as for our troubles, they began about three weeks after we first met. In fact, I should have cut it off a long time ago, but I was weak, I let you control every aspect of our life, and I wasn't happy. But now, even with getting shot at, I'm still happier than I've been in a long time, so what do you' think of that."

Apparently she didn't think much of it because she hung up on me and that suited me just fine. Besides, it was time to head for town, and that was something else that made me happy.

The trip to town gave me ample time to think about everything that was happening in my life, this life, and the one we were delving into in the past. There always seems to be parallels between the two, and unless we learn from the mistakes of the past, then we will more than likely repeat those same mistakes in the future. I also believe that until you overcome your downfalls, the higher powers will set the same stumbling blocks before you again until you get them right. My hope is that these sessions with Dr. Miller will help me to recognize some of those mistakes, and then compare them with where my life is now, and thus avoid a lot of hassles and heartaches.

Dee claims that one of us always dies early when we are at the height of our relationship. It almost happened already, and I don't intend to watch it happen again anytime soon. I'm looking for the story ending that says, "And they lived happily ever after." I hope that saying is more than just a fairy tale.

I arrived at Dr. Miller's home about a half an hour early, and was parked outside of his house on the street, lost in my own thoughts when Dr. Miller came out of the house and waved to me to come inside. As I walked up to the house he spoke to me.

"Hello Henry, my last appointment cancelled, so if you're interested, we can get some extra time in today."

"You bet," I said, as we went inside, me to my easy chair and Jim to his chair across from me. I settled in and made myself comfortable just as I had so many times before, listening to the sounds of the stream, and to the birds chirping, while the slight breeze circulated throughout the house. Just this little bit of peaceful stimulation had me ready to go under hypnosis before we were even ready. Finally, Dr. Miller broke the spell by asking how my week had gone, so I proceeded to tell him about everything from the fireworks sales, to the fight with Jane, to the continued relationship with Dee, and then to the shooting.

"It looks like we need to get some answers for you real soon," Jim said, "I'm glad we have some extra time today, so lets get started, shall we."

"I'm ready," I said.

"Okay Henry," he started, "lean back, close your eyes, and relax. Listen to the birds chirping. Imagine yourself in your private place in the mountains, lying beside a cool mountain stream, with a slight cool breeze gently blowing on your face. Now, feel yourself relaxing even more, feeling yourself getting heavier, sinking into the cushions, aware of every nerve, every pore, every inch of your body. Relax even more now, sinking deeper, deeper, deeper, deeper, deeper."

Chapter 8

"Ethan my love, it's time to wake up."

Mara was tracing my eyebrows with her finger, which had the opposite effect than what she wanted, I was totally paralyzed from the eyeballs down, except for my mouth, which barely managed the words to tell her if she kept doing what she was doing, I would never be able to get my eyes to open. I did manage to get one eye open to look around the room enough to figure out where I was, and then both eyes opened so I could see the beautiful lady lying next to me.

"Good morning gorgeous," I said, as I rolled onto my side to face her. "I was having the craziest dream again; remind me some time to tell you about it. Meanwhile, do you want to make love?"

"No, you horn dog," she said teasingly, "you've worn me out now, and besides, we have a lot to do today, and we need to get started. We'll make love tonight, okay."

"Oh my love," I said, "you're killing me, you're absolutely killing me."

Mara just laughed as she jumped out of bed, flinging the covers off of me as she did so, making sure I would have to get up. The view as she walked away from the bed had me mesmerized, and all I could do was stare at her while she cleaned up and brushed her hair. Finally, she realized I was staring at her, and with a twinkle of embarrassment in her eyes, she said.

"Would you stop staring at me and get out of bed, we have to get a move on; you can bet the Gog army isn't lounging around in bed right now like you are."

"I suppose you're right," I said reluctantly, "but I could go to my death more readily if we could make love one more time." I tried to sound dejected to get more sympathy, but it didn't work, because her reply was.

"Ah, but you need to stay alive and healthy my love, so we can make love again tonight, otherwise, how else am I ever going to keep you motivated and on task."

"That's motivation enough for me to stay alive," I said as I climbed out of bed to join her in getting cleaned up and dressed. "And each night, when I've lived through another day, I'm going to make love to you like there is no tomorrow, because truly, you never know if there is going to be a tomorrow. So you better hope I don't get killed today, or you'll be sorry that you didn't make love to me this morning."

I was trying to sound as pathetic as possible, which almost worked, because she did turn around, embraced me in her arms and said.

"When this is over Ethan, I will make love to you night and day if you wish, but until this army is defeated, we may not have a future together, and that's what scares me. I love you, and I adore you, and I always will, in this life, and the next. Right now Ethan, before it's too late, we must make a pact with each other, that upon our deaths, we will seek each other out throughout eternity, to return to the earthly realm at the same time, and to find each other, no matter what it takes. Will you promise me that Ethan?"

Mara was almost in tears as she spoke these words to me, and I responded by saying.

"I promise to you Mara that I will also seek you out in every lifetime that I return to this earth, and that I will love you throughout eternity."

With that promise, we kissed each with a kiss that would span the ages forever, a deep, longing, desperate kiss, one that epitomized the state of danger that we were about to face from two distinct enemies, one from the outside, and another one closer to home.

As we broke off our kiss, we continued to hold each other until finally; it was my turn to break the spell.

"We better get on down to the kitchen to meet with Balon, Valik, and Marta to see how things are progressing, and to make plans for today, are you ready to go."

"I'm ready my love," she said, and gave me a quick kiss on the cheek, and as soon as I had wiped the last tear from her face, we were off to the kitchen.

When we arrived, everyone was already seated, having breakfast, and making small talk. We exchanged a quick greeting to everyone and then we sat down to join them. Marta clapped her hands for one of the servants to bring us some breakfast, and soon we had a wonderful breakfast sat before us.

Marta still seemed cold and distant, so I tried to speak to her as often as I could to loosen her up. It is not a wise move to have dissenters among your ranks; in fact, it can be dangerous, if not fatal.

"Marta," I began, "how is it going with the procurement of food and supplies?"

"It is going as well as can be suspected, without drawing too much undo attention. The venders are certainly happy, but I fear it may take several days to finish. I will go to town today to go right to the sources, and have the supplies sent up here. I should be back tomorrow, and my handmaiden Sophie will take care of the supplies when they arrive."

"Very good, Marta," I said, "and I trust your judgment that Sophie is a trustworthy ally. Please be careful when you are in town and at the first hint of trouble, get out of the city and head back up here, understand. We slowed them down yesterday, but not for long."

"Yes my Lord," she responded, "I understand. Did you say that you slowed them down yesterday Ethan? Do you mean to tell me you've actually seen the Gog army?"

"Yes we did see the Gog army, and we destroyed an advanced patrol in the Talon Pass. We also created a minor obstacle in the Pass to slow them down, but it will only take a day or two for them to breach that, and then another two days to reach the King's castle, and lay siege to it, if they even have to lay siege to it. From everything I could gather there may be a large number of spies already in the city, which could wreak havoc on the troops trying to secure the castle in the face of an advancing enemy. That is why you need to be on your guard at all times when you are in the city, and to not let anyone know of our plans of defense up here."

Marta had a look of disbelief on her face, and then she said. "You mean to tell me you were at the Talon Pass yesterday, engaged the enemy, and returned back here, all in one day? How can that be possible?"

"Just trust me when I tell you that we have our ways, which will be revealed to all in due time, so please, do not ask me any more questions that need to remain secret. Just do as I ask, and we will take care of the rest, fair enough."

"Yes, my Lord," she replied, "now, if I may take my leave, I will get started for town."

"You are excused Marta," I said, "and thank you for being my loyal friend, and partner."

Maybe I shouldn't have said that last part, because even though she did not turn to face me, I heard a catch in her breath, and thought I noticed a tear in her eye as she walked away.

Next, I removed the key and the lanyard from around my neck, and handed it to Valik, who had a puzzled look on his face, and then I said to him.

"Mr. Valik, take your two men, go down to the cavern, take the Horn of Gideon off of the chariot, but take the Dragons Breath weapon, and go once again to the Talon Pass to check on the progress of the Gog army. Do not engage them unless it is unavoidable, just observe, and report back to me in a few hours. And by the way, is there any word from Captain Sardon lately?"

Valik spoke. "There has been no word from Captain Sardon my Lord, and as a matter of fact, no one has seen him since he left the castle two days ago. I fear whatever he is up to is not in our best interests."

"You are probably right," I agreed, "and continue to have your men monitor his actions if he does return. Also, what is the consensus amongst your men to pledge allegiance to me when the attack begins?"

"Most of the troops will back you without question," Valik began, "but there are a few troopers whose families live in the city, and I feel that their loyalties will of course lie with them. Perhaps if we had them move their families up here, they would have an increased sense of urgency to defend this castle."

"I think you are right as always," I said. "Please arrange for them to bring their families up here until the conflict is decided."

"Thank you, my Lord," Valik replied, and as he rose to leave, he stopped, and turned back to speak to me.

"And thank you my Lord for trusting me with these great tasks, I won't let you down."

"You're welcome, Mr. Valik," I said, "and I know you won't let me down, now, off with you."

"Yes sir," he said, turning briskly on his heel, and headed out the door into the courtyard.

"And as for you Balon, my friend," I said as I turned to Balon, who all of a sudden had a blank look on his face like he had hoped I hadn't seen him. "I want you to go to the gate with a note that I will write now, and instruct the gate keepers to question everyone who comes to the gate today, with full authority to turn away anyone who doesn't have a good reason to be here, except for the regular venders, and the families of the troopers we spoke about earlier. I want them to close the gates early tonight, and raise the drawbridge. Tomorrow, they are to be even stricter, letting no one inside the castle except for venders that Marta has instructed to deliver to the castle. Time is running out, and we must be ready to secure the castle at a moments notice."

As I wrote the note, I asked Balon if he had any questions, to which he replied 'no.'

"Very well then," I continued, "when you are done, meet us in my chambers. Mara and I are going down to see the dragons, and then we'll meet with you, understand."

"I understand," he said, as he took the note, and waddled on out the door into the courtyard.

"Shall we go see the pets, my dear?" I said, taking Mara's hand in mine, and leading her to the stairway down to the dragon pens.

"Lead me, my love," she responded, giving me goose bumps, and making my heart leap inside my chest. Then off we went, down the stairs to the dragon pens, which were, of course, at the gate, staring through the bars as we approached. As we approached, we were being flooded with images, and questions, all originating from the dragons, and almost in unison, Mara and I replied back to them, without speaking, to be calm, and to take turns communicating with us.

Most of the dragons' questions had to do with the things they had seen yesterday, the flying chariot, the Dragons Breath weapon, the horn of Gideon, and then of course, the presence of the Gog army, and what their own role would be in all of this. They were concerned that they had already lost two of their number, and were very uncertain about their own futures, now that man had the ability to destroy dragons almost at will. They were concerned the new weapons might be used against them some day. In their hearts they knew their own days were numbered, we were now entering the age of man, and they were almost bitter, bitter at mankind in general, upset that when man becomes the dominant species, they tend to destroy everything around them, including each other.

Now it was our turn to respond. We tried to assure them that when this battle was finished, the weapons would again be hidden away from the world like they had been for all these hundreds of years. I assured them that as long as the weapons were in my possession, they would never be used against a dragon, and as for the Gog army, they were still only to observe their movements, and report back to us about them. The dragons would be of much better use keeping the Gog army nervous than actually attacking them directly. It was time for men to battle it out with each other now, and for dragons to watch from the safety of the skies and cliffs. It was time for dragons to look out for themselves. We also let the dragons know that Valik and a couple of his men would be going to the Talon Pass by way of the Valley of The Dragons, and to give them safe passage and protection.

The dragons seemed to be feeling a little better about things, but it was obvious that they were never going to be completely secure again. After this battle was completed, no matter what the outcome, I wanted the dragons to know they were free to go, to live wherever, and however they pleased, to live as dragons, not as pets. Now, it was time for them to go out and hunt, to hunt for food, and to watch the enemy, the Gog.

I opened the outer gate, and Mara hugged each dragon in turn, telling them to be careful, and we watched as each one crawled through the opening and dove into the abyss below, only to spread their wings, and soar back into the air, twisting and turning like acrobats, reveling in the fact that the one thing they have over mankind is the ability to fly, unencumbered.

We watched as they flew away into the distance, wondering to ourselves how many would survive the coming conflict, and for that matter, how many of us would survive. I broke the silence by suggesting that we needed to get back to my chambers to meet Balon, and to check out a few more surprises that I had in store for the Gog clan. They will indeed wish they had stayed home by the time we were done with them. Closing the inner gate to the hallway, we climbed the stairway back to the villa, and then down the hallway to my private chambers, where Balon was already waiting for us.

"Did the guards get my note?" I asked as we approached.

"They did indeed," Balon replied.

"And what was their reaction?" I inquired.

"They were a little nervous about it," Balon replied, "but they said it will be done. They also said that they knew I couldn't tell them, but they all sensed something is in the wind, given all the recent activity, and they did affirm that they would obey your every order. I think they know in their hearts that their Captain Sardon is an untrustworthy rat."

"Very good," I said, "now, let's go inside, I have some more fun things to show you."

Once inside, we locked the door behind us, and then proceeded to the bedroom, where I unlocked the door to the pharmacy, going inside first to light the lantern, again revealing shelf after shelf of jars, urns, and barrels of powders, plants, and specimens.

"What is all this stuff?" Balon asked, staring in wonder and bewilderment.

"This is just some of the hidden knowledge of our world, forgotten by some, and never known by most. Some of these potions can cure the world; others can destroy it, that's why only a few people on earth today know anything about it, and also why it is under lock and key. In fact, you had a little taste of what some of these potions can do the other day when I had to put the dragons to sleep. That's an example of the good that can come of this knowledge, but, put it in the wrong hands, it can just as easily be used for evil, and sometimes only the Gods can tell the difference."

Continuing on, I said. "I'm only going to show a few potions today that we plan to introduce to the Gog army, the first is the one you've already experienced Balon, the sleeping potion, not too exciting in itself, but an enemy encampment with everyone asleep, including the sentries, are vulnerable for the opposing army to walk right in and kill them in their sleep, not very fair, but then again, all's fair in war."

"And love," Mara interjected. Balon and I stopped and looked at her, and she just shrugged her shoulders, and smiled.

"Continuing right along," I started, "the next item is a little bit messier, and noisy." Moving over to a large barrel, I carefully pried the lid open, and then reaching inside, I used a small scoop to gather up a small amount of the black powder. Then I again closed the lid tightly.

"You can't be too careful with this stuff," I said, "and don't ever get a flame near this barrel, and only near the powder when you're ready to use it."

Taking the sample to the table, I grabbed a small metal orb about three inches in diameter, with a small hole in the top. Then using a paper funnel, I poured the powder into the orb, rolled a length of string in the leftover powder, inserted it into the small hole, and then dribbled a small amount of melted wax on top to further seal the hole.

"Now," I said, "let's go try this out, I think you're going to be impressed by what you see."

Holding the small orb in one hand with the string covered, I told Balon to grab a large clay pot from the hallway to bring along, and then I lead the way back down to the caverns, stopping in front of a small empty cavern.

"Balon," I said, "place the pot in front of the cavern, right in the middle of the hallway. Then, I want the two of you to stand back down the hallway about fifty feet, and cover your ears, because this is going to be loud."

Then, when Balon and Mara were safely down the hallway, I took the small orb inside the small cave, placed it on the ground, and then using a flint, I lit the string, ran out of the cavern and down the hallway to where Mara and

Balon waited. Looking back at the cavern, and the clay pot, there was suddenly a blinding flash of light and a thunderous boom. In the blink of an eye, the clay pot was nothing more than broken shards scattered about in the hallway. Mara and Balon stood there with their mouths open, and their eyes wide in disbelief. Balon was the first to speak.

"That was incredible Ethan, let's do it again."

"That was awesome," I agreed, "but, if you're the clay pot on the battlefield, it's not quite as fun, in fact, it's quite deadly. We're going to make about a hundred of those to toss into the midst of every gathering of Gog troops that we can. It will kill out to about fifty feet, and wound out to a hundred feet. And better yet, it can destroy catapults and chariots, bridges and siege works, and even blow holes in walls, so it's definitely not a toy to play with carelessly."

"Balon," I continued, as we walked back to my chambers, "I want you to take one of the orbs to the blacksmith, and have him build a hundred more of them. Then, when Valik returns, I want you to take the barrel of powder to him, show him how to build the thunder balls, and stockpile them down in the cavern where they won't hurt someone if they go off. And Balon, be careful."

"Yes, my Lord," he responded

Just as we started to leave my chambers, a soldier came running down the hallway, definitely excited about something, and nearly too out of breath to speak.

"My Lord, something terrible has happened," he said, trying to catch his breath.

"Slow down," I said, "take your time, what is it that's happened?"

"Refugees," he began, "refugees are coming to the gate, coming from the valley below. The city is falling, and the castle is under siege. The Gog army is attacking the city. What are we going to do, my lord?"

"First thing we do sergeant," I responded, "is to get some troops to the gate to process those refugees, one at a time. I don't want any Gog clansman to infiltrate this castle like they did the city and the castle below. Also, send one trooper to the tower to blow the horn that will recall the dragons to the castle. I want them to stop any Gog troops from approaching this castle until we're ready for them. At the first sign of trouble, raise the drawbridge, now go, you have your orders."

"Yes my Lord," he responded, "it shall be done." He turned and rushed off down the hall.

"I guess we didn't slow them down as much as we thought," I mused, more to myself than anyone else. "Unless, there were already troops through the pass when we ambushed them. We'll have to wait until Valik and his men return from their scouting trip."

Turning to Balon I said. "Balon, you have your orders also, grab an orb from the pharmacy, and get over to the blacksmith. While you get the orb, I'll write out my orders for the blacksmith. Tell him to make haste with these, because lives could depend on it."

"Yes my Lord," Balon said obediently, and went to grab the orb while I wrote the note for the blacksmith. When he returned, I handed him the note, and told him to get a move on it, which sort of worked, as he waddled down the hall toward the door to the courtyard.

Finally, I turned to Mara, who had a stressed look on her face, but still managed a smile, and said.

"My love, I need you to greet the dragons when they return. Instruct them to circle the castle, and patrol the road leading to the castle. They are free to attack the scent of any Gog clansman who tries to approach this castle. But remind them to stay clear of any weapons they don't understand, especially the giant crossbows. As soon as that's done, come back here to our chambers, and lock yourself in until I return, do you understand."

"Yes my love," she responded, "but where will you be, I want to be by your side."

"I'm going down to the gate to be with the troops so we don't have a riot within the castle, at least until Valik returns. Right now, the people need good, strong leadership, and this is my destiny. If I am to be the next King, I better start acting like it. As for you, I don't want any harm to come to you, so I would prefer that you would stay in the safety of our chambers. I will send a guard to stand watch outside our door. Now please, do as I have asked, it wouldn't look good for people to start disobeying me before I even become King."

Mara looked a little dejected, but nodded her head in agreement, and then headed back down the hallway to the stairs leading down to the caverns. As I headed for the courtyard, I heard the loud blast of the horn in the tower, sounding out the call for the dragons to return to the castle.

My heart was pounding as I emerged into the bright sunshine of the courtyard. There were people running to and fro in a panic, at least until they saw me heading for the front gate, at which time many stopped in their tracks, and some even followed me back toward the gate, which then drew a following of its own, so that by the time we got to the gate, there were nearly a hundred people with me.

The scene at the gate was not much better, with troops trying to hold refugees back while they checked each individual out prior to allowing them into the castle. As I approached, everyone sort of stopped what he or she were doing and went quiet, except for a few children who continued to cry. The throng parted as I approached the gate. Climbing up on the wall, I held out my hand for silence so I could address the crowd.

"Dear friends," I began, "do not panic, things are totally under control, and so let me explain before you start a panic. My partners, the soldiers, and myself have been planning for this conflict for weeks, we knew the Gog army were coming, and we have a plan in place to defeat them, so please, do not panic. This castle is impregnable to attack, so you will be safe within these walls."

I continued. "We have been storing food for just this occasion, and, we have unlimited water supplies in the caverns below. The dragons are on their way back to the castle as we speak, and they are to patrol the area around this castle. They have been taught the scent of the Gog clansman, and they will attack anyone with that scent. As for those of you who have come from the valley below, we will get you inside the castle as soon as we make sure there are no Gog clansmen in your midst. So, look around you, if there is anyone you don't recognize, or anyone who looks suspicious, point them out to the troops now. When the dragons come, do not be afraid, if you are not a Gog clansman, you will have nothing to fear. Give the dragons plenty of room to sniff out the intruders, in fact, the dragons are returning as we speak."

With that announcement, everyone's eyes turned to the skies to see the five dragons soaring overhead, circling, and swooping low above the crowd. Just then, a trio of men broke away from the center of the mass of people, and started running in a panic back down the roadway.

"Archers," I shouted to the men on the wall, "shoot them down."

The archers managed to hit two of the infiltrators, and as the other one was able to run out of range of the archers, one of the dragons swooped down and snatched him up in his talons, taking him high in the sky, where the other dragons joined in tearing him to shreds. Some of the women and children were whimpering as I raised my hand to address the crowd once more.

"As you can see, the Gogs fear the dragons, and the dragons hate the Gog. The dragons will kill any Gog clansman that ventures near this castle, and unless you are a Gog, you have nothing to fear while you are in this castle. So, please calm down and the troopers will process you into the castle in an orderly fashion.

Now you see why it's been taking so long. The Gog have been infiltrating the city and castle below for months, and have already been caught within this castle. Here you see three more who were attempting to get inside to raise havoc. I implore all of you to be vigilant in this time of crisis. Watch out for anything out of the ordinary, and let a trooper know. Meanwhile, we will keep preparing the castle's defenses. Troopers, you may continue with your work, and people, be strong."

With that said, I backed away from the edge of the wall, and then, using only my mind, I concentrated on communicating with the dragons, instructing them to go to their pens to communicate with Mara, who was waiting for them there. Obviously, they got the message, because they soon were diving over the back wall of the castle to the cliff face and into the cave openings to their pens.

I turned back to watch the progress of the troopers who were screening the refugees, when it suddenly dawned on me that Marta had gone to town this morning and had not returned. My heart sank within my chest, and I prayed that she would be safe. Even though we were having some differences right now, she was still one of my oldest and dearest friends. If anything bad has happened to her, a thousand Gog clansman will pay with their lives, this I swear.

As I watched the proceedings below, I could see Balon approaching from his mission, so I called to him, and waved him up on the wall with me. Just as he got up to me, the dragons suddenly appeared again overhead, some circling the castle while others soared down the mountain following the roadway leading up to the castle. I turned to Balon and said.

"It looks like Mara got the message to the dragons. They are now on patrol to protect this castle, and I wouldn't want to be a Gog clansman right now."

"I heard you already had a little excitement up here," Balon said, looking beyond the castle walls to the two dead clansmen who were lying face down on the road.

"Yes we did," I replied, "and it was a very good training tool I might add."

"And timely too," Balon said with a slight grin on his face.

As we stood there, we heard a distant blood curdling screeching in the sky, and turned just in time to see two of the dragons dive from the sky and disappear from sight down the mountain.

"It looks like our friends have found something else to play with," I said with a hint of excitement in my voice.

Sure enough, soon the two dragons were climbing into the sky, one with two human bodies in its grip, the other one holding a single, struggling soul. Just as quickly, the other three dragons joined them in the sky to tear the victims to shreds, pieces of human bodies falling from the sky, some to be snatched up again by fellow dragons like a cat playing with a mouse, and other parts falling to the depths of the mountain gorges, probably to be eaten by other scavengers.

As we continued to watch, I suddenly became aware of another person on the wall beside me, and turning with a start, it was Mara standing there.

With slight annoyance, I said to her.

"I thought I told you to wait for me in our chambers." That was probably not the right thing to say, because she instantly retorted.

"I am not one of your subjects, or concubines that you can order me around, Ethan. I am your partner, your lover, and I plan on being at your side through danger or peace. I will not back down from anyone or anything, so don't ask me to."

"You're right Mara," I said, "forgive me for belittling you; for you are my equal in every way, I am sorry."

Mara put her arms around my neck, and as I put my arms around her waist, I suddenly became aware that the courtyard had become quiet, and everyone was staring at us.

"Well, I guess now is as good a time as any," I said, and, turning to the crowd, my arm still around Mara's waist, I addressed the crowd.

"People, I want to introduce to you my new Queen, Mara."

When I spoke those words, the crowds below let out a yell that shook the walls of the castle, and sent shivers up and down our spines.

"Hail to the Queen," they shouted.

"Hail to the King," was the next shout, and then repeated over and over until I held my hand up for silence.

"I want to thank you for your support," I started, "I know I have been out of touch for a long time around here, but I'm back now, and I'm stronger than ever, thanks to Mara. We have a devilish plan for the Gog intruders, and believe it or not, we now have them where we want them, on our lands, where we can get at them. I plan on destroying the Gog clan so far down that they will not consider leaving their own borders again for another thousand years."

With that, the crowd roared again, yelling, "Hail to the King." Again I raised my hand for silence, and continuing, I said.

"Some of the things we have planned for the Gog will require your assistance. Don't fear, we will not put your lives in danger, but we will require logistical support. My partner, Balon will talk to you about what we will need help with. I will leave him here to talk with you while I attend to other matters."

Then, to the soldiers below, I spoke next.

"Troopers, I have promoted Valik to be your commander. Captain Sardon was a traitor, in league with the Gog, and he has since disappeared. If he tries to return, I want him arrested, and brought to me, unharmed, do you understand?"

Another roar went up from not only the troopers, but also from the crowd.

"Hail Valik, Hail Valik."

Raising my hand one more time, I said. "Valik is out on patrol, monitoring the movement of the Gog army, and will return soon. As soon as he arrives, he will take over as your commander, so please give him the respect he deserves. If anyone of you have a problem with that, feel free to leave now, because if you agree now, and then change your mind later, I will consider you a traitor, and will give you to the dragons, do I make myself clear."

"Yes, my Lord," they all said in unison.

"Carry on." I said, and turned back to Mara, and said.

"Shall we go down and mingle with our subjects, my love?'

"Yes, my Lord, we shall," she said, giving me a little seductive smile.

"Oh, so now I'm your Lord again am I, how convenient," I said as I swatted her on the bottom as she headed down the ramp from the wall, causing her to laugh teasingly.

Once down in the main courtyard, we talked with all who wanted to speak, consoling the worried, discussing strategy with others, and getting as much information from refugees as we could on what had happened in the valley below.

Apparently, an advance contingent of the Gog army had already been through the pass, so when we ambushed the second scouting party, the Gog decided to attack the city itself, utilizing the troops they had snuck into the city over the past few months. It had caused such confusion for the inhabitants of the city that the city fell within hours. The castle was in such disarray from lack of discipline over the years, that they had simply retreated to the castle and closed the gates. It is my guess that when the rest of their army arrives, the infiltrators within the castle will strike the guards, and then open the gates for the rest of the army to march inside without much of a fight. Knowing the diminished mental status of the general Gog clansman, someone else must be behind the planning of this attack, and it's probably Sardon. In fact, a couple of the refugees thought they had seen someone that looked a lot like Sardon riding with the Gog army outside of the city prior to the attack.

The last of the refugees were now inside the castle so I instructed the drawbridge to be raised, effectively sealing my castle off from the world below. Stragglers would be dealt with as they arrived, and the dragons would protect anyone who was not a Gog, even if they had to wait outside the gate until the next time we accepted refugees. Local families were taking refugees under their wing, and the others were to be sheltered in the large meeting hall in the center of the castle grounds. So for now, we were secure, and it was time to go inside and make plans for our counter attack on the Gog army.

"Balon," I said, "grab a few locals, go to the blacksmith, and take all the orbs he has done so far, and then get the barrel of powder from the pharmacy. Take it to the kitchen and start filling them with powder, and prime them with fuses. Then stack them on the walls to toss at the Gog army if they make it this far. Use the slings to get better distance on the toss. And Balon, remind everyone that they have to be lit first."

Mara and I went back to our chambers to put together a few more potions to use on battle wounds, and to treat infections, making about fifty portions of each into individual pouches, and then put like potions into separate satchels labeled with a tie tag to know what was inside. Then we made up separate satchels with potions to use as weapons, one of those being the sleeping potion, with enough to put an area to sleep the size of a small town or castle, given the right wind conditions. The other potion was deadly, and had to be treated with the utmost respect. This one will put you to sleep, permanently.

We had just finished putting the satchels together when Valik and his men arrived, obviously out of breath from hurrying up from the caverns. As soon as he could catch his breath, he told me what they had seen at the Talon Pass. It appeared that the Gog army had made a single pathway through the rubble of the landslide we had created the day before, and were streaming through, single file. The good news was, they had to leave the giant mobile crossbows, and their large siege works behind, along with a large number of troops to continue widening the path to make it big enough for the large equipment to pass. The bulk of the troops were hurrying through to finish laying siege to the King's castle.

Apologizing profusely, Valik said it was just too good of an opportunity to pass up, having all of those siege works, and giant crossbows backed up, waiting to be taken to the battlefield, so they used the Dragon's breath weapon, and destroyed all they could see, as well as most of the troops working the pathway. Valik was extremely apologetic, feeling he had disobeyed my orders, but felt it was a great strategic victory. When he was done, I spoke.

"There is no need to apologize, Mr. Valik, you are a military man, and I trust your judgment. Even though this weapon is no longer a secret, there will be no defense against it that I can envision right now. Anyone or anything within our vision will be subject to its power. You did a great job, but now, on a more serious note, this castle is now on lockdown. The drawbridge is up, and we have a large number of refugees within the walls. The Gog army has already taken the city, and laid siege to the castle, which will probably fall as soon as the bulk of the Gog army arrives. I'm sure there are enough infiltrators within King Malok's castle walls to overthrow the guards at the gates."

"The dragons are patrolling the road to the castle, and have already attacked several would be infiltrators, including three we killed just outside the gate as they were trying to sneak in. I have already announced your promotion to commander of all the troops, so be prepared for a great celebration from your troops, as well as the populace."

"Balon has some new weapons to use from the walls, so have him demonstrate how they work. Other than that, you are in charge of organizing our defense of the castle. Later on, I may require use of these two soldiers to go down through the caverns with me, and out through the falls to check on the siege of the valley. Congratulations 'Captain Valik, now go check on your troops."

"Thank you, My Lord," Valik replied, turned to leave, but stopped abruptly, handed me my key to the secret doors, and rushed out to the courtyard to begin his new duties.

"I think you picked the right man for the job," Mara stated.

"I believe you're right, my Queen," I said, turning to take Mara in my arms, "just as you and I have made the right choice to pick each other for all eternity. If anything happens to either of us, we can take relief from the fact that we will see each other again in the next life. We just have to be sure that we find each other a little quicker next time."

We held each other for a little longer than usual this time; uncertain of what the immediate future might have in store for us. This time the spell was broken by a rising crescendo of shouts, and chanting from outside in the courtyard, which spooked us a little at first until we realized the chanting was for Valik.

"It looks like Mr. Valik has been spotted by his peers," I said, ending our embrace. "I guess we should finish up here, and then go outside to see how things are shaping up. After that, I think we should take the chariot for a ride beyond the falls to check out the valley, and maybe raise a little havoc ourselves, what do you think partner?"

"I think that could be a lot of fun," Mara agreed.

"You do," I mused, "perhaps you do have a streak of deviltry in you after all, I'll have to watch myself."

"Only when it comes to someone trying to kill me," Mara replied. "Or my man," she also added.

Taking Mara on my arm, we went outside into the courtyard, and made our way to the gate, greeting all who passed by. Arriving at the gate, we climbed the ramp to the wall where Balon was explaining to Valik the inner workings of our new toys, like he was some sort of expert now on bomb making. Oh well, everyone deserves his day in the sun, and this was Balon's, so we let him talk, and pretended to listen in earnest. Then it was time to demonstrate what the bombs would do.

Balon lit the bomb, and just as he went to throw it over the wall, he dropped it at his feet. Everyone just sort of watched it roll around their feet, except Mara and I, who went into a frenzy trying to get a hold of it before the fuse reached the hole. Finally, I grabbed hold of the bomb, and threw it as hard as I could over the wall, yelling for everyone to duck down. Everyone but Balon ducked, being a little slow on the uptake about how dangerous these things really were.

The explosion was deafening, having went off in the air about forty feet away, peppering the outside of the wall with hundreds of pieces of metal shards. As soon as we had gained our wits again, it became immediately clear that Balon was injured, lying on his side on the causeway, holding his hand over his face, moaning, with blood showing between his fingers. At first, I was angry with Balon for being so careless, yelling at him as I helped Mara to her feet.

"Balon, these things aren't toys for your amusement," I said as I kneeled beside him, moving his hand away enough to see that he had lost one of his eyes, which in this case he should consider himself lucky.

I was just about to chastise him further when the rush of wings drew my attention. All five dragons made a low flying pass directly overhead. They had obviously sensed the danger to Mara and myself, and were ready to attack anyone who was a threat. Forcing myself to calm down, I sent a message to the dragons with my mind, as did Mara, that everything was okay, and that we just had a little accident. We further instructing the dragons to keep a safe distance while we practiced with some new weapons. Then turning back to Balon, I continued.

"Do you realize we all could have been killed just now? You have got to be more careful, and that goes for everyone."

Mara was now kneeling beside Balon, holding a piece of cloth over his eye, and said.

"I'll take him inside and get him patched up, Ethan. When you're done here, come pick me up before you go to the falls, okay."

"Okay," I said, finally starting to calm down from the near death experience. As Mara led Balon back inside, I thought to myself, I don't think anyone else realizes just how close they came to dying just now, so, as I stood there with Valik and a few troopers, I had them lean over the side of the wall to look at the damage to the wall itself from the metal shards. Only then did they begin to realize the devastating power these bombs were capable of, so, I decided to fill in the blanks that Balon had left out.

"These bombs," I began, "will kill anything out to about fifty feet. Then, from fifty to hundred feet, they will seriously injure everyone else. They are extremely dangerous my friends, they are meant to kill people and destroy walls and buildings, nothing else. Now, since we probably need more distance on these, I plan to use these large slings that Balon brought along."

The sling was a simple device about three feet long, made from a forked tree branch, with a strap of dried goat gut stretched between the two forks, and a large pad made of animal hide sewn in the center of the strap. The sling was most effective when the tree branch was still fairly green, so it would have extra spring to the wood. The sling handle was then placed in a hole in the top of the wall, drilled there a hundred years ago by my father for just this type of occasion.

"Okay my friends," I began, "watch and learn, because your lives may depend on it."

Placing the sling handle in the wall, I grabbed another of the bombs that were being stacked on the causeway, then, placing a bomb in the large pad at the center of the straps, I grasped the bomb in the pad, pulled back on the straps as far as I could, told Valik to light the fuse, and let the bomb sail out away from the castle wall. This time the bomb went over a hundred yards, landing on the road, and then skipping another fifty feet before exploding with a great roar, and a large cloud of black smoke. A cheer went up from everyone on the wall.

"That should discourage most intruders from venturing too close to the castle I would think, don't you Mr. Valik?" I asked.

"That it should," Valik replied, "that it should."

"Continuing, I said. "I will leave the castle in your hands, Captain, and if I may, I would like to take two of your men with us to check out the activity in the valley. We will be back about dark, at which time we'll have a meeting to discuss our strategy for tomorrow."

Valik assigned the same two troopers to us who had accompanied us before, and off we went to find Mara. We found Mara in the kitchen area, just finishing up with Balon, where she had put a paste made of herbs and pollens on his damaged eye, removed the piece of metal, covered his eye with a patch, and then gave him an herbal tea to keep away infection. Both of them rose to go with us to the caverns, but I turned to Balon and said.

"I'm sorry my friend, but I'm afraid you're going to have to sit this one out. We may have to move fast, and with you being injured, you may put all of our lives in danger, do you understand."

Balon looked upset, but he had to agree with me, he would stay behind on this trip. It felt odd, because for all of my life, Balon had been assigned to watch out for me, and now, when the real danger arrived, it was I who needed to save him.

"Balon," I said, "while you're here, check on the progress of the blacksmith, and make sure the bombs are made correctly, but please, let the others handle them, you just be in charge of them. And watch for the dragons to return safely. We'll be back in a few hours."

I patted him on the back, and, after shouldering one of the satchels, off we went to the caverns, down the stairs, past the lower pens, through the secret door, and down to the main cavern.

Once we reached the cavern, we boarded the chariot, where I assigned Mr. Damon the command of the vehicle again, since he seemed to have a natural ability to fly the craft, then, opening the back door to the cavern, we headed down the long pathway to the Falls door, leaving the back door open until our return. Once we reached the Falls door, I had the others wait inside while I opened the door, and walked out beyond the falls, just in case there were refugees, or for that matter, enemy troops nearby. Sure enough, I could hear voices beyond the waterfall.

Sneaking back to the craft, I asked the troopers to investigate who might be out there. The troopers chose to take their short bows with them because of the lethality of the weapon at a greater distance, and they also had their daggers on their side for close combat. I would follow them to just behind the waterfall, so I could rush out to help, or rush back inside the caverns to safety. Mara would wait just inside the cavern with the craft.

The troopers went first, and were gone only a short time when I heard shouts, not shouts of fear or combat, but shouts of stern instruction. So, I decided it was safe to venture out far enough to see what was happening, and when I did, I saw Mr. Damon and the trooper speaking to a family of refugees. I hailed to the troopers so as not to spook them, and they waved me forward. As I approached the small group, I recognized the bartender from the saloon where I had met Mara. He also recognized me, and said.

"Oh thank the Gods, Dragon Master, we are so glad to see you, we thought we had been caught by Gog troopers."

"How did you get here?" I asked, looking around nervously to make sure there were no other surprises lurking around.

"We escaped from town when the first uniformed Gog army troops showed up, and since you told me to come up to the safety of your castle, that's what we were trying to do. But, the Gog army had a contingent of troops guarding the road up the mountain, so we just side hilled around the base of the mountain until we ended up here. We reached a dead end here, so we have just been hiding here, hoping not to get caught. But, how did you get here my Lord, there is no way over the cliffs above?"

"I'll explain that soon enough," I replied, "but for now, have you seen anyone else up here, friend, or foe?"

"No one else, my Lord, the Gog have a large encampment down below on the plateau, with sentries on constant patrol. There is no longer any escape from the city, and no travel allowed by anyone."

"Tell me more about what has happened within the city," I asked, "and what of the King and his castle?"

"You were right master," he began, "the Gog had infiltrated troops all over the city, and as soon as the first uniformed troops showed up, they killed all of the King's troops that were outside of the castle walls, and then killed all the government officials they could find. It was over so fast. My family and I were all ready to head for your castle, so we slipped out of the city in the confusion, and were on our way until we saw that the road to the castle was cut off, and that's how we ended up here."

"But what of the King?" I pressed.

The shopkeeper continued. "As far as I know, the King is still safe inside his castle. Apparently, a couple of the King's troops were off duty, and when they saw what was happening, they made it to the main gate in time to warn them to close the gate. Unfortunately, those two troopers were killed outside the gate, but I did hear the warning bugles blaring inside the castle, so I know the message got through. I'm sorry, my Lord, that is all I can tell you."

"Thank you," I said, "you have been of great service. By the way, what is your name?"

"My name is Galen," he replied, bowing before me, "and I am at your service Master."

"Thank you Galen," I started, "now here is what I need you to do. My friends and I are going to raise a little havoc with the encampment below. You are about to see some things that you must never speak of, do you understand, do all of you understand."

"Yes Master," they all replied.

With that, I walked back through the waterfall, had Mara pull the craft through, and then closed the door. Then, climbing aboard, we moved out into the open and approached the group standing with the troops. The looks on their faces gave the impression they had just seen a ghost. Pulling up next to them, the two troopers climbed aboard, with Mr. Damon taking over the controls, and then, as I unmasked the Dragons Breath weapon, I spoke to the group.

"I want you to wait here until we return. We may be in a hurry, so be ready to jump on board. Right now, we have work to do, so stay hidden, and stay quiet, because that's how we found you. If you see any enemy troops, find a way to warn us as we return, does everyone understand."

"Yes master," they replied.

"Okay," I said to my group, "let's go."

Mr. Damon took us on over the face of the hill, gliding effortlessly over the rocks and bushes, not making even a whisper of a noise. First, we skirted side hill until we came near to the troops guarding the roadblock, and before they could react, the Dragons Breath weapon cut them down to a man, leaving their lifeless bodies maimed and smoldering. The weapon also caused the surrounding vegetation to catch fire, giving the impression of hell on Earth. Then, Mr. Damon turned and took us straight down the road and onto the plateau, then along the edge of the Gog encampment.

Keeping the camp to the side of the chariot that the dragon's breath was on, the fiery stream belched out death to everything it touched, men, horses, tents, and wagons. Anyone who happened to be on the other side of the chariot were dispatch by the other trooper with his short bow.By the time we broke off the attack, a three hundred yard swath of death and scorched earth lay behind us. The remainders of the troops on the plateau were in a panic, and, not knowing what was happening to them, they turned and ran in full retreat, running back toward the city, fearing another attack.

Since we had the advantage, we decided to make one more pass the other direction, so I quickly moved the weapon to the other side of the chariot, and as we passed the rear of the fleeing troops, the Dragon's Breath killed or maimed another swath of troops and horses. It was time to get out of there while the Gog army was still in a state of chaos, so, we turned and headed back up the face of the mountain to the falls above.

Just as we thought we were clear, a lone Gog clansman, who had hid in the bushes at the first attack, stood, and let loose an arrow, striking our extra trooper in the chest, knocking him off of the chariot. Just as quickly, I turned the weapon on the clansman, holding the weapon on him until there was nothing left but an overcooked mass of smoking flesh.

Mr. Damon started to slow down to retrieve the fallen soldier, but I told him to keep going, because there would likely be a lot more dead within the castle walls before this was done, and they too would have to be disposed of less dramatically to prevent disease. So, we continued on up the face of the mountain to the falls, where Galen and his family were waiting. Just as we pulled up to Galen and his family, the sound of distant explosions echoed through the canyons from the mountain above. Our castle was under attack.

We quickly loaded the seven refugees onto the chariot, and moved on through the waterfall, stopping in front of the seemingly solid rock wall. As I jumped down from the chariot and walked up to the stone wall, Galen spoke up.

"Is this where you've been hiding out, in a small cave under the waterfall, because if it is, it won't take long for them to find us?"

"You don't seem to have much faith in me," I said as I put my key into the hidden lock, and magically, the stone door slid away to reveal the cavern within. Galen and his family were still staring ahead, mouths agape as Damon moved the craft through the door, then closing the heavy stone door behind us, and I climbed back aboard the craft.

"Let's make haste Mr. Damon, and everybody hold on tight," I said, and then held on tight to the rail as Damon raced back up the pathways, with lights on and the narrow walls rushing by. When we reached the wizards cavern, Damon started to slow to a stop, but I told him to continue on up to the main level because we didn't have time to waste. Stopping at the last doorway before the dragon pens, I instructed Damon to shut down the craft while I opened the door, then I instructed everyone to climb down, and go through the door, at which time I closed the door behind us, leaving the craft just inside the secret door to the cavern.

Mara volunteered to escort Galen and his family while Damon and I rushed ahead to help out, but Galen said he would like to go with us also. All help was welcome so he kissed his wife goodbye, and the three of us rushed up the stairs, through my villa, and out through the courtyard to the castle walls, which were surprisingly quiet. It was obvious there had been a battle because there were several slain and wounded troopers lying about the courtyard, with the wounded being tended to by some of the civilian women.

Valik and most of his troops were still positioned along the walls, bows at the ready. Daylight was fading fast, but from what I could see beyond the walls was a scene of utter death and devastation. There were dozens upon dozens of dead and dying Gog soldiers and their horses lying scattered along the road. As I approached Valik's side, I spoke to him.

"It looks like you had a little excitement here Captain, what happened?"

"Well," he began, "a large contingent of Gog troops marched right up to the abyss in front of the gate, and demanded that we lower the drawbridge, and surrender."

"Yeah," I asked, "then what?"

"Then I threw a bomb at the arrogant bugger," Valik chuckled, "and the fight was on."

"Nice response Captain," I said between chuckles, "I like that."

"How did the Gog troopers make it all of the way to the castle without being attacked by the dragons?" I asked, more to myself than to Valik.

"I believe," he began, "that the dragons did not attack them because they kept themselves hidden in the forest when the dragons flew over, and then made the final push here when the dragons flew back to their pens for the night."

"The Gog seem to know our routine even better than we do." I mused. "It just reinforces my suspicions that the Enemy had spies within our walls. They just hadn't counted on us raising the drawbridge so quickly. Usually it would take several hours for word to reach us from the city below, but we knew the Gog were here days ago."

"Not to change the subject, my Lord, but how'd you do down below?" Valik asked.

"I'm afraid we lost one of your troopers Captain," I said humbly. "I beg your forgiveness, but we had to leave him behind."

"No need to apologize to you my Lord," Valik responded. "This is war, and I would have done the same thing. And how did you do raising havoc on our friends, the Gog army?"

"Quite well," I started, "I believe we killed several hundred, and the last we seen, there were only a few horses left still running for the city."

"Fantastic, my Lord," Valik said, and then his face lit up when I told him of the details of the raid, and also of Galen and his family. Valik looked past me to address Galen, who was standing quietly behind me.

"I thought you looked familiar sir, I'm glad you could join us. We will find a place for you and your family to stay. Meanwhile, if you'll excuse me, I need to check on my wounded troopers."

"By all means Captain," I said, "I'm sorry to keep you away from your duty. Come talk to me in the kitchen when you're secure up here."

We followed Valik down the ramp, and then Galen and I went on to the kitchen where Mara had taken Galen's family to get them something to eat after their flight from the city, and a night sleeping in the mountains. After they had eaten, I instructed Galen on how to find the meeting hall, and sent him and his family on their way. When they had gone, Mara turned to me and said.

"I need to go down to the dragon pens to speak with the dragons. They were very hyper, and upset as we went past the pens. I was only able to let them know that I would be back as soon as possible. Will you be able to join me my dear?"

"I will join you as soon as I speak with Valik about tomorrows plans." I said, "and thank you for all your support, I couldn't have gotten this far without you." Mara gave me a quick kiss, and then she headed for the dragon pens.

I grabbed a piece of fruit, and was nearly finished when Valik came in, and as he sat down, I slid the bowl of fruit across the table to him. He helped himself to the fruit, and ate ravenously. When he was done, I began to speak.

"I think we've given the Gog army more than they bargained for today, from your attack this morning on their men and equipment at the Talon Pass, to my attack on the lower plateau, and finally the defense tonight of the castle. By my calculation, I figure we killed six to seven hundred of the Gog clansmen, not to mention horses and equipment. We know the dragons have also killed a few today, and probably another hundred or so on the plains of Migido. So all in all, I'm quite pleased at our progress. Tomorrow, we will need to hit them even harder."

Continuing, I said. "My plan is to load the Horn of Gideon onto the chariot, along with the both of the Dragon's Breath weapon, then go out through the castle gate, clear the road all the way down to the plateau, sweep the plateau again, then turn up the hill to the falls, where I want you to meet me with as many troops and volunteers as we can muster. Then we're going down to the plateau overlooking the city and the King's castle, and set up the Horn of Gideon where it can't be seen. Then, we show ourselves to the Gog army, and invite them to come out and play with us. When the Gog troops get far enough away from the city, we play them a tune with the horn, and when they're incapacitated, we send the troops down to finish them off, while I stand guard with the chariot. If we get a big enough response from the Gog army, we'll give them everything we've got."

"What about defending the castle while we're gone?" Valik asked.

Responding, I said. "With the drawbridge up, even a handful of men on the walls with bombs and bows can hold off a sizable force. Besides, once I clear the road, there won't be many Gog troops left to attack the castle. How many troops do you have in the castle captain?"

"We did have two hundred," he responded, "but that was before Captain Sardon disappeared, along with a few of his followers. Then we lost two dead, and three wounded on the wall, and you lost another one, so roughly, I'd say we have about a hundred and eighty five uniformed soldiers. Do you think we can enlist some of the locals to fight with us Ethan?"

Responding, I said. "I'll call an emergency meeting in the meeting hall, and ask for volunteers. It doesn't take much to learn how to shoot a bow, or to stick a sword into an incapacitated soldier. There may be some with moral issues in that respect, but I'll bet we can get plenty of volunteers to man the wall, and to throw bombs or shoot arrows. That would free up a lot of your troops to fight down below on the plateau."

Looking a little concerned, Valik continued. "You know we're still going to be severely out manned?"

"I do," I said, "But, we have some superior weapons on our side, and I'm hoping that when the defenders of the king's castle see the Gog troops being decimated, they will come out of the castle and join us."

"That's going to be kind of a stretch, don't you think?" Valik asked, still not completely convinced.

"Yes I do," I responded, "but we can hardly stay up here while a new regime takes over the land. We have to drive them out once and for all, or kill them to a last man. If it looks like they are going to overrun us, we retreat back to the falls, and escape back into the mountain and regroup. What do you think Captain?"

"I think it's hard to get used to Captain before my name," he responded, "other than that, I think you're right, we don't have much choice. The Gog troops aren't going away without some encouragement, and it doesn't look like we're going to get much help from the king and his troops. They're going to try to wait out the siege as long as possible unless we do something to encourage the cowards to come and help us, so, I'm with you Ethan, let's have a meeting."

"Thank you Valik, have one of your men sound the horn in the tower, and that will call all the people to the meeting. I'll be there in a little while, but first, I need to go down to meet Mara at the dragon pens. I want to know what the dragons think about what's going on, because I feel a sense of uneasiness coming over them, even a sense of wildness returning to them, which can be good, and bad. I won't know until I speak with them, so give me a half hour, and I'll see you at the meeting."

"That sounds good," Valik said, "I'll see you there." And with that, he turned and left for the courtyard, while I headed down to the dragon pens.

As I approached the pens, I was being flooded by images and emotions that were almost too much to bear, so much so that I had to cover my head and ears to try to block out some of the hidden noise, and with my own mind, I yelled back at them to slow down, that they were hurting me. Almost immediately it went quiet, and Mara rushed around the gate to see if I was okay. Only then was I able to uncover my head and ask.

"What was all that about Mara is everything okay?"

"No, Ethan, everything is not okay," Mara responded, tears in her eyes. "Feron is gravely wounded with a spear from one of the giant crossbows, and the rest of the dragons are extremely upset, upset with humans in general, and I don't blame them, I'm upset with the way humans act too. Why must we fight and kill each other? Why can't we all just live in peace Ethan, like it was in the early days of Atlantis, before the sons of darkness came to the earth, why Ethan, why?"

Mara leaned her face into my chest and cried exposing emotions I had not seen in her before. She had seemed so strong, so tough up until now. It seemed that something had been bothering her over the last day or so. I could sense that something was not right. I could feel her emotional strife, a sense of impending doom, and it was overwhelming me to the point that I now had to block her out also, and just to keep focused on the crisis at hand. Looking up, I saw the faces of four dragons leaning around the corner, concern in their eyes, and concern in their minds, which I was now allowing back into my own mind.

Taking Mara in my arm, we walked into the dragon pen, the dragons giving way, as we walked up to Feron, lying on her stomach, head outstretched on the floor, alive, breathing heavily with a grunting sound, and an audible sound of air hissing from the site of the spear that protruded from her side. She raised her head to look at us as we walked up to her, and then laid her head back down again. Mara sat down on the floor beside her, laying her own head on the neck of the dragon, with an arm over the dragon's neck. Tears still streamed down Mara's face, falling onto the dragon's head and neck, causing one to fall from my own eye as well. It was then that I turned to address all of the dragons.

"My friends," I started, "I beg your forgiveness for what we've done to you, for what I've done to you. You and I have been together all of our lives, and if I were truly your friend, I never would have allowed this to happen to you, and so, I will not ask you to do anything more on behalf of men, no more fighting for us in our wars, no more killing on behalf of a man who would call himself a King, when he is really only an idiot, myself included. This is not your fight; it is man's fight, one evil against another for a piece of earth that really doesn't belong to any of us."

Continuing, I went on. "Men are inherently evil from the start, they lie, they cheat, they steal, they kill themselves, and they kill everything else around them. They ruin their environment until even the earth itself fights back and tries to shake them off like a dog trying to shake off fleas, and still we don't learn from our mistakes. We just keep doing the same things over and over, win one war, then start another one over some other errant word or deed, and for what, who will remember, who will even care in a few short years?" Still speaking, I added.

"So, my friends, you are free to go now, never to return to the evil that is man, free to live your life as you see fit, not as I want you to. This fight is man against man, and if the Gog should win this fight, you will need to flee for your lives anyhow, so now is the best time to go, for tomorrow we go to face the enemy on the battlefield, to kill or be killed, it will all be decided tomorrow, and I don't want any more of you to die. Man will go on, no matter what happens tomorrow, man will still survive, but dragons will not, not if man has his way. Your only chance at survival is to be wild, on your own, answering to no man, only to the spirits who made us. Now go, we will take care of Feron as best we can, that I promise to you."

None of the dragons moved a muscle; they just stood and looked at me, as if analyzing every word I had said. It was almost unnerving, until finally they started communicating with me one by one, as slowly as they could, and this is what they said to me.

"Our friend, we do not hold you responsible for what has happened to us. We know in our hearts that our time on earth is almost done. It is time for the man creature to rule the earth, and all that is within it. To fight against that would be to fight against the Gods themselves. We recognize that the worst of the evils are the Gogs, for they do wish to destroy the creature, which is dragon, and they do grieve Mother Nature greatly. A time is coming again soon when the earth will again shake her back to try to rid herself of the flea called man, and for a time, what is left of man will behave, until he again populates the earth, and gets so full of himself that he thinks he is equal to God, and repeats all the same evils again, for truly, there is nothing new under the sun, history repeats itself over and over again, God has seen it all, and will see it again, that is how things work."

I was so amazed at the things the dragons were telling me that I had the impression that dragons were somehow tied directly to god, and even privy to his wisdom. Why had I not listened to them before, why did it take so long for Mara to come into my life to teach me the way of the dragon? Just as I was pondering these things, another of the dragons spoke to me.

"We will continue this fight until the end Ethan. The Gog is our enemy as well as yours, and if they are allowed to take this land, the end of the dragons will come all that much quicker. But with them gone, those of us who survive will at least be able to live out the rest of our time on earth in relative peace. When this battle is done, those of us who are left will leave this place, never to return, and the time of man can go on until the earth rebels against him, and puts him back in his place. We all have our time on this earth, just as the dragons did for thousands of years, and just as the giant beasts did before us, so now is man's time. Tomorrow, we will fight, maybe to die; maybe not, only tomorrow will tell. So now, please leave us with our sister, we need to make peace with ourselves, and with the powers that be."

Mara, who had been lying beside the dragon, rose to my side, and, with my arm around her, we left the dragons to themselves, our hearts feeling empty inside, the reality setting in that a new era was upon mankind, upon dragon kind, maybe even upon the earth itself. Fate was ready to play itself out, and I felt like a pawn within a larger game, played by forces beyond my control, but sensing that the outcome was already decided, that it only awaited action on my part to get the game rolling, and tomorrow, that game was going to be played out, to a conclusion that was already decided, no matter what I did. So, there was a small measure of comfort to know that whatever would be would be. All I had to do was show up, give it my all, and pick up the pieces that were left. It was going to be a glorious day tomorrow, I was going to fulfill my destiny, we would all fulfill our destiny, whatever that destiny happened to be.

Arriving at the meeting hall, most of the inhabitants of the castle were already there, except for the troops guarding the wall. All eyes were upon me as I walked to the front of the hall and walked up on the stage, Mara at my side. Addressing the crowd, I began.

"My friends, I know you are all worried for your safety, and unsure about the future, but let me assure you, everything is under control, and I further assure you that you are totally safe inside this castle. This castle was designed for just this type of conflict, a siege. I saw this conflict coming quite a while ago, and my partners and I have been preparing ahead for it. We have plenty of food and water, and we are completely impregnable. We could stay here for a long time, but, if the Gog army defeat King Malok, then the Gog will be here for a long time, and that is something we can't outlast, so, I have a plan to drive the Gog out of our land once and for all, and that is where I need your help."

Continuing. "I would like volunteers to help fight the Gog army. Now I know you are not soldiers, and many of you have families, so I'm only asking you to defend the castle so the troops here can be free to help me attack the Gog in the valley, although anyone who wishes to fight the Gog with us would be greatly appreciated. Captain Valik and his troops will train you to shoot the bows and arrows, and also to use the bombs. By the time we use our new weapons to clear the road and the plateau; there won't be much of the Gog army left to defend against."

By the time it was done, nearly three hundred men, women, and teenagers had stepped forward to volunteer, with fifty or so willing to go with us to fight in the valley. Anyone can shoot a bow, or throw a bomb, and with some good pointers from the soldiers, they can learn to use swords and spears effectively. It was a rag tag army at best, but it was all we had, and it would have to do.

"Alright volunteers," I started, "follow Captain Sardon to the armory to get your weapons, and begin your training. I know its dark outside now, but I want you to know the basics of handling your weapons just in case we have visitors again tonight, and I thank you all."

As everyone filed out of the meeting hall, I put my arm around Mara and led her out the door and into the courtyard. She seemed very subdued and pensive, only speaking when spoken to. I know she is upset about everything that had happened lately, but this was different, Mara was tough, battle and death itself would not bother her like this. It had to be something else, and I needed to find out what was bothering her.

Mara and I walked in silence until we got to our chambers, and after we were inside, I sat down on the bed beside her, and asked.

"Mara, my love, I know that something is bothering you, and I know it's not because of the battles, or the deaths, because it is something that you've seen and experienced before, so it has to be something else. Please trust in me, as I am part of you, I can feel your emotions, and it is hurting me to know that you're hurting, so please, tell me what you are feeling."

With a tear rolling down her cheek, she looked at me with beautiful, yet sad eyes, and said to me.

"I'm scared Ethan, I'm scared of dying, I'm scared because I don't want to lose you now, not so soon after we've found each other again, and it's more than I can bear."

"You are not going to die, Mara," I said, "I won't allow anything to happen to you. I will protect you, and the dragons will protect you with their lives, and if you stay in the castle, no harm can come to you, this I promise."

"You don't understand Ethan," she replied, "first of all; I am not going to stay in this castle while you're risking your life on the battlefield, because I'm also here to protect you, or to perish with you. Secondly, I know in my heart that I'm going to die soon, I can feel it coming for me, and it scares me Ethan. I can't bear the thought of it, I can't go into the next life having to try to find you again, and I can't do it. What if I can't find you again, how could I bear it?"

She was crying openly now, her face in my chest, my arms around her, holding her tight, and it was my turn to speak.

"Mara, I don't know what tomorrow, or the future will bring, but if death is to separate us, we need to make a pact right now as to when, and where we will try to seek each other out again."

"I know the where," she responded, a glimpse of hope returning to her eyes. "I want us to meet in the land of the library, the land of the pyramids, the land of the great lion. I feel that place is calling to us Ethan, and we need to do it before the next great earth movement, the one our scientists predict will happen within the next three or four hundred years. So, whoever dies last, given our ages right now that should put our reunion in about one hundred and fifty years, right?"

"It's a date then," I replied, and while still holding her tight, we kissed for what seemed like an eternity, and when we did break it off, Mara surprised me by saying.

"Let's make love right now, my darling, because we don't know what tomorrow will bring, and if one of us should die tomorrow, I don't want it to happen regretting not having made love one last time."

"I'm up for that," was all I could say, and, picking Mara up in my arms, I carried her to the bed, where we hastily stripped off our cloths, and fell back on the bed, making love with an earnest that only comes when life hangs in the balance, when the uncertainty of the future gives way to the passion of the moment, and when we had spent all the energy we had left, we fell asleep, a fitful sleep, reliving the battles of the past, and playing out the strategies for the battles to come. It will all culminate tomorrow; the final conflict will be played out, for better, or for worse, but tonight was spent in lovemaking, and sleep, precious, revitalizing sleep.

Five, Four, Three, Two, One, Snap!!!

Chapter 9

This time, my eyes opened a little slower than last time, not knowing for sure which life was being played out at the moment, but, with a sigh of relief, tinged with regret, I saw Dr. Miller sitting across from me, notebook in hand, a fleeting look of concern on his face.

"How do you feel, Henry?" he asked.

"I'm not sure doc," I responded, "I feel a little uneasy about my life, now, and in the past. I must admit, I'm a little bit scared to see the outcome of the battle to come, and the possibility of seeing mine, or Mara's death. How will I respond to it, will I still be okay when I wake up, or will the shock kill me in this life also? There are so many things to worry about; do you know what I mean?"

"I understand completely, Henry," he replied, and then continued, "we can call it quits right now if you'd like, but I can also assure you, if you do want to continue, if I sense any problems occurring while you're under hypnosis, I will snap you out of it in an instant, but it's up to you."

"You know I have to keep going Jim," I said, "I wouldn't be any better off if I didn't see the outcome, or get closure to the bad dreams I've been having, so, same time next week doctor?"

"Then I'll look forward to seeing you next week Henry." Dr. Miller said, as we both stood, and after walking with me to the door, he shook my hand, and bid me farewell.

I felt numb inside as I walked to my truck, still reflecting on the events that I'd just witnessed during my hypnosis session, and even more disturbing was what I might learn at next week's session, and if history does indeed repeat itself, then what's in store for us all in this life, for Dee, myself, Scott, and

Mike? Knowing the answers to some of these questions could definitely determine how we should live our lives this time around. And another question would be, can you change your future, can you avoid the mistakes of the past? Here is what I feel about that question.

I would like to think that it all depends on knowledge first, and then on how intelligent you are in dealing with that knowledge. Let's take Scott for instance; he is a happy go lucky kind of character. His current life is following exactly in the footsteps of his past. He lost an eye in the past life by an accident with a bomb, and in this life, he has already lost an eye to a simple firework. Does he not have what it takes to avoid losing his eye again, or is it simply because he didn't have the knowledge of his past, so that he could have avoided the same mistake in his future? Then of course the next logical question is, given the knowledge of the past, do we have the intelligence to act upon that knowledge and make a difference, or is history really a double edged sword that cuts you coming, and going. The coming days, months, or years will tell the tale, so we will certainly find out.

The drive back down the valley was again spent in quiet reflection, so much so that I nearly missed the turnoff to my house. When I got to the house, Scott was already there, sitting on the deck in the shade drinking a beer, so I grabbed one for myself and joined him on the deck. He was anxious to hear about my session with Dr. Miller, so over the next couple of hours, I related the story up to date, including the part where he lost his eye to the bomb shrapnel, which seemed to put him in a slightly pensive mood, pondering if it could really be true that he would be doomed lifetime after lifetime to lose one of his eyes. That's when I decided to lighten it up a bit, so I said to him.

"In your next life Scott, do not play with anything that blows up, okay."

"You've got a deal," Scott replied, smiling, as he finished his beer.

"I thought I'd invite Dee and the kids over for hamburgers tonight, Scott, what do you think?"

"I think it would be a good idea, Henry," Scott replied, "that way you can tell her about the hypnosis session. While you give her a call, I'll start making some hamburger patties, and slice some onions and tomatoes. In the mean time, can I get you another beer?"

"You bet I'll take another beer," I responded, and then picked up the phone, and called Dee at work to ask her to come over for supper. She gladly agreed, and asked if she could bring anything.

"Just bring your gorgeous body, my love," I said, trying to be clever, but added, "and also some potato salad, if you don't mind."

"I'll see you in a couple hours," Dee said, and hung up.

In the meantime, we got everything ready, set the table outside, made some lemonade, and ran to the store for hamburger buns, and by the time we had finished preparations, Dee and the kids had arrived. Dee and I gave each other a big hug, and made our way out to the barbecue where Scott had already started cooking burgers. Meanwhile, the kids headed off to play video games until the meal was ready.

"Okay Henry," Dee started, "I want to know everything that happened when we were together back in the days of the dragons, and don't leave anything out."

"Well then," I replied, "you'd better get yourself a beer and a chair, because this is going to take a while."

So, she did just that, and while Scott cooked the burgers, I told Dee all about the escalating adventures from the days of the dragons, including the part where her counterpart, Mara, said that she felt as though she was going to die soon, and the pact we'd made to meet each other again in the land of the pyramids at a predetermined time in history. Dee got a far away look in her eyes, and then spoke.

"That explains a lot about the other dreams I have once in a while, and also explains my fascination with ancient Egypt, the pharaohs, the pyramids and their builders. When you get all the mysteries solved about our life with the dragons, you can start with our Egyptian life, what do you think?"

"That was my thoughts exactly," I replied. Then I continued to tell her about the battles we had fought already with the Gogs, and how Scott's counterpart, Balon, had also lost his eye in a similar way as Scott had in this life. Dee was mesmerized by the things I was telling her, and admitted that she could see it all in her mind, just as I was describing it, reaffirming the fact that we had spent a previous life together. Dee was zoning out when I broke her trance by speaking.

"You know, my love, we need to make an iron clad pact right now to meet again at a certain time and place, just like we did all the times before, especially given the things that happened at the fireworks booth with Mike. You just never know when death will come to claim you. So, when, and where should we meet in our next life my dear?"

"Well," she began, "I've always wanted to live in Australia, so lets meet there, and given our ages right now, along with our life expectancy, let's meet in about forty years, and don't be late Henry."

I looked at her with a sense of awe, because that was exactly the way Mara had talked when she made the pact with me about our meeting in Egypt. When Dee noticed my bewilderment, she smiled, and said.

"I was just kidding about the 'don't be late' thing, darling," which then snapped me back to reality.

"I'm sorry love," I replied, "I was just amazed about how you sounded just like Mara when you spoke about our ages and life expectancy. Mara said it exactly the same way."

"Of course, silly," Dee added, "Mara and I are the same person you know, so we would naturally talk the same. So, lover, do we have a date, forty years from now?"

"We do indeed, and since we have our reunions down to being born under the same zodiac sign, we should be able to shave off a few years in age difference too. Now, give me a kiss to seal the deal."

Pulling Dee to me, we embraced and kissed a kiss that would leave an impression on each other that would last for another lifetime. When we finally broke off our kiss, it left us both weak in the knees, and I too had to sit down.

"That was weird," I said, catching my breath. "I've never had that happen before."

"Now you know what you've been doing to me all this time," Dee replied. "It looks like our souls are starting to meld together all over again. That should ensure our reunion in the future, don't you think?"

"Hell, I may never be the same right now," I stated, "let alone in the future. My head is still spinning, so what is that all about?"

"I'm not sure, my love," Dee said, "but, I'm sure that after your next session with Dr. Miller, we'll probably find out."

It was Scott who finally broke our déjà vu by announcing that the burgers were ready. Calling the kids down to the table, we had a wonderful meal, with laughter and jokes, small talk, and a sense of ease that could only have come from our decision about plans to reunite in our next life. It was like getting a new life insurance policy, where you knew that yours and your spouse's future was secured. It took a load off of both of our minds.

After the meal was done, Scott, Dee, and myself all went out on the deck to sit, drink, and talk, while the kids both got into the hot tub. Around ten, Scott announced that he was going home tonight, and would see us tomorrow, and after he left, Dee and I continued to sit and talk about the past, and the future. The kids went off to their respective rooms to play video games, or watch television, and about midnight, Dee and I went to bed, first to make love, and then to sleep a sound, peaceful sleep. Life would be perfect if we just knew the whereabouts of Mike right now. He still had not been caught, and we could never be completely at ease while he was still loose.

Morning came bright and early, and while I fixed coffee and a light breakfast, Dee got ready to go to work, and the kids reluctantly got up and had breakfast. As Dee got into the car to head out for work, she gave me a kiss and a big hug, and said she would call me tonight. She had work to do at home tonight, and I had to go to work the day after tomorrow, so we would not see each other for a few days. Of course that would make our next meeting all that sweeter, but until then, I would be going crazy.

I watched as Dee drove away, waving to them as they went. All the while there was a nagging feeling in the back of my mind, and I was unable to shake the feeling. I've had these feelings many times in my life, and in every single case, there was some sort of crisis taking place, or soon would be, and that was the impression I was getting now. Unfortunately, I never know what the problem is until it's over. Maybe in one of my previous lives I had the ability to predict, or interpret what the feeling meant, but in this life, I seem to have lost that ability. That's what happens when modern luxuries ruin old talents, and each sojourn on earth moves us farther and farther away from those abilities. Maybe there's a way the hypnotherapist can reawaken those talents, it might be worth a try.

I walked back into the house to clean up the breakfast dishes, and was lost in thought when the phone rang, nearly scaring me out of my socks, and snapping me back to reality. Picking up the phone, I was shocked to hear Jane's voice on the other end, which caused me to stutter when I asked her what I could do for her. There was venom in her voice when she spoke, and it sounded as though she had been drinking.

"So, I hear you already have a live-in girlfriend, you jerk. You didn't even let our bed cool down, did you?"

"What business is it of yours?" I asked, "since you're the one that left me', not the other way around. What I do now is none of your concern, so I would appreciate it if you didn't bother me again. And besides, this house was my family's home long before you ever moved in, so you don't have any say here. You already cleared your belongings out, so if you continue to harass me, I'll file a restraining order against you, is that clear?"

Responding in drunken anger, she said. "It's too bad that bullet didn't kill you, maybe the next one will." Then she hung up, leaving me standing there, mad, and frustrated.

Although I really didn't believe she was actually threatening me, after the attack by another jealous individual, I won't ever take my safety for granted again. It's probably just the alcohol talking, but I'll keep my guard up, at least for a while. Having to look over my shoulder all the time is going to take all the fun out of my life, and give me an ulcer besides. There's no use worrying about Jane right now, but if she gets out of hand, I'll have to let the law deal with her. I swear, she's Marta reincarnated all over again.

After finishing the dishes, I busied myself with mowing the lawn, cutting weeds, trimming trees, and getting caught up on all the things that I had neglected while I was selling fireworks. Later that afternoon I paid a few bills online, and went to see my parents on their ranch. About suppertime I met Scott back at my house where we decided to go out for dinner. I figured that I would call Dee when I get back home, but I wasn't ready for the surprise I was to get when I returned home, a surprise that was to change my life forever.

Scott and I finished dinner around 8:00 pm and when we got back home, there was a message on my answering machine, not from Dee, but from Mike. The disturbing part was that the caller I.D. stated the phone call originated from Dee's house. A cold chill ran down my spine as I listened to the message. This is what he had to say.

"Henry, my friend, I have your girlfriend here, or should I say, 'my girlfriend,' you know, the one you stole from me. The only thing is she doesn't seem to enjoy my company anymore, thanks to you."

As I stood there in a state of shock, the phone rang again, and again nearly scaring me out of my socks. Out of habit, I looked at the caller I.D., and saw that it was Dee's phone number again. With panic in my heart, I jerked the phone out of the cradle and yelled into the mouthpiece.

"Dee, are you okay?"

The voice on the other end made my blood run cold, for it was not Dee, but Mike who spoke to me from the other end.

"She's okay for the time being," Mike responded, "but she won't be for long, unless you come over for a little chat."

My response back to him was. "Let her go you creep, it's not her fault. I'm the one you want, so why don't you come over to my house, and we'll play."

"Not hardly," he replied. "You've totally ruined my life Henry, and now I'm going to ruin yours. I can't even show my face in public anymore, thanks to you."

"Thanks to me?" I said in amazement, "did you forget something; you're the one who shot me, not the other way around."

"Apparently I didn't do a good enough job, now did I?" He responded venomously, "But I won't be making any more mistakes like that, so why don't you come over here so I can finish this once and for all."

"You know what, you little weasel," I replied, "I think I'll do just that, now let Dee go, because this is between you and I."

"I don't think so," he said smugly, "I'm going to keep her and the kids here for good measure."

Enraged, I blurted out, "You have her kids there, you moron, what the hell is wrong with you, you're going to scar them forever, now get them out of the house before they see you do something that no child should ever see. I'll be there in half an hour, now let them go, or the deal's off."

You could tell he was responding to my authoritative talk, because he said he would let the kids go, but not Dee. You could hear the kids screaming and crying in the background, saying they didn't want to leave their mother, but Mike was yelling at them to get out of the house before he did something bad.

Mike was weak, mentally and physically, so maybe I could work him even more before this got totally out of hand. Soon, Mike came back to the phone, and said.

"Alright Henry, I've done my part, now you do yours, I'm not going to wait all night long for you. If you don't get here within an hour, I'm just going to shoot Dee, and then come looking for you. You'll never know when the next bullet is going to get you, and trust me, I won't miss the next time, now get over here, and don't call the cops, or I'll kill Dee right now, do you understand?'

"I understand Mike," I replied, "but I want to talk to Dee to make sure she's okay, or I'm not coming anywhere near that place."

"Fair enough," he said, and soon, Dee's voice came onto the phone, a little shaky, but still strong.

"I'm okay Henry, but don't you dare come over here, or he'll kill us both."

"Don't worry about me," I assured her, "I'll take care of myself. Now, just say yes or no to my questions so he doesn't know what I'm asking, understand?"

"Yes." she replied.

"Okay," I started, "are the kids out of the house, and safe?"

"Yes," she replied.

"Does Mike have a gun?"

"Yes."

"Are you injured?"

"No."

"Was he already in the house when you got home?"

"Yes,"

Then abruptly, Mike was on the phone screaming at me for trying to talk to Dee in code, and told me I was running out of time, and then the phone went dead. As soon as I hung up the phone, I called 911, and told them what had happened, and that it was the guy who had shot me earlier. I also told them that he had a hostage, and had threatened to kill Dee if I called the cops. I also told the detective who came on the line that Mike was expecting me within an hour, so they would have to be in place around the home before I got there, and to not let Mike see them.

They agreed, told me to be careful, and under no circumstances should I go into that house. They needed me to lure him outside, or at least to the door, where a sharpshooter could get a shot at him. I agreed to do what I could, but as a security measure, I decided to put my own pistol down the back of my pants in case things went bad, and maybe I could get a chance to take him out myself.

The ride down the valley this time was the longest drive I think I've ever taken in my life, with a million thoughts racing through my head, thoughts of the present, and reflections from the past. Does a crisis have to be involved in every one of my sojourns, I asked myself as I drove. I wished I had gotten far enough in the hypnosis sessions to maybe see this coming. Both Dee and Mara had warned me that our relationships were always cut short throughout history, and it would seem that this lifetime was going to be no exception. Why don't I listen?

As I approached Dee's trailer park, it was obvious that the police had the area cordoned off, and were evacuating as many people as they could from the trailer homes near Dee's house without being noticed. I was stopped at the roadblock, but the detective in charge recognized me, and waved me on, but stopped me long enough to give me a few last minute instructions before sending me on my way. He didn't think any of his officers had been seen, and he had snipers in place.

I was totally annoyed as I pulled away, because surely there was no way on earth that Mike would not have known something was up outside of the trailer unless he was a total idiot. So, with a heavy weight on my heart, I drove ahead and into the trailer park, where I pulled up in front of Dee's house. I remained seated in my pickup, hoping Mike would stick his head out of the door where a sniper could end this ordeal once and for all.

Unfortunately, it was Dee's head that looked out from an only partially opened door, and it was obvious that Mike had a hold of her from behind, making sure she would not run away. Mike yelled to me from the safety of the house.

"I told you not to call the cops Henry, but you didn't listen. Now Dee's blood is going to be on your hands. Now get out of your truck where I can see you, or are you a coward?"

As I started to slowly get out of my truck, deliberately keeping the front of my truck between Mike and myself, I responded to his threats with a few insults of my own, hoping to make him so angry that he would forget about Dee, and come far enough out of the house to challenge me.

"You're calling me a coward," I said tauntingly, "you're the coward, you pathetic piece of crap, hiding behind a girl, holding her hostage, threatening to kill an unarmed, helpless woman. Why don't you come out and fight me like a man, no cops, just you and I, man to man. How about it you pussy?'

Well, that did it, Mike let out a scream of rage, and immediately raised his gun to take a shot at me. That's when Dee kicked Mike in the shin, then when he let go of her, she pulled away from him and ran from the house toward me. I jumped out from behind my truck to run toward her before Mike could recover his senses, pulling my pistol from my rear waistband as I ran toward Dee. Mike and I were raising our guns at the same time, and when all the guns went off, it sounded like thunder.

I blinked my eyes, feeling almost stunned, but I grabbed Dee as she started to stumble, and as both of us fell to the ground, I saw several bullets striking Mike, who had been standing in the doorway a split second ago, but was now being spun sideways, and backwards against the door jam, and then falling over the porch rail to land in a heap on the ground, lying in a anatomically incorrect position, obviously mortally wounded.

It was only then that I became aware that I was lying on top of Dee, trying to protect her. Rolling off of her, she was face down in the grass, and it was then that I noticed the growing bloodstain on the back of her shirt. Screaming NO" at the top of my voice, I rolled her over, cradling her head in my arms and lap. She coughed, and blood spattered my chest and face. Her eyes opened, and she looked up at me, with nothing but love in her eyes, and she spoke to me.

"Henry, my love, please watch out for my kids, tell them that I love them, and know that I love you, and I don't regret a thing. I'm thankful for the time we were able to spend together."

Tears were streaming from my eyes, and all of a sudden, the cops were rushing in to secure the scene, making sure Mike was incapacitated. The detective kneeled down beside me, and said an ambulance was on its way, and asked if I was okay. I nodded yes, and he moved on.

Then I heard more screaming and crying as Dee's kids struggled to get to us, and when I motioned for them to come up, the police that were restraining them, released them, and they came up and kneeled down with us, holding their mom's hands, crying, and telling her that they loved her. Dee coughed again, and blood ran down her chin, but she managed to continue speaking.

"Kids, Henry, I know I'm going to die," which caused her daughter to cry even harder, but, putting her finger to her lips, she continued.

"Don't be sad now, because you know that this is only the end of this life, and the beginning of the next one, and before I go, we need to make a pact between us. Henry and I will meet again in Australia, in about forty years, and if any of you kids should die before then, you will meet us there too. Otherwise, if you live to old age, and mine and Henry's next life goes to full age, then lets all meet again in one hundred and fifty years, in England, at Stonehenge. We may not know why we are drawn there, but follow your hearts, promise me, kids, promise me, you too Henry."

We all promised Dee that we would meet again at the specified times, and as we were making our promises, Dee coughed again, this time emitting a large gush of blood, and choking. I tilted her head to the side so the blood would not cause her to choke, but I noticed that she had gone still. Placing a finger along side of her neck, I could feel the pulse fading, and it was only then that I had noticed the ambulance had arrived, and the paramedics were moving in to take over care of Dee, while the police were helping the kids move out of the way.

My partner Dan was on duty, and when he looked at me for a sign of her condition, he could tell that there was not going to be much hope for Dee, but, like a good paramedic, he performed all the necessary steps to try to save her life, if nothing more than for the benefit of her children, and the onlookers. As they loaded her into the ambulance, the started performing CPR. Holding an arm around each of Dee's kids, we watched the ambulance roar away, lights and sirens blaring.

The spell was broken once again when another screaming woman broke through the police line, and rushed toward the kids and me. As a policeman grabbed her to restrain her, we saw that it was Dee's mother, hysterical, screaming for Dee, screaming for the kids, so we waved for the policeman to let her go. She ran up and grabbed the kids in her arms, screaming to know what had happened, and saying that she had warned Dee to stay away from me, that only trouble would follow.

I wanted to tell her that she should have warned Dee to stay away from Mike and not me, but at this point, it was all mute. There would be no sense in arguing with Dee's mom at a time like this. As she started to tow the kids away to take them back to her house, Chelsie broke away and ran back to me, throwing her arms around my waist, sobbing uncontrollably, and saying she wanted to stay with me. As her grandmother screamed at her to return, I kneeled down to speak with her, face to face, saying.

"You need to go with your grandmother right now; you know your mom would want it that way. Your grandmother is your family, and I'm not, so the authorities would never allow you to come stay with me. But you know my phone number, and you can call me anytime you need to talk and the same goes for your brother. For now, the police are going to need to talk to us, and they are going to be asking a lot of questions from all of us, so you need to be strong, strong for your mom, and strong for me, okay."

She nodded, still crying, so I continued.

"Don't ever forget the pact we made with your mom, that we will see her again, in another life. Don't mention the pact to your grandmother, she wouldn't understand, and she would tell you not to believe in such things, and she may even convince you that it can't happen. But you and I know the truth, and that's all that matters, so be strong, and don't ever forget, okay."

"Okay," she responded, the tears getting lighter, She told me she loved me, and then releasing her grip from me, she walked back to her grandmother, who gave me a look of disdain, and then hustled the kids away to a policeman, who was waiting to take them to the station for questioning.

I felt bad that Dee's mother hated me so bad, she just needed someone to focus her frustration on right now, and I guess I was that outlet. The object of my frustration was lying in a heap on the ground just fifteen steps away, dead and departed from this world, Mike, and good riddance to him.

But then it hit me, it hit me like a rock, and the thought of it nearly made me ill. Mike and Dee just went to the next life together. That's why Mike, Sardon, and who knows how many other names he is known by, that's how he continues to plague us lifetime after lifetime, because he manages to get killed at the same time as Dee, the same time as Mara, time after time. How could I have been so stupid? I will need to find a way to change that in his next life. I will have to ask Dr. Miller to help me to figure out how to do it during one of our hypnosis sessions.

The look on my face must have made the detective think I was injured, or sick because of the shooting, because he came over to where I was standing, and asked me if I was okay, or if I needed an ambulance. He saw all of Dee's blood on the front of my pants, and was concerned that I may have been shot also. I assured him that I was okay physically, but not so good mentally right now. Then he asked if I needed to see a psychiatrist or anything, and I told him no, that I already see a doctor every week, and that I would be okay until my next appointment.

The detective then asked if I was ready for my debriefing, and I said yes. Meanwhile, he reached down to pick my pistol up from the ground, and told me he would have to keep it for now as evidence in the case, and to see if my bullet had also struck Mike. I told him that I understood, and followed him to his car. I looked back as the coroner was taking pictures of Mike's body, and then covered the body with a body bag. All I could think of was the fact that now I would have to see Mike again, in another life, and probably under similar circumstances.

The interview with the detective took about an hour, going over everything from my relationship with Dee, to my first meeting with Mike at the fireworks booth, then to the first shooting at the fireworks booth, to the phone call today, and finally to my part leading up to the shooting a short time ago. The detective wanted to make sure this little fiasco wasn't a preplanned event on my part to get back at Mike for something. I was slightly offended at his accusations, but I did understand his concerns. After he had all the information he needed, he said I was free to go, but to be available if he had anymore questions.

I walked back to my truck in a virtual state of shock, and to the onlookers, I'm sure I looked like death warmed over. I was covered in blood, my face was pale, and I shuffled my feet like I had been beaten. The drive home was just as depressing as the gravity of the situation sunk in. I would never again in this lifetime see the woman I loved, I would never feel her touch, taste her lips, feel her body next to mine, hear her voice, or look into her eyes. I felt lonelier now than I ever had in my life, and a tear found its way to my cheek, only to run down my chin, and fall onto my blood covered lap. It was almost too much to bear.

I had no sooner pulled into my driveway than Scott came out of the house to greet me. He had already heard through the grapevine about what had happened, and as soon as I saw his face, another tear found its way out. Scott put an arm around my shoulder, and told me he was sorry to hear about Dee. I told him thanks, and walked with him into the house. As soon as I had changed cloths, and cleaned up, Scott asked.

"Would you like a gin and tonic, it'll help take the edge off."

I told him I would love one, and I went to sit on the deck while he fixed the drinks. When he came back, he handed me a drink, and sat down in a chair opposite from me. Neither of us said anything for several minutes, until Scott finally asked me if I was willing to tell him about what had happened. I told him yes, and as soon as I could gain my composure, I related the story to him, beginning with the phone call from Mike, and finishing with the shooting, and finally the interview with the detective. When I was done, Scott could only shake his head, and say he was sorry that he wasn't there to help out.

After another drink, I told Scott I needed to go lie down for a while, but asked him to stick around in case I needed to talk some more. He said he would watch television until bedtime, but wanted me to know that even after he went to bed, that I could wake him up if I needed to talk. I told him thanks for being such a good friend, and then I went to lie down, falling asleep almost immediately.

Sleep tonight would prove to be anything but restful though, with images of Dee being killed in a nondescript trailer park outside of Hamilton, Montana, to the screams of Mara being killed on an ancient battlefield. The images of dragons circling overhead, mixed with images of Mike holding a rifle, lights, sirens, laser beams, and singed flesh was just about all I could take, and I suddenly bolted upright in bed, drenched in sweat, looking around the room, half expecting to see the battle still raging. Nothing but the bedroom walls were to be seen, and instead of dragons screeching, only the birds were chirping.

It was hoping it would be a long time before I'd have these dreams again, and I was hoping they were done, but obviously, I still had a ways to go. There are still unfinished issues to be dealt with on a subconscious level, issues of guilt perhaps, the guilt of not being able to save the woman I love, lifetime after lifetime. Surely this can't be all there is to our existence, doomed to follow the same pathway, over and over again. I have to figure out how to break the cycle, or the next sojourn on earth may well be spent in an asylum.

As I swung my legs over the side of the bed, my feet resting on the cool floor, I thought about all the people who were locked up in asylums, and I wondered, how many of these poor souls are in there because of something in a past life, something so terrible that it was easier for them to withdraw into there own minds, to push out reality, to fight the demons within their own souls. It would explain a lot of things if therapists could delve into the dark recesses of the troubled mind, and repair it from the inside, out.

Shaking off all of the weird things going through my head, I forced myself to get up and get dressed. It would be too easy to let this incapacitate me to the point of listlessness. I have to force myself to keep moving, to keep doing something to occupy my mind, to keep my life moving forward, if only to find answers to the mysteries of my own past. I wish I could get back in to see Dr. Miller before next week. In light of everything that's happened, maybe he can get me in sooner.

Forcing myself to get up, I dressed and went downstairs to start a pot of coffee. By the time the coffee had finished brewing; Scott was coming down the stairs, drawn by the smell of fresh brewed coffee. He asked me how I had slept, since I didn't wake him up during the night. I told him about the dreams I'd had, and how I felt like I needed to go see Dr. Miller again. He said that might be a good idea. I agreed to give the Doctor a call later today when the rest of the world woke up, since it was still only 7:00am.

"Fix yourself some breakfast before you head out Scott," I said, as Scott got ready to leave. "There's some frozen waffles in the freezer if you like that sort of thing."

"I think I'll take you up on that," he said. "Can I fix you something too?"

"No thanks," I responded, "I'm not feeling very hungry yet today."

"Okay," Scott replied, "but you need to eat something later to keep your strength up, physically, as well as mentally."

"I will," I promised, not feeling at this point that I would ever be hungry again.

Scott finished his breakfast, then headed out to mow lawns, and to check the car wash. We agreed to meet again here this afternoon when it got too hot to mow. I told him I would try to make an appointment with Dr. Miller for late this afternoon, and maybe Scott could ride in to town with me. He said that would be good, and off he went to work. If I couldn't get in to see the doctor in the next day or so, there's no way I would be able to go back to work at my own job, as my mental state would be a detriment to good patient care. In fact, I'm considering taking a leave of absence for a while until I can get my head on straight again.

It's amazing how guilty one can feel after something like this happens.

Dee was killed trying to protect me, because that bullet was meant for me. I'm the one that should have been dead twice over, once at the fireworks booth, and again at the trailer court. I guess fate had a hand in it, because for some reason, I'm still alive, and Dee is dead, just like she predicted, and just like she predicted thousands of years ago in the time of the dragons, a death that I'm still going to have to face, again. I don't think I like this past lives therapy anymore. It's like having to experience yours, and your loved ones' deaths, over and over again.

After Scott had left, I took a cup of coffee out to the deck to sit on the porch swing. The morning air was cool and fresh, and as I sat there, I watched the clouds passing overhead, marveling at the mountains that framed both sides of the Bitterroot valley, and I listened to the birds in the trees. The whole thing was quite therapeutic, and the next thing I knew, I must have dozed off, because I woke with a start to the phone ringing. Gathering my wits, I rushed to the phone before the answering machine could pick up. The remote phone is on a stand just inside the door of the house, so I didn't have far to go to get to the phone. When I picked up the phone, I was surprised to hear the voice on the other end, it was Dr. Miller.

"Henry," he began, "this is James Miller. I hope I'm not disturbing you."

"Not at all Jim," I replied, "in fact, I was just about to call you to find out if I could get in to see you again as soon as possible. I'm having kind of a rough time, and need someone to talk to."

"So I've heard," Dr. Miller stated, "I heard about it on the news Henry, and I want to tell how sorry I am to hear about Dee's death. How are you holding up my friend?'

"I've been better doc," I replied, "is there any chance I can get in to see you today?'

"That's why I called you," he replied. "I have an opening at two o'clock if you can make it. I knew you would be needing some help Henry, and I have some other interesting things I'd like to share with you too, so, can you make it at two?"

"I certainly can doctor," I said with a glimmer of hope in my voice.

"Very well then," Dr. Miller responded, "I'll see you at two."

"Thank you so much Jim, I really appreciate this," I said, and as I hung up the phone, I thought to myself, what an incredible coincidence, or was this fate guiding me along, just like it has time and again.

Scott walked in the door at about noon, and I couldn't wait to tell him about the phone call from Dr. Miller. He too was amazed by the timing of the phone call, and by the thoughtfulness of Dr. Miller. We both wondered though at what he meant when he said he had some other interesting things to tell me. Usually it's the patient who does most of the talking, not the doctor, so, with my interest peaking, I kind of pushed Scott a little hard to hurry and get cleaned up and changed so we could get going to town. While he cleaned up, I made him a sandwich to bring along so we didn't have to take time out for him to eat.

We were on the road by one o'clock, and it was decided that Scott would go do a little shopping while I had my session with Dr. Miller, and then be back to pick me up after a couple hours. That should be about how long the session would take, and if either one of us got done early, it was a nice day to sit around outside.

On the way to town we talked a lot about what had happened in the last few days, and if there was any way we could have prevented it from happening, especially knowing what we know now. The conclusion was still the same, there was no way to change the outcome, one of us was predetermined to die. The only variable might have been which one of us died first. Sometimes I think that all I would have needed was a few more sessions with Dr. Miller and I would have known exactly what had happened in each of our past lives. Perhaps then I could have recognized a pattern about what was going to happen in this lifetime. Maybe then I could have changed the outcome, but now I'll never know.

By the time we had hashed out all of the different possibilities over and over, we were pulling up in front of Dr. Miller's house. I noticed right away that the 'Session in Progress' sign was not out, so I knew I could go right up to the door without waiting. I told Scott I would see him in a couple of hours, and off he went to do some shopping, which I'm sure would be trips to all the local sporting goods stores. As I turned to walk up the pathway to the house, Dr. Miller opened the door to greet me.

"Hello Henry," he began, "how are you doing my friend, I'm so sorry to hear about your loss, please, won't you please come inside."

"I'm hanging in there Jim," I said as I walked past him into the house.

"And how's your side doing from your bullet wound?" he asked.

"It's healing nicely," I replied. "It itches a little though, but I'll deal with it, given what the outcome could have been."

"I'm glad you could come in Henry," Jim said as I took my place in the easy chair.

"I'm glad you could get me in," I said.

"Actually, Henry," he started, "I cancelled some of my appointments today so I could fit you in. I have some interesting information for you that I learned from another patient, but please understand, this is confidential information. I usually don't share anything a patient tells me with anyone else, but this is so fantastic, and so relevant, that I felt that you have to know."

Dr. Miller definitely had my interest and attention right now. I had no idea what it was he could want to tell me, but I was ready to hear anything right now, so I said to him.

"What is it doc?"

"I have another patient with whom we are exploring his past lives, and to make a long story short, he was a monk in a monastery in an area now known as the Swiss Alps. He said the monastery is located on top of a mountain peak, and was once apparently an ancient castle that the monks took over about four thousand years ago. The monk said the castle had been there for eons before that, and was in a bad state of erosion before they restored it."

"That's definitely interesting," I said, "but what's that have to do with me?"

"Here's where it gets interesting," he replied. "it would seem that when they excavated the grounds, they found one room in particular that appeared to be a library, and maybe a pharmacy combined, with lots of herbs, plants, potions, and earthen jars, some of which contained the preserved remains of baby dragons."

My mouth was wide open, and I must have looked like I was in shock, because Dr. Miller asked if I was okay, and after acknowledging that I was okay, he continued.

"It would also seem," he continued, "that there was a journal inside the room that talked about the inhabitants of the castle, including the owner of the castle, a person known as King Ethan, the Dragon Master."

Chills ran up and down my spine when he said that, and my arms broke out with goose flesh. I thought I was going to faint, but I managed to tell him to continue, which he did.

"The man was very specific in describing the contents of the journal, and that journal became the basis for their whole belief system, and those words are still taught to the monks to this day. The best part is that the 'Order of The Dragon' is still alive and operating to this day Henry."

My head was swimming with images and possibilities, and after a minute, I nodded for him to continue.

"Henry," he continued, "the monks are waiting for the Dragon Master to return, to be reincarnated, to return to the monastery to confirm their beliefs, to teach them what has been left out of the journal, and to show them the secret chamber."

"I don't know if the world is ready to see the things in the secret chamber." I said.

"The monks don't want to show anything to the world, in fact, they have other technologies that they have been studying that they will never share with the world, including a direct communication with the people who have died, and are waiting in the other world, waiting to be reborn and return to the earth, and that includes Dee, or should I say, Mara."

This last part was almost too much to grasp, and I placed my face into my hands to try to stop my head from spinning, but Dr. Miller continued.

"Henry, the monks are waiting for you to return to the castle, to your castle, and it may well provide you the opportunity to talk to Dee again, maybe to say something you didn't have a chance to say, or maybe just to coordinate yours and her mutual return to earth, what do you think."

When I looked up from my hands, there was a tear in my eye, but I managed to say.

"Yes doc, I feel that I should go there, and that feeling is very strong. I've always felt that I had some purpose to my life, but I didn't know what it was, until now. I have a little money set aside, and now would be as good a time as any to take a leave of absence from work, under the guise of personal grief. If I find what I'm looking for there, maybe I'll stay, and if not, I'll have a month to find out."

"Now you're talking Henry," Jim said, "and now, are you ready for your trip back in time?"

"I'm ready doc," I stated, "let's do it."

"Okay Henry," he started, "lean back in your chair and get comfortable. Listen to the stream babbling through the rocks, a cool, clear stream, flowing back in time, back to the time of the great dragons. And the birds, listen to their songs, they're talking to you, telling you a tale of days gone by, days when the flying creatures ruled the skies, ruled the earth itself. Now, feel the breeze on your face, the same breeze that blew across the face of the earth for thousands upon thousands of years, a breeze that has carried the breath of millions of creatures, human and dragon alike, a breeze that has passed through your own lungs one lifetime after another. Feel those past lifetimes coursing through your lungs, through your veins, and remember those lifetimes, one of which we are going back to visit right now, the life you know as the Dragon Master. At the count of five, you will be on your journey. One, two, three, four, five.

Chapter 10

A knock on the door jarred me out of my sleep, and as I sprang out of the bed, my hand immediately gripped the handle of my sword, expecting anything, but as my eyes focused on my surroundings, it became obvious that I was still in my chambers, and when the knock came again, I was coherent enough to ask who it was. The voice beyond the heavy wooden door was the voice of Balon, stating that Valik was waiting in the kitchen for the orders of the day. I told him I would be there in five minutes, and I turned to see Mara, awake, leaning on her elbow, looking at me, but with a vacant look in her eye.

"Good morning my love," I said, as I put down my sword, and leaning forward to kiss her on the lips. She grabbed me around the neck and held on tight.

"Don't go Ethan, stay here forever, stay in the castle forever until the Gog die of old age, please." Mara seemed desperate.

"You know I can't do that Mara," I said, "I have to finish this today, because this is my destiny. Please promise me that you will stay here in the castle where it's safe."

"And you know that I can't do that either," she responded, "because I also have a date with my destiny today, and it is waiting for me."

"Please don't talk like that Mara," I said, getting slightly annoyed by all of the talk of death. I felt that I could protect her from anything, which is probably just male ego speaking, but I felt if she would stay in the castle, she would be safe. Why wouldn't she listen to me, why does she have to be so stubborn? I suppose I could have her forcibly detained here, but that would certainly strain our relationship, so I guess we will go to battle together, to whatever end is in store for us.

"You go on ahead," she told me, "I'll be along shortly, but do not leave without me, or I'll walk to the battlefield."

"Yes, my love," I responded, and quickly dressing, I headed to the kitchen for our briefing.

When I arrived at the kitchen, Captain Valik was there, with a couple of his men, along with Balon, and a couple of civilians. As I approached, Valik hailed me and introduced the men with him. The two soldiers that accompanied Valik were his next in command, each one commanding a hundred troops, and the two civilians were going to be in charge of the castle guard while we were away from the castle. Valik assured me that these men have had prior military experience, and were quite capable of commanding the volunteers, as well as defending the castle. His soldiers had been up most of the night training the volunteers in weapon use, including bows, and the explosives. A few soldiers were to be left behind as instructors and support.

After a short while, Mara joined us, and soon we had our plan of attack ready to implement, and we were ready to proceed. I was to go below, take the chariot down to the caverns, mount a second Dragon's Breath weapon on the chariot, load the Horn of Gideon, and bring the chariot back up to the castle grounds. Then, I would go out through the main gate, and clear all enemy troops off the road from the castle all the way down to the valley floor.

Meanwhile, Captain Valik and his troops were to march down through the caverns and tunnels to the gate at the falls, engage any enemy that may have been brave enough to venture into that valley, and then wait for me to meet up with them there. Then we would proceed down to the plateau overlooking the town, and the King's castle, and set our trap for the Gog army. I gave Valik a key to the hidden gates below, and told him not to ever let it get into enemy hands, a charge he accepted wholeheartedly.

The sight of the chariot coming through the castle grounds was going to cause quite a stir among the populace, but it was probably going to be the boost in moral that the people would need. It was time to put our plan in action.

We all shook hands, gave each other hugs, and words of encouragement, and separated to execute our orders. I told Mara to gather some food from Sophie, distribute first aid kits to Valik and his troops, and then meet me in front of my villa when I returned with the chariot. Then, we would ride the chariot through the castle grounds together as King, and Queen.

Valik had left Mr. Damon to be my chariot driver, as well as three other troopers, one was to man the second Dragons breath weapon, and the two others as archers to shoot down any enemy troops we may happen to miss with the weapons. Balon would accompany Mara and I in the chariot. He has been my friend and confidant for as long as I could remember, and whatever fate awaited us, we would all meet it together. After giving Mara a quick kiss, Balon and I hurried down the stairs to the caverns below.

Looking into the dragon pen as we passed, they were empty, except for Feron, still alive, but looking very weak. I greeted her in my mind, but the only acknowledgement in return was a sense of defeat and loneliness. I felt bad, but I also felt I had to keep going, to avenge her injuries, and to avenge the deaths of the other dragons, not to mention the death of my father at the hands of the Gog clan. The Gog had much to pay for, and today was their judgment day. As we continued on, I caught a slight mental picture from the injured dragon, which only said, "Good Luck."

I opened the first hidden door to the secret caverns, and there was the chariot, right where we had left it in our haste the day before. Balon lit a torch, which when brought on board, immediately started charging the crystals in the floor. As soon as we were both aboard, we glided the craft down the long pathway to the main cavern, and while Balon loaded the Horn of Gideon, I went to get the other Dragon's Breath weapon. The hatch to let in sunlight was still open, so the cavern was awash in sunlight. I figured we might as well leave it that way so the troops with Valik would be able to see their way down the corridors. Won't the new troops get an eyeful when they see the mummified dragons encircling the cavern? I hope they all have strong hearts.

As soon as I returned to the chariot, we quickly mounted the second Dragon's Breath weapon in its receptacle and headed back to the surface. Just as we reached the lower level of caverns of the castle, Valik and his troops were descending the stairway. Some of the troops' eyes went wide with fear and amazement as they cleared a way for us to pass, but as Valik bowed his head, the rest quickly regained their composure, and followed suit, bowing their heads. I yelled good luck to them, and guided the craft up the steep stairways, level by level, until I reached the main castle hallway.

Balon climbed down to open the massive double doors which would lead us out to the main castle grounds, and as I guided the craft out into the courtyard, Mara, Damon, and the three troopers were waiting for us. Civilians in the courtyard stopped in their tracks to stare at us, some dropping whatever was in their hands, and some even ran away screaming as if a monster was suddenly in their midst.

As soon as everyone was aboard, Mr. Damon maneuvered the craft through the courtyards and on to the gate, where we got the same response from everyone we passed. I stopped for a moment to address the crowd, and to quash their fears. I told them that because of these things, they would never have to fear the Gog again, and, telling the crowd to watch, I instructed the gatekeepers to open the gate. Then, to give an example of what the weapon would do, I aimed one of the Dragon's Breath weapons out through the gate at a rock cropping across the gorge, and fired the weapon at it.

The intense heat that was generated against the rock caused it first to start to melt, and then to explode from trapped gasses and steam within the rock. At first, the crowd went totally quiet, faces ashen, but then slowly, and with growing excitement, they started talking, then laughing, and then cheering. I told them we have already been attacking the Gog with these weapons, and we were now on our way to confront them again. I encouraged them to be brave, and to guard the castle until our return. Then, instructing the gatekeepers to lower the drawbridge, we went out through the gate, crossed the drawbridge, and then waited until the gatekeepers had raised the drawbridge, and closed the gate.

Slowly we made our way down the road, past the dead bodies of the slain Gog troops, some of which were being picked at by birds and rodents, and all of which would have to thrown into the gorge when this conflict was done. The roadway made its way down through winding valleys, and along steep cliff faces, so each wide spot was a potential ambush spot. Here and there was evidence that the Gog had attacked and killed peasants and peddlers who had tried to escape from the valley below, apparently showing no mercy, and that was exactly what they would receive from me, no mercy.

Our first confrontation came about a mile below the castle. As we came silently around a bend a group of about a hundred enemy troops were camped in a small meadow, along with a giant crossbow, probably the one that had wounded Feron. By the time the enemy saw us, it was too late as both dragons breathe weapons unleashed hell upon troops, horses, crossbow, and equipment. As a small group tried to outrun us down the road, the archers cut them down.

Mara happened to notice a sentry trying to hide behind a rock bluff above the camp. As soon as we stopped to train our weapons on his position, he came out of hiding, hands above his head, trying to surrender. No Mercy' was the only thought that went through my head, and firing the dragons breath weapon at him, his scream was cut short when the super heated air cut him in two at chest level, and left him a burning, quivering mass. As I turned to look at each person on the chariot, there was no response from anyone.

This is war, everyone understands that, and prisoners would only complicate things. These people showed no mercy to those that they had raped and murdered in cold blood, and when they entered this land for that express purpose, they will reap what they have sowed. It was time to move on.

I knew there was another large meadow about half way down the mountain, and another one where the mountain valley gave way to the wide-open expanse of the plateau, and the Valley of the King Below that. Those two places would be where we would encounter our next concentrations of troops.

As we approached the first large meadow, it was obvious that there was going to be a large concentration of troops to deal with. The first sign was a sentry post about a quarter mile up the road from the camp, manned by a dozen enemy soldiers. Since they didn't seem to be expecting traffic from the direction of my castle, they too were caught unprepared. The Dragon's Breath weapon killed them quickly, but the fire, screaming, and rush of activity alerted the camp. As we approached the encampment, some of the troops were trying to rally themselves together for a counter attack. The two Dragon's Breath weapons spouted fire and death as the chariot moved down the road toward the camp, which was now stirred up like a beehive.

Some of the enemy were even managing to launch a few arrows at us, but most fell short, as our weapons were killing them at a much farther distance. As we entered the large meadow, there were enemy troops on both sides of us now, and the two Dragon's Breath weapons were raking both sides of the road. Everywhere the Dragon's Breath touched the grasses and trees would burst into flames, adding to the confusion. Men were running in every direction, some stopping to fight, others running for their life.

Suddenly, a giant spear launched from a crossbow whisked past the front of the chariot. I quickly backtracked its trajectory, and spotted the launcher hidden in the trees. As the enemy troops were working to reload it, I fired the Dragon's Breath into the midst of the troops, trees, and the crossbow, turning the whole place into an inferno. Soon it seemed that the whole meadow and the surrounding forest was on fire. Enemy troops were running around in panic like ants in a fire. The conflagration was now doing most of the work for us, and at this point we were just picking off stragglers as we moved through the meadow and continued down the road.

In the smoke and confusion, we hadn't paid attention to the fact that we had approached the lower sentry position, and the first warning came as the soldier manning the opposite Dragon's Breath weapon was hit in the chest with two arrows, throwing him back into one of the archers before he collapsed to the floor of the chariot. In an instant, Mara rushed to the weapon, and, as a dozen enemy troops rushed the chariot, Mara cut three of them in half with the Dragon's Breath, and the other archer killed another one.

I was on the wrong side of the chariot to reach the attackers with my weapon, so, as several of the enemy soldiers jumped up to grab the rails of the chariot and tried to clamber aboard, Balon and I rushed over to fend off the enemy with our swords. Our other archer managed to kill two more, while Balon and I dispatched the other three who tried to climb on board the craft. Another had lost his grip and fell off, and just as he regained his feet behind the chariot, Mara cut him in half with her weapon. The two remaining troops on the ground tried to flee back the way they had come, but were also cut down as Mara swept her weapon across them. They died face down in the dirt, their cloths still burning as we passed.

We were all in a slight state of shock as we cleared the encampment, and about a half mile down the road, I instructed the driver to stop on a long, straight stretch of road, flanked on each side by a cliff wall, one above us, and another below us. This was a good place to regroup, as we could not be approached from either side, and there was plenty of defensible distance ahead of and behind us.

We all took a deep breath, and then took some time to gather our thoughts and go over what had happened, both right, and wrong. The first item was to push the dead soldier off of the chariot so we didn't continue to trip over him. Balon and I pushed him to edge of the railing, and let his body fall over the cliff into the abyss. Then, we passed around the water jug, and a loaf of bread, which everyone tore off a chunk of, and ate it greedily.

"Nice work with the weapon Mara," I stated, not really expecting a response.

"Thanks," she replied. "I've used one before, just not under this kind of pressure."

"Do you want to have someone else take over for you?" I asked.

"No," she responded, "we need archers for just the sort of occasion that just happened, and Balon turned out to be good swordsman, which also helped immensely, so I think I'll stay here where I can be of use."

"Fair enough," I said. "Let's be more alert next time okay, we forgot there would be sentries above and below each camp. The next camp is going to know something's up, with half the mountain on fire, so I suggest from here down, we move slow, kill everything as far out as our weapons will reach, and herd the rest out onto the plateau where we can cut them down in the open, agreed?"

"Agreed," they all responded.

"Then let's move out," I said, and took up position at my weapon. The archers each knocked another arrow, and Mara was already at her weapon. Balon brandished his sword like he was ready to take on the world, and even though he didn't look all that dangerous, his determination would carry him through. Motley crew as we were, we had just annihilated several hundred of the Gog army regulars, and I'm certain we would kill a lot more before this day was done. It wasn't even noon yet, and we were just getting started.

We proceeded down the mountain road with a lot more caution and stealth this time. The last encounter got a little intense there, and we didn't want to lose any more men, or women. It's making me a nervous wreck having Mara with me on this foray, let alone having her right on the rail manning a weapon. If we do get out of this alive, I need to have a serious talk with her about who's supposed to be the boss around here. Of course I already know the answer to that one.

As we approached the plateau, our senses were heightened to the point of overload. We were already getting a little jumpy when we made contact with the first enemy forces, a sentry post that had been reinforced due to the billowing smoke up on the mountain. It looked like nearly a hundred men, and a giant crossbow. The crossbow was a little unnerving, due to its long-range trajectory, and indeed, before we could even gather our wits, the enemy fired the weapon at us. Mara and I reacted at the same instant and fired both of the dragons' breath weapons at the incoming projectile, totally vaporizing it in mid air. Then we kept the weapons firing as we lowered them to cook the crossbow, and all of the troops manning the sentry post.

As we approached the sentry post, we noticed that the road was barricaded with logs and wagons. Apparently they didn't know the chariot could rise as high in the air as fifty feet, which is what we did now. All of a sudden, I wondered why we hadn't done this sooner, as the view from higher up was definitely to our advantage. We could see far into the encampment, and even out onto the plateau. There were enemy troops everywhere, and about the same time that we saw them, they also saw us, and that's when the party started.

Staying as high as the craft would allow, we bore down on the hapless Gog troops, firing our Dragon's Breath weapons at everything that moved or breathed. Enemy troops were firing their bows at us in a constant barrage, only to bounce off the bottom of the chariot. Once in awhile an arrow would arc over the top of the chariot, and if the barrage got too intense, we just moved back away from the railing until we could get clear enough to resume firing.

Balon was picking out giant crossbows for us to target when all of a sudden, one of the giant bolts hit the bottom of the craft, nearly coming all the way through the hull, and almost knocking a couple of us over the side. The spear had shattered a few of the crystals, which caused the chariot to lose some altitude, but it was not a noticeable difference. After a quick chastisement of Balon for not spotting that crossbow a little quicker, Mara and I both vaporized it with our weapons.

The plateau was now in complete chaos, with enemy troops running back toward the city on foot, while others were riding full gallop on horses, and still others tried to stand and fight, only to be scorched by the Dragon's Breath weapons, and still others trying to escape up toward the hidden valley by the falls. Won't they be in for a surprise when they run into Valik and his men?

Just when it seemed there wasn't enough chaos for the routed enemy troops, four dragons swooped out of the sky to randomly attack every group of enemy soldiers they could manage, sometimes swooping down simply to rake troops with their talons, some being knocked over with their spiked tails, while at other times the dragons just grabbed up small groups of men in their talons, only to take them high in the air where they would release them to fall to their deaths. It was truly a terrible, awesome spectacle, and if I was on the wrong side of this battle, I think my heart would probably fail me for fear.

Since most of the crossbows seemed to have been destroyed, we left the remainder of the immediate battlefield to the dragons, and we turned to attack the rear of the troops fleeing up the mountain to the hidden valley. We had to stay out of bow range of the enemy troops because even though we were fifty feet in the air, we were now at the same level as the troops climbing the mountain. It was a good thing that our weapons had such long range, because we were able to kill the enemy from beyond their bow range.

It was at this time that we noticed Valik and his troops coming over the break of the hill, attacking the enemy from a direction they had not even expected. It didn't last long as Valik's archers killed most of the panicked enemy troops, and his swordsmen finished off the rest. We hung back covering the surrounding area so as not to be surprised again, occasionally picking off a straggler, or a small group trying to hide or escape. We waved

Valik and his troops to proceed down the mountain to the rendezvous point on the plateau overlooking King Malok's castle and the surrounding city, all the while covering for them from above.

What a day this had been thus far, as we have completely routed the Gog army. We know that we will be unable to roust the enemy from the city or from the castle if it had been breached, but our plan was now to lure those troops out to attack what is going to look like a vastly inferior army. If we have to go into the city, it was decided that we would use the Horn of Gideon to incapacitate everyone within the city, and then send our troops in to kill everyone who was not a friend, but first things first.

As Valik and his troops gathered below us, Mr. Damon lowered the chariot, but as we tried to settle down, the spear from the crossbow that was stuck through the hull would not allow us to settle to the ground. Valik took out his sword, and hacked away at the bolt until he had chopped it in half. Then we set the chariot down on the plateau, back away from the crest of the hill overlooking the city and the castle, so as not to be seen by the enemy forces. Valik sent a few of his men ahead to keep an eye on the enemy's movements, as well as posting sentries out from our perimeter to prevent a sneak attack.

Jumping down from the craft, I embraced Valik, and asked how his journey through the falls had gone. He stated that they had surprised an enemy soldier who was relieving himself behind the falls, quickly dispatching the poor soul, who soiled himself when the side of the mountain opened up. Then they proceeded to sneak out from the falls and ambush a group of about a hundred enemy troops searching the area. He did regret losing two of his own troopers, but all in all, it was a very successful campaign.

With the troops they had killed at the break of the mountain from the falls, he estimated they had killed about a two hundred and fifty of the enemy troops. Add to that the estimated eleven or twelve hundred troops we had dispatched on the road from the castle, and another two thousand or so on the plateau, I would think that the enemy is probably having second thoughts about their conquest of our lands. We still don't know if the castle had fallen, nor how many enemy troops the castle guard may have killed. Our goal so far has been to kill everyone we've encountered so that there are no survivors to warn their comrades about our advanced weaponry. We want to draw the bulk of the enemy army out of the city and away from the castle, and then into the open where we can kill as many of them as possible.

Gathering the troops around us, and still out of sight of the city and the castle, we set our plans in motion. We have about a hundred and eighty soldiers with us, which we plan to spread out all along the crest of the plateau in a skirmish line, each man about an arms length away from his comrade. This is to give the illusion of a larger army than we actually have, but yet small enough to draw out the bulk of their army. Then, once the enemy is far enough away from the city, we will attack them with the Dragon's Breath weapon, hoping to kill as many as possible, with our troops staying on the plateau for safety. My hopes are that the King's troops defending the castle will then come out to attack the enemy from behind, a good plan if it works.

Next, it was time to set up the Horn of Gideon on the crest of the plateau, with its bellows wide open to the valley. The intent here is to incapacitate the approaching enemy if there are too many of them for us to handle. The plan is to leave ten men with the Horn of Gideon, half to keep the drumbeat steady, and half to keep moving the bellows of the horn to face the greatest threat. As soon as the horn was set and ready, it was time to spread out the troops and begin the ruse.

As the troops began to spread out, I gazed to the sky to see if the dragons were still there, and though I could not see them, I knew they were there, I could sense them, staying out of sight until the attack began. The dragons were getting smarter, and seem to be developing tactics and strategies, instead of simply responding by instincts, instincts that up till now have nearly made them extinct. Times are changing, and only time will tell if those changes are good, or bad.

When the troops had finished forming their skirmish line, a couple of troopers were held back as signalers, to let those of us on the chariot know when to begin our attack. This time Mara would be a rider on the chariot, and not handle a weapon unless it was necessary. In fact, this time Valik himself was going to ride the chariot, and handle the other weapon. His next in command would take charge of the troops on the ground, and all had orders to escape back to the falls if our tactics failed. One trooper had been left behind the falls to hold the key until we returned, so it would not fall into enemy hands. It was now time to begin our attack.

Valik's troops marched to the break of the plateau, in plain sight of the city and the castle, and the sight below was enough to make the heart stand still, there were thousands of enemy troops encamped below, with hundreds of tents, thousands of horses, wagons, and new siege works being built.

At first it seemed that the enemy wasn't even aware of our presence until our own troops started chanting, and taunting the enemy troops below. Then, as if in slow motion, wave after wave of enemy soldiers turned to face the plateau behind them, the one they thought was occupied and well guarded by their own countrymen. The effect though was exactly what we had hoped for, in fact, the whole scene below us was what we had hoped for, thousands of troops in the open, backed up against a closed and defended castle.

There was some evidence of a previous conflict within the castle, with the smoke from several fires still smoldering within the walls, one of which appeared to be in the area of the King's villa. If I had to guess, I would say that the enemy troops who had infiltrated the castle and the city, had initially had some successes in their initial attack, but the fact that the gates to the castle were secure, and the enemy was building siege works, it appeared the enemy had been defeated within the castle, with the rest driven out.

The effect of our presence behind the Gog army was one that caused a lot of chaos, as enemy troops started milling about, looking for possible escape routes, ignoring their officers, who were trying to gain control of the situation. I'm sure they were confused at how so many of their troops guarding their flanks could have been defeated by what was supposed to be only a small garrison of troops guarding my castle, yet here we were, behind them, with no warning from their fellow countrymen, so of course it would be a little disconcerting. Unfortunately, that wasn't to last long, as the officers gained control of their troops, and with further assessment, they figured out we were only a small force, certainly one that could be easily defeated.

Soon, the enemy troops started a chant of their own, which of course drowned out the chanting of our own soldiers, and it was enough to send chills up your spine, if it wasn't for the fact we had our chariot and Dragon's Breath weapons hidden out of view of the enemy. That was going to be quite the surprise for the overconfident army which now faced off against us, many of whom were beating their swords upon their shields, pounding their chests, and making obscene gestures our way. Then, as their commanders got them organized into a huge skirmish line, they started their march up the slope of the plateau to engage us.

You could see our own troops starting to fidget and shuffle their feet at the menacing sight approaching them, but our own commanders were doing a wonderful job calming them down, encouraging them to stand fast, and reminding them of the surprise we had waiting for the intruders. This had the desired effect on our troops, and soon, our own small army were beating their chests, and giving back a few of their own obscene gestures, much to Mara's delight, who only got embarrassed when I gave her a funny look, but she was still smiling when she turned her head, and I could only shake my head.

All too soon, the signalmen raised their flags that it was time for us to engage the enemy, so without further ado, Mr. Damon lifted the chariot into the air, and over the crest of the hill we went, to the cheers of our own troops. The effect was immediate, and quite the opposite though on the enemy troops, who had no idea what was coming at them, and then only had a split second to think about it before the dual Dragon's Breath weapons started incinerating them.

It was like the whole of the enemy army stopped in its tracks, mesmerized by what was happening, dozens upon dozens, then hundreds upon hundreds of their fellow comrades dying before they finally got the idea to break ranks and try to save themselves. By then we were cutting a huge swath of destruction and death right down through the center of their forces, first killing all directly in front of us, and then swinging the fiery death from the Dragon's Breath weapons out to each side to mow down enemy soldiers like the peasants harvesting grain from the fields. Everywhere the Dragon's Breath touched, row upon row of enemy troops and horses fell to the ground, screaming, burning, and dying.

I guess I had never really noticed how noisy war really was, sword against sword, armor against armor, men yelling, screaming, and some even crying. And the smells of battle, the smell of smoke, oiled leather, the musky smell of the thousands of animals used in warfare, and the smell of burning flesh. It may sound sick, but I love that smell. I'm betting right now that the Gog troops aren't sharing my fondness for the war, as wave after wave of the hapless souls went to the next life.

I instructed Mr. Damon to turn the craft across the face of the hillside so we could more effectively use our weapons against a larger number of targets, and also to prevent many of the enemy troops from reaching our own soldiers. We had to be careful not to injure our own men with the Dragon's Breath weapons. It was not going to be possible to prevent the entire enemy from reaching our troops, but I'll bet any that do still have the heart to engage our men will be easily dispatched by our own men.

After the initial penetration of the enemy lines, and the subsequent sweep across the hillside, most of the remaining enemy forces were in full retreat back down the hillside, so we turned the chariot down the hill, and made another sweep across the hillside, killing as many of the enemy as possible before they could get to the safety of the city.

Once we reached the outskirts of the city, we had to be aware of the crossbows, and hidden soldiers, so it was quickly decided not to pursue the enemy too close to the city. Instead, we destroyed everything of use to the enemy that was within range of our weapons, including tents, wagons, siege works, crossbows, livestock, and any troops that tried to challenge us. Our own troops were venturing down the slope, engaging, or dispatching any enemy stragglers left to fight, and the dragons themselves were picking off any enemy troops who had run from the battlefield, thinking they could escape. It was now time to break off our attack, regroup, and plan the liberation of the city.

Retreating back up the slope, we rallied our troops together at a new meeting spot considerably down the slope from the Horn of Gideon. I waved for the troops manning the Horn to bring it down the slope to set it up in a place where it would have the optimum effect on the city below, and once that had been done, our next plan of attack was put together, well within sight of the enemy troops in the city, and the defenders of the castle. It was like bait, trying to lure the wolves out of hiding, only to kill them, though I believed the enemy didn't want anything more to do with our toys.

As the troops gathered around the chariot, everyone was encouraged to eat and drink while they had the chance, because we would all need our strength if we had to go in and clear out the city. We were all standing around, eating, drinking, laughing, and enjoying our victory, when one of our troops yelled out a warning. A group of men were coming out of the city, and they had a white flag. Could the Gog army be surrendering, it was almost too good to be true.

Quickly, I grabbed a spyglass, and trained it on the group working its way up the slope toward our position, and my heart sank when I saw who was coming. It was Sardon himself, which in itself would have been a welcome sign, but the rest of the party is what caused me great discomfort, for they had Marta with them, as a prisoner, held fast between two soldiers, obviously going to be use as a bargaining tool for some nasty plan Sardon has cooked up to save his own hide.

Sardon had about fifty men with him, and behind him, you could see several hundred enemy troops standing at the gates of the city, unwilling to venture far from the safety of the city walls. The enemy party stopped at the base of the hill, and waited for our response, so addressing our own group, I said.

"Okay, listen up everyone, because this is very important, and the outcome of this may determine the fate of everyone here, as well as everyone within the city, and the castle. I'm going down to talk to Sardon, and try to work out a deal to save Marta. I'm going to take an equal number of men with me as they have down there, so they won't attempt to take me prisoner. I want one of the signalmen to come along to signal you up here if things go bad down there. If things do go bad, I want you to use the Horn of Gideon to incapacitate everyone on the battlefield, including myself, then, if possible, swing down with the chariot and pick up as many of us as possible, does everyone understand."

Everyone nodded in agreement, even though I could tell it was with reservations. I wanted everyone to know that it would be best to disable all of us, and then send the troops down to sort us out afterwards, rather than allow all of us to be killed or captured, only to be used later as bargaining chips. The damage done from the Horn of Gideon was a less permanent problem than the alternative. Continuing to address the troops, I added.

"If things do indeed go badly, I want you to retreat back to the falls with the chariot and the weapons. No matter what, they are not to fall into the enemies' hands, understand?"

Again, everyone nodded in agreement, but even less wholeheartedly than before, although they all knew it was the way it had to be.

"Mr. Valik," I said, "I want you to stay with the chariot, I know you will do the right thing, and I trust you to rule in my absence, and Mara, I need you to stay here also, I don't want anything to happen to you."

"Oh no," she responded adamantly, "wherever you go, I'm going with you."

"My love," I started, "I don't plan on anything happening to me, but if it does, I want to be able to try to protect myself without having to worry about the distraction of trying to protect both of us, am I making any sense to you Mara. I love you and don't want anything to happen to you, so please, promise me you'll stay here out of danger."

"I'll stay here only as long as you aren't in danger, Ethan," she replied.

"Fair enough my love," was all I could say?

"What about me?" asked Balon.

"I'm sorry my friend," I started, "but with your injury, I need you to remain behind too. The same thing applies to you, if I have to watch my back and yours, I'll lose the edge I may need to survive, do you understand."

"Yes, my Lord," he responded with his face lowered to the ground in humility.

"Okay then, people," I said, "it's time for us to go, and the rest of you get ready to defend us from here."

Waving for a group of about fifty men to come with me, we set out down the slope to meet with Sardon and his misfits, to see what sort of terms he wanted for the release of Marta, as if we were going to make a deal with him in the first place. I was really hoping he would just surrender and let it go at that, but somehow I didn't think he was going to be that cooperative. He probably had some sort of scheme up his sleeve, but, so do I. If things went bad, my friends are going to play a tune on the drum, turning us all into jelly, and then come down to pick up the good guys, and of course, kill all the rest, at least that was my plan.

As we were descending the hillside to meet with Sardon, Valik, Mara, Balon, and the others were manning the weapons, ready to dispense a taste of hell on the inhabitants of the valley, which unfortunately now included me and a few other good guys. So, let's hope it doesn't come down to that.

Drawing near to Sardon, and his men, we stopped short of their party, with about ten feet separating our parties, each group sizing up the other, with Marta in the middle, held fast by her wrists by a couple of ugly looking characters. All the players were tense, swords drawn, at the ready, and as we stood there facing each other, Sardon was the first to speak.

"So Ethan, it is true about the chariot, and the Dragon's Breath weapons. You certainly have raised havoc with the Gog army, and I fear they will never be quite the same again. Now, if you would be so kind, please call off the dragons, so nothing unfortunate happens to dear Marta."

"Sardon," I said as I alone approached him and the soldiers holding Marta, "Marta, and myself are the only thing standing between you and the wrath of the dragons, so don't threaten me. The dragons know you were responsible for the deaths of their sisters, and they haven't forgotten, and no matter what happens to me, you and the dragons have a date, and I can't say I'm sorry about the Gog army, but they should have stayed in the land of Magog where they belong, because I plan to kill a lot more of them before I'm through, for my father's sake. Now, you filthy traitor, I want you to release Marta to me, and maybe I'll let you live."

Sardon stood there and glared at me, hatred in his eyes. If anything was going to happen, it would happen soon, because Sardon was a spoiled little weasel, used to getting his own way, and when he didn't, he usually did something rash, and that's exactly what I wanted him to do, so I just glared back, waiting for him to make his move.

Meanwhile, up on the hill, Mara, and Valik, had a good view of the whole battlefield, unlike our small viewing area where we stood, and it was Mara who noticed something wrong with the scene we were playing out. She had been watching us through the spy glass when she noticed that Marta was not really being restrained at all, it was just a ruse, and Marta had a dagger hidden in one of her hands, one of the hands that was supposedly being restrained.

Valik was just about to give the order to use the Horn of Gideon, when Mara jumped down from the chariot and started running full bore down the hillside, screaming at the top of her lungs that it was a trap, but with the wind blowing, by the time I heard her screams, and turned to see what the problem was, two of Sardon's soldiers raised their bows and loosed their arrows, both striking Mara in the chest. She stumbled and fell, almost at my feet. She was supposed to wait on the hill, why hadn't she listened to me?

I turned to face Sardon, my face flush with rage, and as I turned, there was a sharp stabbing pain high in my chest, just below my right shoulder. I looked down at the dagger protruding from my chest, and thought to myself, that doesn't look right. When I raised my eyes to see who had been so treacherous, I couldn't believe my eyes, it was Marta, of all people, Marta.

I backed away from Marta and Sardon as the whole world seemed to erupt around me as both groups of men attacked each other. For a moment I was swallowed up in the confusion, and when I found my beloved Mara, I fell to my knees beside her. It was then I heard a sword being unsheathed for a final strike, but somehow I found a surge of strength, pulled my own short sword, turned, and thrust it upward at my would-be slayer. My sword found resistance as the blade penetrated flesh, muscle, and bone, and then I twisted the handle hard and withdrew the blade. I looked up into the face of a disbelieving Sardon as he collapsed to the ground. He was so sure that he had destroyed us both, so sure his little plan had worked perfectly, and indeed, it almost had.

Turning again on my knees, I sought out the hand of my beloved Mara, and when I had found it, it felt so cold, so clammy. She looked up into my eyes, not with fear, but with love and adoration. I sat down beside her and cradled her head in my lap, my own eyes feeling tired, and it was so hard for me to keep them open. A noise soon jarred me back to my senses, a screeching sound that would make your blood turn cold within your body, and looking up, I saw a dragon, on the ground, coming directly at us, as fast as it could crawl, knocking over soldiers from both sides as it made its way right up to us, and then it stopped next to us.

It was Feron; she had come out of the pen in the castle, even though she was mortally wounded. Now she had even more wounds, with arrows and spears protruded from her body like quills, and then she too collapsed on the ground beside us, her head lying beside Mara, her breathing labored, raspy, blood oozing from her mouth and nose, just as it was with Mara, and I suppose even from myself.

Meanwhile, the battle raged around us, each man engaged in his own life and death struggle, unaware, and uncaring about anything but his own survival. It seemed like there were a lot of troops from both sides all of a sudden, and I finally realized that the castle had opened its gates and counter attacked the Gog army, who, between the Kings army on one side, and the Dragon's Breath on the other, and the other four dragons swooping down to shred even more of their comrades, the result was a full fledged retreat by what was left of the shattered Gog army, retreating back toward the Talon Pass, fighting and dying for every inch of ground they stepped foot on.

Looking back to Mara, and the dragon Feron, I spoke to both while life was still in them, and this is what I had to say.

"Feron, my good and faithful friend, you have served me well all these years, and now, as you pass into the next life, I need you to serve Mara, to serve, protect, and guide her throughout eternity, to be her spirit guide and mentor. And to you Mara, my queen, I will see you again, in three hundred years, in the land of the library, the land of the great lion, the land of the pyramids."

Mara and the dragon were lying almost face to face, Mara's head on my lap, Feron's chin on the ground, and as the dragon exhaled her last breath, Mara breathed in her last, part of the dragons breath filling her lungs, one last time. A single tear fell from Mara's eye onto the bloody face of the dragon, and I believe, those two things sealed the two of them together for all eternity.

It seemed like a dream from that point on, as the last real thing I remembered was being lifted up and placed on the chariot, rather roughly I thought, by Balon and a couple of troopers, at least I think it was Balon and a couple of our troopers, and I remember shouting at them to please get Mara, and to not leave her behind. Everything else is a little hazy, except for yelling, screaming, armor clanging, and the occasional flash from the Dragon's Breath fire streaking across the battlefield.

I do remember how rough the ride back to the castle was though, and almost rolling off of the side of the chariot a few times. Beyond that, the next thing I remember was waking up in my own bed back at my villa, and wondering how I had gotten there. Opening my eyes to the bright light caused a bit of a headache, and at first I thought maybe I had gotten drunk again, but then the realization of the battle started to sink in, and then I remembered Mara.

"MARA!" I screamed as I bolted upright in bed, which then of course reminded me I had been stabbed in the chest by Marta, the bitch, and as I laid back down in pain. Balon, who had been sitting with me ever since I had been brought back to the castle, rushed to the bedside, and told me to lie back down and relax. I looked at him with the patch over his eye, and smiling, I said.

"Balon, my one eyed friend, aren't we a sight." And as the pain in my head subsided, I added.

"Remind me to fire Marta," at which point we both chuckled, which didn't do my head any good, but it felt good to the soul.

"I would love to fire her Lord," Balon said, "except no one seems to be able to find her."

"You mean she got away?" I asked, concerned about a future run in with her.

"Oh no," Balon started to explain, "it's just that the dragons packed off her body when they saw what she and Sardon did to you, and we haven't seen either one of them since, except maybe a few parts of them here and there, but then again, there are so many parts out there, it may be hard figuring out what belongs to whom."

"So, what happened down there," I asked, "who won the battle, or are we holed up here under siege, because I don't remember much of anything after you guys threw me on the chariot."

"Sorry about that my Lord," he began, "we were in kind of a hurry. You should have seen it Ethan, as soon as you and Mara were struck down, our troops clashed with Sardon's men, at least until you killed Sardon, and then they tried to surrender, which of course did them no good. When the enemy troops outside the city walls saw you struck down, they thought they had a chance, and they tried a counter attack, only to be cut down by Valik and myself with the dragon's breath. Then, the castle gates opened up, and the King's troops counter attacked the enemy too, and amidst all that confusion is when we got you back to the safety of the castle."

"But what of the battle's outcome?" I pleaded.

"I was getting to that," Balon continued. "It seems that it was a full fledged rout of the enemy, with the King's guard on one side, and our troops in the middle, the dragons overhead, and even the inhabitants of the city took to the streets, killing every Gog trooper and tribesman they could find. I would be willing to say that very few if any of the Gog tribesmen were able to escape back through the Talon Pass. It was an overwhelming victory Ethan, thanks to you. You're a hero Ethan, and everyone's waiting to hear from you."

"And what of King Malok?" I asked as I forced myself to sit upright, with a little help from Balon.

"The King was killed by the initial infiltrators of the castle. They thought that would cause the rest of the King's guard to quit fighting, but it didn't. They fought to get the gates closed, then fought it out inside the castle until they secured the castle. If it hadn't been for us harassing the Gog army so bad at the Talon Pass, enough of the Gog army would have been there to take the castle completely. Once the castle was secure, the castle guard settled back to hold off the siege for as long as possible. Then, when they saw what we were doing to the Gog army, they came out to help finish them off. Ethan, it was incredible. But now, if you can manage it, there is something I need you to see, and the people need to know you are alive, do you think you can you make it?"

"I can make it my friend," I replied, "with your help, I can make it."

Balon helped me to my feet, my good arm draped over his shoulder. My head did a spin for a second or two, but as soon as that went away, we continued on.

"How long have I been in bed Balon?" I asked.

"About a week," he responded.

"A week," I exclaimed, "how could you let me sleep that long, I have too much to do."

Balon just shook his head, and muttered something about that being gratitude for you, and we continued on into the hallway, where servants and staff were standing in lines, as if waiting for something. When they saw me emerge from my quarters, a cheer went up, with smiles and laughter filling the halls, some even dancing arm in arm, and when it finally calmed down a bit, I addressed them, with a bit of deviltry to make some fun, saying.

"All right now, doesn't anybody work around here, why's everyone standing around, get busy doing something."

With that, everyone tried going every direction at once, and it looked like chaos, but my smile gave me away, and everyone started laughing and giggling as they went back to there respective jobs, some saying 'welcome back' as they went past. It did make my heart rejoice at the support I got from them, and as we headed out the door to the main courtyard, I couldn't help but to ask Balon.

"What have you done with Mara's body?"

"It has been taken down to the main cavern, and placed upon a throne beside yours, to rule with you after death, for all eternity. The shopkeeper from town built it for her, and it is truly a throne built for a queen."

"Thank you my friend," I said, "I knew I could count on you. Now, let's go see the people."

As we pushed open the massive doors to the courtyard, the first vision I beheld was of a somber mass of people, milling about listlessly. They too were apparently waiting on my return from the edge of death, and when they saw me emerge from my villa, the cheer that arose from the throng of humanity was deafening, with cheering, chanting, crying, and dancing, all of which hurt my head, but I wasn't going to say a word. Soon the chaos turned to a group chant of.

"Long live the King; long live the King," and "Hail King Ethan, hail King Ethan."

For a few moments, my heart threatened to burst out from my chest, and before long, there were tears running down my face. I was afraid my legs were going to turn to mush, but Balon held me upright until the waves of emotion had passed. Then with a wave of my hand to quiet the crowd, I addressed them.

"My friends, I thank you for all of the support you have given me during this time of crisis. I know some of you have lost loved ones, and I am sorry. I know how you feel, and I too share in your loss. We have won a great victory, but let us look at it with humility, knowing that the victory is tempered with great sorrow also. Much has been lost, in terms of human life, and in terms of the near extinction of the dragons. They may never recover from this ordeal, and soon their kind will be gone from the earth. We all need to learn a lesson here about man's place upon this earth. We are stewards of life on this planet, we can nurture it, or we can destroy it. Let's work on nurturing life, because it is way too easy to destroy it. If we get lazy in our stewardship, soon the life form we lose may be our own. So go now, live in peace, and I will try to rule wisely, with your help."

Again, the cheering was deafening, and the crowd continued to cheer as Balon and I made our way down the steps. Balon wanted me to come to the castle walls now to address the soldiers, and to another sight that awaited my return. Moving through the crowds, I tried to acknowledge as many of the people as I could, many of them simply reaching out to touch me as I passed, and it made my heart lift as they did so, my strength growing with each moment, to the point where I could now walk on my own.

As we approached the castle walls, I could see Valik and the troops lining the roadway leading to the gate, all standing at attention, shields at the ready. It was an impressive sight for such a small contingent, but what struck me as odd, was the fact that the castle gate was still closed. I didn't have time to dwell on that, because with such a small contingent of troops, it appeared that we must have lost a few men during the last fighting. As I approached Captain Valik, he raised his sword into the air, and the whole contingent of troops, both on the ground, and on the walls, raised their voice into a chant, saying.

"Hail to the King, long live King Ethan."

My heart swelled again as they chanted over and over again, and as I came abreast to Captain Valik, I embraced him with my good arm, and then hand in hand, together we raised his sword aloft. Then he and Balon nodded in the direction of the walkway along the castle wall, and I assumed they wanted me to go up there to give another speech, so, with Valik in the lead, we ascended the walkway to the castle wall, stopping just short of the causeway, where Valik raised his hand for quiet, and then he turned to me to speak.

"My Lord," he started, "what you are about to see, and the decision you make in regard to what you see, will decide the fate of your entire Kingdom. Beyond this wall is nearly the whole of former King Malok's castle guard. They wish to serve you, as their new King, heart, and soul. They have been waiting outside the walls for nearly a week to hear from you, to decide their fate. We refused to allow them inside until you could make that decision, because of their previous loyalty to King Malok, and because of their inactivity in helping us to fight the Gog until the end of the battle. It is your decision my Lord."

"What is your opinion about their loyalty Captain?" I asked.

"I think with the right discipline, and some new training from myself, and my aides, they could be a welcome asset to your kingdom, but again my lord, the decision is yours. You have lost the most because of their lack of discipline under king Malok."

"I trust your wisdom my friend," I said to Valik, "and I will trust you to train them the right way. Now, let's go welcome them to my kingdom."

We climbed the remaining steps to the causeway, and as I looked out from the wall, the sight before me was as awesome a spectacle as I have ever seen, hundreds upon hundreds, in fact, there were nearly two thousand troops, standing at attention, row upon row, backed up as far down the road as I could see, eyes fixed upon the castle wall, and when they saw me step forward into view, this time the cheer was beyond deafening, with the same chant as the others.

"Hail to The King, long live King Ethan."

The cheer resounded over and over again, and then the same cheer was sounded behind me by the troops within the castle, and then taken up by the civilians who had gathered all around, and soon, even the mountains were echoing the chant, threatening to cause a landslide. I held up my hand to quiet the crowds, and after a minute or so, when it was quiet, I addressed the troops waiting outside the walls.

"My friends," I began, "I hold no animosity toward you for the events that have recently overtook our lands. You were governed by a worthless King, and commanded by even more worthless commanders. The job you did defending the castle below against overwhelming odds was outstanding though, and I commend your resilience. If you will dedicate your loyalty to me as your King, and Captain Valik as your commander, then I promise to be a benevolent and understanding King, and I'll rule with fairness and equality for all. If you do not dedicate your loyalty to me, feel free to leave the kingdom now, no questions asked, because neither I, nor your commanders will tolerate misbehavior later. What say you?"

The cheer was unanimous, and quite boisterous, again making the mountain rumble, and with each cheer, the resounding echo seemed as though the mountain itself had a voice, and was also declaring its loyalty to the new king. If this scene wasn't enough to make the human heart swell with pride, then the next scene was sure to do so.

As I stood there enjoying a unity that this land had not seen in quite some time, four shadows passed low overhead, causing large shadows to fall across the ground, and causing the entire crowd to go quiet. Looking up, the four remaining dragons circled, swooped, twisted in mid air, and dove toward the ground only to swoop back up again. After several minutes of this, one by one, each dragon landed on one of the parapets of the castle walls, wings open wide, looking proud and menacing, and then one by one, each dragon folded his wings, and then sat quietly, at least quietly to all of those around me. But to me, they had a message.

"Ethan, master of dragons, slayer of our enemies, and King of all the land, we are happy to see you back among the land of the living, and we mourn the death of your mate, and our friend Mara. You are truly great among men, and we will always respect your wisdom and strength, but we can no longer live among your kind. The Earth is now entering the time of man, and your kind has truly became strong and powerful. Man no longer needs us, you no longer need us, and the only way for our kind to survive is to move far back into the wilderness where man has not yet set foot, and that is what we go to do now. We will never again pass this way our brother, so we wish you good luck, and wise rule."

"Thank you my friends," I responded back, "good luck, and happy journey."

With those words said, The dragons lifted off of their perches, rising into the air on the prevailing wind currents, circling and circling until they were soaring high in the air, and just before they disappeared from sight, I caught the glimpse of a fifth dragon, larger than the others. It appeared to be a big male, and as they disappeared from sight, I thought to myself, maybe they have a chance to survive, if only they stay away from mankind.

Turning back to look at the crowds, they were all staring at me, knowing that I had spoken to the dragons with my mind, but I decided it was something I should keep to myself, just in case someone, someday, decided to challenge my rule. Speaking to the gatekeepers, I said.

"Open the gates and lower the drawbridge so that our brothers can come in."

With that, another cheer rose up from the crowds, and as the troops filed in to visit, I turned to Valik, and said.

"The army is yours my friend, rule with wisdom and strength. Are all the weapons secured below?"

"They are my Lord," he replied.

And with that he handed me his key to the secret caverns, which I added to the one around my neck. Then I gave Valik a hug, and asked Balon to take me back to my quarters so I could rest.

Along the way, I greeted many soldiers and citizens, thanking them all for their part in our victory, and as I ascended the steps to my villa, I instructed my new house master, Sophie, to instruct the kitchen staff to kill ten fatted calves to feed the masses at the castle tonight, and then Balon helped me to my chambers. Once I was safe inside my quarters, I bid Balon good night, and told him I would be okay for now. And when he had gone, I opened the secret compartment under my nightstand, and dropped the keys to the caverns inside. I was not ready to see Mara in the state she would be in, not for a long time. And when the keys were hidden, and the nightstand replaced, I lie down on my bed, and fell fast asleep.

Five, Four, Three, Two, One, Snap!!!!

Chapter 11

I opened one eye at a time, waiting to see where I was, and who I was. Instinctively, I reached up to rub my chest where the dagger had been, but found nothing but a bad memory. This whole ordeal was beginning to take its toll on me, mentally and physically, and I'm not sure if I am better off knowing what had happened or not. Only time would tell, would I now be able to sleep at night, or would the new memories of Dee being killed take the place of the dreams of Mara being killed. I was almost afraid to find out.

"How are you feeling Henry?" Dr. Miller asked with a little concern in his face.

"I feel okay doc," I responded, "just a little overwhelmed with the whole thing."

"That's understandable, given the circumstances," he said. "That was quite the adventure this time Henry, and to the average everyday person on the street, I'm sure it would be quite far fetched, but to us, and having it confirmed by the monks, we believe it's actually true. There's only one way to be sure Henry, and that's to go to Switzerland, and find your castle, what do you say my friend?"

"I'll going to make arrangements as soon as I get back home," I said as I got up from my chair, feeling a little weak, as though still feeling the effects of the dagger.

I shook Dr. Miller's hand, and wrote him a check for what I owed him to date, saying.

"Just in case I don't make it back, I want to have everything squared up between us, and I want to thank you from the bottom of my heart for all you've done for me doc."

"You quite welcome Henry," he replied, "and the pleasure has been all mine." I've learned as much as you have, and it has been very enlightening. Good luck on your quest my friend, and if possible, let me know how it went. But I guess in this case, no news will be good news. Good bye Ethan the Dragon Master."

I smiled at him when he said that, and said.

"Good bye Jim."

When I walked down the sidewalk to the street, I could see Scott was sound asleep in the passenger seat of the truck, and when I checked my watch, I was surprised to see that it had been nearly three hours since I had entered the house. No wonder I was worn out, and no wonder Scott was sleeping.

As I opened the door, Scott woke with a start, looking around as though some unseen enemy had attacked him. Perhaps he too had dreams about the past. Why does it seem that some people are plagued by their past, when others never seem to have any recollection of anything but their present life. It doesn't seem fair to those of us who have to relive their past over and over again. Perhaps it's only those of us who have unfinished business from the past, or maybe because of the tragic endings that happen in those past lifetimes cause us to deal with them over and over until we get it right. Maybe the monks will be able to tell me what I seek.

On the drive back down the valley, I told Scott everything I could remember about the hypnosis session, including what Dr. Miller had told me about the monastery in the Swiss Alps, and then about my plans to go there as soon as possible. Scott had a pensive look on his face, so I asked him what he thought about the session, and of my plans to go find my castle. He hesitated before he answered, and then he spoke.

"As you told me the story of our battle, I could see it in my minds eye, as if I were recalling my own memories of the events, so I truly believe we were there, exactly as you told it. I'm skeptical about the castle in the Swiss Alps, but with all that's happened over the last few weeks, I won't doubt anything. All I ask is that you be careful, and to look at everything adjectively. And if indeed your castle is there, don't be so quick to reveal all of the hidden secrets without knowing the intentions of the supposed monks who seek to find those secrets. You never know who else has been reincarnated into the present day, and wish to use those secrets for their own gain, including a few modern militaries."

"Scott," I began, "you are my very best friend on earth, now, in the past, and I trust, in the future. I trust in your advice, and I have indeed thought of all of these possibilities. Most militaries have technology far in advance of the weapons we used back in those days, but modern day terrorists could raise terrible destruction on modern citizens, so your concerns are well founded. Trust me when I say that I will not reveal anything to anyone unless I feel they are completely trustworthy, and, to make sure I behave myself, I want you to accompany me to Switzerland, what do you say?"

Scott's eyes got wide, and a sparkle told the story before he even answered my question, but then a look of concern came over his face, and he spoke.

"I would be honored to go with you Henry, but I have a couple of problems. The first being that I have no money to go with, and the second problem is that I wouldn't have a job to come back to if I did leave for a month, so I'm afraid I'm going to have to pass."

"You won't have to worry about money Scott; I have enough money in my savings and retirement accounts to pay for both of our airfares, and enough for food. All you'll need is some cash for any incidentals you may want along the way. I'm hoping that the monks will provide us with everything we need once we get there, since they're supposed to be waiting for my return. As for your job, I'm sure you could find a friend or relative to cover for you while you're gone, and as long as the lawns get mowed, and the carwash gets cleaned everyday, why should your boss care what you do. In fact, if you tell him you're getting a free trip to Switzerland, he'll probably be elated to see you go on such an exciting trip. I just wouldn't tell him all of the details."

Scott's eyes were sparkling again, and he said.

"I think this will work, I have a nephew who could cover for me while I'm gone. He could use the extra money, and I have a few hundred dollars in savings for mad money over there, so yes, let's do it."

A high five sealed the deal, and as soon as we got back to my house, I got on the phone to my ambulance supervisor to request an emergency leave of absence, and then contacted my retirement company to cash in my retirement, also under emergency measures, and after a few detours through various people within the company, everything was arranged. The money would be transferred directly into my bank account so I wouldn't have to rely on snail mail, and a final call to my bank had my savings transferred into my checking account.

Tomorrow I would go to the bank and withdraw my money as traveler's checks, and then go to the Travel agency to buy our tickets. Meanwhile, we both had a lot of loose ends to tie up before we could leave, like calling my mother to have her, and my siblings watch over the house while I was gone. They would have to make sure no one bothered the house, and bring in the mail each day. My bills were all on automatic withdrawal, so I wouldn't have to worry about that, and the only other thing they would have to do is water the lawn. Scott's nephew could even keep my yard mowed while I was gone, so things were falling into place like it was meant to happen. Perhaps fate was in control after all.

I hung out at the house the rest of the afternoon while Scott ran errands, checked the car wash, and contacted his nephew to offer him the part time job. It felt odd to be alone again, but now I felt an inner peace just knowing I was going on this journey, this journey back into the past. I didn't feel any anxiety at all about going on this trip, that's why I feel it was meant to be, it was my destiny, and to deny your destiny is when you feel the anxiety. I was ready to go; in fact, I couldn't wait to get started.

Scott made it back to the house about 8:00pm, and it was obvious that he too was excited. Everything had worked out perfectly for him too. His boss agreed to let him go on the trip, and agreed to let his nephew cover for him. Scott had taken his nephew down to meet his boss, and to show him everything that needed to be done, so he was set, except for packing and securing funds for the trip, which we would take care of tomorrow. As for tonight, we were just going to relax, drink a few gin and tonics, and think about our next great adventure.

We went to bed that night so excited that we could hardly sleep, and if it hadn't have been for the drinks, I'm quite sure I wouldn't have slept at all. All I could do was lie on the bed for a long time thinking about the monks living in my old castle, and I wondered how many of them had been reincarnated from my lifetime with the dragons. Would I recognize any of them, would they recognize me, or would they think I was an intruder trying to sneak in and steal their secrets? And what about Scott, would those same questions apply to him? I think I already know the answers to my questions, if they are indeed waiting for me, then they will know me when they see me.

The next thing I knew, it was morning, the sun was up, and the birds were singing louder than I remember, as if they were telling some sort of story, or a parable from long ago. I wish I knew what they were saying, but try as I might, I didn't have a clue. It used to work with the dragons, but then again, these aren't dragons, are they.

I looked at the clock and was surprised to see that it was already 9:00. I haven't slept this long in quite some time, and as I thought about the things I was going to do today, I remembered the trip we were going on, and I got excited all over again. Jumping out of bed, I dressed quickly, and headed for the stairway, calling for Scott to get his lazy butt out of bed as I went past his room. As I descended the stairway, I recall hearing him moan something about now wanting to go to school today, but I ignored it and continued down the stairs to the bathroom to clean up.

When I emerged from the bathroom, Scott had the coffee started, and was sitting at the table reading the newspaper. Jokingly, I asked him if he was ready for school, at which he just smiled and kept reading the paper. After a couple of cups of coffee, our blood pressure was up enough for us to tackle the day, so we decided to head for town, get the tickets squared away first, and then catch a late breakfast at the café.

We both had our birth certificates for the tickets and visas, so we headed straight for the travel agency. Everything went so smooth at the travel agency that I started to think I was not the one controlling my own destiny anymore, and that maybe I was just along for the ride, but, if that's the case, so be it, let the ride begin, I'm ready.

Isn't it funny how things work out in your life? Let's take this trip for example, here I am going back to explore my roots, roots that are founded in a land that bears the ancestry of my current forefathers, for I am Norwegian, Swedish, and German.

Apparently my forefathers must have liked the area and didn't stray too far away from my old castle, probably not more than a few hundred miles in any direction, at least until my recent sojourn in America. I would have to guess that transportation of that day was not conducive to long range travel, not to mention the fact that all throughout history; Europe and Asia were involved in one era of warfare and conquest after another. That type of thing takes all the fun out of moving around the countryside very far from the protection of a castle or city, and I still don't like to travel very far from home to this day.

With our travel visas and airline tickets in hand, we left the travel agency and headed for the restaurant for breakfast. So much had happened within the last couple of days that I was still in a minor state of shock, and I was beginning to have second thoughts about whether I was doing the right thing here, chasing ghosts and fairy tales. The normal person on the street would have said I was crazy and locked me up in a Looney bin, but the more I thought about Dee, about Mara, the more I was able to convince myself that this was the right thing to do, and once the initial guilt trip had passed, I sat down to enjoy a wonderful breakfast.

As we ate our breakfast, we talked about the upcoming trip, and what all we would need to take. It was decided that since we knew we were going to have to do a fair amount of hiking in the mountains, we would each take an internal frame backpack, packed with extra socks, underwear, t-shirts, and a couple of pair of pants. The rest of the space would be for freeze-dried food, water, rain gear, a small tent, and ultra light sleeping bag. We would dress in layers with a light jacket over the top, and add or take off clothing as the weather dictated, and anything else we needed, we would pick up along the way.

Any money or valuables would be kept close to our bodies, and then only in small, separate bundles of cash so no one would think we were carrying a large amount of cash. It would spoil the whole trip if we were to get mugged along the way. Most of our money would be in travelers' checks, and we would only convert it to Swiss francs as we needed.

We were due to depart from the Missoula airport in two days, with a couple of layovers in the states before the long trip across the Atlantic to our first stop in France. We would be tired of airplanes by the time this trip was done, but there wasn't time to worry about that now because we have some serious shopping to do before then.

A stop at the local sporting goods provided us with a large selection of freeze dried foods, along with a lightweight, collapsible pot for cooking, as well as reusable dishes and utensils. Both of us already had sleeping bags and pack frames, and I had a small tent, so the only thing else I needed was a small camp stove and propane bottles, and after looking through the selection, I chose a small single burner unit that would stow away nicely.

When we got home, we gathered up all of our supplies, packs, sleeping bags, and so on and laid them all out across the lawn to see what we had and what we were missing. Then once we had everything we needed, the packing process began, fitting everything into place to maximize storage. Our packs have plenty of pockets and tie downs on the outside of the pack for matches, lighters, flashlights, extra batteries, and water bottles.

By the time we were finished, it was almost suppertime, so we went to the store to get a couple of steaks to put on the grill. This would be one of our last good meals, so we decided to make it a nice one, adding baked potatoes and steamed asparagus to compliment the steaks, and a nice bottle of red wine topped it off perfectly.

As we sat down to enjoy the meal, I raised my glass for a toast, saying.

"To a great adventure, my friend, may we find what we seek, and no matter the outcome, may we find closure to the issues that confront us."

We raised our glasses, touched them together, and took a hearty swallow of the fermented elixir, and without another word to one another, we ate heartily, each of us left to our own thoughts, our own perspectives, and when we were done, and the table cleared, we retired to the deck to finish the bottle of wine, and still no one spoke. There was too much for each of us to think about in regard to this trip, and to what the outcome of such a trip would be. I can only speak for myself, but I can tell you that I was searching deep within my soul, asking myself hard questions about what I truly believe in, and asking myself if I truly want the answers, and my response was yes, I needed to know.

Sleep that night would not come easily, as my head was filled with working out the details of the trip, and just the anxiety of going on a trip to an unknown country, seeking an unknown place to find answers to questions that may or may not be real. What the hell am I doing? About two o'clock in the morning I finally got frustrated by my lack of sleeping, and had to get up and make a cup of herbal tea. It was not that the tea had any special properties to help me sleep, it was just that it was soothing to the soul to sit in the quiet of the night sipping tea, and after about an hour, I was tired enough to go back to sleep.

It was nearly nine o'clock before I woke up, and I could smell the coffee brewing, so I knew Scott was already up. As my senses also came awake, I was aware of another smell, the smell of bacon cooking. There is nothing on this planet that will get you motivated to get out of bed like the smell of bacon, and as I descended the stairway, my stomach started to growl just thinking about it.

When I reached the kitchen, Scott was just putting the bacon onto a plate, along with scrambled eggs, and hash browns.

"It's about time you got out of bed," Scott said as he saw me coming down the stairs.

"I know," I said, "I was awake most of the night, but now I was sleeping great until I smelled that bacon cooking."

"I kind of thought that would bring you around," he said, "so grab yourself a cup of coffee and meet me on the back deck."

Breakfast was as wonderful as it smelled, probably because I didn't have to cook it, and as we sat at the table, we discussed any last minute details about the trip. It was agreed we would go our separate ways today, making sure all our bills were paid up ahead of time, getting hold of our families to pick up mail, and so on. Then we would meet back here this afternoon, eat an early supper, and get a good nights rest. We would have to be at the airport at 6am, so there would be no late night drinking out on the deck tonight. I doubt that I'll be able to get much sleep, but I'll have to try.

The day went well, and I finished everything I could think of that needed done, but as you know, there will always be something that you forgot to do, and if there was, then I can always call my mom, at least up to a point, if there is anything I remembered later. Otherwise, I think we're ready for the journey of our lifetime.

Scott showed up about 7pm that evening. He had a little trouble getting everything set for his nephew, but it looked like everything was ready to go now. Once the trip was started, his nephew was on his own, and how he performed would decide whether or not Scott had a job when he got back. It was a little stressful to him, but he was too excited about the trip to worry about it for long. We'll worry about things here when we get back, and for that matter, if things are good over there, we may decide not to come back. After all, it is my castle, and that's where Scott, or should I say Balon, and I spent at least one of our lifetimes. I doubt it will hold the same fascination for us that it did before, but who knows, I'm open for anything at this point.

We ate a light supper of frozen burritos heated up in the microwave, with a side order of potato chips, and washed it all down with a couple beers. That's what you call a man's dinner, a real six-course meal, consisting of two burritos, a bag of potato chips, and three beers, boy howdy.

We managed to make it to bed about eleven o'clock, after going over our checklist one more time, and double checking our packs. We were definitely jazzed about our trip, and neither of us got much sleep that night. The alarm was set for 4am, but both of us were up ahead of that, so we decided to drive in to the airport early, and have breakfast in the airport restaurant. There was no use delaying this any longer, so we headed for town with our spirits soaring. This was going to be the biggest adventure of our lives, at least this lifetime.

We arrived at the airport at about a quarter to five in the morning, checked in our bags, and went to the restaurant for breakfast. We ordered light because we were both a little too nervous to eat, and I wouldn't want to have a nervous stomach while on the plane. I also went easy on the coffee, because when I drink too much coffee, I have to make a lot of trips to the rest room.

We hung in the restaurant until we heard the first boarding call, at which time we headed up the stairs to the boarding gate, going first through the security gate, and then waiting in line for our seating to be called. We had side-by-side seating so we decided to take turns sitting by the window, and since I'd flown before, I let Scott have the window first. Besides, I planned on taking a nap, and wouldn't see anything but the backs of my eyelids for a while anyhow, and that's what I did. I slept all the way to our first stop in Minneapolis, where we had an hour layover before catching our next flight to New York.

The layover in New York was considerably longer, about three hours before catching our next flight, the long flight across the Atlantic to France. Now that was a long flight, with nothing to look at but water. At first you might see a ship once in awhile, but after that, nothing, which provided another good opportunity for a long nap, which both of us did. By the time we get where we're going, we'll have had plenty of rest.

The pilot announced when we were getting close to the French shore, and when we did, it was a beautiful sight, not only aesthetically, but also because I'm afraid of water, and we had just flown over a lot of water. We had about an eight-hour layover in France before catching a smaller plane to Switzerland, so we wandered around the airport, checking out all the shops, and enjoying the cultural differences between America and Europe. At one of the shops I picked up a German, English dictionary, so I could try to muddle my way through the local languages.

Switzerland speaks about 63% German, 19% French, 7% Italian, and the rest a mixed bag of languages from nearby countries, so I figured German was the best language to work on, and besides, I've always wanted to speak German. We would have to have people speak slowly to us, and have them help us look up the various terms so we could understand them, and hopefully we would find a few people who spoke a little English.

We waited at our boarding gate until it was time to board, and from here we took a commuter flight into Bern, Switzerland. This was to be the starting point for our journey. The rest of the trip was going to be by bus, rail, and then finally on foot. I knew the general whereabouts of the castle, or should I say monastery, and I figured that when we got closer, I'd start asking for better directions. I'm hoping that once I got to the area, I would recognize the surrounding countryside. Unfortunately, according to the reincarnated monk in Dr. Miller's office, earthquakes, and a polar shift have greatly changed the look of the area, so everything will look a little different. My castle is not quite as far up the mountain as it used to be, and of course the points of the compass are no longer the same as they were when I lived here, but still, I'm holding out great hopes.

Once we arrived in Bern, and retrieved our packs, we asked around about hotels, or even hostels, and were delighted to meet up with a young fellow who spoke very good English. He gave us directions to a very nice hostel in town. He even helped us to hail a taxi, and then told the driver where to take us. Paying him the proper amount of cash was interesting, and we had to take his word for it that we paid him the correct amount.

Just as we were pulling away from the airport, I had the oddest feeling, and as I turned to look out the back window of the taxi, I noticed a man dressed in a long robe with a hood pulled over his head that was standing by the wall of the building. I wasn't sure, but it seemed as though he was looking in our direction, although it was hard to tell with the hood and all. I know this country has a few old monasteries, so it wasn't out of reason to see a monk, but I just had a weird feeling about this one that I couldn't shake. I turned back to look one more time, but he was gone, and I turned to Scott, and said.

"Did you see that monk standing back there by the building?"

"No, I sure didn't," Scott replied as he turned to look, but by then of course, the monk was already gone.

Turning back to face the front, I simply shrugged my shoulders, and thought to myself that the monks must hang out here at the airport begging for money like the Hari Krishnas do in the airports at other places. I quickly forgot about the monk and enjoyed the rest of the drive to the hostel, marveling at the beauty of the mountains, the homes, and the buildings, and before long, we were pulling up in front of the hostel.

The hostel was a beautiful, old two story stone house, which had probably been built well over a hundred years before, and once inside, it was even more incredible, showing the rugged architecture that Switzerland is most famous for. The first room we entered was a huge open area, with several overstuffed chairs and couches placed around the room, all facing a giant rock fireplace. Large, hand-hewn beams accented the open ceiling in the center of the room, and the ceiling had to be well over forty feet to the peak. Around this great room, both on the ground level, and the second floor, were rooms for the guests, and along one wall was a desk where you checked in.

After we got over the initial awe of the structure, we went up to the desk, and rang the bell. Soon, an attractive young woman came out of the room behind the desk, and spoke to us in German, which caught me off guard, and as I fumbled around in my pocket for our translation dictionary, I muttered to myself, and apparently the young woman heard my English, and spoke back to us in fairly good English, much to our delight.

"May I help you?" She asked.

"Yes," I replied, "we need a room for the night, and I'm so glad you speak English. I haven't learned much German yet."

"We get a lot of English speaking tourists here," she continued, "so many of our people speak the language. Now, would you like one room or two?"

"One would be fine," I replied, "if you have a room with two beds."

"I do," she said. "Please sign in, and that will be ten dollars, American that is."

"That's wonderful," I replied, pulling a ten-dollar bill from my pants pocket.

I had brought some American cash along, because I've heard that a lot of places here like to get American currency instead of Swiss Francs. It seems that American currency is accepted all over Europe because it has been a stable currency around the world for so long. In Europe of course, they are trying to switch over to the Euro' as the standard currency, which has met with a little resistance. Now, when we are away from the larger cities, I'm sure the Swiss franc is going to be the currency of choice.

"Where are you gentlemen traveling to?" she asked as we were picking up our packs to go up to our room.

"We are going to find a monastery in the mountains outside of a town called Sierre," I replied. "Do you know of the place?"

She had an odd look on her face, and then replied. "No, I'm afraid I haven't heard of a monastery down there, but there are some other, quite famous ones in our country, if you're into that sort of thing, but good luck, and have a safe journey."

She started to turn away, but stopped, and said. "By the way, there will be breakfast ready in the kitchen when you wake up. It is self serve, and if you'd like, you can leave a tip in the jar. Good night now, and enjoy your stay."

"Thank you," I said, and shouldering our packs, we climbed the magnificent stairway to our room. The stairway was nearly six feet wide, and was made out of hand hewn logs, split in half, with the flat side sanded and polished to become the steps. Each of these log steps were then fitted into rounded notches cut into enormous logs spanning the distance from the first floor to the second, and an incredible pole railing, varnished and made smooth from tens of thousands of hands over the years completed the structure.

'What a wonderful country,' I thought to myself as I climbed the stairs to our room, 'I could probably enjoy living here.' I truly felt at peace here, and it was probably because I had spent several lifetimes in this area over the eons.

Our room was very nice, very basic, but nice, with two small beds, a shared dresser for extended stays, and a window facing out into the street. As I glanced out the window, for a fleeting moment, I swear I saw the same monk disappear into the shadows of an alley across the street, but it was dark, and it could have just been a pedestrian passing by, bundled against the chill of the high mountain air. I shook my head and told myself I must be getting tired, and starting to see things, so I closed the curtain and turned back to go find the bathroom.

There was a communal bathroom down the hall, as well as a shower room, and towels had been left on each bed so you could clean up when you wanted to. It was already getting late, so we decided to skip the shower and go straight to bed. We would have to get up early to catch the bus to a town called Spiez, where we would then catch a train for the next leg of our journey. We had a long ways to go, so the local sights would have to wait for the return trip, because for now, I was ready for bed.

I must have been tired, because as soon as my head hit the pillow, I was asleep, and the next thing I knew, a beam of sunlight was coming through the curtain and hitting me right in the eyes. Looking at my watch, and taking into account the time change, I knew we needed to get going right away, so I woke Scott up, grabbed our gear, and headed down the stairs to the kitchen for a quick bite to eat, and oh what a delightful sight it was.

The table was piled high with fruit, fresh baked bread, jam, and pastries, and there was a steaming pot of hot tea on the counter. There were a couple of other young folks in the dining area, all traveling like we were, and it seems they were all from different countries, going different directions. We nodded to each other, attempted to speak to each other, and finally gave up and ate our breakfast, an activity we all understood. When we had finished, I left a tip in the jar, worth about five dollars.

On the way out, I stopped at the counter and asked the girl about directions to the bus station, which she said was within walking distance of the hostel, and, after pointing us in the right direction, we set off, packs on our backs, just like we knew what we were doing. The bus depot was a large sprawling place, with signs all over the walls, telling which bus was going to which town, and at which time, and with the help of our pocket translator, we found the right terminal, muddled through the ticket purchase, and found our bus, the bus heading for Spiez, about five hours southwest.

The bus ride was picturesque, following a major highway through country that you would only see on postcards, and, after another nice nap, we arrived in Spiez, another wonderful little town at the foot of the Alps. The backdrop for this town was stunning, with the mountain range rising up into the clouds. What an incredible sight it was.

The bus station was directly across the street from the train station, which was convenient for us. Unfortunately, our train doesn't depart for another three hours, so we have a little time to kill. We decided now would be a good time to check out the local shops, and what a treat that turned out to be.

The Swiss of course are known for their clocks, and I have never in my life seen such ornate pieces of craftsmanship. These clocks were truly works of art, and came in every size, shape, and design as you could imagine, from huge grandfather clocks, to mantle clocks, to wristwatches, with prices to match. It was fun to look, but we weren't here to buy a clock.

From here, we checked out the camera store. The other thing the Swiss are noted for are their optics, which means expensive cameras, binoculars, and telescopes, all of which I dearly love. It was tempting to buy a couple of these toys, but I had to remind myself what I was doing here and perhaps on the return trip, maybe I'll take home a souvenir.

By the time we had checked out a couple of the other shops, and had a bite to eat at a nice little bistro, it was time to catch our train southeast to a town called Brig, which is in a high mountain valley about four hours from here by rail. It's not that it's a great distance from here, but it's almost all uphill, winding up mountain passes, and through high valleys so lush and green that it almost hurts the eyes. There is a road that goes to Brig, but it's very winding and bumpy, whereas the train is quicker, and a lot more comfortable. Besides, the train has a dining car, and a club car that serves alcohol, now we're talking.

As we boarded the train, I had that weird feeling again, so this time I started looking around, and sure enough, about five cars back, I spotted the same monk boarding the train, and now I was sure he was following us, or at least keeping track of us. I wondered if he was from the monastery we were looking for, and if he was, how on earth did they know we were coming. This was starting to get a little weird. I wasn't nervous, or scared, in fact, I was beginning to believe there really was a monastery, and perhaps a castle as well, my castle.

We found our berth, stored our backpacks, and waited for the train to get underway. As soon as we were moving at a good steady place, we decided it was time for a drink, and off we went to the club car, which was just a couple of cars ahead of ours. It's an interesting experience stepping from one moving train car to the next, but, after the initial hesitation, it went fine, although we better not have too much to drink before trying it on the return trip.

We found a seat in the club car, and ordered a couple drinks from the menu, not knowing exactly what it was going to be, but, as it turned out, it was some sort of local wine, and was quite tasty. When we had finished our drinks, we managed to convey to the waiter that we would like to have dinner in the dining car, and would like another round of drinks sent to us there. So far, so good on this language barrier problem. By the time I leave here, I may even be able to understand what I just said.

The waiter in the dining car spoke some broken English, so we had a little better luck figuring out what to order, and after a nice meal we made our way back to our berth without incident, even though the drinks we had were a little stronger than anything I was used to. The drinks must have affected Scott even more than me because he tried to go into the wrong berth, much to the dismay of an elderly woman changing her cloths. It was a good thing she wasn't a very good shot with that shoe, and after a hasty retreat, we ducked into the safety of our own berth, chuckling all the way.

It was then that we decided another nap was in order, and before we knew it, the train was slowing to a stop, causing us to wake up rather abruptly, and wonder who, and where we were. Oh yeah, train, Switzerland, castle, wow, those drinks were strong.

As soon as the train had come to a complete stop, we grabbed our packs, and on slightly wobbly legs, we exited the train, and as I did, I quickly scanned the people exiting from the rear cars to see if I could spot the monk. Unfortunately, there were too many people on the boardwalk to get a good glimpse of anyone in particular.

The train was not going to continue on until morning, so once we got inside the station, I asked as best I could where the nearest hotel or hostel might be, and again, as luck would have it, there was a hostel within a few blocks of the station. I think they have it very well planned to have hostels close to the train and bus stations.

As we walked down the street to the hostel, we got our first glance at the surrounding countryside. We had gained considerable elevation, and the evening air had a chill to it. I was glad we had packed a light jacket with us. The view of the mountain peaks, and high mountain valleys was breathtaking, and it touched something deep within my soul, stirring up emotions that I couldn't explain, almost a feeling of déjà vu. In fact, I was having such a feeling of déjà vu that I nearly walked past the hostel, and if it weren't for Scott, we probably would have.

This hostel wasn't quite as fancy as the first one we stayed at in Bern, but it was comfortable, and that's really all you can ask for, especially in a foreign country, and best of all, they're quite inexpensive compared to the hotels in the larger cities. In towns like this that are way off the beaten path, the tourist trade doesn't drive the economy, so when guests do come into town, the welcome mats come out.

You'll never go hungry in a small town, no matter what country you're in, because the locals believe in serving a big meal. Even the complimentary breakfasts laid out by these local hostels are a feast fit for a king. If it wasn't for the fact that we were going to be hiking high into the alps, we'd probably end up getting fat on this trip, and we haven't had to even touch the freeze dried food in our packs, thank God for that. Freeze dried food will sustain you when you're hungry, but it's definitely not the most flavorful meal you've ever eaten. So for now, we'll eat hearty while we can, and go lean when we have to.

The night in the hostel was very peaceful and relaxing, and the cool mountain air made sleeping a refreshing experience. In the morning we showered, changed our cloths, and ate a great breakfast. Then it was back to the train station for the last leg of our motorized travel, a train ride to a town even further up into the mountains, a town called Sierre. From there, it would be all foot travel through rugged mountains to what we hoped was my old castle, and what is now a monastery. Something inside me was starting to come alive, I could feel it. I didn't know what it' was, but I could feel it just the same.

We checked in at the train station, got our tickets punched, showed our travel visas, and boarded the train. There weren't quite as many people on the train for this trip, so I looked around for the monk that seemed to be shadowing us, but he was nowhere to be seen. Maybe I was just imagining things all along, being paranoid, but I didn't think so. I could feel a presence, a bond of some sort, a bond with the monk, with the land here, it was something I couldn't put my finger on, but the farther we went, the stronger that feeling was getting.

The train ride would take about six hours, so we settled back into our berth, and this time I watched the scenery passing by outside as we continued to climb into the mountains, through the Sierre Pass, and into the narrow valley beyond to the town of Sierre. I think I was starting to get a little mesmerized by the trees, and rocks whizzing by the train when all of a sudden I was jolted out of my trance by a sight that caused my eyes to open wide, my mouth to drop, and my heart to skip a beat, and I nearly scared Scott out of socks when I yelled at him.

"Balon, look, we're in the Talon Pass!"

Scott's jerked to his feet out of a sound sleep, eyes wide open, and then looked around to see where he was, and then he turned and looked at me, and said.

"Did you just call me Balon?"

I looked back at him in shock, and then I realized that I had indeed called him Balon, which caused my heart to skip another beat, but I quickly recovered, and said to him in an excited voice.

"Look out the window Scott, don't you recognize where we are, we're in the Talon Pass, where we ambushed the Gog troops so many thousands of years ago. Look at the rockslides on that side; in fact, the tracks were laid over the top of the rockslide, the rockslide we caused with the Horn of Gideon. And look at the places where the rock cropping are barren of vegetation, you can still see the lines of melted rock where Valik used the Dragon's Breath weapon on them, isn't this incredible."

Scott was looking out the window, but he was not seeing what I was seeing, and then it dawned on me that the only reason I was remembering it was because I had relived it through the hypnosis sessions over the last few weeks, so it was still fresh in my mind. Scott had no recollection of his past life, and for whatever reason, not everyone is in tune with that aspect of his or her pre-existence, but Scott did say that the place looked vaguely familiar. He said he would have to take my word for it, and then he settled back into his chair for the rest of the trip. As for myself, I was now more alive than I had been in my entire life, at least in this lifetime, and I was excited, because I now knew where I was, and I knew where I was going.

Once we had topped the pass, it was downhill from there into the valley, the valley that had once been the valley of the King, King Malok that is. Now it was the valley of the town of Sierre, a peaceful little town in modern day Switzerland, a town that had no idea of its past, no idea of the great battle that ultimately helped bring about the demise of the dragons, a battle that used ancient weapons so advanced that they didn't come back into existence for nearly twelve thousand years, and you know, I hope they never find out.

The train had picked up considerable speed on its downhill trek, and the squeaking of the brakes were a reminder of the remoteness of this area, exactly the reason my father of old chose this place to live, and now I'm back. It's beyond my comprehension as to what I'm going to find, what I'm going to learn on this trip, but fate is leading me on, I can't deny it, all I can do is enjoy the ride, and that is what I intend to do.

As we pulled into the station, I almost expected to see the castle of King Malok still standing, but there was nothing to be seen but a low hill where I thought the castle should have been. The hill was covered with houses, but the more I looked, I thought I could see some old pillars sticking out of the ground, and it appeared there was some sort of geological excavation going on, I'll have to ask the locals about it. I wonder what had happened to bring the castle down so low that the earth itself had covered it up until now.

After we got off the train, we decided that we had better get something to eat before we started our trip up the mountain. It was mid afternoon, and I would like to at least get up on the plateau before dark, maybe even to the base of the mountain where we could set up camp. As we turned to find a bistro, there was the monk, or at least a' monk, walking down the street, and as I started to get excited about him being out in the open, I noticed two more across the street, loaded down with heavy bundles on their backs, making their way out of town, headed in the direction of the plateau, and no doubt the mountain beyond. They must have come to town for supplies, and were now headed back to the monastery. At least I knew I was in the right area.

I watched the monks for a few more minutes, and as I did, the lone monk whom I believe had been shadowing us crossed the street to intercept the other two, and as he hailed them, they dropped their bundles to the ground, and rushed to greet him with hugs, and what appeared to be a very excited conversation, at which time the other two monks looked over their shoulders in our direction. That confirmed it for me, they knew we were coming, and as I watched, the first monk helped them pick up their bundles, and all three hurried down the street toward the end of town. Following suit, Scott and I walked down the street in the same direction, but first we needed something to eat. Our inevitable meeting with the monks would have to wait a little longer.

We chose a small bistro on the main street going through town, and chose a seat by the window. A charming older woman waited on us, and with the help of our dictionary, and some very broken English on the part of our waitress, we ordered our meal. When she came back around, I asked her about the excavation going on up on the hill. She was able to convey to us that a few years ago; workman had discovered the ruins of an ancient castle as they were digging the foundation for a new house.

No one really knew how old it was, but it was guessed that it was only a few thousand years old, since most of the castles in Europe were about four thousand years old. It was supposed that an earthquake may have destroyed it, but no one really knew, or cared for that matter. It was more of a nuisance to the workman than anything, because there was so much rubble, it was almost impossible to dig through it to build a foundation. And as I sat there and ate my meal, I thought to myself, if these people only knew the half of what that castle stood for, there would be teams of archeologists from all over the world digging there. Then I thought to myself, it's better off this way.

We finished our meal, paid the lady at the counter, shouldered our heavy packs, and headed out the door and down the street toward the mountains. Everywhere we went, people stopped to stare at us, whispering to each other, no doubt wondering what a couple of Yankees were doing so far away from home, and so far off the beaten path. We just nodded our hats at them as we passed by, and kept walking, right out of town, toward the plateau, and the mountain beyond.

The mountain didn't look quite the same as it did so many eons ago. Now, heavy timber covered the slopes, whereas when I was here last, the mountains were relatively new, having been thrust up from the earth only a short time before, geologically speaking. There was a lot of brush, and some trees at that time, but now the mountain was covered with thick, dark timber, kind of foreboding if you thought about it. Instead of rough, jagged peaks, everything was rounded off, weathered, and eroded over time. From what I have learned from my sessions, and from other studies, the earth has changed it's polar axis since I was here last, and the resulting earthquakes and seismic activity have smoothed things out a bit. It will be interesting to see how my castle has held up, given the state of the castle of King Malok.

We climbed high out of the valley throughout the afternoon, finding the narrow winding trail up the mountainside. It would appear that only foot traffic goes beyond the plateau, as numerous landslides over the years have destroyed any old roads that happened to be here before, and now, all that remains is a well worn foot trail, obviously having been used for many thousands of years by the monks.

It was just before dark when we reached a large flat area, which I guessed used to be one of the meadows the Gog troops were camped in when we attacked them. Now, even though you could tell it was a large flat area, it was overgrown with brush and timber, except for a nice grassy area next to the creek, and it was here we decided to make camp for the night. There was no use attempting to hail the residents of the monastery during the dark of night. This way we'll get to the monastery around noon, just in time for lunch.

By the time we got the tent set up, gathered a little firewood, and got a fire going, it was pitch dark out. In the mountains, with heavy timber, when it gets dark, you can't see your hand in front of your face without the aid of a flashlight. A campfire is always a welcome friend when you're camping. It beats back the darkness, keeps the animals at bay, and the flames always seem to mesmerize you, giving you a sense of security in a place where you' are the stranger, and since I don't know what sort of animals live here anymore, I'll take all the security I can get.

As soon as the fire was roaring, I took out the camp stove and fired it up, while Scott used the flashlight to get a kettle of water from the creek. Then we heated the water to a boil, took out a couple of freeze-dried meals, added water, and enjoyed a scrumptious camp meal. I am kidding of course about the scrumptious part, but it was a meal, and as you know, us guys can eat most anything and believe that we're living like kings. For some reason, when you're camping out, everything tastes good, just as it did tonight.

At this elevation, it got a little chilly during the night, but we had pretty good sleeping bags, and the tent kept the wind and morning dew off of us, and when morning came, we waited inside our bags until the sun hit the tent. Then we got up, brewed some tea water on the camp stove, and ate a couple of granola bars. Washing our faces in the cold creek water was a wake up experience though, and by the time that was done, we packed up camp in record time. We were anxious to get started on our hike, if for no other reason than just to warm up, and after a change of socks, we were on our way up the winding trail.

I marveled at the landscape as we continued the steady climb up the mountains. Some of the surrounding valleys and peaks looked familiar, yet far removed from the way they appeared in my hypnosis sessions, but that was to be expected since over twelve thousand years had elapsed. It was hard to imagine twelve thousand years had passed; I had only just recently relived the experiences a few days, and weeks ago. They were still so fresh in my head that this was almost a culture shock. I was having a little difficulty grasping the whole concept, yet here I was, seeing it with my own eyes, strange as it was. I could still see the battles vividly, but as I passed by each area where we had battled, there was no sign that this land was anything more than what it was right now, a peaceful, serene, and majestic alpine mountain.

I was deep in thought and recollection as I walked, that Scott finally asked me if I was okay, and if anything was wrong. Scott was actually the lucky one here, not having any recollection of this part of his existence. I just replied to him that I was okay, and that I was just reliving a lot of old memories as we traveled, and the closer we got to the castle, the heavier those memories weighed upon me, including some very painful memories of Mara, and of Dee.

As we approached the chasm in front of the castle, I was shocked to see a rope and wood footbridge across the gorge instead of the drawbridge, but lord knows that drawbridge rotted away thousands upon thousands of years ago, and a footbridge can be changed every few years as the need dictates. I do have to tell you though, that during one of my lives, I became none too fond of heights, and crossing that footbridge was causing me some major pucker power.

The castle walls were no where near their original height or grandeur, having crumbled over the centuries due to earthquakes and erosion, and then I suppose a lot of the wall was scavenged to replace other crumbling structures within the castle. All in all though, the castle looked pretty good for as old as it was.

Interestingly enough, the main gate was open, or perhaps there wasn't even a gate there anymore, which made sense since the footbridge was deterrent enough for most folks, not to mention the fact that they probably didn't get many visitors up here anyhow. Unless they replace the gate every fifty years or so, it would just rot away, and my guess is, if they locked the place up, someone would think there was something to hide here, and we certainly don't want anyone snooping around.

Walking across a swinging footbridge is always an interesting experience, and it's not for the faint of heart. You have to watch each step you take, and hope there's no loose boards to fall through, and keep your hands on the guide rope to steady the swinging, not to mention the fact you want to have a hold of something in case you fall through, all good fun for a guy that's scared of heights.

I pretty much took baby steps all the way across the footbridge, as I wasn't about to take any chances being a daredevil. Scott on the other hand just waltzed right across like it was no big deal, but then no one ever accused him of having good sense. Once across I paused to let my heart stop racing, and as soon as Scott was across, we walked through the gate into the castle, and the sight that awaited us was enough to make your heart skip a beat.

Chapter 12

As we entered the castle, there before us were nearly two hundred monks, lined up across the courtyard, side by side, four rows deep, with three more monks spread out in front of them. Each monk wore the traditional brown colored, hooded robe, with a thick, rope waistband. As we entered the compound, all the monks bowed before us, only to raise their joined hands in unison, shouting, hail to the Dragon Master, hail to King Ethan. My heart almost stopped in my chest, and I turned to Scott, and said.

"Do you think they were expecting us?" at which he replied.

"It would seem so."

As we approached the formation of monks, the three in front walked up to greet us, and with a bow, the lead monk pulled back his hood, revealing a strangely familiar face, and as I was standing there pondering why that face was familiar, he said.

"We have been expecting you master; you have been gone a long time. Please come inside to greet the brothers."

It suddenly dawned on me that I had understood every word the monk had just spoken. How could that be, we were in a foreign country? It just reinforced my notion that I am supposed to be here, for whatever reason I don't know, at least not yet, and as I stood there thinking about it, the monk jarred me back to reality.

The head monk clapped his hands, and everyone broke ranks and hurried off toward the main building, which even though it had changed, was roughly in the same place as my old meeting hall, but now it served as their chapel. The monk motioned for us to follow him to the meeting hall, and as we did so, I looked around the grounds of the castle, trying to get a perspective of how

I remembered the layout, as compared to how it looked now.

The castle grounds itself covered roughly sixty to eighty acres, and appears as though the mountain top had been hollowed out on top, with the walls of the castle being part of the original rock. That makes sense when you realize that an ancient volcano formed this mountain, and all of the caverns below it, including volcanic vents that were later sculpted out by water. My ancient ancestors did the rest of the finishing touches mostly by hand, but I suspect with a little help from the lasers to cut rock, and the Horn of Gideon to move large stones.

Off to the sides of the chapel, and all along the back wall of the castle, were what appeared to be living quarters for all of the brethren, and to one side, stood another large stone structure, which was where my villa had once stood, even though it seemed to be somewhat smaller than I had remembered. Now, it was apparently the main dining hall, as part of it had been when I lived here.

Back in one corner was a stone tower with four small open windows cut through the walls, hardly big enough to provide much of a view, or ventilation. What purpose that served, I would have to ask later. On the opposite side of the compound was another stone tower, and this one had no windows at all, just a wooden stairway going half way up one side. I don't remember either of those towers being there from my hypnosis sessions.

All of the buildings were very plain and simple, unadorned by anything fancy or frivolous, at least on the exterior, but once we were inside the main chapel, it was obvious that there were some superb artisans within the fellowship. The walls and ceilings of the chapel were adorned by incredible artwork, which depicted dragons, castles, and epic battles of good versus evil, while seven wooden support columns were carved into ornate serpentine dragons. The floors were chiseled into the stone of the mountain itself, and were polished to a shine like glass.

The chapel was lined with hand hewn wooden benches, each adorned with carved dragons at both ends, and at the front of the chapel was a beautiful wooden podium, varnished and polished to a rich tone, while the front of the podium was carved in relief, depicting seven dragons, and I wondered if they represented my' seven dragons.

As we entered the chapel, Scott and I set our packs down against the back wall, and as the head monk led us forward, the rest of the brothers quickly sat down on the benches. I assumed that he wanted us to address the congregation, but I really didn't know what I was going to say, at least until

I reached the podium. Meanwhile, Scott was shown to a bench at the front of the hall, and then I was led up to the podium, standing beside the head monk while he addressed the crowd, and again, we understood everything he was saying. I'm not sure if he was speaking English, or if somehow, we understood the language he was speaking.

"My brothers," he began, "we have waited a very long time for Ethan to return, but we believed in the oracles that he would return to us, and now he has indeed returned. We welcome him with open arms, open hearts, and open minds. I know he has as many questions for us as we have for him, and I trust we will have many days together to explore those questions. I would have him speak only briefly to us now, and then he must rest, and eat. Dragon Master, if you could please say a few words to the brothers before we show you to your quarters."

The monk bowed, and backed away, and as if I knew what I was doing, I stepped forward to speak.

"My friends, I'm not exactly sure what I'm doing here, but I know that I have been led here by fate, and so, I am here, to learn from you and you from me, and I'm anxious to get started."

I turned back to face the head monk, who stepped forward to address the congregation once again.

"Brothers of the Dragon, we have waited a long time for Ethan to return again, and now he has come. We look forward to completing his training and hope that we will learn a great deal more from him also. For now, we need to show the Dragon Master and his friend Balon to their rooms, and get them food and drink. Later this afternoon, we will begin our training."

The monk clapped his hands, and two young monks rushed forward to grab our bags, and then motioned for us to follow them. As we walked down the aisle past the seated monks, all eyes were upon us, and each monk was smiling at us like we were the some long lost Gods returned to earth, which maybe in a way, that's what we were.

We followed the monks out of the chapel and across the courtyard to what I assumed was my old villa, or at least what was left of it. It seemed to be a lot smaller than before, and there was a smaller building off by itself, not far from villa, which I don't recall being there at all, but after this many eons, that was not surprising.

Once inside the villa, we were led down a short hallway, past a heavy wooden door, which was closed and bolted, and finally to the end of the hallway to two small private rooms. In the corner of each room was a small bed and a trunk to put our private effects in, as well as a small table with a single chair. On the table was a large bowl of water to wash up with. This sure isn't the way I left the place, but, now I'm just a guest in a foreign land, and beggars can't be choosy. This was now home away from home, and it would have to do.

The monk who had accompanied us spoke to me in whatever language I was understanding, and told us to clean up, rest, and then come to the dining room for some food and drink. I was all for that, so after cleaning up, I sprawled out on the bed, and before long, I was sound asleep.

A knock at the door woke me up, and as I swung my legs over the side of the bed, I called for them to come in. It was one of the monks who had escorted us to our rooms, and now he was requesting our presence in the dining hall. I glanced at my watch, and I was surprised to see that I had slept for nearly two hours. I must have been more exhausted than I thought. There was another possibility though, and that being that I was at peace in this place, the place of my ancestry, the place where I had spent at least one long lifetime, and who knows, maybe more.

As I followed the monk out into the hall, Scott was already waiting for me, and said.

"It was about time you woke up, I'm starving."

"You're always starving," I replied, smacking him on the shoulder as I walked by.

Scott had to hurry to catch up with us, and we followed the monk down the hall to the dining room, and when we entered, most of the monks had already arrived, and were seated at the long wooden tables, eating bread and cheese, and drinking wine. The din of everyone talking was almost deafening, until I noticed that no one's mouths were moving. That's when it struck me, I understood everyone with my mind, not my ears. It was just like the old days, except I couldn't tell if I was hearing them on my own, or if they were projecting their thoughts to me, but either way, it was a little disconcerting.

The head monk was seated at a separate table with the two other lead monks, and when they saw us enter, he raised his hand, and everyone went quiet. Then I heard him say.

"Welcome Ethan, welcome Balon, please come and sit with me, and have something to eat and drink."

He waved us forward, and we took our seats at the head table, I beside the head monk, and Scott across from me. Almost immediately two young monks brought us bread, wine, and cheese, and as we sat there savoring the wonderful fare, the head monk spoke to us, and to the rest of the congregation.

"First of all, let me tell you how wonderful it is to see you again Ethan, it has been a long time indeed."

I stopped him at that point, and asked him how it was that he knew who I had been, and how he knew we were coming, and he replied.

"We have followed you since you reentered the earthly realm nearly fifty years ago, and we've followed your progress ever since, and when fate had played out it's hand one more time, we sent a messenger to show you the way home."

"A messenger?" I asked.

"Yes," he replied, "the monk who spoke to your Dr. Miller."

It all made sense now, everything had played out just as it undoubtedly had so many lifetimes before, and then when it was all done, and I had no where else to turn, I was led here. All of a sudden, I was angry, and I spoke up.

"If you knew what was going to happen, why didn't you warn me, why didn't you stop it from happening?"

The monk raised one hand just to calm me down, and in a soft voice he said.

"There is no one on earth who can change your destiny except you alone, and even then it is nearly impossible to accomplish once you're back on earth, since most people don't know that their life is following a predetermined path. You had the perfect opportunity this time around because you knew that something was going to happen, yet you still weren't able to prevent it."

With a feeling of resignation, I asked.

"Do you mean to tell me that you can change your destiny before you come back to the earthly realm?"

"That's exactly what I'm saying," he replied, and then he went on. "After we die, our spirits go to a place of waiting, a place of reconciliation if you will. In this place we study our past life, figure out what we did right, and what we did wrong. Old injuries, both physically and mentally need to be repaired during this time period. If we come back too early, before we've had time to repair our souls, or before we've had time to learn from our mistakes, then we are more than likely going to make all the same choices and mistakes again that we've made in the previous life, and this is where your lesson begins Ethan."

A lump formed in my throat at the thoughts going through my head, but I fought those back for a moment and with a change of subject, I managed to croak out.

"My name is Henry, and I would appreciate it if you addressed me by that name right now, as it still feels very foreign to be called by the name of Ethan."

"Very well, as you wish Henry," he said, and then continued with his dissertation.

"You and Mara, I mean Dee, have been chasing each other around the universe for so long that neither of you have taken the time to heal your souls. Both of you came back to the earthly plane this time less than 15 years after your previous deaths, as did tens of millions of other souls following the end of the two world wars. There were so many people killed early in their life from those two wars that most of them couldn't wait to get back into the earthly realm. The problem with that is, if you return too quickly, you bring all that baggage right back with you because you didn't have time to heal, and that's why there are so many messed up people in the world today."

"That's beginning to make a lot of sense," I interjected. "Dee was so afraid of thunder that I often wondered what had happened to her in a past life."

"The reason she is so afraid of thunder," he resumed, "is because she was killed by German bombs in London during World War II. The thunder she fears so much was the thunder of thousands upon thousands of bombs raining down on London, and the winds caused by the infernos of the burning buildings, the same buildings that toppled down like falling trees. She should have stayed in the place of peace for at least a century, and maybe even two centuries to heal from the mental and physical damage from that death alone, but no, the two of you made a pact to come back as soon as possible, and now you see what the result were."

"Oh my God," I started, "we made a pact again to come back within thirty years of our combined deaths. Will we have to go through all of this again?"

"Not necessarily," he said. "We know of a way to change that part of your destiny from here if you so desire."

"I do desire it, tell me how to do it," I pleaded.

"We will discuss that tomorrow," he said, and stood to leave, but I stopped him and asked.

"May I ask what your name is, or by what name I used to know you?"

"You have known me by many names over the eons, but the best recollection you will have of me right now is the name, Valik, Captain of your castle guard. The two other head monks here with me are also know to you, or at least they were know to you a very long time ago."

Both of the men with Valik stood as he introduced them.

"This man here you knew as Mr. Damon, my second in command when we fought against the Gog. He was also the main pilot of the flying chariot."

The man stepped forward to shake my hand, and said.

"It is my honor to serve you again my Lord."

"Thank you Mr. Damon," I replied. "I'm glad you could make the trip."

"And this man you knew as Galen, the shopkeeper whose family we rescued from the Gog down by the falls. He has been a big asset to our monastery, many lifetimes over, for he is the artisan who has carved all of these beautiful dragon pillars, the benches, and the podium. He is also responsible for the incredible stone floor in this chapel. We look forward to his return for each sojourn on earth."

I stepped up to shake the man's hand, and then I said to him.

"I am so glad to see you again Mr. Galen. I never got a chance to thank you the first time around for the throne you built for my beloved Mara, but now I can. I thank you from the bottom of my heart."

I gripped Galen's hand for a little longer than necessary, in a show of gratitude to a great master craftsman, but all he could say was.

"It was my pleasure Ethan, I mean Henry."

It was Valik who spoke next, breaking the awkward spell.

"We must go now Henry, but we'll speak again tomorrow."

With that, he bowed, and walked away, followed by the entire assembly, leaving Scott and I sitting there speechless, with our mouths agape, and as he walked away, I thought to myself that there was some resemblance there, but just like with myself, we all change dramatically over time. What a wonderful treat it was to see Valik, Damon, and Galen again, and I wondered how many more of my old comrades were here.

Instead of going back to our rooms, Scott and I decided to do a little exploring, and our first destination was to look over the castle grounds. Once outside, we checked out the perimeter of the castle, walking the walls, and peering over the side into the Valley of the Dragons. It still looked as menacing from this height as it did before, but now, instead of the jagged barren rock walls and peaks, the whole valley was carpeted by heavy forests, with the occasional glint of water from a hidden creek on the valley floor. What a change it was from the vision I have in my head from all those thousands of years ago.

Next, we wandered around the inner castle grounds, checking out the barracks style living quarters, and finally to the first of the two strange towers

I had seen when we first arrived. We walked up the winding steps outside of the first tower, the one with the four windows, and as we entered the main room we were awestruck by the engravings on the walls, ceilings, and floor, engravings of all the signs of the zodiac, and of all the various stars and constellations in the night sky.

Each area of the wall had a star pattern to match a different time of day or night, and in the center of the room was a large round table with a huge star chart carved into solid granite. Along the base of the tower walls, several more stone charts rested on end, leaning against the wall, covered in dust, with some starting to crumble from lack of care.

By standing next to the star chart in the center of the room, and then looking up at the wall, you could see slits angled up through the stone wall of the tower. From different vantage points around the chart, you could view each constellation as it came into view through the slit at its corresponding time of day, month, or year. It was very ingenious, but what purpose did it serve.

As I stood there pondering the question, a monk entered the room, and asked if I understood what I was looking at, and I responded by telling him that I had a good understanding of star charts and constellations, but I didn't understand why they were so interested in them.

He went on to explain to me that throughout the history of the earth, geological changes happen at regular intervals, with one of those changes being a repositioning of the earths poles every twelve thousand years or so. He explained that the earth of course is on a slight tilt, and that when the ice at the poles reached a certain mass and weight, that the poles became so heavy that the earths crust slipped on the molten magna until the weight equaled out, putting the old poles at roughly the level of the equator, and creating a new set of poles, much to the chagrin of whoever now lived at the new poles, that is if they survived the trip.

It was easy to imagine the destruction that would be caused by the earths crust slipping on its core, with the earths crust breaking open along huge lengths of the tectonic plates, causing massive fields of molten lava to spill out upon the earth. Add to that the monster storms caused by superheated updrafts of evaporated oceans, lakes, and rivers, taking that moisture so high into the atmosphere that the only way it could fall back to earth was as giant frozen hailstones the size of automobiles.

Then when you think about the earths crust slipping, you have to think about the oceans. They don't just slide with the crust; they tend to rush backwards across the landmass like a giant tsunami, destroying everything in its path. You can imagine that life on earth would not be a quality experience during times like those.

"But what is the significance of that now?" I asked.

"Because," he explained, "we are again entering the geological time period for those changes to take place again, probably within a few hundred years, more or less. And that is why we continue to monitor the heavens."

"When was the last time this happened?" I asked, thinking I already knew the answer.

"It happened not long, geologically speaking, after your first sojourn in this place, and a couple hundred years after Mara's death."

He stood there, waiting for me to ask another question, which was not long in coming, and so as not to disappoint him, I asked another question that had been bothering me for quite some time.

"There are similar observatories such as this one in the South American jungle, what can you tell me about those."

"After the cataclysms from the last polar shift, the human remnants were scattered about the earth seeking out habitable lands, and one of those places was South America. Some of the ancestors of the old Atlantean culture had settled there from the previous cataclysm, and having experienced the same event twice, they developed a simple way to monitor the heavens, so they could keep track of the subtle changes preceding the polar shift."

"Are you seeing those subtle changes now?" I asked.

"Yes," he responded, "we started seeing the changes back in the early 1960's, very slight, but definitely increasing."

"How much time do we have?" I asked.

"It's hard to predict," he started, "it usually takes a hundred years or so under normal circumstances, but things are different this time around."

"How's that?" I asked.

"Pollution," he said, and then continued, "pollution has caused global warming that has been melting the ice packs at the poles, thus reducing some of the weight and slowing down the slippage."

"Wow," I said, "man definitely has an effect on the planet, whether it's good, or bad."

"Yes he does, and sometimes it's hard to tell the difference," he said as he turned and left us to our thoughts.

There was the other tower on the opposite side of the compound, slightly taller and wider than this one, maybe sixty feet tall and thirty feet in diameter, so that was our next destination. As we walked across the courtyard, we marveled at how some of the old stonework had held up over the centuries, but I'm sure that the monks had something to do with the state of repair it was in, having found, and lived in this place for nearly four thousand years. I wonder how far they've managed to excavate into the old caverns below.

As we approached the tower, I was getting a feeling that the tower was alive somehow, and if I didn't know better, it seemed that it was glowing. Nearing closer, you could hear a barely perceptible humming sound coming from the building itself, and it gave you a very disconcerting feeling, almost to the point of dizziness.

"Do you hear voices?" Scott asked.

"I think I do," I said, but I was still not quite sure.

I hadn't really noticed it before, but Scott was right, I could hear voices, strange sounding voices, not quite mechanical, but distorted somehow, and it was definitely coming from this tower.

We climbed the steps to a heavy wooden door that was about twenty-five feet above the ground, and the voices, as well as the humming, were definitely coming from behind the door, and within the tower. There was also a slight glow emanating from under the door, and with some slight trepidation, I opened the door to a feast of sight and sound that was enough to overload your senses.

Stepping inside the tower you were found yourself walking on a suspended wooden platform, and all around you, from the floor below you, to the ceiling high above your head, everything was made of crystal, or crystals. It was hard to tell if the walls were solid crystal, or made of thousands of crystals, since the whole place glowed, and hummed, making the whole experience overwhelming to my senses. In fact, I had to hold onto the railing, as did Scott, because I thought at first I was going to pass out. A voice out of nowhere snapped me back to reality saying.

"Just close your eyes when it gets too much for you. It's a little hard to get used to at first, but once you do, it'll be very enlightening."

I looked around for the person who spoke, but we were alone in the room, and it was only then that I figured out that the voice had come from the walls themselves, and as my senses came back to some semblance of normal I started to see the reality of what the tower was all about.

From the floor below, to the ceiling above, the walls were imbedded with tens of thousands of crystals, with a six inch thick layer of granite separating each section of crystal wall at intervals of about six feet, and there appeared to be six of these sections. The floor and ceiling were also solid crystal, with the only imperfection being a large metal loop in the center of the ceiling. The wooden platform, on which we stood, was placed slightly less than half way in the tower, allowing a view of the entire inside of the tower. It was only after my eyes were able to focus properly on the crystal walls that I figured out what I was hearing and seeing.

Each section of crystal wall acted as a screen, much like a television screen, though not as clear of course, but I was able to make out with fairly good clarity, the image of a man standing before me, and once I had made that distinction, he continued speaking.

"We welcome you back Dragon Master; you have been gone a long time. Is Balon okay?"

It was then I became aware that Scott was still down on one knee, his head buried in his hands, and he was moaning. It was obvious that he was having problems with all of this sensory input, so I excused myself for a moment while I helped Scott to his feet and helped him back out the door so he could clear his head, and then I went back inside and closed the door.

When I again turned to face the man who had spoken, I was now aware that there were a dozen or more men standing to face me from all areas of the tower, all were wearing the same brown, hooded garb of the order of monks, and, since I had an entire audience, I addressed them all.

"Forgive my inquisitive nature, but, what is this place, and who are you."

"My name is Fallon, and I am the head monk in Haden monastery in Peru. The other men you see around you are from some of the other monasteries around the world dedicated to the order of the seven dragons. The tower you are standing in is made of pure, flawless crystals, arrayed in such a manner that your tower matches all of the other towers exactly. The men before you are all standing in their own respective towers, in their own countries, and all can speak and hear everything the rest of us have to say."

"All of this is very cool," I said, "but don't you think it's a bit behind the times, after all, there are more modern ways to communicate, like radios, and satellite phones."

"On the contrary," he responded, "once you realize that all of these monasteries are in areas so remote that there will never be electricity, and the fact that these towers were constructed nearly twelve thousand years ago, I think they are quite amazing, as well as cool."

I stood there amazed as the gravity of this place revealed itself to me. Even though the design of the towers was simple, having a basis on the design of the crystals used in two-way radios of the twentieth century, the design itself was even more amazing, given the fact that it required no electricity of any kind, and the fact that it was built so many eons ago. As I regained my composure, I spoke once again, this time with a little more humility.

"Please forgive my rudeness. I guess I never realized just how incredible this place really was until just this minute. Tell me, who built this tower?"

"Why, you did Ethan," he responded, "after you returned from the library in the land of the pyramids, in what is now modern day Egypt, the library under the Sphinx. After Mara's death, you traveled to Egypt on a mission to find the library, and when you returned many years later, you built this tower to talk to Mara from beyond the grave. Unfortunately, you died before it was finished."

"What do you mean when you say; to talk to Mara?" I asked.

Continuing, he said. "It is believed that you can communicate with the dead from this place, but we have not been able to figure out how it is done yet, and we have not been able to find access to your secret cavern to check out the library down there for the information we need to accomplish that task. That is where we hope you will be able to help us."

"And what will you do with such information?" I asked cautiously.

"Unlike the other secrets surrounding this place," he began, "that knowledge is to be used to help those like Mara, who are waiting in the place of rest until they once again return to earth. They are encouraged to wait until they are truly ready to return. But there is another side of this that we hope to accomplish, and that is to prevent the evil souls from returning to the earth to kill and destroy, those such as Adolph Hitler, and Stalin, and if they do return, we hope to learn when those souls returned to the earthly realm, and identify who and where they are in the present day."

"And what will you do when you do identify those 'Evil Ones?" I asked.

"We plan to monitor their activity," he began. "We plan to modify their environment if need be to lead them in a different path."

"But, you know as well as I do," I said "that we are all led by fate, and that it can't be changed."

"On the contrary," he responded, "human will supercedes fate, and we all have the right to choose which path we take. Even God will not force us to do anything we don't want to do, allowing us to follow the path of our own choosing. As for us, we feel that we can help direct that 'will' in the cases that warrant it."

"That's interesting," I said, "and disturbing, in the fact that my own human will probably helped lead to Dee's death because I didn't think I could change the outcome. I believed that she had to die again just like she had every other time. How could I have been so stupid? We need to find that book on conversing with the dead. Now please, tell me more about this place, and how it was you were able to find it."

"Thousands of years after you left this place, brothers reincarnated from the time when the dragons ruled the earth found this place again, through dreams, parables, and rumors, and restored the castle into a monastery. Over the centuries, more and more of the brothers found their way back here, and they have dedicated their lives to the preservation of those times, those beings, and what they represented in respect for the influence man has upon this planet and its creatures. There are secrets here that the world shall never know, lest they somehow use them to do evil, and that's why we are here, to preserve and protect those secrets."

"Now," I started, "I know that some of you are from other monasteries around the world, and you all seem to have a common bond with this one, but can you tell me what that bond is?"

"That bond," he began, "is Atlantis, and as you know, the Dragon Master's great grandfather came to this place from Atlantis before the great catastrophe, and the wizard who brought the chariot and the weapons used to destroy the Gog army, he also came from Atlantis, leaving there just prior to the catastrophe. It seems that the survivors of Atlantis spread out all over the earth, and the places where these monasteries are, is where the most highly evolved communities took up roots. Each of these monasteries have secrets of their own, every bit as fascinating as the secrets within the monastery in which you are standing, and the brothers residing there were reincarnated from those communities, just as you were from the one you're standing in.

"Fascinating," was all I could say, and as I stood there thinking about all of the things we had talked about, the monk addressed me one more time.

"We have many things to talk about Dragon Master, and many things to learn from each other, but for now it is getting late, and the evening training is about to begin, so I bid you good evening, and we will speak to you again very soon."

He and the others were already turning to leave before I even said goodbye, so I let it go at that and went outside to check on Scott, who was now sitting at the bottom of the steps, being attended to by a young monk. As I approached, the monk bowed, and said that Balon was feeling much better now.

"I do wish they would call us by our proper names," I thought to myself, but I let it go. In some ways it was unnerving, but at other times it felt totally natural, and when you come to think about it, I was Ethan the Dragon Master, and this was Balon, and these folks were living proof that everything I had seen in my hypnosis sessions was real. I'm not sure if I'm here because I miss Dee, or if I'm searching for something deeper, but only time will tell.

I helped Scott to his feet, and said there was a training session about to start, and asked him if he would like to go with me, but he declined, saying he was still feeling a little light headed, and was going to lie down for awhile, so I bid him good night, and headed over to the meeting hall.

When I entered the building, the room was full, and quiet, with all the monks seated, heads bowed, meditating. My entrance of course put a stop to that, and the head monk, aka Valik, who was sitting at the front of the hall motioned for me to sit up front with himself, Damon, and Galen, and when I had done so, he addressed the brothers.

"We are pleased to have Ethan join us here tonight, and we hope that he will be enlightened by all that he hears and sees, so I see no reason why we shouldn't get started. As you know, Ethan was known to us as the Dragon Master, and he ruled this castle as King nearly twelve thousand years ago, he and his seven dragons. He accomplished many wonderful things during that lifetime, as well as many lifetimes after that, some of which we already know and use, and some of which we are yet to see and learn."

"Although Ethan has been here several times throughout history, only now has he come with the knowledge he needs to reveal the secrets that have been lost to us for all of these thousands of years, the secrets of the hidden caverns, the dragons, and the rest of his library, including the guide book to the crystal tower and the afterlife."

"We have waited throughout eternity for this day to arrive. All of us having returned here from time to time throughout eternity, not knowing why, but knowing that we must return, and return we have. Nearly every one of us who lived and died during the reign of the dragons has returned to fulfill our destiny, and we will fulfill our destiny by changing the future of destiny itself."

"The return of the Dragon Master was the key we have all waited for, the man with the full awareness of who he was and what he has accomplished, not the man named Henry, not the man who was known as John, or Liam, or Lozeau, or any of the other surnames he was given over the courses of his sojourns on earth. The man we have waited for is Ethan, the Dragon Master, and he is here, here once again."

Valik turned and held his hand toward me, and when he did so, the crowd stood and cheered, sending chills up and down the full length of my spine, so, doing what anyone who didn't know what the heck he was doing would do, I stood up, embraced the monk known as Valik, and nearly feinted, only to be steadied by Valik until I could get my bearings, and then I addressed the crowd.

"My friends, I have already learned a great deal in the short time I've been here, and I think I'm beginning to realize the purpose of my visit here. I know how to get to the secret caverns, and I know where the key should be to open the doors to the cavern, and even though there are still some blank spots in my memories, I have a feeling those memories will all be coming back to me quite quickly as we delve deeper into our past. In fact, I think we're all going to learn a lot about ourselves in the near future, and with that knowledge, I hope we can change the course of the future, not only our own futures, but the future of the world itself, and I'm anxious to get started."

When I had finished speaking, I stepped back and embraced Valik, and when I did, the crowd roared again, and kept on until finally Valik stepped forward and raised his hand for quiet. The brothers were well disciplined and calm was restored within moments, each man taking his seat, smiling, but quiet, and then Valik spoke once more.

"My brothers, thank you for your loyalty and dedication throughout the eons. We have worked long and hard to bring about this day, and even though it is within our grasps, we need to exercise patience, restraint, and caution. We are undertaking a great responsibility, and not only our future, but also the future of mankind is at stake, so we will not undertake this task lightly, or foolhardily. So tonight, enjoy yourselves, partake of wine in celebration, and tomorrow we begin our quest for that which was lost, now go, and enjoy yourselves."

As the crowd left, they were so excited that it looked like a bunch of high school kids getting out of school for the summer. When they had gone, Valik asked me to join him in his study for a glass of wine, and some conversation, so I agreed, and followed him to his quarters, a small, but quaint villa set back against one wall of the old castle.

It would seem that once you reached a certain level of authority, or hierarchy, that you also graduated up to a larger living quarters, one in which you didn't have to share those living quarters with a dozen other men. There were nearly a dozen of these small villas, one for Valik, one each for the other two chief monks, and the rest were vacant, no doubt held in reserve for other monks to establish themselves as worthy of better things, or perhaps they were for visiting dignitaries.

There was one villa in particular that stood out from all the rest, somewhat larger than the others, and set slightly farther away from the rest, and when Valik noticed me looking in that direction, he said.

"That is your quarters Ethan, for as long as you decide to stay with us. Inside you will find all the comforts you deserve, as well as a few surprises."

"Thank you," I replied, "you are very kind, but what of Scott, or should I say Balon."

"He is in the quarters next to yours," he responded, "in fact he was shown to his quarters while we were in our meeting, and I believe he is feeling better now. Would you like for me to have him join us?"

"No," I replied, "I'll see him later before I go to bed, but for now, we need to talk alone."

"Very well then," he said, "but let's have a glass of wine while we talk."

"Lead the way," I said, and followed him inside.

The inside of the Valik's villa was very plain, definitely a single man's home, with no frills. There was a fireplace, a bed with a side table, a dining table with two chairs, an overstuffed easy chair with a footstool, a bookcase, and a very well stocked wine rack. As he was pouring us each a glass of wine, I commented.

"You have a very nice stock of wine. Is it all local wine?"

"It is indeed local, we make it right here at the monastery. This collection is just my own personal collection, much like the collection in each of the villas, and also the barracks. But the real collection is down in the caverns, now there is a sight to behold. We sell and trade our wine to the locals in town, mostly to provide ourselves with the things we can't produce up here, and occasionally to buy something frivolous. We have chosen to live simply here so as not to draw a lot of attention to ourselves. We really don't want the rest of the world to be snooping around."

"You do know that they found the old castle of King Malok on the outskirts of town, and are beginning to excavate the site?"

"Yes," he responded, "but they have been working at it only half heartedly for many years now, and mostly out of necessity just to build a new house on the spot of the digging. Besides, I don't think they would ever find anything to get very excited about anyhow."

"You're probably right," I said, and sat down at the table to sip at my wine.

"This really is incredible wine, my friend," I said, marveling at the flavor and bouquet of the drink.

"Thank you," he said. "We save the best reserves for ourselves, and sell the rest to the townsfolk."

"So tell me," I asked, "what happened to me after Mara was killed, because I never went that far in the hypnosis sessions?"

Valik leaned back in his chair, and started his story, or should I say, my story.

"According to your journals, you had been wounded, and were unconscious for several days recovering. Meanwhile, we took Mara's body to the caverns to be interred with your father, grandfather, wizard, and the dragons. Your body healed, but not your heart, and during the next few months, you grieved pretty hard for Mara until one day you found her satchel, and decided to look through it, and from that day on, you were a changed man."

"What was in the satchel?" I asked.

"It was Mara's diary," he replied, "and within that diary were notations from her life at the library under the sphinx in ancient Egypt, fantastic notes about the wonders stored there, including books, manuscripts, and most of all, the instruction manual on how to communicate with the dead. That's when you decided you were going to the library to find out how to contact Mara again. We all tried to talk reason with you but you weren't having any of it, so, off you went on your journey, and poor Balon trailed along with you to protect you. The only problem was, Balon never returned with you, he was killed in a freak accident somewhere between here and the library."

I hung my head in shame even now thinking about it, my best friend killed following after me and my foolhardy ideas, just like now, and then I thought to myself, oh my God, just like now. Here I've followed in the footsteps of my destiny once again, wandering off on a fool's errand to chase down Mara, or Dee, or whoever, and it was my own will to do so. I could have said no, I could have let things be, but I didn't, that's how strong fate can be, so how do these people think for a moment that they can change it. Then I turned my face back to Valik, and asked

"How did Balon die?"

"According to your journals, he fell to his death from the trail of a high mountain pass. It seems that when he stepped aside to let some other travelers pass by, that he took a step backwards, and fell over the cliff."

"That's incredible," I stated, "because to this day, Scott still backs up all of the time without looking behind himself. He is always stumbling backwards over something, or someone. I am going to have to break him of doing that before he gets killed the same way in this life. Besides, there's not much glory in dying a death such as that. Now, please tell me more about my trip to Egypt, and the Library.

"You returned to the castle after a couple of years, a changed man, a determined man, but a man with new insights, insights that you had gained studying at the Library, and you put those plans into reality. One of those plans was the crystal tower that you visited today, a quite marvelous invention, both then and now. It was quite by accident that we who were left found out how to use it for communication, when one day, one of the men was standing inside and heard a voice, and saw the image on the wall speaking to him. He nearly fell off the catwalk, and the rest is history, we use it to talk to other monasteries all over the world. Unfortunately, we have never been able to figure out how to use it to speak with anyone who is dead, and you died of a heart attack before you finished it, and before you ever got to try it out."

"I did all of that huh?" I queried.

"Yes you did, Ethan," he replied, "and we knew that one day you would be back to try it out once again, to try to talk to the woman you have loved throughout eternity, and we have waited for you, century upon century, to learn what the tower is truly for, but for a totally different reason than yours. Our reasons are not for personal gain, but to create a better world, and now you are here, and we rejoice in your coming."

With that, Valik raised his glass for a toast, and when I raised mine, I said.

"I hope we can all live up to expectations, because the outcome can have devastating consequences."

After I finished my glass of wine, I bid Valik good night, and on my way back to my villa, I made a detour to check on Scott. There was a candle lit inside, so I knew he was up, and after a knock on the door, Scott answered the door looking perkier than I had seen him in a long time. As I stepped inside, I said to him.

"What happened to you, a little while ago I thought you were going to die, but now you look great. Maybe this mountain air agrees with you."

"Maybe so," he replied, "I feel so alive here, so at ease and at peace with myself. I can't explain it, but I think I belong here, and I've done a lot of thinking about this Henry, and I don't think I want to go back to the states with you when you go. There really isn't anything there for me, but I feel alive here, does that make sense to you?"

"More than you can imagine, my friend, more than you can imagine."

I patted Scott on the back, and told him I would see him tomorrow morning, for it was going to be a busy day. Then I went back to my own villa, where a small oil lamp was burning low so I could find my way around, and when I turned up the wick, the glowing light revealed treasures right out of my dreams, or in this case, right out of my hypnotic dreams.

All around me were bookcases filled with ancient books, journals, drawings, jars of spices, herbs, and teas, and another one which made my heart stand still, a jar filled with liquid, and inside the liquid was a baby dragon. 'My God,' I thought to myself, it's true, it's all true. I had to sit down before I fell down.

The rest of the night was spent reading my old journals, and looking through ancient manuscripts about potions, elixirs, manuals on how to train dragons, but most exciting of them all was the personal journals I kept from the times of my life, including the battle with the Gogs, Mara's death, and my trip to Egypt. But that's where it ended, so where is the other journal, and the book about the crystal tower. They must be together, and I'll bet they are in the secret cavern, but where is the key to the cavern. Surely if they found all of this, they must have found the key also, unless; that's it; I always hid the key in the secret compartment beneath my nightstand, not in my private library and pharmacy. They didn't bother excavating outside of that room, outside being where my old bedroom used to be, but tomorrow we'll remedy that. Tomorrow I will fulfill my destiny once more.

I was nearly too excited to sleep, but, reading always makes me tired, and somewhere during the night, I fell asleep, dreaming once again of Mara, dreaming of seeing Dee one more time, and reliving my life as Ethan, the Dragon Master.

Chapter 13

A knock on the door woke me up from a sound sleep, and when I opened my eyes, I found that I had fallen asleep in my chair while I was reading. Stiffly, I stood up and made my way to the door, and opened it to find a young monk standing there. He bowed, and said his master, Valik, requested my presence at breakfast. I told him I would wash up and be there shortly, at which time he bowed again, and then hurried away.

I left the door open to enjoy the cool mountain air while I cleaned up and changed my shirt. Then I headed off to the cafeteria for breakfast, and what I hoped would be a very exciting and productive day. As I walked across the courtyard, I looked back to see Scott sitting on his porch. I called to him to ask if he was coming to breakfast and he said he'd already been there and back again. He also informed me that I was the one who was running late. I guess I must have slept in, but then again, I was up all night reading my own journals.

Entering the dining hall, I found Valik, Damon, and Galen, as well as a couple of other monks sitting at a table drinking hot tea. When Valik saw me enter, he hailed me over to sit down, and then clapped his hands for a young monk to bring me some breakfast. I sat down next to Valik, thanked him for the tea, and apologized for sleeping in. He said it was okay, and that he had expected it since all of my journals were there to read, and then he told me to eat, which I did, eating greedily.

Breakfast consisted of waffles, home made jam made from local berries, fruit, and hot tea. Maybe it was the mountain air, or the fact that I was a long way from home, but this food was the best food I'd ever eaten in my life. I'm sure the others must have thought I hadn't eaten in a week because they seemed to stare at me while I ate, so, not to make a spectacle of myself, I pushed the plate away for the young monk to take, but I kept the cup of tea handy, and when he was sure I was satisfied, Valik spoke.

"Please forgive our impatience to get started on our quest to find the secret caverns, but we have waited so long for this day to arrive, and we can hardly contain our excitement. Did you learn anything from your journals on where to find the key to the caverns?"

"I learned a lot from my journals," I said, "but they didn't enlighten me on the location of the key."

Each man looked dejected, and I waited a few seconds to let the effect sink in before I went on.

"Like I said, I didn't learn the location of the key from my journals, but I did figure out where it was."

That got the effect I was looking for, as each man's face brightened with expectation, and then I went on.

"I always kept my key in a secret compartment under my nightstand in my bedroom, and that was outside of the area that you excavated to find the pharmacy. All we need to do is excavate the area a little farther out, and we should be able to find it, so what do you say Valik, can you lend me a few men to finish the dig today?"

Excitedly, he jumped up, patted me on the shoulder, and said he'd meet me at the site in a half an hour and he'd have the entire population of the monastery there to help. With that, he rushed out of the cafeteria, with the other monks close on his heels. I drank down the last dregs of my tea, and then I too headed out to find Scott.

Stepping outside, the whole place was a frenzy of activity, looking more like a schoolyard than a properly reserved monastery. Apparently word travels fast, because there were monks everywhere, gathering shovels and picks, buckets and baskets, and all heading over to the general area of my old villa. Stopping by Scott's villa, I told him what was going on, and asked him to join me later at the dig site. From there I headed straight to the dig site to supervise so that some overzealous young man didn't destroy the exact thing we were trying so hard to save.

By the time I got over to the new dig site, Valik was there with a large contingent of his fellow monks, and when I arrived he said they were ready to start digging at my direction. I asked him to wait quietly for a few minutes while I looked the area over, and oriented myself as to how the villa looked during my hypnosis sessions, and when I had figured it out as best I could; I picked an area for them to start digging. Unfortunately the new dig site was a large pile of debris placed here from the excavation of my old pharmacy and personal library, and would all have to be moved. It was a good thing we had plenty of help.

The monks were tireless workers, moving tons of large stones that were once a quite large and magnificent villa. The stones were dumped over the cliff face into the once named Valley of the Dragons, now simply an unnamed mountain valley. It's amazing to me just how much dust and dirt can accumulate on a site over twelve thousand years, but with nearly the whole contingent of monks hauling away stones, and buckets of dirt, we were fast approaching the area of my old bedroom where my secret compartment should be. Now was the time to go slow and easy, being very careful not to ruin any documents or artifacts we might come across.

It was about mid afternoon when one of the workers announced he had found the edges of what appeared to be a large, sunken stone box. The lid itself had broken and fell inside of the box, effectively sealing the contents beneath it. Now the monks worked slowly and meticulously removing chunks of stone, and brushing away dirt and debris with small brushes, exposing first the entire outline of the storage box, then working their way down inside of the box, and after another two hours, the first relics were being unearthed after thousands of years. Much care had to be taken now to ensure their safety.

The first item out was what was left of an old tattered rag, wrapped around a metal dart. One of the young men started to unwrap it haphazardly when I blurted out for him to be careful with it, as it was deadly poisonous, having been the dart that killed the first dragon, Gahenna. That now made the dart a sacred heirloom to this group of dragon worshipers, and it was whisked away, to be placed in a stone vault somewhere in the catacombs beneath the monastery.

The next item out of the hole was a small vial, with the stopper long rotted away, and the contents dried up. I also emphasized caution in handling this artifact, since it was the vial that contained the poison used to kill the dragon, and even a small amount of water added to the bottle would reconstitute the poison. That vial was also taken away to be revered as a sacred artifact.

Other items which made their way back into the new world were my old dagger, sword, and shield, a large amount of gold, silver, and bronze coins, which, even though they were valuable beyond belief as they were, could never be allowed into the public domain because of the ramifications of where those coins had come from. They were either going to have to be hidden away in secret vaults forever, or melted down into bars that could be used on the current world market. That was something we would decide later, and for now, they were taken to a secure area by one of the chief monks.

Then, we found the first real item of treasure that we had searched so long and hard for, one of the two keys to the secret caverns below the mountain. It was in a bad state of rust and decay, but Valik said he would have his metal workers make a more modern copy of it, and it too was taken away in a soft velvet lined box. We found only a piece of the other key, it having been outside of a protected area under the collapsed lid, but it too was taken away with reverence, to also be used as a guide to build the new key in case part of the first one was missing. I certainly hope the manual for the crystal tower hasn't met the same fate as the second key.

The rest of the hole was excavated slowly and meticulously so as not to destroy the book if it was there, but by the time we had reached the bottom, it was obvious that the book was not there, both to my disappointment as well as my relief. If indeed the book had been there, chances are that it would have been long reclaimed back to the earth. Now, we could only hope that the manual was in the secret caverns where it would be sealed away from all of the destructive influences of erosion and time.

Turning to Valik, I told him I was going back to my villa to clean up, and because of the late hour, I felt it would be better to wait until morning to venture into the caverns below, to which he agreed. We would meet again for dinner in an hour, and then meet for the evening service to discuss the proceedings of the day, and decide what our actions would be tomorrow. Scott and I went back to our villas to clean up.

As soon as I had gotten cleaned up, I read through my old journals until it was time to meet Scott for supper, so I put down the journal and headed for Scott's villa, and together we headed to the cafeteria for supper. As soon as we arrived, it was obvious that the atmosphere was much more jovial than the last time we were here, with the brothers laughing, joking, and having a good time. In fact, it was almost too noisy, and when we walked in, the noise level went up by several decibels, at least until Valik raised his hand for quiet, which had an immediate effect. The brotherhood was definitely well disciplined.

As we crossed the room, I patted a few of the young men on the back, or the shoulder, which pleased them greatly, and then we sat down with Valik and the other monks. We made small talk while we ate dinner, and then after dinner we had about a half hour until the evening gathering. The evening gathering was where we would discuss the plan for entering the caverns tomorrow, as well as how many men would accompany us on the initial foray below. No business was ever discussed in the cafeteria because here was a place to rejuvenate the soul and the stomach. The stress of everyday business was not good for the digestion.

Nothing is discussed in secret within the monastery, which was why this evenings gathering was so important. All of the brothers would know every move, every decision, and every plan. Outside of the monastery was a different story, and no one was to ever speak to any outsiders about anything that happened within the monastery. The only thing the outside world was to ever know about the monastery was that they were a religious order that made some really great wine.

After the evening meal, we had just enough time to stop by our villas to freshen up, and have a glass of wine, and then it was off to the nightly gathering. This time I arrived a little early and had time to visit with Valik and a few others before the bulk of the brothers arrived, still jovial from the events of the day, and the expectations of tomorrow. As soon as the hall was full, Valik raised his hand for quiet, and everyone took their seats, and relative quiet settled upon the congregation. Then, when all was quiet, he stood at the podium to speak.

"My brothers, it is a great day indeed that has set upon us, for we have found the key to the secret caverns, and even though the manual for the crystal tower was not with the key, we feel confident that we will find the book down below, sealed away from the ravages of time. Ethan has described to me that the caverns provide the perfect median for preserving any artifact placed within them, be it animate, or inanimate objects, so we feel confident that if the book is there, it will be in good shape."

Continuing, he went on.

"We will descend into the caverns in the morning right after breakfast, but for the first trip, since we don't know exactly what we will find, or what state the artifacts will be in, we only plan to take a small number of brothers with us."

That statement caused a slight grumbling amongst the brethren, but Valik held up his hand once again to quiet them down, and then he explained.

The first group to go into the caverns will be Ethan, Balon, I, the three head monks, and the head of each of the ten barracks. Once the caverns and their contents are deemed safe, each barrack and its leader will take turns visiting the caverns. Meanwhile, anytime there is a group down below, life will go on within the monastery as though there is nothing out of the ordinary. We do not want to be surprised by unannounced visitors, and in fact, the footbridge is to be withdrawn for repairs until each group has returned from below, is all of this understood?"

Everyone within the hall acknowledged his understanding, and each man looked excited. Then, Valik continued.

"We are on the verge of fulfilling our own destinies, and changing the outcome of the future of our world, thanks to the arrival of our brother Ethan, the Dragon Master. The whole world will someday owe him a dept of thankfulness, even though they will never know that they had been helped. Our dreams have become reality this day, and we owe it all to this man. Ethan, if you will speak once again to the brothers."

Valik held out his hand to welcome me to the podium, and I shook his hand, and took my place at the podium. I was really starting to feel the part of all this, it felt natural to me, for I knew I had been here before, in this place, and tomorrow would prove it. I was excited, yet nervous at the same time about the things I would find down below, especially my own mortality. How will I react when I see my own body preserved for centuries, or that of Mara, or my long dead ancestors? How would I feel when I saw the dragons, beings that were not supposed to exist? There were a lot of unanswered questions waiting for us below, and those questions were going to have the biggest impact on me alone, and I wasn't sure I was ready for that yet.

Standing at the podium, I spoke.

"Brothers, we are all here for the same reason, and that is to know our pasts, to know who we are, and where we came from, and within the next few days, you will become part of an elite group of men who will have that opportunity, and very few men on this earth can make that claim. The things you are going to see will be both wonderful, and disturbing, so enter the caverns with an open mind, and you will behold some of the true wonders of our great earth, things that have long been forgotten about our past, and things that this world is not yet ready to see."

"You are all going to embark on a journey that will change the future of our world. You have a great leader in Mr. Valik. I trusted him with my life all those thousands of years ago, and I trust him with the lives of everyone on the planet today, as well as you should all trust him with your lives. I cannot emphasize the importance of what you are going to attempt to do in the future.

Do not take this charge lightly, for the future of the world is soon to be in your hands. Accept that charge with all of the seriousness it deserves, and best of luck to you. Now, I want to speak to you about the trip in to the caverns tomorrow."

"The artifacts we will be seeing tomorrow are likely to be extremely fragile, so please do not touch anything without checking first with myself or Mr. Valik. We do not want anything destroyed out of carelessness or over zealousness. The air is going to be very stale and very low on oxygen until fresh air rushes in when we open the heavy stone door. From the time the fresh oxygen rushes into the caverns, decay will immediately begin to break down the artifacts, so we need to let everyone take a look at the caverns, remove only those artifacts that are absolutely necessary, and then close up the caverns once again. Then, those artifacts we do bring back need to be kept in sealed cases when they are not being examined. In fact, I would suggest that your artisans make copies of every document that we exhume from the caverns below, to ensure that the information lives on, even if the original is destroyed. That is all I have to say for now, so I'll turn this back over to Mr. Valik."

I walked back to my seat, and Valik took the podium to address the brothers.

"I want the leaders of each barracks to assign duties to your wards for tomorrow in your absence, with someone assigned as charge while you are gone. Make sure someone is assigned to withdraw the footbridge and someone on the wall to act as a mediator to any visitors who wish to enter the compound. The rest of you need to act as if nothing out of the ordinary is going on, and have patience until it is your turn to visit the caverns. As for tonight, relax, have some wine, and rejoice in the fulfillment of our dreams, now go, and enjoy yourselves."

As soon as the brothers were dismissed, the place became even noisier than it had been before, and as the men departed, they were talking and laughing again like schoolboys just getting out of class. I bid Valik good night, and told him I would see him at breakfast, then Scott and I went back to our villas, saying good night to each other, and then going off to our respective rooms, Scott to his to enjoy the peace he had found here, and I to my villa for a few glasses of wine, some deep soul searching, and to continue reading my old journals. Tomorrow would be quite a day, quite a day indeed.

I was awake early the next morning, even before the sun had come up. Anticipation mixed with uncertainty kept me from getting good nights sleep, so I paced the floor of my villa until I heard the bell toll in the tower, calling the brothers to greet a new day. I washed my face, and shaved a several day old beard, and then after waiting as long as I could stand, I headed for the cafeteria for breakfast, and the promise of an adventure of a lifetime.

Apparently Valik was as excited as I was because he looked as though he hadn't had much sleep either, so I walked up to join him at his table to join him in a cup of tea while the brothers filed in from their barracks. As I sat down across from Valik I said.

"That was about the longest night I think I've ever spent, how about you."

"You know it," was all he had to say, and then went back to sipping his tea.

The rest of breakfast was spent in silent anticipation, and when it was done, Valik called for the heads of barracks to get their charges lined out for the day, and to remain behind for the trip to the caverns. When they were finished, they all gathered around our table for a final briefing. There was an air of excitement that filled the room until it was going to be difficult to hold it back, so I made my speech short and sweet so that we could get started on our journey.

"Okay now, listen up," I began, "when we get into the caverns below, be very careful not to touch anything, as it is likely to be very fragile, if indeed anything still remains. We don't know what state of preservation everything is in, and we don't want to destroy any precious artifacts, so please be careful. If there aren't any questions, let's get going."

It was sort of a controlled stampede to get out the door, and I have to admit that I was just as excited to get going as everyone else, and I'm sure each one of us had his own reason to meet their past, mine to not only prove that my past here did indeed exist, but also to find out if I can change my future by not leaving my karma to chance, and thereby reliving mine and Mara's fate time and time again.

Valik led the way out a back door and down a well-worn pathway to a small wooden building with a very large padlock on its heavy wooden door. The building scarcely looked big enough to hold us all, but I was quite sure this was about where the stairway should be to the first three levels of caverns below the castle. My old villa used to stand above the stairway, and the stairway was only accessible from inside of my villa. Time has a way of changing things, and now, a nondescript building is all that hides the most wonderful secrets on earth. And how fitting that should be, an old wine cellar in an old monastery on top of a mountain, in the middle of nowhere, hiding the secrets of a time long forgotten. I couldn't have planned it better myself.

Valik unlocked the door, and as we entered the room, there before us was the wide stairway leading down to the caverns. Several of the monks grabbed torches from a barrel and lit them from a single oil lamp placed on the wall, a lamp which I came to find out was constantly monitored so it would never run out of oil or wick, and had already burned for many eons, and I trust would burn for many more.

As we descended the stairway, I marveled at how the stone stairway had withstood the ravages of time, looking much the same as I remembered from the hypnosis sessions. I'm sure Valik and his men had restored them to their present condition, but basically, they had held up quite well. There was some evidence of old earthquake damage within the caverns themselves, with cracked walls, and a couple of the old chambers buried completely. I do hope that the secret cavern itself has remained intact. It would be very disappointing to find it caved in after all of this time.

We descended past small caverns full of grain, corn, and other food-stuffs, and still other caverns full of barrels of lamp oil, but when we reached the second level, that was where it got interesting, because here was where they stored their wine. My mouth dropped open when I saw the enormity of the operation, as there were cavern after cavern of wine barrels stack one upon the other, thousands of them by my estimate, and more caverns which had heavy wooden doors across the front to keep the tens of thousands of bottles of wine at a steady temperature for proper aging. It was an incredible sight, and I had to speak out.

"Valik, this is a winery to compete with the finest wineries in the world, how old is some of this wine?"

"These bottles here," he responded, "are only a couple of hundred years old, but we do have a private stash that is around five hundred years old locked away for a special occasion,"

"Who was the Vintner of those old bottles?" I asked.

"Why we were," was his response. "You will find each of these bottles signed by the vintner, and a record is kept in our vault, of whom that vintner was then, as well who he is now, and that makes the study of the wine itself all the more interesting?"

When he saw the look of disbelief on my face, he continued.

"Most of us have been back here during several lifetimes. We have preconditioned ourselves to seek this place out each time we return to the earth, much like you and Mara have tried to do over the eons. But unlike you and Mara, we have sought to do much more than chase each other around the universe to fulfill a love affair We have had a purpose in mind, the purpose to which we are about to see fulfilled."

"You mean the guidebook to the crystal tower?" I asked.

"Yes my Lord," he responded, and then he continued speaking as we descended to the third level, the level of the dragon pens, and of the doorway to the secret cavern.

"The crystal tower will allow us to seek out our brothers in the afterlife when they are waiting to drop back into the earthly realm, thus guiding them to us more predictably than the hit and miss approach of letting our inner consciousness lead us here lifetime after lifetime."

"There are some amongst us who have it down pretty well, and are able to return here lifetime after lifetime, usually by the time we are old enough to leave home legally, and these are the men who stand here before you, the heads of each of the barracks. Others return only once in awhile, with one, or two, or even more lifetimes in between visits. That makes it hard to continue our work here, but now, we are on the verge of changing all of that, of changing the future itself, and it's very exciting, don't you agree."

"I do indeed, Mr. Valik, I do indeed," I said as I rushed past him, knowing exactly where I was, the hallway to the dragon pens.

I rushed ahead to the doorway to the pens, almost expecting to see the dragons inside, but, much to my despair, the pens were long empty, never again to see the likes of the creatures that once resided here. The iron gates had long since rusted away to be reclaimed by the earth herself, and I felt a sadness creep over me, chilling me to the bone. All of a sudden I realized I really didn't belong here anymore, that none of this was how I had left it. What had I expected to find here, everything had long ago died away, and the only thing left for me here was memories, and just about the time I was ready to turn around to leave, Valik put his hand on my shoulder, and said to me.

"I know what you're felling Ethan, we've all went through it the first time we came here, but remember this one thing, if you truly want to see Mara again, and someday live a full, meaningful, and happy lifetime with her, then we have to find that book and get on with our work here. It's a good and worthy goal, and if you don't give up now, I think you'll see that soon."

Then, he reached into his pocket and pulled out a key, and handed it to me saying.

"Show us the way my Lord."

I held the key in my hand, much like I had so many years ago, and my inner strength was renewed right there, so I smiled at Valik, told him thank you, and quickly led the way down to the end of the hallway where I knew the hidden door would be. A lot had changed over time, and it took all of us nearly a half an hour to claw and scratch away thousands of years of dust and debris until one of the monks said he had found what he thought was the keyhole Then, after another ten minutes of cleaning out the hole itself, I inserted the key and turned it hard to the right.

At first, nothing seemed to happen, but just as we started to think all was in vain, a slight rumble started within the wall, and then a vibration, followed by a cascade of dust and dirt, and then a large section of the wall rolled away, causing a gush of air to rush past us into the darkness beyond, almost like a giant beast taking a huge breath of air. The thought that went through my head at that time was that the mountain, my mountain, had indeed breathed back to life after twelve thousand years.

The rush of air that went past us into the cavern was so powerful that it blew out our torches, so, before we could proceed, we had to search our own pockets for a match to relight the torches. Luckily, Scott still had matches from our campfire on the trail up the mountain, and after giving him a high five we ventured forth into the dark abyss, and the secrets that lie below.

We proceeded very slowly and deliberately, not knowing what amount of damage may have occurred to the pathway over the centuries, especially as we got closer to the main cavern where the pathway hugged the wall on one side, and where there was nothing but air on the other. The pathway was still in relatively good shape, except for a couple of places where sections had crumbled away during an earthquake. Before long we were standing in the main cavern, our torches barely penetrating the thick darkness.

While the others waited, I moved to the back wall just as I had during my hypnosis session, found the chain that would open the louvers high overhead, and pulled with all of my might. There was a lot of resistance so I had Scott come to my aid, and as the centuries of erosion and decay broke loose, the more we moved the chains, the lighter it became within the cavern. It didn't take long before you could hear the gasps being emitted from the group of men standing back at the bottom of the pathway. I knew exactly what they were seeing before I ever turned around to look myself, 'Dragons'.

Scott and I turned around slowly to behold a sight that would make a normal man's heart stand still, and even though I had seen the sight recently under hypnosis, it still sent chills up and down my spine. When I turned to look back at Scott, his jaw had dropped open, and his face was white as a ghost.

"It looks like everything's just the way I left it," I said as I started to walk off, Scott staring at me incredulously as I walked away.

I walked past dragon after dragon, not even pausing, it was as though they were something one would see everyday. I had only one thing on my mind, and that was to see the throne room, and to see Mara. Nothing else mattered at this moment. It was a different story with the others though, they were completely mesmerized by the menacing diorama of the mummified dragons, each one standing upright, wings spread wide, head facing down at the lowly humans before them as if ready to send a deadly stream of fire or venom down upon the hapless soul. It was a very humbling experience to be in the presence of such a mighty beast, an experience that these men would not soon forget.

I approached the throne room with a slight amount of trepidation, not being sure if I was strong enough to handle seeing not only Mara, but of seeing myself, or what used to be myself so many eons ago. So, taking a deep breath, I turned the corner, and entered the throne room, and even after all these years, the sight was still breathtaking. There before me was a line of ornate wooden thrones, four men, and one woman. The throne on the far left was obviously the old wizard, the next one was Ethan's grandfather, then his father, then I, or should I say Ethan, and then Mara. My heart was beating so hard, I thought it would leap out of my chest, but I forced myself to move forward to look more closely.

I forced myself to go first to the old wizard, and to lean close to see every aspect of his being. He was remarkably preserved in this environment, as were all of the denizens of this place. It was as though the cavern had been hermetically sealed for all of these eons, preserving everything within it. Unfortunately, now that it had been opened again, everything would start to decay fairly rapidly, so we would have to make our trips short, taking with us all of the artifacts we could, to be copied and preserved by the monks above. The rest of the monks would have to make their trips through here over the next couple of hours so the cavern could be resealed to preserve the remains.

Even in death and mummification, the old wizard was a noble and powerful presence, and even with his eyes long closed, you felt as though he was still looking right through into your soul, reading your thoughts like they were written on the pages of an open book, and who knows, maybe he was. There is a lot we don't know about the spiritual world, but hopefully, with the manual for the crystal tower, we may indeed unlock those mysteries.

Next in line was my grandfather, and even though he looked very old, he still held a majesty that demanded reverence. He was the man who founded this place, carving a home out of a world that up until that time was only suitable for the dragons that lived here before he arrived. If it wasn't for his foresight, and his understanding of the natural world, none of this could have been possible.

Next, I faced my father, Ethan's father. He was a large and powerful man, powerful as in strength, not like the wizard, who was powerful in a magical sense. My father was powerful in a warrior sense, a man not to be taken lightly when it came to battle, or in dealing with man or beast. All three men held sepulchers in their hands, the wizard's hands long and slender, and my father's, large and powerful. The sepulchers were made of an unknown wood, tall, twisted, polished, and each with a crystal dragon's head mounted atop the shaft. Here again, even in death, and with sightless eyes, my father seemed to be looking straight through into my very soul, and his presence gave me goose flesh just being close to him, so, it was time to move on.

As I moved over to stand in front of my own body, I felt a slight dizziness and nausea, almost to the point of fainting, but, I was able to shake it off, telling myself that this body before me was only the clay vessel that once held my soul, the essence that is now within this body I have now, and when I was finally able to put it into that perspective, I was able to look at this whole experience more scientifically, and then I was able to continue.

Looking at my past self, I noted some very interesting facts that I had not realized could be a factor, the first being that I used to have a full head of long, wavy, dark hair. My, I used to be a handsome devil, a bit unkempt, but handsome. And I appeared to be a lot taller than I am now, so what happened? The answer was quite obvious.

Each sojourn back to the earthly realm is totally dependent on what family you are reborn to, and what those family traits have to offer you. There are a lot of souls trying to get back to earth at any given time, and it is more or less a crap shoot as to where or to whom you are going to be born, and in my current life, I happen to be only of average height and weight, and given to premature balding. Now don't get me wrong, I love my parents, but next time, I want to be born tall, dark, handsome, with a full head of hair, and while I'm at it, I just as well be born into a rich family. And if this manual to the crystal tower works out, these possibilities may not be all that farfetched.

As I looked more closely at the man who was Ethan, I noticed that he too held a sepulcher like the one held by my father, grandfather, and the wizard, and as I looked down, that is when I noticed that Ethan held a book in his other hand, and from what writing I could see, I could make out parts of the words,

"Crystal Tower." We had found the book we were looking for, and as I turned to call for Valik, I stopped in mid sentence, realizing that Valik, Scott, and all of the others were standing behind me at the entrance to the throne room, staring at me, and at the royalty seated before them, each man quiet as a mouse, at least until I told them the book was here. Then they became a bit more excited, still trying to be quiet like they thought they were going to rouse the beasts within the cavern, or perhaps disturb the men before them.

I summoned Valik forward, and together we worked the book loose from Ethan's fingers, fingers still pliable after all of this time. In place of the book, I quickly wrote a short note on a piece of paper from my own journal, which simply said, "I have returned," and put today's date on it, rolled it up, and placed it in Ethan's hand. I then handed the book to Valik, who in turn handed it to another monk carrying a small wooden box lined with velvet. Valik sent him back to the surface with the precious artifact to be copied, restored, and preserved. Now, it was time to meet Mara, and my heart was threatening to collapse within my chest.

Mara was stunning, even in death, long, with thick, flowing blonde hair, hanging down in the back, and a lock of hair from each side drawn back from the front to be tied at the back. Her face was flawless, even now; even in death she was beautiful. Her arms were long and slender, her hands delicate works of art, her fingers the tools of the Gods themselves. Her counterpart in this life was Dee, and though Dee was also slightly shorter, she was still slender, delicate, and very beautiful in a natural way, unadorned by makeup. Some things change, while other things remain the same. Seeing Mara made me realize how bad I miss her, and how I miss Dee. With renewed enthusiasm I vowed that I must get that crystal tower up and running so I could speak to her once again.

I leaned forward and kissed Mara on the forehead, and then turned to face the others.

"I have made my peace," I said. "Let's quickly look at the remainder of the cavern so the rest of the brothers can see it too. Then we need to seal the cavern again before all of this starts to decay."

As I walked past the men several of them reached out and touched me on the shoulder, showing their support for my grief, and before a tear could expose my humanity, I hurried on to the next place I wanted to see, the library. The men hurried their pace to keep up, and even though it was just a short distance, my emotions were in check by the time we entered the library. As I entered the library, the sight before me stopped me in my tracks.

Before me was a metallic box, about four feet in diameter and five feet tall. I thought to myself, 'I don't remember that thing." I approached the box, examining it from all sides until I noticed a small handle on a barely perceptible door. Reaching forward, I turned the handle and opened the door, and when I did, the inside was glowing as if by magic, for it was made of hundreds of perfect crystals, just like the ones in the crystal tower, and I knew in my heart that this was a major part of the puzzle that we sought.

Inside the cubicle was a seat, also made of crystal, configured in such a way so that when you sat on it, you were semi reclined for comfort. On top of the cubicle was a large metal ring, and I suspected it was made to hang the cubicle somewhere we would have yet to learn. On the sides of the cubicle were metal rings at each corner, and about halfway up the side, the presence of two long metal poles confirmed that this was how the cubicle was transported, much like the ancient pharaohs were carried around by slaves. I turned to speak to Valik who was standing there mesmerized like the rest of the men, and said.

"This is part of the crystal tower, and probably the piece that makes the whole thing work, so we need to get it to the surface as soon as possible."

Valik quickly snapped out of his trance, and instructed four of the men with us to start carrying the cubicle to the surface, and another monk to hurry ahead to get more men to come down to help them. The men slid the long poles through the rings on the side, and with a man on each end, they lifted the cubicle into the air and started their journey back up the long pathway to the surface with their prize. Then we turned our attention to the rest of the priceless items within the library.

There were dozens of books strewn across the table, as if they had been looked at and then haphazardly stacked or laid on the table, probably to be looked at later on. The only problem was, I never returned to look through those books, because I died before I was finished with them, and before I could finish my work on the crystal tower. It has taken a long time, but now I was back, and I plan to finish what I had started.

The books were covered with a fine covering of dust, and I'm sure they were extremely fragile. Care would have to be taken in transporting them to the surface, so once again, Valik instructed one of the head monks to go to the surface, get all the monks in his charge, and return here with protective boxes for the books. Then, each book would be taken to the surface to be restored, copied, and sealed away for eternity in sealed cases, away from everyone except the monks within this faith, a faith which apparently includes a few other monasteries around the world.

These books represented knowledge that for its time, would have been considered magic, and even though some of the works are now common knowledge, the volumes dealing with what was at that time ancient history, would now be called heresy, mainly because the modern world does not acknowledge that intelligent life, human life, nor dragons, existed during this early time period. Other books chronicle practices that still haven't been perfected in this day and age, like levitation, and other psychic abilities, which had flourished in the days of Atlantis, only to be lost for twelve thousand years, and which only now are being explored with any seriousness.

The next stop would be the armory, mostly out of curiosity, since there was no need for weaponry in this place, at this time in history. My need to see the chariot and the crystal lasers was fueled more out of the need to confirm the things I had witnessed during my hypnosis sessions, even though there could be no doubt in my mind, given the things I had already seen. But you know the hearts of man, unbelieving even when it's in front of your face.

Entering the armory, the first thing to be seen was the chariot, since it was the biggest and most dominating presence within the small room. It must have been quite a menacing sight to the enemy as it moved about the battlefield, lasers flashing death and destruction to anyone within sight. Now, it looks rather archaic, but I'd be willing to bet that to the unsuspecting, it would still be quite a surprise. The only problem is that a lone soldier in this day and age, armed with a shoulder fired rocket launcher could destroy the chariot within the first few minutes of battle.

The only thing this craft would do if it was made public now would be to mess up the entire worlds point of view about the ancient past, and since we don't want the world to know about the secrets here, the chariot will have to remain here for another twelve thousand years. Now the lasers are a different story, they could still have very strategic value, since their design is strictly Atlantean in nature, and we really don't want the world to be aware that this technology came about from that culture. It's best that the world believes that they designed the laser in the 1950's.

The lasers were still mounted on the chariot, having been there since the battle with the Gog army, but now, one of the Dragon's Breath lasers was tipped forward, the front lens having fallen off, and several of the light concentrating crystals had spilled out on the ground. The crystals were covered in eons of dust, and out of curiosity, I picked up one of the gems, wiped it off, and held it up to the light to examine it while Valik and his men examined the other items within the armory. The crystal was about three inches in diameter, and about the same in length, configured in such a way that the crystal behind nestled perfectly into the crystal ahead of it. It was while I was examining the crystal more closely that I came to the awesome realization that these were more than just crystals, they were diamonds, perfectly formed, matching diamonds. I felt the color draining from my face as I realized how much these diamonds would be worth on the world market and what some men would do to possess these diamonds.

Quickly looking around me to the men milling about, I slid the crystal back into the tube of the laser, followed rapidly by the others lying on the floor of the cavern. I slid the last one into place, and was replacing the outer lens just as Valik walked up to me to see what I was doing.

"You don't really plan on using that weapon ever again do you Ethan?" Valik asked as I tipped the end of the Dragon's breath weapon upright once again.

Recovering quickly, and with a slightly shaky voice, I replied.

"I see no reason to remove the lasers from the chariot, since the chariot is not leaving the cavern, and neither are the lasers. Besides, the lasers will make great visual tools for future history lessons for the brothers during their group sessions. Future meetings are going to become very interesting at the monastery, don't you think?"

"I certainly do, Ethan, I certainly do," Valik responded with a large grin on his face.

Turning once again to address the brothers, I decided to myself not to tell anyone about the diamonds. That kind of wealth could corrupt even the most devoted of men.

After explaining the basic workings of the chariot, and the lasers, we moved ahead to the Horn of Gideon, the sonic weapon. Unfortunately, time had not been so kind to this weapon, as the animal hide covering the drum head had long since rotted away, and the wood of the horn itself had become brittle to the touch, almost crumbling at first touch. Valik stated that his artisans could probably duplicate it from diagrams they would make here at the site, and only for historical restoration, not for anything strategic. It may prove to be kind of useful, and fun to use it to move around some big boulders with the sound vibrations.

The belief here at the monastery is that anything to do with the time period of the dragons, and anything to do with Atlantis, needed to be preserved for all time, and to be cherished as a priceless artifact that could never be replaced. This particular weapon was developed in Atlantis primarily as a way to move heavy objects around by sound vibration, and then out of need, it was later developed into a lethal weapon. This is also a weapon that the world would be very interested in right now, but here again, because of its origin, the world must never know of its existence. So, here it must remain for all time. If the world is to develop a weapon such as this, it will now have to do so on it's own.

After looking over a few more items in the armory, it was time to go, but I wanted to see the dragons one more time, to look upon the creatures that so influenced my very existence, the creatures that spawned a near religious following of these monasteries around the world, and the creatures whose past existence is going to influence the future of the world as we know it, through these monks, and the crystal tower. And speaking of the crystal tower, all of a sudden I was very excited to get back to the surface to resume work on the tower, and the cubicle. It was time to go.

Passing by the dragons on the way out, I marveled at their majesty, their power, and I was even more amazed that they were a beast that tolerated mankind, even to the point of comradery, maybe even friendship. Add to that the fact that they could communicate with me on a subconscious level, and it made you realize that they were the more intelligent being, not us. The dragon's only drawback was that they were not able to adapt, probably because of their size, otherwise, the world today should be inhabited by dragons, not by humans.

As we hurried up the pathway to the surface, other groups of monks were hurrying down the pathway to retrieve books and artifacts before the inrush of fresh air could start decomposing the delicate artifacts. Time was against us, we needed to get everything we needed out of the cavern within twenty four hours, so we could reseal the cavern, and who better to do it than a bunch of dedicated and ambitious monks. I knew that the future of the artifacts were in good hands.

Back at the surface, we paused only long enough to get a drink of water and a bite to eat, and then we hurried to the building where the artisans were restoring the manual to the crystal tower. I wanted to be there as each bit of information became available. I watched as each page was gently turned and separated, and then treated with a light oil and paraffin mixture to make the page pliable, yet not allow them to stick together. As each page was turned, I made a mental note of the drawings and writing on each page. By the time the small manual had been completed, I already had a good working idea on how the crystal tower, as well as the cubicle, would function, and I couldn't wait to get started. The only hold up now was a manpower problem. All of the monks were in the process of rotating through the cavern, bringing out artifacts, or some other assigned task. We were going to need a small army to get the cubicle into the tower, and then to get it suspended from the ceiling into the very center of the tower. As excited as I was, it looked as though I was going to have to wait until tomorrow to see the tower up and working, so, it was time to go to my villa for a glass of wine.

I bid farewell to Valik for the time being, told him I would see him later for dinner, and then I headed back to my place to do some drinking, and thinking. I felt a little anxious at the prospects of hearing Dee's voice again, what would I say, how would she look, would she know me, and would this contraption work at all? There were a lot of questions that I just didn't have the answers to, and wouldn't until I could get inside of that cubicle.

As I approached my villa, I saw that Scott had already made it home, and was sitting outside on his porch, drinking a cup of tea. I hailed him, and told him I'd be over to visit after I got a glass of wine. I quickly grabbed a partial bottle of wine, a glass, and hurried over to Scott's villa, finding him still sitting on the porch, and he seemed to be in a little bit of a daze. I asked him if he was all right, and he said he was, it was just that all of the sights he'd seen today had him in a state of overload. He just couldn't imagine how all of this could be true, and how he himself had been a part of it. It was just too much for him to comprehend, so here he was, sitting, thinking, and trying to sort it all out.

We talked about everything for nearly two hours, watching the groups of monks coming and going into the caverns below, some emerging with the same distant look that Scott had, while others were so excited that they just babbled constantly among themselves, gesturing with there hands about the things they had seen. It was very interesting to watch, and I noticed a great number of small boxes being carried to the artisans place, undoubtedly books from the cavern. I felt sure that the books were in good hands, and there was only the one book I was interested in, and that was the manual for the crystal tower. I really didn't need it anymore, having noted the pages as they were being preserved, but just in case there was something that had been missed, it was good to have the book on hand as a reference.

Scott and I sat on the porch until we noticed several of the monks heading for the cafeteria, and when we checked our watches, we were surprised to see that it was time for the evening meal. So, we got up, stretched, and headed for the cafeteria. As soon as we approached the door to the cafeteria, you could hear that the place was very festive tonight, and when we opened the door, the volume of the people talking was almost deafening. When the brethren saw Scott and I enter the building, the noise level went up several fold, until Valik pounded his cup on the table, and even then it took several long minutes for the din to die down. As the noise died down, Scott and I found our way to our seats.

The food was served, and even though the noise level again rose dramatically, it was to be expected, and Valik let the men have their say for now. They were excited, and you couldn't deny them that. Many of these men had been here many years; some most of their life, and all of them had waited patiently for this day to arrive. It's not everyday you get to see prophesy fulfilled, so it's not something you can stifle by simply pounding your cup on the table. Besides, we're not here to stifle anything. We're all here to learn, to learn something about ourselves, and the world around us, the world we can see, and the world we cannot see.

As soon as the meal was done, the brethren were dismissed for wine and rest until the evening gathering, so Scott, Valik, and myself went back to my villa for some more wine, and to discuss the day's events, as well as the topics for tonight's message. We were deep in discussion when we noticed it was time to go to the meeting. Scott said he was going to remain behind, so Valik and I headed to the meeting. Along the way, Valik asked me if Balon was doing okay, and I told him that Scott was just a little overwhelmed by it all, and that he would be fine. He was just doing some deep soul searching of his own. Valik said he understood how Balon felt, because even though he knew what to expect, the reality of seeing it all with his own eyes was a little disconcerting to everyone, some just a little more than others.

Entering the meeting hall was as noisy as the dining hall had been, but the head monks quickly brought their charges to order, obviously having spoken to them during the break. Valik and I made our way to the front, and I sat down while Valik addressed the congregation. He spoke about all of the sights and wonders they had seen today, about the fulfillment of their dreams, and what the future was going to hold for them, including the brothers spreading out around the world to influence world events. He reiterated the need for secrecy, especially about the artifacts they had retrieved, and how they would all be taught everything that was within those books. Finally, he spoke about the cubicle, and what its importance held. It was at this time he turned the meeting over to me, so I took the podium to speak.

I told the congregation what I had observed about the cubicle, and then I told them what I had gleaned from the manual as I watched it being preserved. Then I told them how the cubicle interacted with the crystal tower, concentrating the signals received by the tower, and focusing it directly into the cubicle. Next, I laid out the plan for hanging the cubicle first thing after breakfast in the morning, and the problems we might face accomplishing that task, and how we might overcome those obstacles. Then, I also touched on the importance of secrecy, and about the importance of everyone within this faith, old or young, great, or small, and how what they learned in the next months and years would influence the way the world moved for ever more, and to not take that charge lightly.

During the time Valik and I spoke, no one made a sound, as each man listened intently to our every word, and when we had finished speaking, each man remained seated for several minutes, reflecting on what had been said, what had been seen, and what the future might hold for each of them personally. And after a minute or so, men began to stand up, to speak to one another, and before long, the din returned to it's previous noise level as the men were filing out of the building, discussing with one another what they had learned, and what they felt, and when they had left, only Valik, myself, and the head monks remained.

When all of the men had left, I asked Valik if he felt we should place a guard on the cubicle until morning, but he gave me a look of mild disappointment, and told me that if he couldn't trust every man within this monastery, then we just as well throw everything over the cliff face, because all that they believed in, and everything that they had strived for would be lost. I told him I was sorry for doubting the integrity of the brethren, and bid him good night, feeling very sheepish as I walked home to my villa.

This was going to be a long night, with thinking about how I had made an ass out of myself just now, to thinking about finishing the tower, and then the possibility of talking to Dee once more. I figured that if I was going to get any sleep tonight at all, I was going to have to get drunk and pass out. Right now, that sounded like a good idea, and that's exactly what I did, just like the old days.

I woke up to someone knocking at my door, and when I finally got the cobwebs out of my head, and figured out where I was, I called for them to come in. When the door opened, the bright light hit me in the eyes, and only then did I realize I had one hell of a headache, aka, hangover. Looking through my hazy eyes, I noticed a young monk standing there, and asked him what he needed. He told me that I was late for breakfast, and that everyone was waiting for me so we could get started on the crystal tower. I told him I was going to pass on breakfast, and that I would get cleaned up and meet them at the tower.

As he started to leave, he turned quickly, and, saying he had almost forgot, he handed me a book, and then left in a hurry. I held the book up to look at it and was amazed to see that it was the restored copy of the crystal tower manual. It was beautifully done, given the fact it had been done so quickly. The artisan who restored the book must have been up all night. It would appear that everyone here is as excited about getting started as I am, so I better get a move on.

I quickly splashed some water on my face, and headed for the crystal tower. The sun was up, and it was going to be a beautiful day, even though the sun hurt my eyes, and my head was still aching. I'm not sure having all of this wine around is all that good an idea, because if I spent too much time here, I wouldn't be able to get anything done but drink. I hope these monks are more disciplined than I am.

Pulling my cap down to shade my eyes, I made my way toward the crystal tower, and even before I got there I could see a flurry of activity, so I knew that the men were working on installing the cubicle in the tower. I'm glad I missed the part of trying to work the cubicle through the door, but it looks like I'm just in time to help with hanging the cubicle from the ceiling hook

I thought to myself that it would be impossible to get a chain all of the way up to that hook, not to mention winch the cubicle up into position while standing on the narrow walkway, but as I climbed the steps and looked through the door, I could see that the chain was already suspended, and that they were preparing to attach it to the cubicle. Only then did I notice the small open hatch in the ceiling, apparently designed for just such an occasion. It looks like Ethan had thought of everything back then, unlike the man who occupies his soul today, namely me'.

There were a half a dozen men standing on the platform already, so I stayed by the door to watch, and when Valik spotted me, he told me good morning, and was glad I could join them. I apologized for my lack of discipline, to which he told me not to worry, because I was new to the scene, and without dwelling on it any longer, he explained what they were doing.

They had known about the hatch from climbing over every inch of the tower over the many years, but they hadn't known its purpose until finding the cubicle. One man had climbed to the top of the tower, opened the hatch, attached the heavy chain, and then lowered the chain to the men on the platform. The manual had told them exactly how long the chain should be, which was about five feet short of the platform, just enough for the cubicle to be lifted up, hooked to the chain, and the result making the cubicle hang approximately one foot above the platform, making easy access to step into the cubicle from the platform. It was simple in design, but the results would prove to be ingenious.

As I watched the men finish hanging the cubicle, I suddenly became aware of the multitude of images staring out from the walls of the tower. It would seem that we had an audience from every monastery in the world, and you could see many of them taking notes, and talking quietly amongst themselves. I'm betting that before long, the rest of the monasteries would be equipped with a cubicle of their own if they can find enough of the proper crystals in the world today. I don't even remember where I secured all of the ones I got, but I'm sure I wrote it down in a journal somewhere, I'll just have to look for it later, although I'm sure Valik's protégés have already done so.

I watched as the men finished securing the cubicle to the chain above, and then four small diameter chains secured the cubicle at right angles to the walls of the tower. When it was done, the cubicle would be quite stable as you climbed inside, and sat in the reclining seat. Once inside with the door closed, you should almost experience a feeling of floating in mid air, probably not a pleasant feeling for someone who experiences motion sickness.

Apparently the diagrams in the manual called for only a small walkway out to the cubicle, one small enough so as not to block the signals picked up by the crystals in the walls of the tower, which then concentrate their entire signal onto, and within, the small cubicle at the center of the tower. So, before we could use the cubicle, the platform to it would have to be partially dismantled, downsized, and secured. That won't take this bunch of people very long at all, and we should be able to try it out right after lunch. Until then, I'm going to go make some strong tea, and maybe take a nap, so, I left instructions for Valik to send someone for me when the tower was ready, and off I went to my Villa.

Apparently I had indeed taken a nap, because around 3 o'clock in the afternoon there was a knock on the door that woke me up, and after a moment of confusion as to who or where I was, I called for the visitor to come in. A young monk stepped inside just long enough to announce that the tower was ready for my inspection. I felt my heart skip a beat in anticipation as I got up from the bed, and I told him I was on my way. Then, I followed him out the door and over to the tower. It would seem that everyone who resided at this monastery was present outside of the building, standing and waiting, as if it were the second coming about to take place, and I guess in a way, that's what this represented.

As I approached the tower, the monks opened their ranks to let me through, staring at me like I was a convicted man ascending the gallows. I guess the way my heart was pounding from the uncertainty of what was about to happen, I did sort of feel like I was climbing the stairway to the gallows. A lot of thoughts were going through my head as I topped the stairs to meet Valik, who was waiting for me there. Together, he and I, and two of the head monks entered the building, closed the door behind us, and it was an eerie feeling indeed.

Now, I realize that there probably wasn't anything to worry about, but you always have thoughts going through your head about what could go wrong, and that's what I was doing to myself as I approached the cubicle. Would this thing even work, and if it did work, would my mind be able to handle what I may soon see? Are we delving into an area that should not be delved into, and would those in the spirit world respond kindly to our interruption? There were so many questions that I should have thought about before I jumped into this venture, but it was too late for that now. It was now time to act; it was time to enter the cubicle.

I hesitated at the door of the cubicle before going inside, a fleeting moment of panic washing over me, and as I looked at Valik, he smiled, and pointed to the walls of the tower. When I looked around, the walls were full of images of men watching from all of the other towers scattered around the globe. It appears that I was going to be the main attraction for today's show, so, pushing back the anxiety that I was feeling, I waved to all of those watching, and stepped into the cubicle. Valik wished me good luck, and said he would remain right outside of the door in case I needed him. Then he closed the door, leaving me alone inside of the glowing, humming cubicle.

At first, the feeling I experienced was one of panic, then dizziness, followed by a short bout of nausea, and then I finally settled in to a less claustrophobic feeling as I started to get used to being inside the confined quarters. It was a bit disconcerting being inside the cubicle in the aspect that you had no real point of focus on which to look at. All of the crystals soon melded into one another until the walls of the cubicle seemed to become invisible, and I had the feeling that I was floating in mid air. In fact, the only thing that looked remotely familiar was my own legs stretched out before me, but even then it seemed like my body was floating in space.

I forced myself to lean back on the reclined seat, and relax, letting my mind wander a little, and then as I watched, the walls once again seemed to go invisible. It was then that I became aware that I was looking out at another world, a very bright world, and one that looked very clean and orderly, almost to the point of being sterile. This world didn't seem to have any boundaries, no sky, and no horizon.

The more I became aware of this other place; I began to see people, lots of people. At least I think they were people. I mean, I'm sure that they were people, but they lacked a definite form like we do here on Earth. I sort of recognized that they had faces, but the rest of their person appears to be like a mist, but with more substance.

I guess it all makes sense when you think about it. The human body is strictly a temporary housing for your eternal soul, having been adapted to survive in the earthly realm, just as the possibility that life elsewhere has adapted a body to survive whatever conditions they dwell in. But here, in this place, there is no need for a physical body, as the vessel in which you lived was discarded at death. So here, in this realm, only the essence that is the soul resides, unencumbered by physical restraints. By leaving the body behind, you also leave behind all of the disease, all of the injuries, and all of the things that wear down your body and your mind, for here, there is true peace, peace of mind, and peace for the soul.

As I continued to watch, I noticed that the souls in this place seemed to float, rather than walk, which also makes sense, if you don't have a body, you probably don't have legs or feet. As I continued to watch, I noticed that some of the souls were just milling about, while many others were sitting in groups listening to tall, majestic looking individuals, dressed in white flowing gowns. I could only guess, but they were probably learning about all of the secrets of the universe, secrets that we could only guess at while we lived on Earth. What else were you going to do during the years that you waited to return to the Earthly realm? This place is a place of rest, of healing, and a place of learning.

I also noticed that there were several different types of beings that resided here, some were much larger than the others, powerful in a sense, but not in a menacing way, and they had less of a human air about them. They were not like the ones who seem to be teachers, but more like a totally different species than humans, and they moved around seemingly oblivious to everyone else around them, like they had specific duties to perform, and were totally dedicated to that mission.

Another being that I noticed was much smaller, and was flitting around what reminded me of a huge fishing net that moved across the sky in an unending line. The fish net structure didn't really have a tangible form to it, as it was sort of opaque, and seemed to be three-dimensional. The beings themselves reminded me of large hummingbirds, or maybe large bees, as they flew to various spots on the net, and then zipped away as quick as a wink to who knows where, only to return moments later to repeat the process. It appeared that every being here, except for the human souls, had a purpose, and were carrying out that purpose tirelessly.

As I floated about, I soon became aware of a presence floating along beside of me, and it gave me quite a start. It was one of the creatures that appeared to be a teacher, and he was tall, maybe ten feet tall, with a kind face, but without substantial form to his body. As soon as I had regained my composure, the creature communicated with me, saying.

"Lucienne do not be afraid, I am Feldore, and I will be your guide. What is it that you seek?"

"Forgive my intrusion," I started, "my name is Henry, and I seek council with the soul known as Dee Ballinger, the soul who was also known as Mara."

Within a heartbeat, one of the small hummingbird type creatures flew up to my guide, and then whisked away, only to return within the next heartbeat. Then Feldore spoke to me again.

"According to the seeker, Tanamara has only just arrived, and she is still quite unstable. I would advise against disturbing her so soon after her departure from the Earthly plane, Lucienne."

"Why do you call me Lucienne?" I asked.

"Lucienne is your given name," he responded. "It is the name given to you before your first sojourn to the place called Earth."

"And Tanamara," I asked, "is that the entity I know as Dee, or Mara?"

"It is the same," he replied.

I looked away for an instant, thinking about what he had said, but I knew I must speak to her, so I said to him.

"I understand the possible consequences of speaking to Tanamara so soon Feldore, but the consequences of not speaking to her would be worse, and more far reaching. You see, for all eternity, Tanamara and I have chased each other from one lifetime to another, only to meet with disaster each time, and as she died this time, we again made a pact to meet up on the earthly plane to take up where we had left off, and we plan to meet again in only thirty years. Unless I tell her not to meet me again so soon, then I have doomed her to another violent death, and I can't bear to have that happen again, so, please, I must speak to her."

The guide was silent for a moment until once again, a seeker zipped up to him, whisked away, and returned a moment later. In the instant that the seeker was near, I noticed that the creature was about three feet tall, with a pudgy face that seemed almost comical, and a body that reminded me of a large bee, but still without a definable form. As soon as the seeker had gone, the guide spoke to me once again, saying.

"The great ones have agreed to let you speak to Tanamara, but only briefly. You must make your conversation short, and to the point. They are afraid that her consciousness may become irreversibly damaged if she is not given adequate time to heal, so, if you agree to be brief, you may speak with her."

"Of course," I replied, "I agree."

I never even knew we had moved, but within an instant we were beside a young female, who was sitting by herself, staring ahead, almost in a trance-like state. Her whole essence seemed to glow, and she looked so pure and ethereal that I found myself staring at her without speaking. She was so beautiful and innocent that I was almost afraid to speak to her, until finally the guide broke my spell by saying to her.

"Tanamara, there is someone here to speak to you."

Tanamara turned to face me, lifting her eyes to meet mine, and I was mesmerized by eyes that seemed to look past me, or perhaps through me. It was like I was looking into a pool of deep, dark water, and the view was haunting. Tanamara looked so different here in this place, partly because the form before me was simply her spirit, and not her earthly body. Still, I was able to recognize her in my heart, so, I regained my composure, and then I spoke.

"Tanamara, forgive me for disturbing your rest, but I need to give you a message."

"A message from who?" she asked, seemingly not to recognize me.

"A message from Henry Olsen, also known as Ethan, also known as Lucienne."

Tanamara blinked her huge dark eyes, and I wasn't sure if she recognized the names or not, so I continued anyhow.

"These entities are all one and the same individual, and they want me to tell you to stay in this place and rest, rest for at least a hundred years, rest until Lucienne is once again able to join you here, and even then, you and he are to rest here together until your spirits are healthy. And whatever you do, do not return to the earthly plane at the time you had predetermined with the entity known as Henry. Do you understand what I have told you?"

"I understand," she said, almost without emotion, which, even though I understood, it still made my heart ache.

"It is time to go," Feldore said.

"Yes, thank you for letting me see her," I said as we started to move away.

As we drifted away from her, I looked back to see her turn my way, and as she did, I saw a tear roll down her cheek. 'She did recognize me,' I thought to myself and my own heart rejoiced, even at the same time that it was breaking.

"I'm ready to go home," I said to the guide, who promptly disappeared.

I closed my eyes for just a brief moment, and when I opened them again, I noticed my feet and legs stretched out in front of me, and this time when I looked ahead, I saw only crystals, not the window to the afterlife. Reaching out to my side, I pushed open the door of the cubicle, and tried to get out, only to find that I was too weak to stand on my own. I kind of fell out the door, and held onto the platform railing until I could get my bearings and regain my strength.

As I emerged from the cubicle and regained my feet, the first thing I noticed was Valik and his two partners kneeling down on one knee with their heads bowed, and when they looked up to see me standing in front of them, their mouths fell open and they just stared at me. The way they reacted kind of gave me the chills, so I asked what the matter was, and as Valik stood up, he spoke.

"Ethan, your hair has turned white, and your face is glowing. Are you okay, are you alive?"

"Now that's a silly question," I said, checking myself out, "of course I'm alive, at least I think I'm alive."

"We saw the whole thing Ethan," Valik continued. "It was all displayed on the walls of the tower, and it was incredible."

Now that was something I hadn't expected, that the whole experience could be viewed on the walls of the tower as well as inside of the cubicle. This whole tower has become a sort of cosmic projector, and the more I thought about the power that this tower represented, the more concerned I became about it falling into the wrong hands. I would have to address these concerns with Valik and the heads of the other monasteries.

Meanwhile, I turned my attention back to Valik, and to the other men whose images were once again on the walls of the tower, listening in, and as I became aware that they were still present, I also became aware that they too were quite excited. They were all talking so noisily amongst themselves, that the tower was becoming a very loud, echoing place to be, so I decided to take control and bring about some sort of order. I held up my hand, and let out a shrill whistle, which had an immediate, desired effect, and quiet replaced the din.

"Gentlemen, please come to order here," I started. "What we have seen here today is truly a miracle, and one that we cannot take lightly, because with the power of this new knowledge comes a responsibility that can truly affect the entire world. I hope you have the right people in place that can handle this responsibility. You need to truly look deep within your own souls to decide if you and the world are ready for this kind of power, because if this falls into the wrong hands, or if the world learns of the existence of these towers, the consequences can be devastating, do you all agree?"

The general murmur throughout the tower signified agreement, so I went on.

"The general impression I got from my experience was that you will always be accompanied by a guide when you enter the cosmic plane, and that you can access virtually any type of information you desire, past or present, through the help of the seekers. The seekers seem to access information through that giant net, or spider web structure that dominates the sky in that place. It seems to hold all of the knowledge of the universe within its webs, with each strand directly linked to the rest. In fact, this gives a whole new meaning to the phrase, surfing the web."

That last statement didn't quite have the desired effect that I wanted, since most of these guys have never experienced web sites, or computers for that matter, so, letting my unappreciated humor slide, I continued.

"There does seem to be a safeguard to that other place, and that is the ones they referred to as the 'Great Ones.' It would appear that they have final say as to whether or not you get access to certain information, or people, as in my case. And it would also seem that unless your motives are pure, you might also be denied access to certain information. So I encourage each monastery to pick one or two exceptional individuals to be their representatives to the other world, and to safeguard access to the towers, lest any thrill seekers go on an unauthorized journey. I do not wish to sound negative about any of your protégés, but human nature is what it is, and no one is above temptation."

I let this all sink in for a moment, and watched the reaction of those observing. It seemed to be a positive reaction, so I continued.

"There is one more thing I need to address, and even though I know you will not like what I'm going to say, but it's something that has to be addressed, for the safety of the world itself. In case there is a breach of security within your monastery, whether it be from the inside, or from the outside, you need to have a system in place to destroy your tower, for it must not fall into unscrupulous hands."

Now that statement got an immediate reaction, with individuals becoming quite vocal about the issue, so I let them vent for a minute or so before I continued, then I spoke up once again.

"I know this would be a tragic thing to have to destroy a tower, but when you go back to your evening meeting, I want you to discuss the ramifications of what would happen if someone was to access the other world for their own desires and agenda. What if the government heard about the towers, and the power that they represented? They would spare no resources, scientifically, or militarily to secure those towers for their own benefit. And what if those governments were an oppressive government, or a terrorist group? The point is that you can't be too careful in this day and age."

"What can we do?" asked one man from the tower walls.

"I suggest that those heads of the various monasteries secretly rig your towers with explosives, controlled from a secret location within your own compounds, a place that could be double locked, with two men each holding a key to the secret place. Then, if the worse case scenario became reality, and then only with the two men in complete agreement, the tower would be destroyed."

Again I looked around the tower to study the reaction of those standing around, and this time the discussion appeared to be positive. They seemed to accept the double jeopardy theory, as well as the fact that there could be a real danger to all humankind if this sort of power were to fall into the wrong hands, and even though it would be a terrible tragedy to have to destroy something so wonderful, the consequences of neglect would be much worse. So, it was agreed by all present that safeguards would have to be taken.

"Now," I started again, "until the other monasteries have their own towers up and functioning, you'll have to coordinate questions for the seekers through Mr. Valik, and this tower here. Mr. Valik, you'll need to assign one or two individuals to be your liaisons to the other world. I don't think it would be wise to have too many outsiders showing up all of a sudden in the hereafter until we know how our intrusion will affect their world. I know both worlds are only a heartbeat away, but they've been separated for a long time, so let's go easy at first, is that understood by all?"

To a man, everyone agreed to the limited conditions of intrusion on the other world. We know absolutely nothing about the other world, so prudence has to be the key for now. I believe there are a few people in the world today that have an unconscious access to that world, and the knowledge therein, but they are few in number. With this new direct link to that world, we are bound to upset some sort of balance, so we must be careful.

"Mr. Valik," I said, "and gentleman from around the world, I leave you now to your discussions and planning. I feel quite exhausted from the ordeal, and I'm going to my Villa to sort through my thoughts. I have many questions to ask the seekers about my own past lives, and I'm going to need all of the strength I have to meet those challenges, so good evening, and good discussion."

All of the men present, in the flesh, and by image, bid me good day, and even before I made it out of the door, they were in heated discussion about what questions would be priority, and which were not as important. As soon as I walked outside, the entire compliment of monks were waiting, some sitting, some standing, some pacing, but when I exited the tower, with my new white hair and glowing complexion, all they could do was stand and stare at me as I walked by, and no one said a word. Maybe they thought I had died, and an apparition was strolling past, I don't know, but it was fun nonetheless. I'm sure if I would have jumped at one of them and said BOO', they would've fainted dead away, but, I kept walking, lost in my own thoughts about seeing Dee again, how radiant she looked, and how distant. I hope she recognizes me when I do finally die and go to that dimension for my rest. I guess that will have to be one of my questions the next time I visit that other place.

When I entered my villa, the first thing I needed was a glass of wine, and with that in hand, I sat down on my chair to think about everything that has happened in my life since this saga began just barely two months ago, from the bad dreams of dragons, and of Mara being killed on the battlefield, to the hypnosis sessions which actually made those experiences real, then the journey to this place which confirmed the reality of all of the theories, and finally the journey into another world, and all of the intrigue that will now follow. It's almost too much for my mind to grasp, and if it weren't for the fact that I was sitting here right now, I wouldn't believe it myself.

So now what, where does it all go from here, have I fulfilled my destiny in this life, and now I'll die from some obscure accident or disease, or is there some new journey for me to go on, and another goal to reach? I'm inclined to think there must be another journey ahead, since our lives seem to be made up of one journey which leads directly to another, only to go on endlessly until we ascend to the lofty goal of perfection. And when will we know if we've reached that state of perfection? Will we make it to heaven, be greeted by a ten foot tall dude dressed in white, and be told that we don't need to go back to the earthly plane anymore that we've passed the test and graduated on to bigger and better things?

Maybe the teachers are the ones who have reached that goal of perfection, and now their job is to teach what they have learned to others. It seems like a boring job to me, but that's probably because I haven't reached that level of perfection, and you know what, I'm kind of glad about that.

I'd much rather keep returning to earth to enjoy the fruits of passion that go along with the nurturing of being in love with someone, or of the joys of eating new and exciting foods, or tasting a great wine like this one in my hand, or the intense feeling of making love to someone for the first time. How am I ever going to experience those sorts of pleasures in the sterile environment of the hereafter?

Maybe I'm missing something here when I think about the hereafter, maybe it's a rocking good place to be, maybe I missed the party spot on my limited journey there, and maybe those are the questions I need to ask on my next visits through the tower. This is probably why I'm still making the journey back to earth so often, because my priorities are still on the pleasures of the flesh, and not on the pleasures of ultimate knowledge.

After a couple more glasses of wine, and just before I fell asleep, I thought to myself, you are what you are, and life is short, so you need to make the most of it, because you never know when it will end, for you, or for someone you love.

I don't know how long I slept, but the noise of the bell above the meeting hall, and a lot of frantic activity outside, woke me up with a start, and thank God, waking up also helped take away all of the bizarre dreams I was having. As soon as I could get my wits about me, I walked over to the doorway, opened it up, and stepped outside. It was still daylight, and the courtyard was in frenzy, with people hurrying to and fro, and it appeared that they were carrying supplies and heavy packs to the meeting hall, so with curiosity getting the best of me, I too headed for the meeting hall.

I had to force my way through the crowd, as it seemed everyone was trying to go both ways through the door at the same time. As soon as men saw my white hair and ghostly face approaching them, they eagerly gave way to me. Once I was inside and working my way to the front, I could hear Valik trying to get some order established, and by the time I was nearing the front, the remaining men standing in front of me had sat down. Right away I could see what the first point of excitement was about, because apparently Valik had also visited the hereafter, and was now sporting the same white hair and glowing face that I was wearing.

As I approached the front of the hall, I noticed six men dressed in street cloths, and my heart sank a notch. I wondered if we had already been found out, but the closer I looked, I became aware that I recognized a couple of the men as monks. Then, I thought to myself that maybe some of the brothers were disgruntled and wanted to leave the faith. As soon as I got close to Valik, who was waiting for me at the podium, I asked him what was going on.

"Ethan," he began, and his voice contained a tone of despair, "Hitler is back on Earth."

The whole thing took me by surprise, and I wasn't sure I understood what it was he had said, so I simply said. "What?'

"Adolph Hitler has been reborn on Earth Ethan," he continued, just as intense as he had before.

"How do you know this?" I asked.

"I asked the teacher if Adolph Hitler was still in the afterlife, and when the seeker returned, he stated that the entity known as Hitler had already returned to the earthly plane, in the land known as Brazil."

Valik was very upset about the news, as was the rest of the brotherhood, and I guess I can't blame them. This is what they had waited their whole lives to prevent, or at least keep tabs on, and now, on the brink of victory, some of the evil ones are trying to get back to Earth while they can.

"So what are you going to do about it?" I asked.

"We're sending brothers out to find him, as well as a few others, as soon as possible," he responded.

"Are you ready?" I asked. "Do you know where to find him?"

"We know the general whereabouts of Hitler," he responded, "and we know his new birth name, so we are confident that we'll find him. With the help of some of our brothers in South America, we have a great support system, and they already know our men are coming."

"Is that what these men are doing dressed up in street cloths?" I asked.

"It is," he replied. "They will better fit in to the real world dressed in the cloths they came here with, and they have everything they need to make the journey, cash from the sale of wine, food, packs, everything, and when they meet with the brothers from the monastery in Chile, they will be supplied with anything else they might need to continue with their mission."

"It looks like you've got things well in hand," I said.

"We have been planning this for a very long time," He replied.

"Do you think you should send six men?" I asked, "because that might draw undue attention."

"Oh no," he said with a start, "only two of the brothers are going to look for Hitler, the other four are pairing up to seek out two other butchers who have suddenly returned to the earthly plane."

"And who are they?' I asked, almost too scared to ask.

"They are Joseph Stalin and Mao Tse Tung," Valik soberly responded.

"My word," I gasped, "why now, why have three of the world's worst butchers reincarnating to Earth at this time?"

"That's what we intend to find out," Valik replied. "It could be that the world is in the perfect ideological state for their type of violence right now with all of the terrorism and genocide going on. I think that evil has a force all of it's own, and it draws like forces to itself like a magnet, even to the point of drawing that evil back to the world from beyond the grave."

"I suppose you're right," I said, "but, how are you going to get your men into China?"

"We have men here from every country in the world," he said. "Just look around you, there are men here of every race, sent here by the monastery in their home country, to learn, and to await your return. Now you are here, the tower is working, and their mission is at hand. They will go back to their own country, to train the brothers in their own monastery, build their own cubicles, and continue the work we've started. This mission is a worldwide mission, and it has tentacles all over the globe. What you have built for purely selfish reasons, we have turned into a tool to better all of mankind."

"Well, I hate to think that I was being selfish, but I understand what you're saying, and I must say Mr. Valik, I am impressed by your foresight, and execution, my compliments."

"Thank you Ethan," he replied, "but none of this could have taken place without you. You were chosen long ago to be an instrument of the Gods, the only problem is that you tend to get a little distracted by wine and women; or at least by one woman in particular."

"I must say Valik; you seem to have more wisdom than I do."

"That's because you have been away for so long, where as I have been here, one lifetime after another preparing for this day."

"Well, I'm here now," I said, "and I have a lot of catching up to do. Starting tomorrow, I'm going to the teachers to follow every one of my previous lives, starting at the very beginning."

"That is going to be incredible," Valik replied. "I can't wait to hear about each and every one, but for now, I must get these men on their way, for there's not a second to lose."

I watched as Valik gave each of the men some final instructions, and double-checked their supplies and cash. Two of the men were obviously Chinese, so I knew where they were headed, two looked to be European, so I suspected they were looking for Stalin, and the other two had a slightly dark complexion, probably from one of the South American countries, and as the whole compliment of brothers followed them to the footbridge, myself included, I thought to myself how so much had taken place over so little a time, that it was almost too much to comprehend.

It was starting to get dark when the six men departed, but they had to leave now to be at the train station in the morning in time for departure. The moon was full, and each of the men had lanterns to light the way. Each man had made the trip to town and back many times over the years, so I trust it would be a safe and uneventful journey. We watched until all we could see was a slight glow from their lamps on the surrounding treetops, and then we turned to go back to our rooms, each man lost in his own thoughts.

Things would become very busy and hectic in the coming days and weeks, with new information being discovered from the teachers, and more men being sent around the world. It wouldn't be long before the compliment of brothers at the monastery would be down to about half, with this number changing only slightly as monks from other monasteries came and went on their missions.

It really was quite an organization, with the sale of wine from each of the monasteries providing the funding to keep the missionaries in the field, and the younger, less experiences monks kept behind to tend the vineyards and produce the wine, until someday it was their turn to go on a mission. And to think it all came about from a simple life as a dragon keeper who fell in love with a girl from his past, his past life that is.

As I sat by the fireplace that night in my villa, I suddenly came upon an idea that would prevent Mike, or Sardon, from ever returning to this earthly realm to ruin mine, or Dee's life ever again. The guide mentioned that newly arrived souls were very unstable, and could be irreparably damaged if you interrupted their souls too quickly, but that's exactly what I intended to do. Tomorrow morning, I'm going to request a visit with my old dead friend Mike. I smiled to myself as I leaned back in my easy chair, and poured myself another glass of wine. We're going to see if you really can change the future.

The next morning I was back in the tower before breakfast, closing myself into the cubicle, and sat back. Before I knew it, Feldore was again floating at my side, saying.

"Lucienne, it is good to see you again, what is it you seek."

"I wish to speak with the entity last known as Mike Gentry, because I forgot that he too has plans to return to the earthly realm at the same time as Tanamara and myself.

"As you wish," he responded, and immediately I found myself beside an entity that I knew must be Mike.

Even though this entity had that ethereal glow about him, he was anything but at peace here, as he paced about, or floated about nervously. He already looked unstable, so it wasn't going to take much to push him over the edge, and as I watched his tortured soul move about, Feldore spoke to him, saying.

"Brekin, there is someone here to speak to you."

He turned toward me in a jerky motion, like we had startled him, and when he did, his eyes looked nothing like Dee's had looked when I had spoken to her. His eyes looked haunting, penetrating, and wild, and as he looked at me, I forced myself to look directly into his eyes with a sternness brought up from deep within my own soul, addressing him as the killer and traitor I knew him to be, and I said to him.

"I am Lucienne, also known as Ethan the Dragon Master, and last known to you as Henry Olsen, Dee Ballinger's lover."

I could see an immediate effect on Mike, his eyes started to widen, and then they turned red, and his entity started shaking violently, so before Feldore could stop me, I continued.

"I am the man who has killed you in every lifetime that you dared to return to the earthly realm, and next time, if you try to return, I will kill you as an infant before you ever have a chance to grow up and destroy mine and Tanamara's life, do you understand me, I don't want you to ever return to the Earth."

This time, he went absolutely mad, screaming and tearing at himself with what appeared to be hands, his whole entity shaking violently. Immediately, two of the giant beings appeared at his side, restraining him with only a single finger from one hand of each being, and just as soon as they appeared, they were gone, as was Mike, or Brekin.

Also immediately, one of the seekers zipped up to Feldore, and just as quickly disappeared, at which time Feldore spoke sternly to me.

"You deceived me with your intentions Lucienne. The great ones have forbid you to ever speak with another departed entity within this realm. Any further visits will only be allowed for information only, nothing else."

"I did not deceive you Feldore," I retorted. "Brekin has followed Tanamara and I back to the earthly realm in every lifetime, and he has destroyed our life in every instance. He would have most certainly dropped back to earth at the time agreed upon by Tanamara and myself, and also before his soul had time to heal. If you would confirm that with the Great Ones, I think you will find that I have spoken the truth to you when I said Brekin was also going to drop back to the Earthly realm with Tanamara and myself."

As Feldore hovered beside me, another seeker zipped up to us, zipped away, and immediately returned, at which time Feldore spoke again.

"You are correct in what you say Lucienne, Brekin would have indeed returned to the earthly realm at the time agreed by yourself and Tanamara, but the Great Ones will now decide on every request in which you seek to speak to an entity in this realm."

"I understand," I said, "and I hope I did not get you in trouble, Feldore.

"You did not Lucienne," He replied. "That is only a condition that happens in the Earthly Realm, not in this realm."

"I'm glad," I said, and then I asked.

"What will happen to Brekin now?"

"His soul is now beyond repair," Feldore responded. "He will never again be allowed to return to the Earthly Realm."

Before I said something that would not be inappropriate, I said to Feldore.

"I'm ready to go back now," and as soon as I had spoken the words, I found myself staring once again at the individual crystals within the cubicle, back in the real world, or at least the current real world, as I know it as Henry Olsen.

As I exited the cubicle, Valik was standing outside on the walkway, having watched the entire scene on the walls of the tower, as did several other monks from the other monasteries. He seemed to be a little upset with me, and said to me.

"I wish you would have told me you were going to do such a foolhardy thing as this. Don't you realize you could have ruined everything that we have waited twelve thousand years for, and for what, personal gain?"

"This was not foolhardy," I retorted. "Just as you want to use the tower to manipulate villains past and future, I eliminated a villain who was just as much a butcher as anyone you are hunting down right now, or did you forget that Sardon was directly responsible for the deaths of thousands of souls in the time of the dragons alone, not to mention how many others have died because of his treachery in countless other lifetimes. I simply took a more direct approach to the problem, so don't lecture me Mr. Valik, for I only did what you are doing on a larger scale. Now, if you'll excuse me, I'm going back to my villa to rest up from my journey, and tomorrow, I'm going to come here to start exploring all of my past lives, one at a time, to repair my own soul, while you work on saving the souls of the rest of the planet."

As I turned to leave, Valik stopped me and humbly said.

"Forgive me Ethan, you are right, and I apologize. We have waited so long for this day that I was afraid we were going to lose out before we could get started. I won't question your judgment again."

"It's alright," I said, patting him on the back, "and you're right about one thing, it was a little selfish, but it got the job done don't you think?"

"It certainly did Ethan. I'll see you later at lunch, but for now, I'm going on a journey of my own to find out about a few more individuals that we want to keep track of, and once again, I apologize for my outburst."

"Forget about it my friend, I'll see you later."

With that, we both went our separate ways, he to the crystal tower, and I back to my villa. I was feeling very good about myself and about the future in general as I poured myself a glass of wine. I believe the future for Dee and I is looking very bright for our next life together, especially with Mike out of the way for all of eternity. Don't get me wrong, I'm not looking forward to my upcoming death, but I no longer fear the afterlife, or the next life for that matter. I wish I could somehow let Dee know that she no longer has to live each life in fear, but the Great Ones have forbade further contact, and besides, she deserves to rest in peace for a while. I'm sure I'll see her soon enough anyhow.

So, with a peace of mind that I hadn't experienced since this whole saga began, I sat back in my easy chair, grabbed one of my journals, and became familiar with myself all over again. It was then that I decided that my next visit to the crystal tower was to seek out my first life on this Earth, the sojourn I spent on the lost continent of Atlantis. After that, we'll just have to see where the journey takes me, and I was excited to get started on that journey.

Later that day, I met with Valik and the others for lunch. Valik's hair was now purely white, as were mine, and our faces were also beginning to pale. They say gray hair, or in this case white hair is a sign of wisdom, and I guess in a way they're right. It would seem that the more we are learning, the whiter our hair is getting. The only problem is, when I go back to the real world, this new look is going to be a little hard to explain. But, with the changing fashion styles in the world today, I may just start a new trend, who knows.

The evening meeting was lively, as new information was found, with new missions being assigned and new strategies being planned. It would seem that the ancient Atlanteans had stockpiled crystals at each of the monastery locations around the world, so those locations would soon be building their own cubicles, in their own towers. The afterlife will soon be a very busy place, and it looks like these guys are going to be busy for a long time to come. In fact, they may need to recruit some new protégées to fill their dwindling ranks, or at least borrow some troops from the other monasteries. But I'm sure they've already thought of all that, so I'll leave those details to the experts. I'm just here to learn about myself, and Tanamara.

Tomorrow, my journey begins, so, I bid Valik and the others good night, and went back to my villa to study, and then to sleep, for I've found over the years that the night passes faster when you're sleeping, and I'm excited for tomorrow to come.

I must have fallen asleep in my chair while I was reading, because the next thing I knew, I was waking up in the chair with a jolt, probably from snoring. Well, the night definitely went by quickly, which suited me just fine. After splashing some water on my face, I headed first to the cafeteria for a bite to eat, and then straight to the crystal tower to begin my first journey. This was going to be interesting, and I was anxious to get started.

As I entered the tower, Valik was just coming out. He had apparently got an early start this morning as well. He looked a bit haggard, but it was hard to tell because of the glow that you acquired each time you went on a journey. As I stepped aside to let him pass, I asked him if everything was okay. He stated that he just had some things to clarify, and then it was back to the meeting hall to send a couple more men out on assignment. Then he asked me what kind of information I was seeking this time, maybe afraid I was going to cause another raucous in the other world.

I assured him that now my journeys were simply to seek out my past, beginning with my first sojourn on Earth in the land of Atlantis. He seemed genuinely interested and bid me good journey. He asked me to fill him in on the details when I could, and then expressed interest in finding his own past when he found time. Then, he was off to the meeting hall, and I was off to the cubicle.

I climbed into the cubicle, closed myself in, and leaned back to relax, letting my eyes close. As soon as I felt myself starting to float, I opened my eyes to find Feldore standing before me, and as I became aware of him, he spoke.

"Lucienne, what is it that you seek?"

"Feldore, I seek to see my past sojourns on Earth, starting with my first one. I wish to see my sojourn in the place that was once called Atlantis."

"As you wish," he said, and the world opened up before me, a beautiful world, pure, white, washed in bright sunshine, with the beautiful blue ocean spread out before me, framed by swaying palm trees to the front, and jagged mountain peaks ringed all around. And as I watched, a strange craft swooped out of the sky to land in the center of the magnificent city, setting down in the center of a ringed arena.

But wait, I'm getting ahead of myself, for that's another story, so I'll see you there.

THE END

Printed in the United States
68382LVS00004B/74

9 781424 148851